THE
GRANITE

Printed in Australia

Cover and internal design by New Found Books Australia Pty Ltd
Images in this book are copyright approved for New Found Books Australia Pty Ltd
Illustrations within this book are copyright approved for New Found Books Australia Pty Ltd

First printing: SEPTEMBER 2024

New Found Books Australia Pty Ltd
www.newfoundbooks.au

Paperback ISBN 978 19231 7241 8
eBook ISBN 978 1 9231 7253 1
Hardback ISBN 978 1 9231 7265 4

Distributed by New Found Books Australia and Lightning Source Global

 A catalogue record for this work is available from the National Library of Australia

More great New Found Books Australia titles can be found at: www.newfoundbooks.au/our-titles/

We acknowledge the traditional owners of the land
and pay respects to the Elders, past, present and future.

THE
GRANITE

ROBERT M. SMITH

While some of the peripheral characters and incidental events are based on real people and occurrences, the main storyline and central characters are entirely fictional. The locations where the novel is set are authentic, although some minor features of the gravelly, scrub-covered titular hill have been altered or enhanced to suit the plot.

*To my parents who gave me
the most idyllic childhood.*

PROLOGUE

He looked down at the gun in his trembling hand. Was this really a solution, or just a way out for a coward? But what did it matter? Life without her by his side would be intolerable anyway. If he was going to do it, now was the time. There was nobody within miles to stop him or talk him out of it. He had made his decision in the lonely hours of the night before and it was time to get it over with.

The crack of the rifle echoed around the hills. Dogs barked in the distance. White cockatoos squawked hysterically as the large flock lifted from the crowns of trees nearby. High above, a wedged tailed eagle soared on the breeze, its wings extended and motionless as it rode the updrafts, totally oblivious to the denouement of a mortal existence far below.

CHAPTER 1

The altercation had started in the carpark a few minutes before Detective Inspector Bowker and his wife arrived. The balding, well-dressed elderly man in a sports jacket and red bow tie was now backed up against the bonnet of a late model Lexus, his walking stick on the ground beside him. Two middle-aged men in dirty jeans and singlets prevented the old man's progress as they shouted in his face and prodded him back against the car. Both had a fishing rod in hand, one carried a tackle box and the other a metal esky. The taller and heavier of the two placed the rod and esky on the ground, opened the cooler's lid and removed two cans of Victoria Bitter. He handed one to his offsider who dropped the tackle box, leant his fishing rod against the car and ripped the top off his beer. He took a long swig then poked the old man in the chest with his free hand. 'You don't remember us, do you *Mr Rice*?'

'We were in your 3E history class,' the other man said. 'You remember 3E don't you, *Sir*? Class for all the dumb-arse shits.'

'I've taught thousands of students over the years,' the old man said nervously. 'I can't possibly remember all who were in my classes.' He stooped down, collected his walking stick and tried to push past them. 'Now if you don't mind, I've a dinner to attend.'

The heavier man blocked his way. 'Noel Sanderson. You remember that name? It should ring a bell, because you wrote me a fuckin' reference.'

The old man shrugged tensely. 'I've written hundreds of those. You can't expect me to recall them all.'

'Well I fuckin' recall mine. I had a brickie's apprenticeship lined up, and all the boss needed was a reference from the school. Well he received one, didn't he?' Sanderson said aggressively, before continuing in a mocking voice: 'At school, Noel Sanderson is lazy and untrustworthy, but may improve in an employment situation.' He feigned a laugh. 'Well I didn't get the chance, did I? The old brickie dropped me like a hot spud and employed that turd Billy Henderson instead. Now he's got his own business, and I'm shovellin' cow shit at the saleyards a couple of days a week if I'm lucky.'

The elderly teacher raised a palm and shook his head. 'Look I'm sorry it didn't all work out, but the staff were instructed to ensure references were honest, otherwise they would have been ignored by employers. That's not fair on the good kids.' He immediately regretted his choice of words.

Sanderson's temper flared and he pushed the old man backwards across the car's bonnet. 'Not fair on the *good* kids eh? What about the others, eh *Sir*? They can all go and get fucked as far as you're concerned, I bet. I've still got that reference at home, *Mr Rice*. Just to remind me how you fucked up my life. I've been inside a couple of times as well, and do you know what I dreamed about while I was in there? Finding you in a quiet spot on your own and then stuffing that reference down your fuckin' throat until you choked to death on its lies.'

'We've got company Sando,' Sanderson's offsider said urgently.

Sanderson felt a hand on his shoulder and spun around to see Bowker towering over him. He looked into the policeman's eyes. 'Who are you fuckhead? And keep your bloody hands off me,' he said as he slapped Bowker's arm away.

The policeman pulled his ID from his jacket pocket and displayed it in Sanderson's face. 'Detective Inspector Bowker. Now what's going on here?'

Sanderson's mate was first to speak. 'Sando and I were walking down to the lake to catch a few reddies and have a quiet beer. We saw one of our old teachers here and thought we'd stop and say g'day. You know, renew old acquaintances.'

'What's your name?' Bowker demanded.

'Glen Brown.' Brown pointed to his mate. 'And this is Noel Sanderson. We were in Mr Rice's class about twenty-five years ago.'

Bowker looked at Rice who was now standing up straight and adjusting his bow tie. There was a look of vague recognition on both men's faces. 'Were they making threats towards you, Mr Rice?'

Rice was keen to put the whole incident behind him and not create more animosity with the ex-students who he knew had consumed a drink or five before the encounter. He told himself it was just the alcohol talking, so why add more fuel to their fire. 'No. We were just discussing what they've been up to since they left school.'

Bowker looked directly into the old teacher's eyes. 'From the bit I heard, I have my doubts about that Mr Rice. And the way Mr Sanderson here had you pushed over the bonnet adds to those doubts.' He paused for a moment contemplating the best course of action. 'But if there's no harm done, I'll take you on your word.' He turned to the fishermen. 'I'm assuming you didn't drive down here. I reckon you'd be well over the limit.'

Sanderson pointed to the south. 'My place is just down there in Garden Street, so we walked. We're not complete dumb shits.'

Bowker sent the pair on their way then addressed the

ex-schoolteacher. 'Let's have your story again, but without the bullshit this time.'

Rice took a deep breath. 'Sanderson was stirred up about a reference I wrote for him that he said cost him a job several decades ago. But you saw him. He was intoxicated, so I don't want to make a big deal about what just happened. He was a bully boy at school but usually his threats came to nothing. I have to live in this town and although I'm probably unlikely to cross paths with him again, I don't need to give him more ammunition to abuse me.'

'Let sleeping dogs lie, you reckon?'

'I think that's best,' Rice replied without conviction.

'Sometimes sleeping dogs wake up and grab you by the throat.' Bowker shrugged. 'But if you don't want to take it further, then that's your decision I guess.'

The ex-teacher nodded but said nothing.

'I think you might have taught me too,' Bowker suggested. 'A few years before those clowns were at school though. Your face and the Rice name bring back memories from somewhere.'

'I do remember teaching a Bowker. An Alex Bowker, if I recall rightly.'

Bowker smiled. 'Alex is my brother. Lives down in Bairnsdale now.' He patted the car's bonnet. 'This your Lexus?'

Rice shook his head. 'I wish.'

'So which is your car?'

'I own a small Corolla, but it's parked in my carport. I'm planning to have a few drinks with my meal, so I'll walk home. Not too far, even for a man with a dicky leg. My house backs onto the lake down near the railway bridge in Arundel Street. Fifteen-minute walk, tops.' He shook hands with the policeman. 'Perhaps I'll see you inside. Many thanks for your help.'

Bowker watched Rice climb the steps of the glassed building

one-by-one before collecting Rachael from their car and making the same journey.

Bowker had little time for school reunions. They always seemed a disappointment. You attended in the hope of hearing about the great lives your classmates had gone on to live after such promising beginnings, or to see how the beautiful people had blossomed. While there were exceptions, the majority of your peers lived an uninspiring existence, often a stone's throw from their place of birth. And the attractive faces from your school days had reached their zenith at an early age and time had taken its toll. The slim and athletic bodies you remembered from your youth had often gone to seed. The fit and lithe had become the fat and lazy. Worst still was the inevitable news concerning the demise of former friends, or their debilitating illnesses or their tragic personal histories.

The detective inspector had another reason to shun these alumni affairs. Bowker was somewhat of a nonentity at school. He grew up on a farm and spent most of his time there. With the exception of team sport, he had little social contact with his classmates. If it hadn't been for a phone call from Ken Phillips, Bowker's best friend at school, he would never have contemplated attending. But he finally relented, deciding to make a weekend of the trip to Benalla to show his wife Rachael his old stomping ground and the farm on which he had grown up.

The trip from Caulfield North to Benalla was an easy two-and-a-bit-hour journey via the Hume Freeway. Long gone were the mile-long truck convoys where overtaking on the old two-lane highway was nigh impossible, and the road toll on this main Melbourne to Sydney link was dominated by those who had tried and failed. Climbing the Great Divide to the improbably named "Pretty Sally" cutting occurred at a frustrating walking pace, and the descent was not for the faint-hearted, with many of the semitrailers leaving the summit in angel gear.

Benalla is now bypassed to the south and gone is the highway traffic up Bridge Street, the main commercial thoroughfare in the small rural city of around ten thousand residents. The town was established in the 1840's at a crossing of the Broken River on the main Hume and Hovell exploration route and has a comfortable laid-back feel about it. This was to change in the next few hours.

The new football club function room housed the reunion dinner, an event aiming to attract ex-students from decades beginning with the 1960's. The spacious second-storey and heavily glassed room overlooked the football ground to the west and afforded spectacular views of the adjacent Lake Benalla to the east. It was still daylight when the Bowkers climbed the steps, with the sun slipping slowly behind the heritage listed grandstand at the opposite end of the oval. The ornate superstructure of the old building cast elongated geometric patterns across the grass as though the oval had been marked out for a giants' game of hopscotch. Bowker immediately recognised two of the organisers who manned the door welcoming each participant as they arrived. Neither remembered him and had to ask his name. Nothing had changed, the policeman thought. Once the paperwork was completed and the nametags and a folder of information collected, Bowker took Rachael by the hand and led her to a circular table where his old mate Ken Phillips was pointing to a pair of vacant seats.

Phillips stood up and shook Bowker's hand and kissed Rachael lightly on the cheek. 'We're lucky, mate. Everyone on this table is from our year.'

Bowker scanned the mélange of faces looking up in his direction. He recognised each one after a few moments, desperately combing his memory and making adjustments for the ravages of time.

'G'day everybody,' he said with a cursory wave. 'Long time no see.' The blank faces told him they had no idea who he was. He pointed to his own chest. 'Greg Bowker. And this is my wife Rachael.' The Bowkers sat down and dragged in their chairs.

'Did you come to the school part way through sixth form,' said a prune-faced woman who Bowker remembered was the centre of a schoolboy crush. Dodged a bullet there, he thought to himself.

Phillips laughed out loud. 'He started with us in first form. Don't you remember? He was in our form all the way through.'

One by one, Bowker perused the wrinkled faces of his former classmates, then glanced at Rachael with a smile. Rachael was three years younger than her husband but looked twenty-five years junior to the women at the table. She was tall and slim and had maintained a high level of fitness after a lifetime in sport and dance. She had an attractive face and deep green eyes. Her hair was cut short and had retained its natural colour, something Bowker felt was unique among the women surrounding him. She wore a long flowing pleated skirt made of a light material that elegantly swung back and forth as she walked. Completing her look was a silk sleeveless blouse and strappy medium-heeled shoes.

'I brought the class photo from Form 5,' a woman opposite said as she removed a black and white picture from her handbag. She placed it on the table and ran an index finger across the smiling faces. 'I can't see you in it, Greg. Perhaps you were away when they took the photo.'

Bowker reached a hand across the table. 'I'll take a look and see if I can spot my boof head.' The woman handed him the photo and he scanned the boys in the back row of the group. He smiled and pointed to a tall lad in the centre with arms folded and trying desperately to push out his biceps. He kept his finger on his younger face as he passed the picture back to its owner. 'That's me. Dead centre of the back row.'

The woman looked with a strained face before diving into her leather bag and retrieving a pair of glasses she had probably hoped she wouldn't have to wear. She viewed the face closely then looked up at Bowker. 'I can honestly say I have no recollection of you being in our form.' She turned the photograph over and read the names on the back. 'Yep. That's you alright. "Gregory Bowker".' She passed the picture to others on the table and the shaking of heads confirmed that Bowker's anonymity was unanimous.

'I could have named just about everyone in this photo, but I wouldn't have put a name to that face in a million years. Sorry Greg,' another mutton-dressed-up-as-lamb frump said.

Phillips smiled. 'I remember you Greg. So at least that's one out of thirty.'

Bowker shrugged. 'I suppose when you were a kid who never got into much trouble at school and spent most of your time on the farm mucking around with horses there's not too much to remember.' Rachael put her hand on his thigh and squeezed it gently under the table.

A small, fat and unfit looking man who Bowker recognised as a bully from his teenage years looked up when there was mention of horses in the policeman's youth. He held up a chubby index finger. 'I remember you now. You were tied up with that business out in the bush. It was all over the *Ensign* at the time. That was you, wasn't it?'

Bowker leant back in his chair and nodded.

CHAPTER 2

t was another magical northeast Victorian spring day. The sky was cobalt blue with the occasional puffy cumulus cloud casting a moving shadow across the rolling green paddocks. It was the type of day Greg Bowker loved lying on his back in the green grass staring up at the passing clouds, watching faces and animals form and disappear in the constantly morphing white billow above him. His imagination transported him to a myriad of transmuting mystical places projected against the sky, all this to a soundscape of whistling birds harvesting the blossoms of surrounding trees and of buzzing bees working the yellow cape weed flowers around where he lay.

Today's adventure for the two boys was a horse ride up to The Granite where they planned to have lunch and shoot a few rabbits for tomorrow night's tea. Hazel Bowker wandered across the mostly bare ground that was laughingly called the back lawn to the netting fence where her sons had tethered their horses under the massive elm trees. The dappled grey, the taller of the two mares, was what Greg termed a total head-case. Contessa, or Connie as he called her, was prone to bolting after the slightest fright. To combat this potentially dangerous reaction, Greg's father acquired a special bit from a rodeo bronc-riding friend that stopped the mare in her tracks before she hit top speed. The downside was her immediate reaction to being restrained. A wild and petulant bucking display. But Greg preferred this to bolting. The only downside to sitting atop a bucking horse was the potential to find yourself hitting terra firma with a severe jolt. But so far, Greg had never been thrown from any horse so the thought of the mare dislodging him never crossed his mind. A bolting horse was an equine of a completely different colour, so to speak. Staying aboard wasn't the worry, it was the unpredictability of what lay in the minutes ahead. Would you cross a country intersection in a full stretch gallop with a truck or car crossing your path? Were the gates you had to pass through only partially open? If a gate was closed, would the horse's perception of its jumping ability bear any resemblance to reality. Greg's younger brother Alexander had no such issues. His coffee-coloured mare, Chiko, with the taffy mane and tail was a pillar of virtue compared with her dappled grey psychopathic companion. Chiko was a class act, both in looks and temperament.

'Where are you headed just in case you go missing?' Mrs Bowker asked as she handed each son a brown paper bag containing a cut lunch.

'Up to The Granite,' Greg replied as he put the lunch in one of the leather bags slung across his horse behind the saddle. 'See if we can shoot a few bunnies.'

'When do you reckon you'll be home?'

'Around dark I reckon. What's for tea?' Greg asked.

'Lamb's fry, mashed potato and gravy,' his mother replied.

'Magnificent,' Alex retorted as he unhitched the reins from the fence, put his foot in the near side stirrup and swung easily up into the saddle.

'Be careful.'

Greg smiled as he mounted his grey mare. 'We're always careful, mum. You know us.'

'Yeah, right,' their mother replied. 'Some of the things you boys get up to on those horses I'm better not to know about. When you're not home before dark, I'm always relieved when I hear the horses galloping across the paddock.'

Things were different back then. The boys, a seventeen and a fourteen-year-old, would be gone all day on horseback, each with a .22 rifle sleeved in a scabbard down the off-side of their mount. It never entered the boys' head, or their parents' as far as they knew, that there may lurk forces of ill-will on the lonely back roads around Lurg and Mollyullah.

The Granite, as the locals called it, was a scrub-covered, rock-strewn hill at Upper Lurg and was visible for miles around. From the Bowker farm, it was seven miles distant, but needing to follow lanes and back roads meant more than a ten mile ride each way for the boys. They cantered through verdant paddocks to the farm's most northerly gate then trotted up Hunters Lane and after a few hundred yards headed northeast along Kennedy's Lane. For the boys, it was hard to imagine a more perfect scene. The sun warmed their back, and the birds seemed to sing to the horses' metronomic hoof beats. There were flies of course, but the sticky insects showed more interest in their sweating steeds despite both horses wearing string veils to protect their eyes. At a bush reserve where Kennedy's Lane swings around the base of a sandy rise a mile or so past Dick Barber's farm house, they shot and gutted two rabbits. These were stowed in a hessian bag to avert fly strikes, although the blowies seemed quite content with the pile of leporid guts on the ground. At this early stage, for the boys this had the makings of a successful day.

The brothers reached The Granite by midday and tethered their horses to the base of sturdy saplings allowing the mares enough loose rein to graze on the native grasses on the edge of the lane. The boys sat on a fallen tree trunk and opened their lunch bags. Mum had come good, as always. Greg tucked into his favoured quince jam and cheese sandwiches, his brother already through his first round containing German sausage and tomato sauce.

'I wonder who lives in that house across the road down there?' Alex asked, pointing down the hill.

Greg shrugged. 'Dunno,' he said as she shoved another sandwich into his mouth.

'Do you reckon he'll get shitty if we start shooting up here?'

'Can't see why he would. We're only shootin' rabbits. Or a fox if we see one. Haven't heard of too many cockies who don't want less rabbits and foxes. Besides, it's a public bush reserve. He doesn't own it.'

Alex nodded but didn't reply. The two boys removed a homemade lamington from their lunch bags in unison. Greg pointed towards the summit of the rocky hill. 'Get a pretty good view from up there.'

'We climb to the top, you reckon?'

Greg nodded. 'Yeah, why not.' He looked at the watch he'd been given for his seventeenth birthday the month before. 'Got plenty of time. I bet you can see our place from up there.'

'You think there's a track to the top or do you reckon we just bush bash our way up?'

'It looks a bit steep to climb straight up. May as well work our way up at an angle and maybe ping the odd bunny on the way.'

Within ten minutes the boys were at the base of The Granite, both carrying a rifle and both with a hessian bag over their shoulder containing a canteen of water and a box of .22 ammo. The climb was tough, even for two country boys who were farm fit. The bushy scrub was prickly, often snagging their shirt or their carry bag. The granite rocks and boulders made footing difficult. As they topped a small spur, Greg put his arm across his brother's chest to halt his progress. He spoke softly. 'Look down in that little gully. A fox.'

Alex peeked over the small ridge then shouldered his rifle and looked down the sights. 'He's too far away to do any damage with a twenty-two,' he whispered. 'We'll have to get a bit closer.'

Greg shook his head. 'He'll see us for sure. Or smell us. See the way he's sniffing the breeze.'

Alex nodded. 'And it's pretty hard not to make a noise in all these stones and rocks.'

Greg took the hessian bag from his shoulder and found what he was after. 'I'll see if I can whistle him up closer.'

The boy had a homemade fox whistle in his hand. A jam tin lid folded in half with a nail hole punched near the crease was all there was to it. Unless personally instructed on how to get a sound out of such a simple device, a novice could try for months without success. In the hands of an expert, the bent tin creates a high-pitched scream mimicking the sound of a rabbit caught in a trap or otherwise incapacitated. On most occasions foxes can't resist investigating. The animal in the gully was no exception. From the moment it heard the whistle it began carefully picking its way up the gully, traversing the slope from side to side and stopping periodically to smell the breeze.

'It's a bit spooky the way it sort of creeps up on us like that,' the younger brother whispered.

Greg shushed him with the wave of a hand. He rested the barrel of his rifle on a flat boulder in front of him and looked down the sights with great concentration. 'Another ten yards and he's dead meat.'

Alex felt a stare piercing his back and turned slowly to look behind him. 'Fuck!' he yelled loudly seeing another fox standing a couple of yards away. The second fox bolted into the scrub and

Alex's yell had the first one scurrying off as well. Alex laid back on the rock holding his chest, his heart seeming ready to jump out.

'Why'd you yell out?' Greg demanded aggressively. 'Another thirty seconds and I would have pulled the trigger.'

'There was another one three foot behind us!' Alex responded breathlessly. 'He scared the shit out of me.'

'A fox won't have a go at you unless he's cornered.'

'Well I didn't have time to think about that, did I?'

They both suddenly saw the funny side of it and began to laugh. 'Big game hunters, us two,' Greg said smiling. 'Which way did your bloke go?'

Alex pointed downhill. 'That way somewhere.'

'My bloke went uphill. How about we split up? You keep going the way we were, and I'll meet you at the top. I'll head up from the opposite direction. With a bit of luck, one of us might see Mr Fox again and be close enough to get a decent shot.'

As it turned out, there were no further sightings of their brushtail quarry. Alex was the first to reach the summit, stopping on a small patch of bare rock just below a slight rise that was technically the top of The Granite. A rabbit was silhouetted against the sky at the top of the knoll. He crouched down on one knee and had a perfect view of the rabbit down his gun sights. He was about to squeeze the trigger when the words of his father materialised from somewhere deep in his subconscious. Never shoot without knowing what is in the background. At that very moment, his brother's head appeared behind the rabbit as he climbed the knoll from the other side. The rabbit scampered away, and for the second time today, Alex lay on the ground shaking and struggling for breath. It wouldn't be the last.

The two brothers stood side-by-side atop the knoll and stared at the view of the countryside to the southwest that melded with the sky way beyond Benalla. They could pick out the pattern of roads and lanes between them and their farm, but the buildings and the boundaries of their property were way too small to see from this distance. When they turned to the southeast, the panorama was even more spectacular. Snow still capped the Australian Alps and the reflecting sun fashioned a ribbon of tinsel across the mountaintops.

Two small stone cairns had been erected at some time past to mark the two highest points of the hill and both sites commanded stunning views in all directions. But time was slipping away and a band of black clouds gathering on the western horizon was a portent to an early onset of darkness. Reluctantly content with the two rabbits they had shot in the reserve on Kennedy's Road, the boys resolved to head home before the weather closed in.

Greg pointed down to the house they had seen when they first arrived at The Granite. 'Connie and Chiko are a hundred yards back from there. How about we just bash our way straight down and see how far we get before we need to go sideways around a gully or rocks or thick bush?'

His brother nodded and they headed directly for the house, being scratched by scrub and scraped by rocks as they went. It wasn't until three-quarters of the way down that they met their first obstacle, a rock face with a fifteen or twenty-foot sheer drop to the scrub below. There was no alternative but to follow the top of the mini cliff until they found a way around it. It was an unexpectedly short distance to where they found the rock face disappear into the gravelly soil and they were able to slide on their backsides down to the level where the rock began its thrust towards the sky. The boys followed the rock face until they were again lined up with the house in the paddocks below. After another five minutes the lane came into view below them and to their surprise they encountered a rough track which seemed to lead from the direction of the house and disappear into the scrubby hill above them.

'Pity we didn't see that when we arrived,' Greg said with a smile. 'Might have taken us to the top without all the scratches and bruises.'

Alex laughed but said nothing, happy to be in sight of their horses and looking forward to a quiet canter home. The track turned and passed under another overhanging rock shelf. Greg heard it before he saw what was still to haunt him some forty years later. The buzz of the flies was louder than he had ever heard before, and he had plucked the wool off many a gangrene dead sheep. And the smell was just as overpowering. But the sight was something no boy, or any person for that matter, should ever see. A wedged-tailed eagle drawing lazy circles in the sky had a better view, but neither lad looked up. A man lay on his side with a rifle in his hand with the barrel near his mouth. Much of his head was blown away at the back. The boys stood speechless, Greg wanting to vomit and Alex again breathing heavily, his heart beat racing well into triple digits.

Greg was the first to speak. 'We need to get help. You stay here so I can find this place again. I'll race down to the house and get somebody.'

Alex was having none of that. 'No way. You stay and I'll go get somebody.'

Greg thought for a moment before agreeing. 'Alright, but don't be long. Yell out if you can't find the way back and I'll give you a whistle.'

Alex was gone in an instant, half running, half sliding down the hill towards the house and was totally out of breath by the time he reached the front verandah. He bashed on the glass door screaming for help, but heard no response from inside. He then sprinted by a lime green Celica parked in the carpark and around to the back of the house where he had a similar response to his door thumping. He hurriedly checked the sheds but found no one. A ute was parked under a tree and a couple of dogs were chained up beside forty-four gallon drum kennels. Their water tins were empty, and the animals strained on their chains, barking as the boy ran past.

The younger brother was exhausted by the time he'd climbed back to find Greg. He explained what he'd found, or rather what he'd been unable to find, and the boys resolved to head back, hoping to find Dick Barber home on the way. But Dick wasn't there and his house was locked so they couldn't even use his phone. Both horses were draped in white foam by the time they dismounted under the elm trees at the back of their house. They sprinted inside and turned the problem over to their shocked parents.

CHAPTER 3

'So it was suicide?' the short fat man asked.

Bowker nodded. 'That's my memory of it. His wife left him a week or so before and he must have decided it wasn't worth going on. So he walked across the road into the bush and ended the whole thing.'

'Why not just do it on the farm?' a woman across the table wondered out loud.

Bowker shrugged. 'Dunno. I was just a kid and don't remember much about it. Don't want to really. My brother and I both had nightmares for years afterward.'

Phillips smiled at his wife conspiratorially then looked at Bowker. 'Maybe you can take another look at the case, Detective Inspector Bowker.'

The others at the table were shocked, several staring open-mouthed at the former classmate they hadn't regarded worthy of memory space.

'I didn't know you were a policeman,' one of the women remarked, the remnants of astonishment still etched on her face.

'Not just any policeman either. A bloody detective inspector with homicide, if you don't mind,' Phillips added. Rachael remained quiet but gently patted Bowker on the thigh letting him know he'd made it at last in his hometown.

There was a series of speeches reminiscing about days of yore and thanking the organisers for their hard work. As a final salute to the old school, a former head prefect led the former students in a hearty rendition of the Benalla High war cry.

Boomalacca Boomalacca hoo ra ra

Upotipotpon zip bam ba

Razzle dazzle razzle dazzle hi jigga ja

Up Benalla High School ra ra ra.

Finally, the fist pumping subsided and guests resumed their individual conversations.

'Upotipotpon?' Rachael asked with a smirk.

'Name of a district out near Goomalabee,' Bowker replied straight-faced.

'Oh, out near Goomalabee,' she replied feigning understanding, 'well that clears it up then.'

Everyone around the table laughed.

Bowker shook his head. 'I've got no idea why it's part of the war cry. Just rolls off the tongue.' It sounded silly to Rachael, but she let it slide. It obviously brought back happy memories for those in the room, and that was the main aim of events like this.

The rest of the night went smoothly, but Bowker was content when it was finally over. He had done right by his mate and put in an appearance. The meal was edible, and renewing old acquaintances turned out better than he'd hoped. He touched base with a few of his former teachers, all of whom were retired and most in their twilight years. In spite of the accolades he accrued for rising to the lofty ranks in the police force, his biggest pleasure came from people's reactions when they set eyes on his tall and elegant wife. He particularly enjoyed the envy of men who were regarded as studs at school and who were expected to marry from the top shelf. Who had the last laugh now? Bowker thought to himself.

The following morning the detective took his wife on a trip down memory lane. She had visited the Bowker home in Hair Crescent many times but had never seen the farm where her husband had been raised. The same year Bowker departed for the newly opened police academy in Melbourne, the remainder of the Bowker family relocated to a freshly built house in Benalla, its construction financed through the sale of the house paddock on the farm.

The trip out Kilfeera Road seemed as familiar to Bowker as it was when he was a boy living on the farm. Everyday he would go back and forwards on the bus, although in his later years he landed an afterschool job at a small mixed business on the edge of town that necessitated him riding his bike in and out from the property. He now smiled at the money he had been paid for his services. Twenty-five cents a week, that was later raised to twenty-seven when he had shown himself to be a good worker. He slowed down passing the retirement village on the edge of town built on a site that was once a camp for refugees fleeing post World War 2 Europe. It was known locally as the Balt Camp in reference to those fleeing the Baltic states of northern Europe to escape Russian annexation after the nightmare of Nazi occupation. All the half-mooned shaped Nissen huts were now gone, replaced with tidy red brick units housing elements of Benalla's retirement population.

Adjacent, the Benalla aerodrome was still there, now called the Victorian State Gliding Centre. A couple of miles out of town the couple passed through a T junction which in Bowker's youth was known as the "Five Roads". There were just three roads now, plus the remnants of a lane running down towards the river. To Bowker's memory, the fifth of the roads had vanished before his time as a boy and he took the word of his father that it had earlier existed. A few miles further along they found the entrance to his old farm. Once it was one of the few gates along this section of road, but now many of the adjoining paddocks had been broken up into ten-acre blocks. New tree plantings, or at least new since Bowker lived out here, further camouflaged the entry to the farm and played havoc with the inbuilt compass that had often guided him home in the dark.

With the death of his parents the farm had been sold, so entering the property for a quick look around was inappropriate. Circumnavigating its perimeter was the next best alternative. He stopped opposite the front gate and pointed to the farmhouse a quarter mile into the paddock. It was circled by large elm trees, but they could still pick out the wide verandah around the side and front, the high-pitched iron roof and the white railing fence enclosing the garden.

'Brings back a lot of memories looking at the old place, Rach. I can remember when dad used to give the council grader driver a dozen bottles to grade our drive when he was repairing the edges on this road. When I was really little, we used to have hawkers come to the farm with their horse and wagon. They sold just about everything. One day we even had an escaped criminal visit the house when dad was down the paddock somewhere.'

Rachael looked across at her husband. 'You're joking, right?'

Bowker shook his head. 'No joke. I can remember it like yesterday, but I would have been pretty little. This bloke walked around the back of the house with a big rip in the leg of his pants and asked mum if she could sew it up. Mum thought he was just another swaggy, so she grabbed a needle and thread and sewed up his strides while he was still wearing them. The bloke thanked her and asked for directions to the Hume Highway. Mum pointed across the paddock and told him it was about three or four miles as the crow flies. He headed off, and about half an hour later a police car arrived and the coppers showed mum some pictures and there was his face. Escaped from Pentridge a couple of days earlier. Mum didn't seem too fazed. Reckoned he was a pretty polite sort of bloke.'

'What did your father say when he got home?'

'Nearly had a fit. But we had a lot of unannounced visitors in those days. Hawkers, the Rawleighs and Watkins blokes with their special ointments. Didn't seem to be as much stranger-danger then.'

'Not that you knew about anyway.'

Bowker pointed across towards the shearing shed. 'See that sand hill over there? In a thousand years, archaeologists are gonna dig there and wonder what sort of strange ceremonies were conducted on that rise.'

Rachael smiled. 'OK, I'll be the sucker and ask why.'

'My little sister's Shetland pony died, and Dad asked Alex and I to bury it on that sandy rise. We towed the horse up there behind the ute and dug a pretty big hole. Big enough to fit a horse, or so we thought. But when we towed the pony into the hole, his four legs were sticking out above the ground and there was no way to get him out again.'

'So did you heap up the sand until his hooves were covered?'

Bowker tapped his temple. 'The Bowker boys are a lot smarter than that. We got a hacksaw out of the ute and cut his legs off and threw them into the hole. Problem fixed.'

Rachael grinned. 'Bullshit.'

Bowker shook his head. 'No Bullshit, I promise. However, we did consider getting a piece of plywood and nailing it onto his hooves to make a table!'

Rachael slapped his arm playfully. 'Now that *is* bullshit.'

Directly opposite the farm's gateway was Standish's Lane. This was a rough gravel track that ran down to a house half a mile to the south. It then continued as a bushy, grass-covered, only half fenced reserve down to the Hollands River. This track and its junction with the creek had been the scene of many an equine adventure for Bowker and his brother during their youth. Fishing, shooting and various exploits on horseback were all part of the fun during a golden age for kids growing up.

As they drove down Hunters Lane at the rear of the old farm, Rachael pointed through her open window. 'Is that the hill you were talking about last night?' she asked. 'Where you found the farmer who'd shot himself?'

Bowker knew where she was pointing without needing to look. 'Yeah, that's The Granite. I'll drive you up there for a squiz. Used to take a couple of hours on a horse, but it'll take us less than fifteen minutes in the car.' He did a U turn in a farm gateway, then turned left into Kennedy's Lane and drove north up past Dick Barber's old house. To his surprise several other residences had sprung up along the lane near the bush reserve where the road circled a small sandy rise and where they had shot rabbits on the day they found the body.

'These houses weren't here when I was a kid,' he said, indicating with the lift of a steering wheel finger. 'Pity. Would have given us a few more places to sound the alarm after we found the dead bloke. We were absolutely shitting ourselves, I can tell you.'

Within a few minutes they were at the base of The Granite and Bowker could see that nothing much had changed in forty years. No attempt had been made to tame the wild scrub and the hill's stony surface continued to render the reserve useless for agriculture. The farmhouse where the dead man had lived was obviously still in use, but Bowker suspected it was a cheap rental for a family on struggle street. The house was now in dire need

24

of maintenance. A missing verandah post and flapping iron on the roof bore witness to a building left to deteriorate at its own pace. A shabby pink tricycle and a cracked, faded plastic sand pit in the front yard told the story of a young family doing it hard.

'Bring back memories, Greg?' Rachael asked, placing her hand on Bowker's forearm.

'Yeah. Causes a few little twitches in the gut. Only the second dead body I'd ever seen. First one with their face blown off, though. Seen a lot since of course, but for a kid it was a pretty big shock.'

'Where did you see your first dead person?'

'In the town beside the river under the bridge,' Bowker replied. 'Kid from school drowned in the swimming hole. The lake wasn't built until the mid 70s. When I was a kid it was just the Broken River running through town and there wasn't a proper swimming pool. Like most towns, everybody swum in the river. There used to be a big willow tree just upstream of the main bridge and that's where the swimming hole was. When they hauled the kid out of the water, he was well dead. Scared the life out of me. But nothing like the bloke up here on the hill.'

'Another sad story to take back to Melbourne,' Rachael responded.

'People talk about the good old days Rach, but hell there was a lot of tragedy. The child mortality was high, people died in accidents all over the place, and crime per head of population was probably higher than it is now.' He patted the steering wheel with two hands and smiled broadly. 'Let's head back to Caulfield, eh? I've done my duty for the old town for another twenty years.'

If only he knew what was to come.

CHAPTER 4

Bowker sat at his desk in the multi-storey police headquarters in Melbourne's Spencer Street staring out the window. The week before he had tidied up the paperwork surrounding a fatal stabbing in the outer suburb of Caroline Springs. It was yet another case of an all-too-familiar scenario, a minor altercation spiralling out of control leaving one dead and another who would spend a significant part of his life behind bars. Now, for the first time in months, the detective inspector had clear air to work on a report he was compiling for the Chief Commissioner on trends in homicides across the state. Just as he opened the folder containing historical crime figures, Detective Sergeant Darren Holmes entered the room carrying a cup of coffee. He wandered over to Bowker's desk. In his late forties, Holmes was only slightly shorter than Bowker and not quite as heavily built. He had receding sandy hair, a brown moustache and sparkling green eyes. He carried a constant smile and put people at ease in his presence.

'How'd the reunion go?' he said as he put down the coffee, pulled over a spare chair and sat down.

Bowker leaned back and knitted his fingers behind his head. 'Interesting, Sherlock. Very interesting.'

'All your former classmates drop to their knees and worship at the feet of another Benalla success story?' Holmes asked with a smile. He took a sip of his drink.

Bowker laughed out loud. 'Nobody even remembered I'd gone to their school. Six bloody years in the same class and no one could place me. And some had been through Primary with me, for shit's sake. Even when I pointed myself out in a class photo, they had no recollection of my existence.'

Holmes raised his eyebrows. 'Are you fair dinkum?'

'Bloody oath I'm fair dinkum.'

Holmes grinned. 'You must have made a big impression as a kid.'

'Obviously.'

'People always remember me when I go back up to Murrayville,' Holmes added with a straight face.

'That's because there were only three kids in each year level up there.' Bowker saw a grin materialise on Holmes's face. 'Yeah, well done. You sucked me in.'

'Many people turn up?'

'Yeah, a couple of hundred probably. One aspect *was* good for the ego, though. A lot of the blokes who regarded themselves as shit-hot studs at school are now little old overweight farts who have spent their lives in dead-end jobs. Rachael said I looked twenty years younger than most of them.'

'Do you think she might be biased?'

'I bloody hope so!'

Holmes chuckled. 'So you had them covered?'

Bowker nodded. 'I'd say pretty comfortably, unless my bathroom mirror is playing tricks.' He paused for a moment. 'One lesson I did learn though. Don't hold on to those rose-coloured images of girls you reckoned were a bit of alright at school. You may get a shock when you see how they've matured. Met a couple of women I thought were drop-dead gorgeous at school. Now you could hire them out to haunt a house.'

Holmes sprayed a mouthful of coffee all over Bowker's paperwork. His senior colleague mopped it up with a handful of tissues.

'So how long did you stay if nobody thought you were worth remembering?' Holmes asked as he wiped down the front of his shirt.

'Once they found out I was a homicide detective they seemed to show a bit more interest. Especially after they figured out I was the kid who found the dead bloke up in the scrub.' Bowker saw the confused look on Holmes's face. 'Haven't I told you about the farmer with a bullet through his skull?'

Holmes shook his head. Bowker spent the next ten minutes describing what had happened all those years ago.

'Bet it stirred you up.'

'Bloody oath it did. Seen a lot worse since, but not a pretty sight for an innocent farm kid.' He stood. 'That coffee looks pretty good. I might grab one for myself. I've still got that homicide trends report to tidy up. It's in that blue folder. Run your eyes over it while I grab a drink.'

As Bowker walked away, Holmes placed his mug on the desk, grabbed the blue folder and leaned back in his chair. He had just finished reading the second page when Bowker's phone rang. He picked up. 'Greg Bowker's phone, Darren Holmes speaking.' The detective listened and shook his head. 'You've got to be bloody joking. He was only up there yesterday. Hold on while I get a pen and paper.' He threw the report back on Bowker's desk and rifled around until he found a biro and a note pad. 'OK, shoot.' Holmes listened carefully and jotted down notes. 'OK, thanks mate. Greg will ring you back.' Holmes looked at the pad and exhaled loudly. 'Fuck me,' he mumbled to himself.

Bowker returned to his desk blowing on his coffee. 'Didn't take you long to read my report. That bad, was it?'

Holmes smiled. 'Didn't really get into it. Your phone rang. What are you doing tomorrow?'

'I'd planned to work on that report. Why?'

'Fancy a trip to Benalla?' Holmes asked with a grin.

Bowker was puzzled. 'Don't tell me.'

Holmes picked up the note pad. 'You'll know the place better than me, obviously. A body was found against the retaining wall at the outlet of Lake Benalla. Major trauma to the back of the head. Vic is a 73-year-old male. ID'd as a Gary Edward Rice of Arundel Street.'

Bowker was visibly shocked. 'Gary Rice?' he asked in bewilderment. 'I was only talking to him on Saturday night. One of those lovable old schoolteachers who wouldn't do anyone a bad deed.'

'Well unless he tripped and fell backwards on a rock or something similar, then someone doesn't share that view. The detective at Benalla is pretty convinced it wasn't an accident. I presume you'll take the case. This being in your old stomping ground and all that.'

'What have you got on this week?'

'Nothing urgent at this stage. I'm waiting for one of the witnesses to the Delany shooting to be located before I can proceed much further with that case.'

'I'd like you on this one with me. Hopefully we can knock it over by the end of the week. I've got a granddaughter's christening in Geelong on Sunday, so I'd like to be home by Friday night if possible.'

'Hopefully, it'll be one of those straightforward jobs that the locals have solved before we get up there.'

Bowker nodded. 'I've can think of two prime suspects already.

When Rachael and I arrived at the reunion, a pair of Rice's ex-students were trying to heavy him in the car park.'

'Nice start to a reunion.'

'These blokes weren't going to the reunion. They were already pissed and heading down to the lake with their fishing gear and an esky stacked with VB cans. One of the blokes, Sanderson I think was his name, had an axe to grind about a reference Rice wrote for him when he left school. Reckons it cost him an apprenticeship with a brickie. He blames that for the rest of his life turning to shit and him spending a couple of stints inside.'

'Big call. Must have been a doozy of a reference.'

'You know what these blokes are like, Sherlock. It's always somebody else's fault. Professional victims.'

That evening, Rachael was saddened when Bowker explained he was returning to Benalla. She leant against the rail of the back deck and was quiet for a moment as she remembered the elderly man with whom she had conversed less than 48 hours earlier. She then looked up into her husband's eyes. 'He seemed like a really nice, gentle, community-minded man Greg. I presume you'll be chatting to those thugs who hassled him outside the dinner.'

'They'll be my first port of call. The body was found against the stone dam wall so it could have entered the water anywhere upstream of that. Given that Sanderson and his mate were fishing somewhere along that stretch, it puts them in the right place at the right time. But Rice's home also backs onto the weir so there's a chance he was accosted at home and his body dumped in the water up that end of the lake.'

Rachael frowned. 'Could it have been an accident? Could he have hit his head and drowned?'

'There's always that chance,' Bowker replied, 'but the coppers in Benalla seem to think it unlikely. We'll have to wait for the coroner's report before we can be sure about anything. It'll tell us the seriousness of the wound and whether he drowned or was already dead when he hit the water.'

'What if it's not those two thugs?'

'Then we'll look for other motives. Was it part of a robbery? Did he have any enemies? Did he owe people money? The normal rule of thumb at Homicide is that you look to the two obvious things first. Money and sex.' Bowker chuckled. 'In his case I think we can probably downplay the latter.'

Rachael threw her arms around her husband's neck. 'I dunno. Getting a bit older hasn't slowed you down, Big Boy.'

Bowker placed his hands on her backside. 'I'm not in my seventies yet, am I?'

'Well we better make as much hay as we can while the sun's still shining,' she said flirtatiously as she led him by the hand into the house.

Bowker collected Holmes from his Preston house before dawn and they were on the Hume Freeway twenty minutes later.

'Sorry to keep doing this to you mate,' Bowker said. 'Weeks away from home last year with the murder up in the Mallee. Now I'm dragging you off to another one of my old stomping grounds.'

'All part of the job, Greg,' Holmes replied, before hesitating for a moment. 'Besides, it won't hurt if I'm out of the house for a few days.'

Bowker looked across at his colleague. 'Trouble in paradise?'

Holmes stared straight ahead. 'Something like that.'

When Holmes didn't elaborate, Bowker let the topic slide. He knew his friend sufficiently well to know he would talk when he felt he needed to. Holmes smiled and changed the subject. 'I'm losing my hair, hand over fist. Don't want to finish up looking like my old man doing his Friar Tuck impersonation. What do you think I'd look like if I started shaving my head?' He ran his two hands over his scalp. 'You know, do a Michael Jordan or The Rock.'

Bowker chuckled. 'Not sure white blokes are as trendy.'

'Better than looking like a modern-day Billy McMahon!'

They both burst into laughter.

Once clear of the city, they turned their attention to breakfast and temporarily left the freeway at Wallan to use the drive-through at an all-night Maccas. Bowker shook his head as he contemplated the enormous suburban sprawl that had now engulfed the area. He remembered the days when once a year, his parents took the family on a holiday down to what is now called the Surf Coast. Their Hume Highway journey passed through places like Wallen and Craigieburn and Beverage and Kalkalo, all mere whistle stops many miles outside the metropolitan area. They identified the start of Melbourne with the Faulkner crematorium and they knew that within minutes came one of the highlights of the trip, seeing the green and yellow trams in Sydney Road. Such has been the continual growth of Melbourne, that the crematorium was now geographically closer to the city centre than it was to the outskirts of the greater metropolitan area.

The detectives arrived at the district police headquarters in Benalla at a little after 8am, several hours too early to register at the motel Bowker had booked across the road. The temperature had already climbed into the thirties with the forecast predicting forty-three by mid-afternoon. The police building is a two-storied brick, concrete and glass rectangular box located on a triangular block facing the wide Bridge Street West which was formerly part of the original Hume Highway. Bowker had visited the police station once before when he obtained his driver's licence. It wasn't the big deal young drivers are put through nowadays. Bowker remembers answering a few questions, then going for a casual drive around the town while his father sat in the back seat chatting about beef cattle with the police officer who had a small farm of his own.

The two detectives introduced themselves to a young officer manning the front desk and they were shown to the CID office area. There they were introduced to Detective Constable Kirsten Larsen and Detective Sergeant Aaron Fleming before being invited to take a seat at a table in the centre of the room. Larsen was a tall, attractive woman with her blond hair tied back in a ponytail. In her early thirties, she had a friendly welcoming smile, deep blue eyes and a peaches and cream complexion. Her name and appearance hinted strongly at a Nordic heritage. She wore skin-tight jeans, a musk pink silk blouse and black medium-heeled ankle-high boots. Bowker suspected she hadn't been with the force for her full working life, since absent was the hard face often associated with officers who have seen things they wished they hadn't. But he was wrong this time. Larsen had joined after dropping out of university and was tough as nails. Fleming was smaller by comparison, with a narrow black moustache and a constant scowl. He wore a charcoal grey suit, white shirt and matching tie. Bowker was to find out later that Fleming's friends called him "Sammy" in reference to his uncanny resemblance to Sammy Davis Jnr. After the usual pleasantries, including the Detective Inspector's connection with Benalla and his attendance at the weekend's reunion, they got down to business.

'What do we know so far?' Bowker asked.

'A seventy-three-year-old male, name Gary Edward Rice, was discovered deceased, floating against the rock dam wall of Lake Benalla early Monday morning,' Fleming replied. 'Massive wound on the back of the skull. The coroner's report will hopefully tell us how long he'd been in the water and whether he drowned or died from the blow.'

Holmes folded his hands in front of him on the table. 'Who found him?' he asked.

'A recently married couple walking their dogs before work. The young bloke ventured out along the rocks when he saw something in the water. At first he thought it was a bag of something, then got a hell of a shock when he took a closer look. He knew it was Rice. The victim lived a few doors down.'

Bowker leaned back in his chair and folded his arms. 'What was Rice wearing?'

'Beige trousers, a navy-blue jacket and a red bow tie,' Larsen replied.

'Same as he was dressed Saturday night at the school reunion up the lake at the footy club,' Bowker said. 'Safe to assume, he was accosted on his way home. He told me he lived somewhere along the lake and his plan was to walk back there after the dinner.'

'His house is in Arundel Street. Pretty close to where he was found in fact,' Larsen added.

'Could have been killed anywhere between the weir and the footy club and his body just floated down on the current,' Fleming surmised.

'Did you find a wallet on him?' Holmes asked.

Fleming nodded. 'Yeah. Inside coat pocket. Money and credit cards still in it so I guess we can rule out robbery.'

'Any sign of his walking stick?' Bowker asked.

'No report of it,' Larsen replied. 'Could be on the bottom of the lake or floating on the surface somewhere. Depends on how heavy it was and what it was made of, I guess. Could even be washed up among the reeds and snags.'

'Probably worth putting it around town that if anyone sees a walking stick near the lake to let us know. Preferably without touching it,' Bowker replied.

Fleming jotted a note on a pad in front of him. 'I'll make sure the *Ensign* includes it in their story.'

'Is he married?' Holmes asked.

Fleming nodded. 'Yeah. His second marriage, according to one of our older coppers who has a bit to do with him at Rotary. The wife's name is Arabella, widow of a prominent plastic surgeon from the city. Bit younger than Rice and likes to think of herself as a class above, apparently. She has a couple of grown-up daughters. They both live in Melbourne, from what we've heard.'

Bowker scratched his ear. 'Did Rice's first wife pass away, or did they divorce?'

'Divorce,' Fleming replied. 'There's a daughter from that marriage. She and her husband work a big property Rice owns on the river flats up at Tatong.'

Holmes raised his eyebrows. 'Did well to buy that on a teacher's wage.'

'Inherited from his father,' Fleming explained. 'Greg Rice was an only child and had no interest in farming, thus the teaching career.'

'Does the first wife still live in Benalla?' Bowker asked.

'Yeah. Well near enough anyway,' Fleming replied. 'She's down at Baddaginnie on a hobby farm. Lives with a hothead called Tony Marshall, who works casually at one of the Benalla tyre places. He breeds and races a few greyhounds. Without much success, I gather. Been done a few times for live baiting. You know the story, possums or rabbits. What the woman sees in him has got everybody beat.'

'Financial security, perhaps,' Holmes replied.

'I doubt it. When she and Rice divorced, I'd imagine there was an asset carve-up.' Fleming shrugged. 'But Rice still owns that big property, so I can't give you much on the ins and outs of any settlement.'

'Just as likely that Rice's father was still alive and the farm still belonged to him when his son divorced,' Larsen suggested.

Bowker nodded. 'Makes sense,' he said as he took a notebook from his jacket pocket. 'Can I run a couple of names past you. Noel Sanderson.'

The Benalla officers looked at each other before Fleming spoke. 'Sanderson is a dumb-arse piece of shit. Petty thief and stand-over merchant. Had a couple of stints in prison for aggravated assault and possession of stolen goods. How have you come across him?'

'Ran into him outside the school reunion,' Bowker replied.

Fleming laughed. 'You've got the wrong bloke, mate. Turning up to school would have been a stretch, let alone a reunion.'

'He was in the carpark heavying Gary Rice,' Bowker replied. 'Half pissed with his mate. They were heading down to the lake with their fishing gear. Sanderson was giving Rice a hard time about some reference he'd written that had cost him a good job.'

Fleming shook his head. 'Sanderson's unemployable except for shovelling shit. He does a bit of that on a casual basis at the sale yards.' He chuckled. 'A reference would have been the least of his problems.'

Larsen pointed at Bowker's notebook. 'If you've recorded names, I take it you must have intervened in the kafuffle,' she asked.

'Yeah. Sent them on their way. Rice didn't want it taken further. Said he could do without the angst.'

Fleming leant back in his chair and folded his arms across his chest. 'But you suspect Sanderson took it further and whacked him on the head later in the night?'

'It's a good starting point,' Bowker replied.

'I bet the bloke with him was Glen Brown,' Larsen suggested.

Bowker nodded. 'Yep. What do we know about him?'

'Dumb as dog shit,' Fleming replied. 'Makes Sanderson look

like Einstein. Stole a hotted-up Monaro from a bloke around the corner and tried to hide it behind the dump where he lives. The owner saw it there and drove it home. Brown was straight on the phone to us complaining that someone had stolen a car from his backyard!'

The four officers laughed.

Fleming looked at Bowker. 'Do you want us to bring in Sanderson and Brown for a chat?'

Bowker shook his head. 'No. I'd like to hit them cold. If we can have their addresses, Sherlock and I will talk to one each so they don't have time to hatch a story together.'

Larsen left the room to chase down the relevant addresses. Fleming checked his watch. At this time of day, you'll probably find them at home in bed. If Sanderson's not there he may be out at the sale yards. I don't think Brown has ever worked, so if he's not home you might find it difficult tracking him down.'

'Maybe he'd be at the sale yards helping Sanderson?' Holmes suggested.

Fleming shook his head. 'I doubt he'd risk getting that close to work.' He looked at Bowker. 'Anything we can do here to help with the enquiry?'

'Be handy if you can track down a list of all the people who attended the reunion,' Bowker suggested. 'Maybe one of them saw something that might be a help.'

Fleming shrugged. 'Big job if you're going to interview them all.'

'Hopefully we'll crack this thing open before we need to do that,' Bowker replied. 'You better show us where the body was found before we talk to Brown and Sanderson.'

CHAPTER 5

In spite of the police car being parked in the shade, the interior was stifling and all four detectives wound down their windows in unison as they climbed in. Luckily, the trip to the lake's stone retaining wall took less than a minute. Fleming crossed the railway line in Arundel street, turned right at the roundabout and parked on the side of the road just short of what was known locally as the stocky. It had likely been years since any sheep or cattle had been driven across the Broken at this point, but the stock bridge's original purpose in times before motorised transport was to allow drovers to cross the river or to give farmers to the west access to the saleyards. The only other place to cross the Broken within miles of the town was the old highway bridge that carried the main shopping street of the town. Town planners had long ago concluded this was not the ideal route for droving sheep or cattle.

The quartet alighted from the car and were met with a dissonance of cicada chirping and frog croaking. Fleming led them fifty metres south through the dry grass along the riverbank and under the steel railway bridge to the lake's retaining wall. It was a modest curved structure comprising many tonnes of rock. A spillway to the eastern end of the wall allowed water to flow into the creek bed below. The detective sergeant scrambled to the top of the wall with the other three following him to a spot about a third of the way along. Fleming pointed to the waterline. 'This is where Rice was found. Face down. Just floating there.'

Bowker shaded his eyes from the sun, feeling its heat burn his face. The reflection off the water caused him to squint. 'Anything else found?'

'Fair bit of rubbish washed up against the wall,' Larsen replied. 'You can see a bit starting to build up now, even though we fished all the stuff out yesterday. It's all bagged up at the station.'

'Anything of obvious interest?' Holmes asked.

Larsen shook her head. 'Nothing that jumped out at us. Mostly chip papers, cling wrap, the odd stubby. Nothing that seems relevant to this case. A lot of it was faded or decomposed, suggesting it had been in the water for a good while.'

'Forensics find any blood on the rocks?' Bowker asked.

Fleming shook his head. 'Nah. Nothing. They don't reckon he was killed here. There'd have to be at least a blood spatter they reckon.'

Bowker pointed south. 'Find anything along the path that led back to the main bridge and the footy ground?'

Fleming spread his hands. 'Until you arrived this morning, we didn't know he'd walked home that way.' With the nod of his head he indicated a house on the western side of the lake. 'He lives just up there. We had no reason to suspect he walked along that path. Hell, we didn't even know he'd been to the reunion until you told us.'

'Surely his wife knew,' Bowker suggested. 'And how come she didn't report him missing when he didn't arrive home on Saturday night?'

'She'd been in Melbourne visiting her youngest daughter who's just had a new bub and was apparently struggling a bit. Didn't get in until Sunday lunchtime. Came home ahead of time because

Rice wasn't answering the home phone or his mobile and she was worried he might have had a turn or something. He was diabetic and he'd had episodes in the past. We had hell's trouble tracking her down to deliver the grim news.'

'How'd she take it?' Holmes asked.

'Devastated, as you'd imagine,' Larsen replied. 'She expected she might find him on the floor when she got home and was relieved when he wasn't there. But that changed pretty quickly.'

'We've had a quick chat with her,' Fleming added. 'The house was locked up when she got home, and we didn't find any evidence of forced entry. Until you mentioned Sanderson and Brown this morning, we had no leads at all. Rather than crashing around in the dark, we thought we'd leave a blank canvas and call in you blokes.' He chuckled as he looked at Bowker. 'That's why you get paid the big money, isn't it?'

Bowker didn't take the bait. 'Can you get a couple of uniforms to search the path beside the lake. Might find something that could help.'

'Kirstin can organise that as soon as we get back to the station,' Fleming replied. 'Anything else, here?'

'Don't think so, Aaron,' Bowker replied. 'Besides, we'll cook if we stay here much longer. The heat coming off these rocks is bloody amazing.'

As they retreated along the wall of the weir, Larsen's heeled boot slipped on a loose rock and she overbalanced. If it hadn't been for Holmes's lightning reflexes, she was destined for an impromptu swim in Lake Benalla. Holmes's arm flew around Larsen's trim waist and he effortlessly lifted her back to safety.

'Lucky for the long arm of the law, eh?' Larsen said looking at Holmes with a wide smile.

'Yeah, luck all round,' he replied.

Behind them, Fleming scowled.

Holmes booked out an unmarked police car, cranked up the air conditioner and followed its GPS directions to Glen Brown's address on the northern side of the main Sydney to Melbourne railway line. It was hard to believe anyone lived inside the derelict weatherboard house, but a rusted number on the half-rotted gatepost confirmed Holmes had the right place. Most of the paint had peeled from the exterior walls and several windows had broken panes and were lined with torn and bleached printed cardboard. The front verandah had been converted into an enclosed sleep out many years ago and the rusting fly wire had large sections missing or hanging limply from the rotting fascia. Thistles grew along the front and the yard was a dumping ground for old cars and various other decaying pieces of junk. Holmes climbed the steps to the front door feeling the springiness of the rotting timber under his feet. The front door was boarded up and the detective quickly assessed this entrance had not been used for years. He picked his way through the disassembled parts of an ancient motorbike in the carport as a scrawny cat crossed his path and disappeared under the house. The backyard was more depressing than the front. Canvas exterior blinds hung from both northern windows, faded and torn. A hole in the ground near the back steps was filled with stagnant greasy water, fouling the air with a putrid fetor. Holmes surmised a drainage pipe had blocked and a hole had been dug to allow the stinking waste to clear the inside of the house. He knocked on the door. A skinny timeworn face appeared, staring through the torn fly wire.

'Fuck off arsehole. How many times do I have to tell you bastards that God's missed his chance with me.'

'Mr Brown? Mr Glen Brown?' Holmes asked.

'Might be. But I'm not interested in religion and I've got no fuckin' money to donate to charity. And if you're trying to get me to change who supplies my electricity, you're wastin' your fuckin time because I don't have the power on.'

Holmes displayed his ID. 'I'm Detective Sergeant Holmes. I need to ask you a few questions.'

'Whatever you're fuckin' on about had nothin' to do with me, mate.' Brown replied quickly.

Holmes smiled. 'I haven't mentioned a crime, Mr Brown.'

'Well you don't normally get a detective in your back yard unless something's happened some-fuckin'-where. I bloody know I've done nothing against the law lately, so whatever you want to talk about had nothing to do with me. End of fuckin' story.'

'Can I come in?' Holmes asked. 'Should only take a few minutes.'

'No, fuck ya. I don't need no coppers lookin' around my house. If we need to talk, we can do it in the yard.' Brown pointed towards the back fence. 'There's an outdoor setting under the tree back there.'

Holmes turned and saw the rusting wrought iron table with accompanying chairs in a patch of stinging nettles under a struggling golden ash. He nodded. 'OK looks like a nice spot in the shade.'

Brown came through the back door with Holmes surprised at how short he was. There was no way he was more than five-foot-six in the old. The policeman suspected Brown had been standing on something inside the door to make himself appear more imposing if confronted with unwanted visitors. His hair was cut very short, a number one or two with clippers, Holmes thought. Probably a self-done job. He was as skinny as a rake and his skin was rough and pallid. In need of a decent drench, the farmer part of Holmes's background told him. Gut full of worms was his rough diagnosis. Brown wore an oversized black muscle tee shirt *sans* the muscles. Filthy torn jeans and bare feet completed a vision of sartorial splendor. Holmes followed

Brown to the old table and chairs, flattening the nettles with his feet to avoid being stung. A brown skink scurried away into the grass while two Asian mynas squawked in the branches overhead. Once seated, the detective asked a few Dorothy Dixers to get the discussion started. 'How old are you Glen?'

'Forty-six next January.'

'You go to Benalla High?'

'Yeah. But shoulda gone to the fuckin' Tech. Taught me fuck-nothin' at the high school.'

'Are you working at the moment?'

'Haven't had a job since I was an apprentice jockey. But fuck that for a job. You can't eat nothin' worth eatin' and you have to be up before daylight. Bloody trainers tellin' you what to do all the time. I'm happy to be my own boss.'

Holmes tried to keep a straight face. 'You know anyone called Noel Sanderson?'

Brown nodded. 'Sando? Yeah, he's me best mate. We went through school together. Both decided to leave at the end of Form 3.' He raised his eyebrows and looked up into the tree. 'Actually, my decision was made for me. Vice Principal asked me if I was going home for lunch. When I said that I was, he asked me if I'd do him a favour. Don't come back.'

'Bit of a trouble maker at school, were you?'

Brown shrugged. 'No more than a lot of others. Pretty boring sitting at a desk all day when you don't understand nothin' and you can't fuckin' read what they write on the board.'

Holmes felt a tinge of sympathy. 'Can you read now?'

'Not much. Overrated fuckin' readin' and writin'. Hasn't held me back.'

Holmes wasn't sure how to respond so he returned to business. 'You know Gary Rice?'

'The fuckin' old school teacher?'

'Yeah.'

Brown exhaled heavily. 'Haven't seen him since I left school and I don't care if I never see the fucker again. He was just like all the other teachers. Always on my back about something.'

'I've been talking to someone who said they saw you with him on Saturday night up at the footy ground. There was some sort of school reunion up there.'

Brown hesitated as he assessed his options. 'Actually, I might have walked past him there. Slipped me mind.'

'Did you go to the reunion?'

Brown burst out laughing. 'What do you fuckin' reckon? I hated school. Do you think I'd be wanting to bring back memories of the bloody place?'

'Did you talk to Gary Rice at the footy ground?' Holmes asked.

Brown hesitated then shook his head. 'Nuh. Just saw the old prick in the carpark on the way to doin' a bit of fishin'.'

'Was Noel Sanderson with you?'

'Yeah, Sando and I often go down the Lake fishing and sink a few tubes while we're there. Need a bit of down time every fuckin' now and then.'

Holmes slapped a mosquito on his forearm then flicked the dead insect away. 'The witness said Sanderson was giving Rice a hard time. Pushing the old man back against a car and accusing him of writing a negative reference and costing him a good job. That ring a bell?'

Brown maintained a po-face. 'Better get yourself a better witness because that never fuckin' happened. Sando might have mouthed off a bit, but nothin' else.'

Holmes chuckled for effect. 'My witness is a detective inspector from the homicide squad who said he had to step in to control your mate.'

Brown stared at the table for a moment then looked up at

Holmes. 'Oh, that bloke. OK there was a bit of a scuffle, but then Sando and me wandered off down the Lake.'

Holmes folded his hands on the table. 'Why didn't you tell me that in the first place instead of spouting all this bullshit?'

Brown shrugged again. 'Sando's me mate. I don't dob on me mates.'

'Dob on him for what?'

'Pushing Rice around. That's what you're here for isn't it? The old bloke's decided he'll put us in.'

Holmes kept his counsel. 'Catch any fish?'

Brown sniffed loudly as he thought back. 'One decent sized reddy and about twenty-five fuckin' carp.'

'What do you do with the carp?'

'Throw 'em up on the bank to die. Sometimes Sando whacks 'em on the head with a tyre lever.'

'Why would you take a tyre lever fishing?'

'Defend ourselves if someone comes lookin' for us. Someone like the fuckin' Trilgonis from up at Wang. Sando's been havin' run ins with them for twenty years. Something to do with drugs. I don't know much more than that. Just know Sando's been belted senseless a couple of times and he's shit scared of them.'

'Which spots did you fish?'

'Started up where the river runs into the lake. Up near the start of the island. Worked our way down to the bridge. That's where we caught the reddy on a spinner.'

'How long did you stay at the lake?'

'Well after dark. We set a few springers along the bank to see if we could catch a big cod. Used Bardi grubs. Stayed till pretty late to see if something took the bait. Those big buggers feed close to the bank at night.'

Holmes was a country boy from just south of the Murray and knew that springers were whippy small-diameter tree branches with a short piece of fishing line attached carrying a baited hook. They could be left unattended and if a big fish took the bait the springiness in the bespoke rod would prevent the fish breaking the line. They were made illegal in most inland fisheries due to their overuse when many fishermen set dozens of such lines. Springers had nothing to do with the sport of fishing. They were a greedy method of harvesting the already scarce Murray Cod.

'See anybody else by the lake?'

Brown shook his head. 'Only a few people fart-arsin' around on the flats on the other side. Didn't see nobody on our side.'

'Anybody from the reunion walk down by the river?'

'Not that I saw. Sando may have seen someone, but he didn't mention nothin'.'

Holmes became more interested. 'Weren't the two of you together?' he asked.

Brown shook his head. 'Not all of the time. When we decided to pull up stumps, I went and checked the springers upstream, and Sando checked the ones near the bridge and down past the wanker's art gallery.'

'And it was dark when you checked the lines?'

'Shit yeah. Couldn't see two foot in front of your face.'

'Where'd you meet up again?'

'Near the footy club. There's some security lights there.'

'Was the reunion still going?'

'There was noise inside, but most of the cars were gone. We walked back to Sando's house and knocked down a bottle of whisky. I bunked down there for the night. Too fuckin' far for me to walk back here and Sando was worried the cops might stop him at that time of night if he'd drove me home.' Brown laughed. 'I reckon he would have blown point one-five at least.'

'You know using springers is illegal, don't you?' Holmes asked.

'That's only in New South Wales and in the bloody Murray,'

46

Brown replied aggressively. 'You can use two lines with hooks down here. Doesn't say anything about springers.'

'But you had more than two each though, didn't you?'

Brown didn't answer.

'Don't worry, I'm not here checking fishing regulations. Fisheries officers look after that side of things, so you better be careful next time.'

Brown didn't like to be lectured, looking up at the sky and sighing loudly.

'Anyway, did you catch anything on the springers?' Holmes asked.

'Not up my end. I think the yabbies' got most of our grubs. Sando said he caught a nine-pound fuckin' carp. Thought he had a cod and was pretty pissed off when he saw what was on the end of the line. Bashed the fuckin' thing with the tyre lever.' Brown chuckled. 'Should have seen the angry bastard. Blood all over him.'

While Holmes spoke to Brown, Bowker was conducting a similar discussion with Noel Sanderson at his rented abode in Garden Street, a more affluent part of town than where his mate lived. The house looked out of place in the leafy street, a cheap transportable cement sheet-clad building dropped on the small block some decades prior with little done in the years since to maintain or enhance its value. The building's footprint was a long rectangle. It had a flat roof and its front was dissected evenly by four square aluminium sash windows. None had fly screens. The front yard was overgrown with weeds and brambles except on two parallel dirt strips that led to a skillion carport attached to the end of the house. Amongst the weeds were piles of junk; old tyres, sheets of rusty weld mesh, a pair of corroded gas hot water units, plus an assortment of other detritus. The building's deep mauve decades-old paint scheme did little to enhance a residence that Bowker felt sure neighbours resented.

As the detective approached the broken down front fence, an elderly man he'd seen checking his letterbox called to him. 'Don't go in there, mate. Angry bastard he is.'

Bowker wandered across. 'Noel Sanderson, you talking about?'

The old man hitched up his trousers. 'Yeah. I wouldn't set foot on the place if I was you. He'd rather have a fight than a feed. Nobody in the street talks to him. And look at the brothel he lives in. Council has tried to get him to clean it up, but he just tells them to fuck off.' The man leaned in closer to Bowker. 'There's suspicion he doctored one of the council trucks after they put an order on his yard. Bloody wheel came off and killed the driver.'

'I'm sure the police investigated,' Bowker replied.

'Couldn't prove anything, they said. I've complained about him on a couple of occasions and after the last time I found a fire burning on my front verandah. I'd like to move out to a retirement village but I can't sell this place. Who'd pay a decent price to live next to that?' He pointed with a shaking finger towards Sanderson's yard.

'Who owns it? Surely they have some control on what's happening with their property?'

'It still belongs to old Mrs Toohey I think. But she's in God's waiting room at the hospital. Dementia, poor old girl.'

Bowker introduced himself and thanked the old man for the heads-up he didn't really need.

Sanderson's front door had frosted glass panels through which Bowker could make out a large cupboard pushed against it, so he walked around to the rear of the house. He passed an old orange Datsun 180B in the carport before being accosted by an angry dobermann-cross which bailed him up, growling with fangs exposed.

'Shut the fuck up, Fuhrer! I told you! It's only a fucking bird!' came a voice from inside the house. The dog growled louder and inched closer to the detective who was now regretting his decision to leave his service revolver locked in his car. Suddenly the back door flew open and Sanderson stormed out, an old golf stick held above his hand. 'I told you to shut the fuck ...' He stood mute on the doorstep when he spotted the police officer. Sanderson was overweight, with a round fat face in which his eyes were set back, a little too close together. There was a long scar above the bridge of his nose and he hadn't shaved for days. Judging by his body odour, Bowker was sure he hadn't showered in that time either. He wore torn baggy shorts that had slipped down exposing the waistband of his faded red jocks. He had indistinct tattoos on his arms and legs. A blue singlet that failed to fully cover a white beer gut, and worn rubber thongs on his podgy tattooed feet completed the look.

'Be a good idea to call off the dog before I put a bullet through the bastard's head,' Bowker said slipping his hand inside his coat.

Sanderson jumped down off the step and laid a foot into the dog's ribs. 'Sit down, Fuhrer!' he screamed at the top of his voice. The animal whimpered then trotted away with its tail between its legs, looking back occasionally as it made its way to shade under an old car body. 'You're the copper we ran into on Saturday night, right?'

'Detective Inspector Bowker,' Bowker replied, not adding that he was from homicide. He'd let that detail sit to see if Sanderson made any assumptions about his visit. Rice's body was found only two days earlier and it was likely the murder hadn't become common knowledge around the town at this stage, particularly among those people who didn't read a newspaper or didn't listen to the news. And especially among those with limited friendship groups and social contacts. Bowker would play it by ear.

'This to do with old Rice, is it?' Sanderson asked.

'Got it in one,' Bowker replied.

'I thought the old bastard said he didn't want to take it any further.'

'His decision, not mine,' Bowker replied without giving anything away. 'Can we talk inside. It's too hot out here.'

Sanderson turned, climbed the steps to the back door and led the detective into a putrid, stinking kitchen. Bowker immediately regretted his request to come inside. Sanderson pulled a chair with a torn vinyl seat from under a cluttered Laminex table and motioned for the policeman to sit opposite. Bowker pushed away beer bottles to make room to rest his elbows. 'Catch any fish?'

Sanderson looked puzzled. 'One decent sized reddy and the million fuckin' carp,' he replied warily.

'How long were you down at the lake?'

Sanderson shrugged. 'Few hours. Near midnight when we pulled up stumps. Headed home when we ran out of piss.'

'Whereabouts around the lake did you drop in a line?'

'Brown Eye tried up at the top of the lake. I had a go down towards the bridge. We set a few springers in between.'

'Springers are illegal,' Bowker said.

Sanderson became annoyed. 'Well we didn't do any harm, did we? Used up all our fuckin' bardis and didn't catch a single cod. Just one monster carp that was better up on the bank than in the fuckin' water. Feral bastards bugger it for everyone.'

'Couldn't agree more,' Bowker replied straight faced.

Sanderson missed the sarcasm. 'Why are you here talkin' about fishin', anyway? If you're gonna charge me with roughin' up Rice, then get on with it. It'll only mean another good behaviour bond.' He feigned a chuckle. 'Mustn't be much on the go if a bloody detective inspector is chasin' up a minor assault.' He looked at Bowker with a smirk. 'Trying to make a name for yourself in the new station? Happy to get down and dirty with the rest of them.'

Bowker smiled and scratched his temple. 'I'm stationed at Spencer Street in Melbourne, Noel. Homicide squad. Drove back to Benalla this morning.'

Sanderson stood up from his chair and his face turned pale. 'Has something happened to Brown Eye?' He shook his head. 'I told the fucker to stay clear of those ice dealers from Shepp. He slept here on Saturday night then walked home Sunday morning. Did they roll him on the way home?'

Bowker stood with hands on hips and stared straight into Sanderson's eyes. 'Gary Rice's body was found in the lake on Sunday morning, Noel. Been whacked on the head. Murdered.' He paused waiting for Sanderson's reaction.

Sanderson stared at Bowker, speechless for a few seconds, before reacting aggressively. 'What's that got to do with me?'

Bowker put his hands on the table and leaned over closer to Sanderson. 'You threatened him in the carpark at the football club on Saturday evening. Then you spent the rest of the night down by the lake getting more pissed by the minute. Gary Rice told me he planned to walk home after the reunion and the quickest route is along the path beside the water. Makes a lot of sense for me to talk to you, don't you reckon?'

Sanderson slumped back into his seat. 'I had nothing to do with any of this. I swear. I was with Brown Eye all night. You can ask him.'

Bowker resumed his own seat. 'Another detective is doing just that as we speak. But you weren't together all the time anyway, were you Noel? You said you were fishing down near the bridge while he went upstream to the inflow of the lake. You could have whacked Rice and your mate would have had no bloody idea.'

'Well I didn't whack the old bastard. Last time I saw him was in the carpark when you told me to piss off.'

'See anyone else at the lake?'

'A couple of people over the other side. Young bloke and a sheila. Down the bank from the Commercial pub.'

'What time was that?'

'Just on dark. They were rootin' around with an old truck tyre.'

'In the water?'

'Yeah. I yelled at them to piss off. They were scaring the fish. The bastard gave me the finger.' Sanderson's face darkened. 'Wouldn't have been so cocky if he'd been over on my side. I would have punched the prick's head in.'

'Like you did with Gary Rice?'

Sanderson shook his head. 'I told you, I didn't see fuckin' Rice.'

Bowker asked a series of additional questions before requesting to see Sanderson's fishing gear. Sanderson led him down an overgrown track in the backyard to a small aluminium garden shed. He inserted a key and the padlock sprung open. Inside were old garden tools that had obviously sat idle for years, a mower which Bowker judged as the first model that Victa had ever produced, old army shell boxes containing who-knows-what, as well as a few suspicious hand tools including screw drivers, pinch-bars, a tommy axe and other bits and pieces that could be put to criminal use if one had a penchant for breaking and entering. Sanderson entered the stiflingly hot shed, clawed at the cobwebs and waved away the flies. He picked up an esky from just inside the door and sat it on the ground. He reached back inside to grab rods and reels.

'No need to get that stuff,' Bowker advised. 'Just open the esky for me.'

Sanderson snapped open the clamp on each end and removed

the lid. The smell was overpowering. 'Forgot to wash it out when I got home,' he said as he took a step back.

'Your mind was elsewhere, maybe?' Bowker asked.

'What's that supposed to mean?'

'Still thinking about Gary Rice, perhaps.'

'Didn't think about him after the dust up in the carpark. Didn't even see him again, so don't fuckin' try and pin something on me that I didn't do.' Sanderson ran his fingers through his dirty hair and looked up at the sky. 'Story of my fuckin' life getting' accused of things I never done.'

Bowker shook his head but didn't comment. He braved the flies that had now found a new target and looked inside the cooler. There was a small tackle box, a couple of small tins that had probably contained bait, and a dozen or more flattened beer cans.

Bowker looked at Sanderson and smiled. 'Kept your empty beer cans, Noel? Glad to see you're so environmentally conscious.'

'May as well throw them in there as in the fuckin' water.' He pointed towards the back fence to a nest of twisted wire all overgrown with dry grass and out-of-control ivy. 'There's an old drum down the back. I chuck the cans in there. One day there might be enough of them to be worth a few bob. The tip's not far from where I work.'

'Over the railway line near the sale yards?

'Yeah.'

The detective removed a pair of rubber gloves from his coat pocket and put them on before kneeling down and removing each item from the icebox.

'Wastin' your time there, mate,' Sanderson remarked. 'Just shit from fishin'.'

By this stage the Doberman Cross had recovered from its kick to the ribs and was reenergised by the smell of blood in the air. It tried to push past Bowker, snarling as the policeman blocked the way with his leg. 'Piss the bloody dog off Noel, or I'll report the bastard as a dangerous breed and get him put down. I should do that anyway, he'll finish up killing some kid who strays into your backyard.'

'No kids ever come near the place. Besides, surely a bloke's allowed to keep a guard dog for protection.'

'One that's properly trained maybe, not some nutcase crossbred mongrel who needs a kick in the guts to take any notice of his owner. You should take him to the vet and have him neutered. Take the sting out of the prick.'

Sanderson was taken aback at such a suggestion. 'You can't do that to a dog. May as well put him down as castrate him. How would you feel about having your fuckin' nuts cut out?'

Bowker smiled in amusement. 'The dog doesn't know it's been done to him. Stop anthropologising the bloody thing.'

Sanderson frowned, struck silent for a moment. 'What the fuck does that mean?'

'It means stop giving the animal human feelings.'

Sanderson mumbled as he grabbed the dog's collar and dragged him to a chain connected to the chassis of an old vehicle.

Bowker reached to the bottom of the cooler and retrieved a tyre lever caked with blood. He stood up and raised the lever in front of Sanderson's face. 'Perhaps you might like to explain this.'

'I carry it to protect myself in case the fuckin' Trilgonis from Wangaratta come looking for me. The bastards reckon I belted up their sister but that wasn't me. One of their mates was rootin' the slut on the quiet while she was livin' here. He was the one who bashed her.'

Bowker pointed at the lever. 'What's with the blood?'

'Fuckin' big carp I caught on one of the springers. It kept jumpin' around while I was trying to get the hook out of the prick and he stabbed me with one of his bloody fins.' Sanderson showed a puncture mark on the fleshy part of his thumb. 'Got me there. Bloody hurt. So I sconed the bastard with the lever. What you've got there is fish blood.'

Bowker threw everything back in the esky and clamped on the lid. 'I'll take this with me and forensics can take a look. Don't even think about leaving town.'

Sanderson placed his hands on his hips and stared into the bright blue sky. 'Fuck!' he screamed loudly, before looking at the ground, shaking his head. 'Here we go again,' he mumbled.

CHAPTER 6

Back at the station, the detectives were allotted a small room on the second floor from where they would run their investigation. The contents were rudimentary. A filing cabinet with one empty drawer, a table with four chairs, and a computer with internet access and printer attached was about all it contained. Larsen had her back to the door and was bent over picking up a stack of old papers when Holmes entered. His eyes widened as he rapped on the open door. 'Knock knock.'

Larsen straightened and turned quickly, tugging down the hem of her silk top. 'Hi Darren. Just setting up the room for the Rice inquiry. It's pretty basic, but I think it's got all we'll need.'

Holmes placed a folder containing his notes on the table. 'How long have you been a detective?'

'Five years,' Larsen replied. 'How about you?'

'Coming up fourteen. Last ten in Homicide.'

'You don't look old enough to have served that long,' she said with the faintest of smiles.

Holmes touched his receding hairline with an index finger. 'Losing your hair is a bit of a giveaway, I reckon.'

Larsen smiled faintly again. 'Sign of virility, I read somewhere.'

A moment passed between them before she spoke again. 'How'd you go with Brown?' she asked.

Holmes inhaled deeply, composing his thoughts. 'Over the course of my career, I've seen the conditions in which some people are forced to exist.' He shook his head. 'But I'm not sure I've seen worse than the place where he lives. Doesn't even have the power on and the sewage empties into a hole near his back door.'

'Did you go inside?' Larsen asked.

'Wouldn't let me.'

'That was a blessing, let me assure you. Stinks to high heaven, old mattress on the lounge floor, bathroom makes you want to vomit.'

'How does he cook?'

Larsen shrugged. 'He has an old gas camp stove, if I recall correctly. Dunno how he heats the place in the winter, though. Or cools the dump on days like this.' She looked quizzically at Holmes. 'Did you interview him in the front street? Won't take long for that to spread around town.'

Holmes chuckled. 'No. He took me down the back yard to what he called an outdoor setting. Rusty wrought iron table and chairs in a crop of stinging nettles. But at least it was in the shade and there was a slight breeze to cool things down a degree or two.'

Larsen handed Holmes a manilla folder. 'I've printed the records for Sanderson and Brown. Brown has a litany of minor offences. Mostly theft and assault. A couple of convictions for possession of illegal substances. Mostly for marijuana, but I think there's one there for ice. Sanderson sheet is a bit more serious. Three cases of grievous bodily harm, one for assault with a deadly weapon and two for breaking and entering. There's also theft of a motor vehicle in addition to multiple drug offences. Spent a total of eight years in jail.'

Holmes sat down and opened the folder. 'So Sanderson's the more dangerous of the two?'

Larsen took a seat opposite and folded her hands on the table, Holmes immediately noticing she had no rings on her left hand. 'By a country mile,' she said. 'If these two rolled Rice, then you can bet that Sanderson did the dirty work.'

'Do they always hang around together?'

Larsen shook her head. 'Not always, no. Both have an ability to find trouble on their own.'

'Are you talking about Sherlock and me,' Bowker said cheerily as he entered the room behind Fleming.

'We were just going through the records of Heckle and Jeckle,' Holmes replied. 'Both petty crims, but Sanderson seems to have a mean streak. Brown is just a poor dumb bastard.'

'Can't disagree with any of that,' Fleming said, moving hurriedly to make sure he took the seat next to Larsen.

Bowker loosened his tie as he sat down opposite. 'After spending twelve years in the Mallee I swore I wouldn't be caught saying this anywhere else. But shit it's hot out there.'

Holmes laughed. 'They'd be wearing jumpers on a day like this in Murrayville.' It was then down to business. 'How'd you go with Sanderson?'

Bowker frowned and shrugged. 'Denies seeing Rice after I broke up their altercation earlier in the evening. Fished until late, caught a big redfin and a heap of carp. He and Brown went back to his place in Garden Street and continued drinking. Brown slept the night there and walked home Sunday morning. Seemed shocked when I told him Rice had been killed and immediately went on the defensive. Appears he and Brown fished separately at times, so he can't vouch for his mate a hundred percent, but reckons Brown wouldn't hurt a fly.'

Holmes folded his arms across his chest and leant back in

his chair. 'Similar story with my bloke. Fished till late, drank a heap of cans, caught one big reddy and shitloads of carp. They set springers trying to catch a cod but had no luck. The two of them were separated when Brown went upstream and Sanderson fished under the bridge near the art gallery. Said he didn't see Rice by the lake. Denied seeing him in the carpark until I told him you'd seen him there.'

Bowker nodded. 'On the face of it, their narratives match pretty well.'

Fleming was unconvinced. 'That's what you'd expect if they spent Saturday night and Sunday morning getting their stories straight.'

'You're already convinced one of them killed old Rice, aren't you Aaron?' Bowker asked.

Fleming nodded and leant forward with his elbows on the table. 'I reckon Sanderson probably did. Bad temper. Been done for serious assault before. I doubt Brown would have been involved unless it was to help roll the victim into the lake. He's a pretty harmless little bugger.'

Bowker nodded. 'OK. You know the pair better than us, but we'll need a lot more before we can charge one of them.' He looked at Holmes. 'Did Brown mention anything about a tyre lever?'

'Yep. Apparently Sanderson used it to kill some of the carp he caught. Brown said his mate cracked it when the carp used up his bait. He'd just snap and bash the fish to a pulp.'

Fleming smiled sardonically. 'Did he explain why Sanderson took the tyre lever in the first place?' he asked. 'Surely when he packed his gear it had nothing to do with killing carp.'

'According to Brown, Sanderson was shit scared of these blokes from Wangaratta. Something to do with drugs.' Holmes flipped the pages of his notes. 'A mob called the Trilgonis.'

'Piece of work that lot,' Larsen said. 'Coppers at Wang are forever crossing swords with the family. Still growing tobacco on the sly up in the King Valley and selling it on the black market as chop chop.'

Bowker raised his eyebrows. 'Sanderson said there was trouble around him supposedly belting up one of the Trilgoni women who lived in his house. But according to him, it was a mate of their family who bashed her.'

'I wouldn't believe a word he says,' Fleming said. 'He's got form for assaulting women.'

'I confiscated his esky and the tyre lever. Both are covered in blood. Forensics will tell us if it belongs to Rice or just some unfortunate marine creature.'

'If it's Rice's blood, then it's all over,' Fleming said with a smile and rubbing his hands together.

Bowker inhaled deeply through his nose. 'Yeah, it'd be pretty hard for Sanderson to explain it away, that's for sure. But while we wait for the forensics we'll have a chat to Rice's wife and see if he had any enemies we should know about.'

Fleming frowned. 'Far be it for me to tell Homicide Squad detectives how to run an investigation, but this case seems pretty open and shut. Surely, we're just wasting our time trying to invent alternative scenarios. A harmless old man is killed just hours after being aggressively accosted by a known offender with a violent temper. An offender who we know was in the area of the murder scene and at the time when the killing took place. It's textbook stuff, surely.'

Bowker had seen this type of tunnel vision derail inquiries in the past, but was keen not to lecture his junior colleague. He leant back in his chair and placed his hands behind his head exposing large areas of sweat-saturated shirt under his arms and down his side. 'You're probably spot-on Aaron, but it won't hurt to collect a few extra bits of information while we wait for the science to arrive.'

'You're the boss, Greg,' Fleming said smiling, 'but it's pretty bloody hot out there to be chasing wild geese.'

The Rice residence was a well-kept Californian bungalow at the north end of Arundel street. Painted light grey and white, it had a large bay window facing west with a verandah traversing half the front of the weatherboard house. Faux stone columns atop red brick plinths supported the roof above a verandah with a waist-high matching wall running between. The garden was well tended, featuring two mature silver birch trees on each side of a paved path leading to a glass-panelled front door. The two detectives entered the property through an ornate steel and woven wire gate set in the exact midpoint of the front fence. A late model deep blue BMW coupe was parked beside a yellow Corolla in a carport to the side of the house. Bowker pushed an illuminated doorbell and heard a crescendo of chimes ring out inside. A cacophony of high-pitched canine barking erupted and after a moment, the door opened to reveal an expensively dressed woman with her face heavily made up as though she was heading to a gala event. Her platinum dyed hair was fashionably cut around a severe face with protruding cheekbones and a sharp prominent nose. Her complexion was without lines or wrinkles down as far as her neck, where the skin was more in keeping with a woman of her age. Her face and her previous marriage to a plastic surgeon gave strength to both officers' initial perception that she'd had work done. And a fair bit at that. The pair of long-haired Pomeranians continued to yelp unabated until finally the woman quietened them with an index finger to her lips as if hushing a small child.

Bowker identified himself and his colleague with both officers displaying their identification. Mrs Rice acknowledged their introductions and invited them through to a large glass-clad extension at the rear of the house that overlooked Lake Benalla.

While the detectives took a seat on a large leather couch, the woman began making tea behind a long marble-topped kitchen bench that ran nearly the full width of the room. The dogs adjourned to red velvet cushions beside an open fireplace.

Bowker passed on their sympathies and explained the routine nature of their visit. 'What time did you arrive home from Melbourne on Sunday, Mrs Rice?' he then asked.

'Around eleven o'clock in the morning,' she replied as she filled a high-end branded electric kettle.

'And the house was obviously empty?' Holmes asked.

'Yes. At first, I was relieved that I hadn't found Gary dead on the floor or in the midst of a hypo. It happened one other weekend when I went away. I came home to find him jammed between our bed and the wall, wet with urine and covered in his own faeces. He was thrashing around and slurring at the top of his voice. He spent over a fortnight in hospital and remembered nothing of that weekend.'

'Did he forget to take his insulin?' Holmes asked.

'Just the opposite, actually.' She leant on the bench. 'He allowed his blood sugar to fall so low that he had little control over his body. It can happen to any diabetic actually. They can become so wrapped up in what they're doing that they forget to eat. By then it's often too late.'

'So when you searched the house and couldn't find him, what were your next thoughts?' Bowker asked. 'Especially after you hadn't been able to reach him by phone.'

She stared at the bench top and shook her head. 'I thought he'd probably let his mobile go flat like he'd done before and was out interviewing people for this family history book he's so obsessed with.' The kettle boiled and she poured the steaming water onto teabags in three matching willow patterned cups atop matching saucers. 'When the police finally located me and explained they'd found Gary's body, I thought he must have taken a turn and hit his head. I was totally shocked when they said the forensic specialist judged the damage to his skull could not have occurred as the result of a fall.'

The woman took a cup and saucer in each hand, walked to the couch and passed them to each officer. Both policemen noticed her wrinkled and spotted hands, so at variance to the smoothness of her face. She retrieved her own hot drink from the bench and took a seat opposite.

'Did your husband have any enemies Mrs Rice? Bowker asked as he jiggled the teabag and placed it on his saucer.

'He was not the sort of person to make enemies, but there was one man who had threatened him several times. A fellow city councillor. Dennis Lowther.'

'What did these threats entail?'

She moved uncomfortably in her seat and the cup rattled on her saucer. 'Knocking his head right off, was the phrase he used to me over the phone. And he grabbed Gary by the throat one night after a fairly heated council meeting.'

'What was Lowther's beef?' Holmes asked.

The woman took a deep breath. 'Rates. Like a lot of rural local governments, the Benalla Rural City has differential charges for different classes of property. A farm attracts a rate that is roughly sixty percent of that paid on a residential property. That's in dollar value terms of course. Gary didn't see why a wealthy pastoralist like Lowther, who owns several thousand hectares of prime grazing land, pays a lower percentage of rates than an old pensioner who lives in a modest house and struggles to put food on the table.'

Holmes looked puzzled. 'I'm inclined to agree with him. What's the counter argument?'

'Lowther claims farmers are asset rich, but income poor. If

his property was rated at the same percentage as the residential category then he'd struggle to make a profit.'

'I would have thought a pensioner owning their own home would be asset rich and income poor as well,' Bowker replied.

Mrs Rice nodded in agreement. 'And Gary wasn't speaking from a selfish point of view either. He owns a substantial farm himself. He just didn't think the system was fair.'

'And Lowther felt threatened by this?' Holmes asked.

'It became pretty personal in the end, I think. At the last meeting Gary told Lowther that if paying his fair share of rates was going to break him, then he mustn't be much of a farmer. Best he sell up his over-valued assets and try another profession. I think that's the night Lowther took to Gary in the council carpark. He was pretty shaken up when he got home.'

'Did your husband report the incident to the police?' Holmes asked.

She shook her head. 'No. He said that Lowther was such a hothead it would only make things worse. The whole thing was a storm in a teacup anyway. The way the council is constituted, Gary's plan wouldn't have passed a vote if it had ever come to that. According to him, the farmers only have two things on their agenda when they run for council. R and R. Rates and roads. Any town-based proposals were always viewed as a waste of money.'

Bowker took a sip from his cup. 'We might need to have a chat with Mr Lowther, I think.'

'Good luck with that,' Mrs Rice said as she daintily sipped her tea with a little finger protruding.

'Did your husband owe money to anyone Mrs Rice?' Holmes asked.

She chuckled. 'I wouldn't think so, detective. He was quite a wealthy man. He inherited eight-hundred acres of prized land from his father. That has to be worth close to two million dollars on its own.'

'That's the property his daughter and her husband farm?' Bowker asked. 'Up in the valley at Tatong?'

A dark look swallowed up her face. 'That is correct,' she said through pursed lips. 'But all that has changed now Gary is no longer with us. He has never seen eye to eye with Ron. That's his gold-digging son in law. If it hadn't been for Gary worrying about alienating his daughter Alison, he would have cashed in the farm already. He certainly had no interest in effectively leaving that property to Ron via her. Our solicitor updated Gary's will just last week so that on his death, the farm will be sold at auction. From those proceeds, a generous but modest inheritance will be bequeathed to his daughter. The rest of his estate will pass to me.'

'And on your death?' Bowker asked, already knowing the answer.

'It will pass to my natural daughters. Those of my previous marriage.'

'Did Gary inform Alison that these changes were in the wind?' Bowker asked.

'I doubt it. He was hoping to keep that secret until he had died,' Mrs Rice replied.

Bowker raised his eyebrows. 'Right.'

Mrs Rice was clearly hesitant before continuing. 'I may have let the cat out of the bag when I saw Ron in the bank a couple of weeks ago after Gary first talked about making the change. Ron was poncing around in moleskins and RM Williams boots as though he's part of the landed gentry. Do you know what his family were? Shearers!' She shook her head in disgust. 'The nerve of the man!'

'So you told him the will had been changed?' Holmes asked.

'No. But I told him Gary was seriously considering it. I doubt they'd assume he'd gone ahead and done it so quickly,' Mrs Rice replied. She then smirked. 'Ron is going to get a big surprise when the will is read and he realises he's fallen from a squatter to a farm hand. I can't wait to see the look on his face.'

Both detectives were shocked at the pretentiousness and snobbery of the woman, but said nothing as they all sipped their tea from the fine bone china.

Holmes was first to break the silence. 'Did you know your husband planned to attend the school reunion on Saturday night?'

Mrs Rice shrugged. 'I remember him mentioning it a few weeks ago, but I'd forgotten all about it once my daughter asked for help with her new bub. She being an older mum threw up a few complications.'

'Were you planning to go to the dinner with Gary?' Bowker asked.

The woman shook her head. 'No. I wouldn't have known a soul there except my husband.'

Not unlike Rachael who had a great time, Bowker thought, but didn't say.

'Not my sort of crowd anyway,' Mrs Rice continued. 'Drunken country yokels.'

This time it was Holmes who had the unsaid thoughts. If you'd climbed off your high horse, your husband may have been still with us. 'Just out of interest, where did you and Gary meet, Mrs Rice?'

'He was a university friend of my first husband. They kept in touch over the years. I didn't fancy being the lonely widow, so when I discovered he and that wife of his had divorced, one thing led to another and here we are.'

Bowker downed the dregs of his tea and placed the cup and saucer on the coffee table in front of him. Holmes followed his lead and the two men stood. 'Thank you for your help, Mrs Rice,' Bowker said. 'We'll be in touch if we need to talk further.'

'Well hopefully you'll find the culprit without delay. The sooner I can leave this God-forsaken place and move back into the house in South Yarra the better.' Her dogs departed their thrones and trailed their mistress as she escorted the officers from the premises.

'Is the old bag up herself, or what?' Holmes said as soon as they were back in the car. 'Didn't seem too upset about her husband having his skull crushed.'

'Always another one out there, I guess,' Bowker replied as he did up his seatbelt. 'Another friend of a friend with the money to give her the lifestyle to which she's become accustomed.'

'But what would any bloke see in her? Her real eyebrows must be halfway down her back.'

Bowker burst out laughing. 'Who can explain the affairs of the heart, my friend?'

'Yeah,' Holmes said pensively.

'If all the evidence didn't point straight to Sanderson and Brown, we'd have to look seriously at Councillor Lowther and the victim's son-in-law.'

'And the daughter?' Holmes asked, snapping home his own belt.

Bowker screwed up his face. 'Perhaps. But it doesn't sound like there was any underlying animosity between her and her father. The old girl said Rice was keen not to alienate the daughter, so you have to assume things were OK between them.'

'Or maybe when Rice said he didn't want to alienate her, that was code for avoiding her cracking the shits bigtime.'

Bowker started the car, did a U turn and returned to the railway bridge near the lake's retaining wall. The plan was a simple reconnaissance mission before uniformed officers conducted a more intensive search. Holmes would walk the lakeside path south towards the bridge while Bowker would return to the football clubrooms to begin a search from where the river feeds the lake. They would likely meet somewhere near the popular art gallery that sits overlooking the water to the east and the extensive botanical gardens to the west. The gardens are the very definition of serenity, cool and shady with extensive rose gardens. In early November, they become the focus of the town's annual rose festival. Extensive parking adjoins on the old highway, and in the centre of the gardens is perhaps the state's most picturesque cricket ground. In the sport's glory days, the oval, ringed by elms and green lawn, was often the venue for country elevens to play visiting test teams when international tours would typically last for several months.

It took Bowker longer than anticipated to search his delegated area. The formed path left the shoreline after he'd walked past the rear of the football club buildings and ultimately wound its way to a footbridge onto Little Casey Island where the river divided as it entered the lake. The detective made the decision to go no further than the footbridge, then follow the shoreline back to the north until he met up with Holmes. His cursory search found nothing of interest, but as he passed under the main bridge and onto a boardwalk below the art gallery, he saw Holmes on his haunches carefully inspecting an area between the timber and the shoreline. Holmes looked up when he saw his colleague approaching.

'Take a look at this Greg,' he said as he circled his finger above an area of grass that had been stained brown. 'Could be dried blood, I reckon.'

Bowker knelt down to obtain a closer look. 'Could easily be, especially judging by the spatter pattern around the main stain.'

'Could be fish blood. Somebody might have caught something and bled it on the grass.'

Bowker shook his head. 'Bloody big fish to pool that much

blood. By the look of the flattened grass close to the water line, a body could have easily been rolled in here.'

The two men stood up and Bowker rubbed the stubble on his chin with his right hand. 'Ring the station and tell them we're gonna need forensics. And get them to send down a couple of uniforms to look after this spot. Once the full story about the murder gets around town, we'll have every citizen detective or rubber-necker stomping all over this.'

Holmes nodded and punched in a number. Bowker climbed the rise to the art gallery, an impressive ivory coloured series of connected cubes with white triangular roofing planes that put Bowker in mind of a poor man's Sydney Opera House. The gallery was the product of benefactor Laurie Ledger's donation of twenty-five percent of construction cost plus his high-quality Australian art collection in 1975. Few regional galleries could boast a permanent collection that included the work of Nolen, McCubbin and Roberts among others. On the lake side of the gallery, the building is supported by stilts and Bowker waved to several patrons sipping coffee on an outdoor deck above him. On the gardens side, the gallery is at ground level. Before circling the building, he wandered across to the "Weary" Dunlop statue and marvelled at the detail captured in this monument to one of the town's most famous sons. By the time Bowker returned to the lake via the gallery's northern aspect, two uniformed police officers had joined Holmes and were driving pegs into the soft ground to support police exclusion tape.

Bowker thanked the young officers for their prompt attendance and led Holmes back to his car at the football club. The detectives hadn't eaten since their early morning breakfast in Wallan and the worms were starting to bite.

CHAPTER 7

It was barely late-afternoon on the first day of their investigation and the detectives had already conducted preliminary interviews with their two major suspects and the wife of the victim. They had also probably determined where the murder took place. The inquiry was moving fast, so fast in fact, that Bowker hadn't found time to register at the motel he had booked. Following a belated lunch of fried chicken from a popular fast-food franchise in the centre of town, Bowker grabbed the opportunity to deposit their luggage and turn on the air conditioning to precool their room. The friendly woman behind the motel office counter took the detective's details and handed him a key to the room he would share with Holmes for the duration of their visit. Bowker hoped that would be no longer than a few days.

Number 17 was a basic, but spacious and clean room that housed a queen bed, plus a single that allowed the room to be used as a twin. Reluctant to pull rank, especially with his good friend, Bowker selected the single bed and tossed the room key and the motel paperwork atop the grey doona cover. He turned on the air conditioner and met his colleague outside to unload their meagre luggage. After five minutes, the two officers strolled across the street to the police building content to leave the car under the shade canopy outside their room. In their makeshift second floor office, Larsen and Fleming were seated next to each other perusing a document on the table in front of them.

'I think we might have found where Rice met his maker,' Bowker said as he sat down opposite the locals.

Fleming nodded. 'Yeah, the duty constable downstairs mentioned you needed a pair of uniforms to guard a patch by the lake.'

'How far along?' Larsen asked.

'In front of the gallery,' Holmes replied. 'Between the boardwalk and the shoreline. There's blood on the grass and a big flattened patch as though something heavy had been rolled across it.'

'Starting to look more and more like Sanderson,' Larsen said. 'Brown confirmed Sanderson had fished down that way while he went upstream.'

Fleming pushed his chair back. 'I'll get the boys in the divi van to bring him in.'

Bowker raised his right hand, palm out. 'Not yet. I want to see what forensics have to say before we talk to him.'

Fleming frowned in frustration. 'Surely there's no doubt now, Greg. It couldn't fit any tighter.' He looked at Holmes. 'What do you think, Darren?'

Holmes screwed up his face. 'My money's on Sanderson, but I agree with Greg. Nothing to lose by waiting for the forensics. Hit him with everything at once.'

'What if he does a runner?' Fleming quickly retorted.

'I'll take that chance,' Bowker said. 'We haven't got enough to charge him at present anyway.'

'We could arrest him on suspicion,' Larsen suggested.

'And give him time to dream up alternative scenarios?' Bowker asked. 'No thanks. We'll just let him think we've got nothing.'

'So everybody just sits around twiddling their thumbs until

the forensic work comes back?' Fleming said, his annoyance becoming more obvious.

'Nope,' Bowker said shrugging off Fleming's attitude. 'I'd like to have a chat with the victim's son-in-law as well as Dennis Lowther.'

Larsen was perplexed. 'Dennis Lowther? As in the Deputy Mayor?'

'That's him,' Holmes replied. 'Had a feud with Rice about the level of council rates charged on farms.'

'And according to the victim's wife he made physical threats towards Rice,' Bowker added.

Larsen tapped the paper in front of her. 'What do you want done with the names and addresses of people who attended the school reunion?'

'Slide them over here and we'll sit on them for a bit,' Bowker replied. 'If we hit a dead end with our other inquiries, we'll need to look at everyone who was in the vicinity the night Rice was killed. There might be a local with an axe to grind who'd had a few too many drinks. Or maybe someone from out of town with bad memories of school.'

Fleming chuckled. 'Like Sanderson, you mean?'

'Yeah, like Sanderson,' Bowker replied without rising to the bait. 'But in the meantime we'll talk to the son-in-law and councillor Lowther.'

'I'm a lot newer to this game than you guys,' Larsen said as she slid the list across to Bowker, 'but I reckon a few drinks at the pub might be a more profitable way to mark time till we get the forensic report.' She winked at Holmes who smiled then looked away.

Wednesday dawned steamier than the day before and by nine o'clock there was already a helix of gliders riding updrafts in the threatening sky to the east of the town. Ron and Alison Cloverdale's farm, or now more correctly the farm belonging to the estate of Gary Rice, was situated along Hollands Creek, close to the tiny township of Tatong, some twenty-seven kilometres southeast of Benalla. Tatong, home to a few dozen residents and a popular local tavern, once boasted a powerful local football team. But in 2014 after years of struggle, the club followed most combatants in the former Benalla and District Football League into extinction. A brief stint in a league based around Wangaratta, and merger discussions with the struggling Swanpool to the west, provided hope that a team may survive in some form, but in the end, it all became too hard. Unfortunately, like hundreds of other rural football clubs, the Tatong Magpies, along with their Swanpool Swans neighbour were consigned to the pages of history. The dusty photos in the few remaining public places provide the only evidence that the two teams had ever existed.

The wide cattle grid entry to the Rice property separated three panels of white timber railing on either side. A professionally scribed sign hanging from the crossbar of an ornate steel stanchion read *Hollands Flat Pole Herefords*. Bowker drove the unmarked police vehicle up the poplar-lined drive before pulling into the shade of an ancient peppercorn tree to the side of the sprawling bluestone farm house. A tower, covered in ivy, thrust up from the centre of the façade and wide verandas circumnavigated the entire house. Extensive lawns and hedges running down to the creek at the rear completed the scene of nineteenth century rural opulence.

'I can see why our Ron wouldn't like to lose this place,' Holmes said as he snapped off his seat belt.

'And why toffee-nosed Arabella used the term "squatter"', Bowker replied. 'The place screams landed gentry.'

The plan was for Bowker to interview Ron Cloverdale while

Holmes spoke to his wife. Conveniently, when the detectives knocked on the leadlight paneled front door and introduced themselves to Alison Cloverdale, they were informed that Ron wasn't in the house, but in the machinery shed servicing a hay bailer. Mrs Cloverdale was a tall solidly built woman but carried no excess kilos. She had a broad plain face but with sparkling eyes and a suspicious smile. Her short hair was a sun-bleached blond and her muscled arms were permanently tanned from years of work outside. She wore a checked sleeveless shirt, faded jeans and badly worn elastic sided boots. There was nothing in her appearance that tallied with either detective's image of a pampered squatter's wife.

After conveying their sympathies, Bowker walked off in the direction indicated by the woman while Holmes followed her down a spacious hallway to a sprawling lounge room with twin bay windows overlooking the grounds. A background of rugged timber-covered hills completed the breathtaking panorama.

'Quite a view,' Holmes said as he sat down in an oversized leather armchair.

'Yes. One of the benefits of living this far out of town,' Mrs Cloverdale replied as she dropped into a matching chair opposite.

'And one of the things you'll miss when the estate is wound up, I suspect?' Holmes suggested.

Mrs Cloverdale looked puzzled. 'The property will officially transfer into my name. For all practical purposes, very little will change.'

'Your father didn't mention he was changing his will?' Holmes asked.

Mrs Cloverdale shook her head. 'Of course not. His wishes have never been a secret. *Hollands Flat* has been in our family since white settlement. Seven generations. It was left to my father by my grandfather and on dad's death it passes to me.'

'According to your stepmother, your father changed his will a few days before his death,' Holmes said watching the woman's eyes.

Mrs Cloverdale's mouth dropped. 'Bullshit,' she exclaimed, staring straight at the detective.

'Mrs Rice said that this property will be sold, with a percentage of the proceeds flowing to you, but with the bulk of the inheritance passing to her.'

Mrs Cloverdale shook her head vehemently. 'No. That can't be right. I would have been told. My father wouldn't keep something like that from me.'

'Your husband hasn't told you that your father was thinking about making a change?' Holmes asked, scratching his temple with an index finger.

'How could he possibly know that? Especially if I didn't?' the woman replied, more a statement than a question.

'Mrs Rice said she'd seen your husband in the bank a few weeks ago and let it slip that your father was contemplating this change to his will.'

Mrs Cloverdale feigned a laugh. 'Well, I wouldn't put much stock in anything she'd tell you, detective. She hates us. Particularly Ron. I can see her making up a story about the ownership of this property just to annoy him.'

'So, your husband didn't mention a conversation with Mrs Rice?'

'No. Probably because it didn't happen. She's an evil woman, detective. And a gold-digger to boot. Used to be married to a big-name plastic surgeon in Toorak before he died unexpectedly. The grieving widow didn't much suit her lifestyle, so when she found out that there was money in our family, she made it her mission to get her hands on it. She pursued dad's affections with a passion. Like a bee around a honeypot. Finally got her way and they were married a few years ago.' Mrs Cloverdale shook her head. 'It's a pity mum and dad didn't stay together.'

Holmes leant back in the armchair and folded his hands in his lap. 'Your mother still lives in the district, I hear?'

Mrs Cloverdale's face relaxed a little. 'Yes. Down at Baddaginnie on fifteen acres.'

'And she has a new partner.'

The woman's mood immediately darkened. 'Yeah, Tony Marshall's his name. A real piece of shit, if you'll excuse my French. Trains a couple of slow greyhounds, drinks like a fish and treats mum like dirt.'

'Why does she stay with him?'

Mrs Cloverdale shrugged. 'Scared to leave I suspect. He's a violent bastard. Especially if he's had a few too many. And that happens fairly often according to mum. She was so scared at one point that she swallowed her pride and asked dad for help. I think he had words with Marshall on a couple of occasions. Not that it would have done any good. Probably would have stirred him up even more.'

'So Marshall and your father may have crossed swords over Marshall's treatment of your mother?'

'At least once, to my knowledge.'

Holmes inhaled deeply. 'Well I think we might add Mr Marshall to the list of people we need to speak to.'

'You won't get any straight answers,' the woman warned. 'He's a slimy little bastard who'd lie to his grandmother if he thought it was to his advantage.'

Holmes took a notebook from his pocket and wrote down Marshall's name with an asterisk beside it. 'Why'd your parents break up, if you don't mind me asking?'

Mrs Cloverdale bit her bottom lip before answering. 'Young history teacher came to the school. Had a lot of trouble with the kids in her classes. Dad took her under his wing. And then under his sheets when Mum visited grandma in palliative care in

Melbourne. Eventually it all became public. Nasty stuff. At the end of the year the young teacher left on compassionate grounds but by that stage Mum had moved out. In hindsight, she'd have been better off staying and giving things another go. Anything would have been better than moving in with the bastard she's with now.' She shrugged and looked Holmes in the eye. 'But hindsight's a wonderful thing, isn't it?'

Holmes nodded and leaned forward, clasping his hands together, elbows resting on his knees. 'Where were you on the night your father was killed?'

Mrs Cloverdale reacted angrily. 'What? You think I murdered my father?'

'No I don't,' Holmes replied calmly. 'I'm just trying to piece together the movements of relevant people.'

'I was here, if you must know. Alone. Ron was playing golf in Benalla. He didn't get home till late. He often stays for a few beers afterwards and occasionally grabs a meal at the club.'

Holmes nodded. 'What time did he get home?'

Mrs Cloverdale shook her head. 'I don't know what time it was. I'd been asleep. I heard him come to bed, but I've got no idea of the time.'

'So, it was late?' Holmes asked.

The woman shrugged. 'I wouldn't have a clue. I worked all day in the garden. There's an open day in a few weeks and I need to get things looking their best. I had a slice of toast and a cup of Milo while I watched the ABC evening news and was in bed by eight-thirty.'

'You didn't go to the school reunion?' Holmes asked. 'I assume you went to school in Benalla.'

'Not the High School. The convent. FCJ College. Our family is catholic.'

Once around the back of the house, Bowker was escorted to a line of sheds by an enthusiastic kelpie that spun in circles around him, occasionally jumping up and thumping his front paws against the policeman's hips as it yelped its welcome. An aging blue heeler trotted along behind, smelling the visitor's legs and occasionally growling its dissatisfaction. A loud disembodied voice commanded the canines to stop barking and get onto the nearby ute. The dogs obeyed immediately and continued their antics on the tray of a Nissan one-tonner, probably anticipating an imminent run around the stock.

Bowker found Ron Cloverdale in a well-resourced workshop applying grease to bearings on an aging yellow hay bailer. As the detective introduced himself, the farmer placed the grease gun on a steel workbench, wiped his greasy fingers with an oily towel and shook his visitor's hand. Cloverdale was a man-mountain both in height and build. He stood several inches taller than Bowker and was broader across the shoulders. He sported a red beard and a shock of red hair. His eyes were a deep green, overhung by bushy red eyebrows. His pale skin was sun-damaged with red blotches and patches of scaly skin on the back of his hands. The rest of his body was hidden under a grimy navy-blue boiler suit. His natural countenance was stern, but deepened further when Bowker moved from pleasantries to questions that the farmer felt bordered on accusations.

'Just for the record, Mr Cloverdale, where were you on the night your father-in-law was killed?'

Cloverdale's eyes narrowed and his jaw tightened. 'What sort of a question is that? Do I look like a bloody murderer?'

Bowker didn't flinch. 'Just routine. No guilt implied. It's a question we ask everyone with an association with the victim.'

Cloverdale folded his arms across his massive chest. 'I was at the golf club on Mansfield Road. Played eighteen holes in the afternoon, had a few drinks afterwards then stayed around for a meal. Fifty witnesses can back me up on that, detective.'

'What time did you leave the golf club?'

Cloverdale shrugged. 'Nine o'clock, probably. Somewhere about then, anyway.'

Bowker nodded. 'What time did you get home?'

'Around nine-thirty, I s'pose. Trip from Benalla to here takes about half an hour.' Cloverdale saw the look on Bowker's face. 'I wasn't over the limit, if that's what you're worried about.'

'I'm not worried about that, Ron,' Bowker said looking the tall man in the eye. 'What I'm worried about is you not telling me that you dropped in at the school reunion after you left the golf club. I saw you there myself, mate. You're pretty hard to miss. Didn't know who the big bloke was until I walked into this workshop.'

Cloverdale's face reddened. 'Weekends all run into one another when you spend most of your time on a farm. Forgot that the reunion was that particular weekend.'

'So you didn't get home at 9.30 that night because I saw you at the function room well after that.'

Cloverdale was caught off guard and ran a hand through his thick greasy hair. 'Yeah, it was probably more like ten when I arrived home that night. Normally it's nine-thirty at the latest unless Alison comes into town and we have tea together at the club.'

Bowker leant against the workbench. 'Did you talk to Gary Rice while you were there?'

'Saw him but didn't speak to him. Just caught up with a few old mates from school that I hadn't seen for decades. Spoke to Sid Wilson about bringing out a buyer to look at some steers I reckon are about ready.'

Bowker waved away a fly as he recognised a name from the distant past. 'Sid Wilson. The stock agent? Works for Goldsborough Mort. Had a small farm in the lane over the road from our place on Kilfeera Road when I was a kid. Must be pretty long in the tooth now.'

Cloverdale nodded. 'Yeah, that's him. In his early seventies and works for himself. Goldsboroughs merged with Elder Smith and now it's just called Elders. Didn't know you were a local.'

Bowker nodded. 'Yeah, until I was about eighteen.' He was keen to move on. 'So you spoke with Sid at the reunion and a few of your old mates. Nobody else?'

'Said g'day to a few locals but there was no chit-chat,' Cloverdale replied before staring straight into Bowker's eyes. 'What are you trying to get at here?'

Bowker ignored the question. 'And you say you didn't speak to your father-in-law that night.'

Cloverdale exhaled dramatically. 'No. I bloody told you that already.'

'Had you spoken to him earlier about his will?'

Cloverdale's eyes widened. 'No. Why would I?'

Bowker put his hands in his pockets and thought for a moment. Wind rustled the leaves in the tree beside him and the dogs snapped at each other on the back of the ute. 'According to Arabella Rice, she saw you in the bank and informed you that Gary intended to change his will and order that this property be sold up and the proceeds be distributed between your wife and herself, with the major share passing to her as his next of kin.'

Cloverdale took a deep breath before dismissing what Bowker had said with the wave of his large hand. 'Oh, that bullshit. I didn't believe a word of it. Gary wouldn't have done that to Alison in a million years. The old bitch hates my guts because she knows I recognise her for what she is. An oxygen bandit and a parasite of the highest order.'

'If you did think he was about to change his will and sell this place from under you, it would provide a good motive to murder

80

him before that could happen, don't you think?' Bowker waited for his reaction.

Cloverdale was matter of fact. 'I agree. But I didn't give what she said a second thought and I didn't kill Gary Rice. End of story, detective.'

'You were in the right place at the right time to do it.'

'So were a hundred others,' Cloverdale retorted quickly.

Bowker returned fire just as rapidly. 'Not with a motive.'

Cloverdale shook his head but didn't reply.

'What vehicle do you take to golf?' Bowker asked.

Cloverdale pointed to the ute. 'The old girl over there. Easy to just throw the sticks and buggy on the back.'

Bowker wandered across to the Nissan and looked on the tray while the dogs tried to lick his face. He opened a metal toolbox but from a cursory glance saw no evidence of blood. The dogs tried desperately to push their heads past him and into the box.

'Looking for a murder weapon, detective?' Cloverdale asked with a smirk.

'Dogs seem pretty interested in what's in here,' Bowker replied as he closed the lid slowly so as not to decapitate one of the canines.

'Dog food. I often keep a bit in there if we're working in the yards all day. Dogs can smell something of interest a mile away.'

'Yes, they can,' Bowker replied with a steely stare as the big farmer nervously removed a cigarette packet from his boiler suit pocket.

CHAPTER 8

olmes was standing with hands on hips taking in the beauty of the crystal-clear and pebble-bottomed creek when Bowker returned to the car. 'Should have brought our rods,' he suggested. 'The water is only a foot deep and you can see the trout swimming among the stones.'

'Don't need rods, mate,' Bowker replied with a grin. 'We could take off our shoes and socks, roll up our trousers and see if we can tickle a few.'

Holmes was puzzled. 'I'm not with you.'

'You wade into the stream and feel under a rock or a fallen limb. If you find a fish, you just tickle their belly. Puts them in a trance or paralyses them so you can grab them and throw them up on the bank. When we were kids, the old man used to bring us up here, or to Upper Ryan's Creek, to tickle a few.'

Holmes chuckled loudly. 'Bullshit.'

Bowker shook his head and spoke seriously. 'No bullshit, mate. Look it up on the internet.'

Holmes smiled. 'I'm not giving you the pleasure. You'll be hanging shit on me for the next six months.'

Bowker took out his mobile phone. 'I'll prove it to you.' He swiped the screen. 'Shit. No mobile reception. I'll show you when we get back to Benalla.'

Holmes still wasn't convinced. 'And I suppose you and your brother tickled a few, did you? Take home a bag full?'

'Not Alex or me, no,' Bowker replied. 'But dad normally got a couple. Tickled a red bellied black snake in Ryan's Creek one day. That scared the shit out of all of us.' He laughed. 'Especially the snake.'

Holmes wasn't about to believe his colleague. 'Cut the bullshit and tell me about your chat with Cloverdale.'

Bowker walked with his colleague to the car. 'He's a big bastard, for a start,' he said as he opened the driver's side door and climbed in. 'Wouldn't look out of place standing on the prow of a Viking boat. Red hair and a long red beard.'

Holmes slid into the passenger seat and buckled his belt. 'Where was he on the night his father-in-law was rolled?'

'Told me he was at the golf club with his mates after playing eighteen holes in the afternoon.'

Holmes wound down his window an inch or two to allow the breeze to enter. 'So, he's got an alibi and plenty of people to back him up?'

Bowker peered over his shoulder as he backed the car from the shade of the tree. 'What he forgot to tell me was that he visited the school reunion after he left the golf club. He got a hell of a shock when I told him I'd seen him there. Obviously, I didn't know who he was at the time, but he stood out like Shaq O'Neal in a jockeys' room.'

Holmes grinned. 'How'd he explain being there? And not fessing up about it?'

Bowker chuckled. 'Catching up with old school mates. He said he got his weekends mixed up when I asked him his whereabouts on the night Rice was killed. Reckoned he was home by ten.' He shrugged. 'But that would have meant he left town at around nine-thirty and my recollection is that he was still at the footy club at ten.'

'His missus said she has no idea when he arrived home,' Holmes said as they made their way through the front gate and onto Benalla Road. 'She said she worked in the garden all day and was so stuffed she just cooked some toast and was in bed by eight-thirty.'

'Surely she must have heard him come in,' Bowker suggested as he slowed to pass through the Tatong township.

'Said she heard him, but has no idea about what time that was.'

'Did she make any mention of her father changing his will?'

'Appeared she knew nothing about it until I raised it with her.' Holmes replied. 'Then wrote it off as just more bullshit her stepmother had fabricated to drive a wedge between her husband and the Cloverdales.'

Bowker dodged a pothole in the bitumen. 'Similar story from Big Red. He gave no credence to the story she spun him in the bank. She's a conniving bitch, according to him.'

'You believe that?'

Bowker shrugged. 'I'd be more inclined to if he hadn't omitted to tell me he was in the same room as Rice on the night he was murdered.'

By the time the detectives arrived back in Benalla, the sky danced with near continuous lightning. Even the glider pilots, who dreamed of steamy days like this with rising columns of hot air that would lift them higher and higher, had decided that discretion was the better part of valour. Their fragile flying machines were now safely stowed in the hangars beside the runway.

'How about we visit Councillor Lowther while we're out and about?' Bowker suggested as they turned into Coster Street and passed the hospital on their right. 'He lives on a farm somewhere in the district. His address should be in that folder on the backseat if Fleming followed up the people I said we were interested in.'

Holmes reached behind him with a right hand and retrieved a blue plastic covered binder. He opened it and found the address on the second page. 'RMB 1298 Goorambat.' He looked at Bowker. 'Where the fuck is Goorambat?'

'Just off the Shepparton road on the railway line to Yarrawonga. My brother played footy out there for a few seasons. Apparently the club is still going and now plays in the Ovens and King League. One of the few teams left standing from the old Benalla and District competition.'

Bowker continued through Benalla, over the main Sydney to Melbourne Railway line and north-west along the Midland Highway. A few miles out of town he veered right onto the Tocumwal road then quickly bore right again onto Moylan Road which ultimately took him to the village of Goorambat. The town was slightly larger than Tatong where they had been earlier in the day, with around thirty houses, a country pub, silos and a couple of churches. The Lowther property was a few kilometres further along the road towards Devenish, the next speck on the map and once the home of The Barbers, the local football team with the red and white striped jumpers. A white painted ten-gallon drum mounted on a vertical length of train rail served as a post box and had the property's RMB address printed in block letters on the side. An ornate wrought iron arch traversed the gateway with scrolled printing informing visitors that they were entering "Nooramunga" a property owned by the Lowther Family Pastoral Company.

'Not surprised Lowther is keen to pay the minimal level of rates,' Bowker said as he steered the vehicle through the gateway and up a long, sealed driveway bordered on each side by white railing fences.

'What do you mean?'

'Did you read the sign? Lowther Family Pastoral Company. Split the income of the place among various family members and finish up paying bugger-all tax.'

The Nooramunga homestead was a disappointment, given the property's pretentious interface with the outside world. The house itself was a recent build and its design went to great lengths to project elegance and wealth. But to the detectives it screamed kitsch and tastelessness, and sat incongruously against its natural backdrop of the Broken Creek. Viewed from the front, the building was a long rectangular cream brick clad box. Windows stretched from floor to ceiling in most rooms with a colonial-look sought via cheap aluminium grids attached to the inside of a single sheet of glass. The roof was low slung with minimal overhang for eaves and the absence of verandas condemned the residence to a heavy use of air conditioning during the summer. The garden was well established, indicating an earlier residence had been demolished to make way for this new construction.

Bowker parked the car with thunder rumbling overhead and with the first few heavy drops of rain blotching the charcoal-coloured path to the front door. Two kelpies barked their welcome from kennels under nearby scrubby melaleucas. Both men barely made it to the faux marble portico before the rain became heavier. The ornately glassed front door was open behind a heavy security door. Holmes pressed the doorbell and a few moments later a tall and wiry, but hunched over woman appeared in the doorway. Her eyes were grey and tired, her face wrinkled and well worn. Her mouth was little more than a narrow slit, her hair was pulled back behind her ears. She wore a light-weight floral dress with a navy-blue apron tied around her narrow waist. Bowker introduced himself and his colleague and explained they were hoping to speak to her husband.

'He's looking at sheep up at Trangie in New South Wales,' the woman explained. 'He'll sleep in Parkes tonight and then he's hoping to buy a dozen rams from a stud just outside Narrandera. He's staying with an old college mate who owns the place, so he won't be home until Friday night.'

'Thanks, Mrs Lowther,' Bowker replied. 'We'll have a chat with him sometime after he gets back.'

'What do you want to talk to him about?' the woman asked as the officers turned to leave.

'We're making a few enquiries about Gary Rice's death on Saturday night,' Holmes replied.

Mrs Lowther slipped her hands into her apron pockets. 'Heard he'd been knocked on the head.' She paused and looked up at Bowker. 'Obviously, you've heard there's no love lost between him and Dennis. That's why you're out here I presume?'

Bowker nodded. 'Apparently there's been a feud about council rates.'

'Not sure feud is the right word.' The woman chortled. 'More like Dennis getting a bee in his bonnet about something that won't come to pass anyway. He's never happy unless he's got someone in the gun.' She frowned and raised her eyebrows. 'I'm just happy that it wasn't me for once.'

'Was your husband home here last Saturday night, Mrs Lowther?' Bowker asked.

'No. He was in Benalla at a council function. He's chairman of a subcommittee that's investigating a sister city arrangement with some big metropolis in China. There was a whiz-bang reception for the overseas delegation. No expense spared. Most of the town's big wigs and their partners were there so I don't think you'll have trouble establishing my husband's whereabouts on that night.' She looked at Bowker and chuckled sarcastically. 'Sister cities is a bit rich when Benalla has a population of around nine thousand and this place in China has twelve million.' She shrugged. 'But there's heaps and heaps of trade opportunities for our primary products, according to my husband. Besides, it gives him another excuse to get out and about. I'd love the same opportunity at some stage.'

Bowker felt sympathy for the woman who he assumed felt trapped and isolated on the farm. 'We'd still like to talk to him anyway Mrs Lowther, so let him know we'll be out. Most probably on Saturday morning.'

The detectives bid their farewells and left Mrs Lowther staring through the security door until they were out of sight.

Back at the station, with thunder crashing and rain tumbling down outside, the homicide detectives adjourned to their makeshift office to update their local colleagues on the day's interviews.

'First up this morning, we interviewed the Cloverdales out at Tatong,' Bowker said.

'Hope you enjoyed the scenery because it would've been a waste of time otherwise,' Fleming replied. 'But go on.'

Bowker was tiring of Fleming's closed mind but didn't let his frustration show. 'Rice's daughter was home on the night of the killing. Sherlock said she seemed genuinely surprised when told of her father's plans to change his will. Ron Cloverdale was in Benalla that night at the golf club, then later at the reunion for a short time. He confirmed that Arabella Rice had spoken to him in the bank recently and that she had made claims about Rice changing his will to include selling the Tatong property.'

Larsen folded her hands on the table. 'What was Cloverdale's reaction to that news?'

'That it was all bullshit designed to split the family.' Bowker shrugged. 'According to him he took no notice of it. Seems he didn't even tell his wife about the conversation.'

88

'Did he seem genuine?' Fleming asked.

'Hard to tell,' Bowker replied. 'But he neglected to tell me that he'd attended the reunion until I told him I'd seen him there myself.'

'How'd he explain the lapse in memory?' Larsen asked.

'Said he'd got his weekends mixed up,' Bowker replied with a smirk.

Holmes shook his head. 'Bit hard to swallow when we're only talking four days ago.'

'Easier to swallow than the crap Sanderson and Brown are trying to shove down our throat,' Fleming retorted quickly.

Larsen saw the look on Bowker's face and sensed his annoyance. 'How'd you go with Dennis Lowther?'

Holmes had also recognised his partner's irritation and answered quickly to avoid a confrontation. 'Didn't get to see Lowther. His wife said he's up north buying sheep and won't be home until late Friday night.'

Fleming failed to read Bowker as well as the others. 'I wouldn't be wasting too much time on him. He's one of the big knobs in the district. Next in line to be mayor. He's hardly going to put all that at risk by killing some old bloke because of a disagreement over council rates. Especially when he had the numbers to veto a change anyway.'

Bowker leant forward and drove his index finger into the desk as he made each point. 'Lowther is known to have made physical threats against Rice, so it appears to me that the victim's rates agenda touched a pretty raw nerve somewhere deep inside the honourable councillor. Plus, he was in town the night that the murder took place. So we *will* be wasting time on him, Aaron. When he gets back from up north, Sherlock and I will slip out to Goorambat and put him through the wringer.' Bowker leant back in his chair. 'Until we prove otherwise, there are more players in this game than Sanderson and Brown.'

Fleming folded his hands behind his head, looked up at the ceiling, but didn't respond.

Bowker lifted his briefcase from the floor beside him and opened in on the table. 'Now let's have a look at that list of reunion attendees.'

For the next hour, the four officers perused every name and address in the ten-page document. Ron Cloverdale's name wasn't there, presumably because he was a blow-in and not an official guest. Bowker wondered how many others were in that same category.

CHAPTER 9

Baddaginnie was a relaxing ten-kilometre drive along the old Hume Highway the next morning. Yesterday's storms had passed, and a stiff southerly cooled what otherwise would have been another sweltering day. Located half-way to Violet Town, Baddaginnie was no more than a hamlet of a few dozen houses, an op shop and the odd small run-from-home business. Bowker turned south from the grandiosely named High Street into Clarendon Street and followed it past the local primary school which, with counterparts at Violet Town, Strathbogie and Swanpool, formed Peranbin Primary College. As the street neared the Hume Freeway bypass of the township, Holmes spotted a rusty letterbox with the remnants of the name Marshall scrawled along the side in spray paint. Bowker turned off the street and stopped in the gateway. A potholed track ran fifty metres towards a dilapidated residence, wheel tracks diverting from the main driveway to avoid the worst of the holes. The house was a relocated suburban weatherboard, cut up in sections at an earlier time and reassembled on the present site. Little had been done to help it nestle into its new surrounds. The stumps on which it sat were still visible with no battens attached to hide its structure. The weatherboards were cracking as the paint fell victim to the sun and rain working in tandem to degrade the look and integrity of the structure. There was no garden to speak of, just the odd agapanthus and a few straggly geraniums parallel to the front wall. The original steps had not been reinstated and the doorway sat half a metre above the ground. A wooden fruit box acted as a step to the front door. Curtains dressed the inside of windows, but torn blinds flapped in the wind outside. A length of guttering lay on the ground to the right of the front door. The only part of the two-acre property that looked well kept was a row of four dog kennels and concrete yards to the south of the house. Two of the yards were empty, the other two housed barking greyhounds standing on hind legs with front paws stretched up against the wire fence. The house paddock was bare of all grass thanks to a lousy, skinny merino wether who stood in the corner rubbing its draping wool against the trunk of a long-dead fruit tree.

'If this is the right place, it's a comedown for the former Mrs Gary Rice,' Holmes said.

'Panoramic views of the Hume Freeway certainly don't match those across Lake Benalla, that's for sure,' Bowker replied as he dodged the potholes in the track.

The front door of the house opened and a short, skinny woman stepped down and walked towards the police car as it pulled up and the two policemen alighted. The greyhounds intensified their barking and an old kelpie sheepdog staggered out from under the house and limped across to see what was afoot.

'Can I help you, officers?' the woman asked in a refined voice. She was well groomed, modestly dressed in clean clothes and shoes, her grey hair cut short. She had a friendly countenance, but her blue eyes betrayed fatigue and melancholy. She wore a suspicious bruise on her left cheek and a cut on her ear. She was the epitome of a woman totally out of place in her physical surrounds.

Bowker introduced himself and his colleague. 'We're looking for Tony Marshall, Mrs err Ms ...'

The woman smiled. 'My surname is still Rice, but best if you just call me Wilma. Tony isn't home. He's taken a couple of dogs to Albury in New South Wales.' A puzzled look crossed her face. 'Why would detectives be looking for Tony? Is this more about that live baiting business? I thought that was over when his suspension finished.'

Bowker shook his head. 'Nothing to do with greyhounds, Wilma. We're making inquiries into the death of your former husband.'

The woman dropped her head for a quick moment then looked up at the policeman. 'What's that got to do with Tony?'

'Probably nothing,' Holmes replied.

'Where was your husband on Saturday night, Wilma?' Bowker asked.

'At the Farmers Arms in Benalla,' she replied sadly. 'Where he is on most nights when he's not at a dog track somewhere.'

'What time did he arrive home?' Bowker asked.

The woman shrugged. 'Well after midnight. I didn't look at the clock, but I knew it was late. Or early, if you look at it the other way.' She looked at each man in turn with a puzzled expression. 'Why would you suspect Tony has relevance to Gary's death?'

Bowker put his hands in his pockets. 'Your daughter told us Mr Marshall has a history of violence towards you. She also said that Gary attempted to intercede on your behalf. Apparently, that merely enflamed the situation.'

'Is that a fair summary, Wilma?' Holmes asked.

The woman looked at the ground and when she raised her head again she had tears in her eyes. She nodded slowly. 'He's a brutal man, Detective. I rue the day I took up with him. I didn't see his dark side until it was too late.' She forced a smile. 'For police, this would be an all too familiar tale, I'd imagine.'

'Why not just move out while he's away?' Bowker asked.

'Where would I go?' the woman asked sadly.

'Your daughter's place has plenty of room,' Holmes replied.

'He'd just come after me. And I don't want them involved,' the woman replied. 'It's my mess, and I just have to make the best of it.'

Bowker hadn't seen Marshall, but was willing to bet that if things became physical he'd be no match for the red-headed Viking from Tatong. 'Well, we're involved now, Wilma. That bruise on your face from him?'

She nodded.

'When is Marshall due back?'

'Tomorrow morning,' the woman replied. 'He's staying in Wodonga tonight. His useless sister lives up there. I'd hate to think how she makes a living.'

'Go back inside and grab what you need. I'll contact your daughter. You won't be here when he arrives back tomorrow, but we will. All this has to stop Wilma.'

By the time Wilma Rice had gathered a few things and the detectives had transported her to Benalla, her daughter was outside the police station waiting for her arrival. Alison Cloverdale hugged her mother tightly while Holmes transferred the older woman's meagre belongings from the police car to the mud-spattered Land Cruiser parked beside it. Bowker took Mrs Cloverdale aside.

'If Marshall comes anywhere near your place, call the police,' he said sternly. 'I'll word up the senior sergeant inside. We'll see if we can get a Family Violence Protection Order made against him.'

Cloverdale nodded. 'Thank you. And thank you for getting her away from that monster.'

'When he gets back from up north tomorrow, Detective Holmes and I plan to speak to him in relation to your father's death. We might also have a quiet chat about staying well clear of your mother.'

The woman put her hand on the detective's forearm and nodded in silent appreciation before returning to her vehicle where her mother was already sitting in the front seat. The detectives stood side by side and watched until the Toyota disappeared over the bridge.

Holmes put his hands on his hips. 'I can't believe Marshall drinks at the pub most nights and hasn't been put off the road. If he had that kind of luck with his dogs, he'd make a fortune.'

'We'll check his record and see if he's ever been done for DUI,' Bowker replied.

Back in the station, Holmes pulled up the criminal driving record of Anthony Marshall of the Baddaginnie address. He raised his eyebrows. 'Twice over the limit in the last eighteen months. Lost his licence the second time. String of driving offences prior to that.'

'Check the LEAP database and see if there's anything on him there.'

Holmes logged into LEAP and his search returned a string of offences. 'Bingo! Long list of minor assaults, petty theft, cruelty to animals. Most recent one involving the use of possums in live baiting with his greyhounds.' Holmes looked at his colleague. 'How does a lovely woman like Wilma Rice get tied up with a dead-shit like Marshall?'

Bowker shrugged. 'Some women go for the bad boy type. Or maybe it was a case of any port in a storm after she split with Rice. Who knows?'

'If you split up with Rachael, could you see her picking up with a prick like Marshall?'

Bowker burst out laughing. 'She'd rip his balls out if he tried to heavy her. Cassie would be the same, wouldn't she?'

Holmes looked back at the screen. 'Probably' he mumbled.

Bowker didn't pursue it further. 'Let's find out who manned the divi-van last Saturday night. See if they came across Marshall in their travels.'

Bowker consulted the duty roster downstairs, and as luck would have it, one of the officers who was on patrol that night was manning the front counter. The detectives introduced themselves to Constable Sam Vernon, a fair-haired young man with a neat appearance and a line of unintelligible tattooed script running down the underside of his forearms. Bowker explained their interest in the Saturday night patrol and quizzed Vernon on whether he and his partner had reason to speak to Tony Marshall. The young man thought for a moment, then shook his head.

'Didn't see Marshall at all last weekend. He drinks at the Farmers Arms and given his history and his likely whereabouts for most of the night, we often pull him over. He's been done at least twice for being over the limit. He always blows something, but he's getting better at knowing when to stop now days.' Vernon chuckled. 'Mind you, he's normally got a six-pack sitting beside him on the front seat. Probably knocks down a couple once he clears town and can't see headlights in his rear vision. Less than a ten-minute trip down to Baddaginnie.'

Bowker leant his backside against the front counter. 'You didn't come across a Noel Sanderson or a Glen Brown in your travels that night?'

'Not last Saturday night, no. The whole town was pretty quiet, actually. Lot of people over at the footy club for the school reunion and there was some sort of a squatters' do at the art gallery. Most of the pubs were nearly empty.'

'Get anyone for DUI after the reunion?' Holmes asked. He pointed to Bowker and smiled. 'Didn't pick up this bastard, did you?'

The constable laughed. 'What? Are the homicide squad supplying guest speakers for social events now?'

'Na. Just another ex-local like most of the guests,' Bowker replied.

Vernon smiled and thought for a moment. 'We booked two or

three as they left the grounds,' he reported, 'but a lot less than I thought there might be. People must be getting the message about a designated driver and all that.'

Bowker nodded. 'I didn't stay till stumps. What time did you run the breathos?'

Vernon scratched his chin with his thumb. 'Half-eleven. Quarter to twelve probably. Did a loop through the grounds around one, and the dining room was locked up like a church. All the lights were off. Followed a bloke in a ute over the bridge and down the main street. Failed to indicate when he turned right at the roundabout at McDonalds. Given the hour and the fact that he had a set of golf sticks on the tray of his vehicle made us suspicious that he might have had an extended session at the golf club before he headed home.' Bowker glanced at Holmes as the constable continued. 'Put the breatho on him and he blew .04 from memory. He was pretty edgy about getting home so late, so we issued a warning about the blinker and sent him on his way.'

Bowker stood up straight and put his hands on his hips. 'And this was a touch after one o'clock?'

Vernon nodded. 'That'd be about right.'

Do you remember the bloke's name?' Bowker asked.

'Not off the top of my head but it will be in the log for Saturday night. Big bastard. Real ranga. Red hair and a long red beard. Looked like Ned Kelly with red hair.'

'How do you want to play this?' Holmes asked as they headed out the Tatong road.

'Make it appear as though we've driven out for a follow up talk with Wilma I think,' Bowker replied as they crossed the Makoan Inlet channel, now disused after Lake Makoan was decommissioned in 2010 to restore the old Winton Swamp wetlands. 'You talk with her and Alison, while I have a heart to heart with

Leif Ericson. Hopefully he won't be with the women and I won't have to manufacture an excuse to have a private word.'

Holmes looked across at his colleague. 'Do you reckon he knocked over Rice?'

Bowker grimaced in thought. 'Dunno, mate. But he's lying about something.'

The afternoon was uncomfortably warm as they parked near the creek. The cicadas were screaming in the gums above, the breeze so gentle as to not disturb the leaves. Two wedge tailed eagles circled above the hills in the distance.

Bowker felt his luck was in when he spotted Ron Cloverdale in the sheep yards a few hundred metres past the back of the house. A barking dog forced sheep up a drafting race manned by the big farmer. 'You go knock on the front door and I'll head down to the yards for a chat with his nibs.'

Holmes nodded and walked off towards the front door of the homestead, waving sticky flies away as he went. A blue heeler strained on a chain under a tree as Bowker strolled past, miffed that he wasn't required to help the kelpie with the sheep. Cloverdale saw the detective approaching and locked the drafting gate across the race. He stepped over three wooden-railed fences and met Bowker in the shade of a white-trunked ghost gum on the perimeter of the yards. He took a cigarette from a packet and snapped open a lighter. He inhaled strongly, the red tip of the cigarette glowing brightly even in the brilliant light of the afternoon. He blew smoke into the branches above.

'Come out to check that Wilma made it in one piece?' the big man asked without conviction.

Bowker nodded. 'Something like that. What can you tell me about Tony Marshall?'

Cloverdale's face relaxed a little. 'First class piece of shit. Does a few hours of casual work at a tyre place in Benalla and a bit of rousying in the odd shed around Violet Town. Also trains a few slow greyhounds. Has the occasional win at regional tracks. People suspect he gives them a sting every now and then to speed them up. Been done for live baiting and had his training licence suspended for illegal substances found in swabs.' He took another drag on his dart.

'What about his relationship with your mother-in-law?'

'Abusive,' the farmer said as he exhaled more smoke. 'He's a violent drunk. Gets pissed, then takes out all his inadequacies on Wilma.'

Bowker folded his arms. 'How come you haven't sorted him out. You're a big boy.'

Cloverdale was silent for a moment as he inhaled another lungful of toxic vapour. 'I've thought about it on more than one occasion, but Wilma always pleads that Alison and I not get involved.' The words came out with the smoke. 'If it was up to me, she would have been living here years ago and I would have knocked Marshall into next week.' He smiled. 'People see me as a gentle giant, but once I do the block, look out!'

Bowker's expression didn't change. 'Is that right?' he asked.

'You blokes must have got to Wilma at exactly the right time. Marshall is away in New South somewhere. And you're cops, so she's got that immediate protection.' Cloverdale shrugged. 'Then again, maybe she'd just finally had enough. Maybe she was scared she'd go the same way as Gary. Knocked on the head.'

Bowker raised his eyebrows and put his hands in his trouser pockets. 'You thinking that maybe Marshall had something to do with Rice's murder?'

Cloverdale spread his palms, smoke rising between his fingers. 'Buggered if I know. But apparently Gary had words with him about his treatment of Wilma. And Marshall's not a man to be told how to behave. Not by an old man with a walking stick, that's for sure.'

Bowker thought for a moment before moving to the purpose of his trip. 'You didn't see Marshall while you were driving around Benalla at one o'clock last Sunday morning, did you?'

Cloverdale frowned. 'I wasn't in Benalla at that time. I arrived home from town around ten on Saturday night. I told you that yesterday.'

'Don't feed me bullshit, Ron,' Bowker said with an edge. 'You were breathalysed around one o'clock by Constable Sam Vernon and his partner in Coster Street. You blew .04. They could have booked you for failing to indicate at the roundabout in Bridge Street, but they gave you a break. Now how about you give *me* a break and explain where you were between the end of the reunion and when the divisional van pulled you over?'

Cloverdale closed his eyes and thought for a moment. 'The officers must have got their times mixed up. It's true what you say about the breathalyser and me forgetting to put on my blinker. But that was around nine thirty. Not one o'clock in the morning, that's for sure.'

'Sorry Ron, that won't wash. You see, when a police patrol pulls someone over, the first thing the officers do is run the number plate details to ascertain whether the vehicle is registered, or has been reported stolen, or belongs to a person they should approach with caution. The time of that inquiry is automatically recorded.' Bowker stared into Cloverdale's eyes looking for a tell. 'It was seven minutes past one on Sunday morning.' He saw the big farmer's eyes flash away briefly. 'So where were you? And no bullshit, this time. With the number of lies you've already told me, I can't help but think you're a man with a lot to hide, Ron. Of all the people we've identified with a motive to kill Gary Rice, you've now moved to the top of the pops.'

Cloverdale reacted angrily and kicked the ground. 'As if I'd murder Alison's father! It's bloody preposterous.'

'Not from where I'm standing, mate,' Bowker replied quietly.

'Alison went straight to the solicitors after your visit yesterday and viewed her father's will. What old Arabella said about leaving this property to her was all bullshit. Gary just made a few small changes to make sure Wilma was properly looked after when he died.'

'Yeah, but you didn't know that until after he was dead, did you?'

Cloverdale ran a hand through his thick red hair. He was now sweating profusely, his eyes darting around ensuring no-one else was in earshot. 'If my whereabouts on that night had nothing to do with the murder, does it still go on the public record?'

Bowker shook his head. 'Only in our notes if the story all checks out and you haven't broken any laws. Our only interest is finding the killer of your father-in-law and building a case for conviction.'

Cloverdale was on the horns of a dilemma and pondered no-win alternatives. Bowker knew it. The farmer was establishing the rules of the game before he committed to play. 'So you're not obliged to inform Alison of things you've uncovered that have no relevance to her father's murder?'

Bowker suspected what might be coming. 'Nope.'

Cloverdale dropped his cigarette and stubbed it out with the heel of his elastic sided work boot. He stared into the branches above him as if waiting for divine intervention. Finally he spoke in low tones regardless of there being no other human ears within a hundred metres. The sound of barking dogs and bleating sheep would have rendered his speech inaudible anyway. 'I ran into my girlfriend from school at the reunion. We got talking about the old days. She's now divorced and lives in Sydney. Real estate agent. Flew down to Albury and hired a car to get her to Benalla and back.'

'And what? You talked about old times until one in the morning? Until well after the reunion had finished?' Bowker asked sceptically.

Cloverdale shook his head and looked at the ground. 'In the cool light of day, I wish that was all that happened. As she left the reunion, she handed me a business card with her phone number printed on it and said she was keen to keep in touch. After she'd left, I turned the card over and she'd written the name of the motel where she was staying. Plus the room number.'

Bowker knew the story but pressed him further. 'So rather than toddling off home to your wife, you decided to drop past the motel?'

The big farmer nodded sadly. 'That's right. We had a few drinks and talked about how full-on we'd been as teenagers. How we'd sneak down to the river and swim in the raw. One thing led to another and before long I'd crossed the Rubicon as they say. Suddenly it became too late for thoughts about Alison and my marriage. You know the old saying. A stiff dick has no conscience.' He exhaled loudly. 'If I had my time over again ...'. He didn't finish the sentence.

Bowker folded his arms across his chest and leaned a shoulder against the trunk of the tree. 'So I assume you've destroyed the card with her telephone number,' he said with a knowing smirk.

'I tossed it into the toolbox on the tray of the ute. Didn't want to risk discarding it where Alison might see it and jump to the wrong conclusion.'

'The right conclusion, you mean,' Bowker retorted quickly.

Cloverdale was suddenly indignant, grasping for higher moral ground. 'It was a one-night stand that I'm not proud of. It won't happen again.'

'That's why you hid the card in your toolbox rather than getting rid of it in Benalla or tearing it into tiny pieces, or better still, burning it with your cigarette lighter?'

'Never thought of it,' Cloverdale replied.

'Bullshit, Ron. You filed it away for future reference. Now can I see the card please? See if it matches with your story. I'll need her phone number too. At the moment, she's your alibi.'

The two men walked to Cloverdale's one-tonner and Ron removed the card from inside a plastic case of drill bits at the bottom of the toolbox. Bowker chuckled. 'Just chucked it in here, did you Ron? Landed in a pretty secretive spot don't you reckon?'

Cloverdale didn't answer. He removed another smoke from its packet and lit up while Bowker copied the real estate agent's details. He turned the card over and confirmed Cloverdale's story about the motel name and room number being scribbled there. He handed the card back to the farmer then pointed into the toolbox. 'Might be more appropriate if you stash the card in that tin labelled "screws".'

The detective walked twenty metres away and dialled the number he had recorded, keen to talk to Cloverdale's dalliance before the big man had time to word her up. After a few minutes of quiet discussion, Bowker walked back to the tree.

'She was reluctant to talk about last Saturday night until I mentioned she could be involved in a murder investigation. The good news Ron, is that she confirmed your story.'

Cloverdale exhaled smoke. 'Thank God.' He looked expectantly at Bowker. 'So there's no need to tell Alison? As I said. If I had my time over again.'

Bowker stared back expressionless. 'Luckily for you Ron, at this stage I've got no need to bring Alison into all this.'

Cloverdale was visibly relieved. 'Thank you, detective.'

Bowker returned to the police car where Holmes was waiting. Holmes had gleaned little further information from his chat with mother and daughter besides being told that no major changes had been made to the Gary Rice will. 'Other than that, there was just further confirmation of what a prick Tony Marshall is,' he explained. 'How'd you go with Big Red?'

'Found out why he lied about what time he left Benalla on Saturday night,' Bowker replied po-faced. 'He was banging an old girlfriend he'd run into at the reunion.'

'Shit. Rendezvous, or just bumped into each other by chance?'

'Just ran into her, according to him. They were an item at school together, apparently. One thing led to another and next thing you know he's back at her motel room.'

'Fuck.'

'Exactly,' Bowker said with a grin.

The men climbed into the car and Holmes wound down his window to allow the hot air to escape. 'If he loves that farm as much as everyone says he does, he's taking a bloody big risk cheating on the woman it belongs to.'

'Seeing the old girlfriend must have brought back memories of his golden days at school when they probably screwed like rabbits.' Bowker started the car and headed up the drive towards the road back to Benalla.

Holmes stared out towards the hills until they passed through the farm gate. 'If you ran into an old girlfriend from school, I bet you wouldn't be tempted to cheat on Rachael.'

'You're spot on there, mate,' Bowker said as he gave way to a ute transporting four rams in a steel mesh cage. 'Besides. I had no childhood sweetheart.' He laughed. 'I told you mate, no one at the reunion even recognised me, let alone a woman trying to ignite an old flame.' He looked across at Holmes. 'What about you? Would you be tempted?'

'Cassie *was* my girlfriend at school. We moved down to Melbourne together. I went to the police academy and she enrolled at Stots secretarial college. She learnt shorthand and all that other shit that technology has now made redundant.' Holmes was quiet for a few moments as they left the township behind them. 'How long have you known Rachael?' he then asked.

Bowker stared at the road ahead as he made the mental calculations. 'Thirty-three years. I was posted to Manangatang the year after we met. We were up there for twelve years and this is our twentieth back in Melbourne.'

'Cassie and I have known each other since primary school,' Holmes replied. 'Probably knew each other at playgroup and kinder as well, but I don't remember that far back.' He gave a half-fake chuckle. 'Bloody long time when you think about it.'

'Yeah, but I wouldn't have it any other way,' Bowker said, slowing the car as he approached a mob of sheep being pushed across the road from one farm gate to another.

Holmes nodded but then changed the subject. 'So, you're convinced by Cloverdale's story about the old girlfriend?'

'Yeah, I spoke to the woman in question before there was any chance of a tip off from Cloverdale. She confirmed his story. And it explains why he was so evasive when I asked him simple questions earlier.'

'He still could have killed Rice before he went to her motel,' Holmes suggested without any real conviction.

'What, murder your wife's father then slip around to an old girlfriend's room for a root? Can't see that happening, mate,' Bowker replied.

'Neither can I. Unless she was complicit in the killing.'

'That'd be drawing a long bow, don't you think?'

'Yeah,' Holmes replied.

With the sheep safely in their new paddock, Bowker waved to the farmer chaining the gate and accelerated to the speed limit.

CHAPTER 10

Much like the Wednesday before, Friday morning dawned hot and humid with dark cumulonimbus clouds building in the western sky. It was anyone's guess what time in the morning Marshall would be back in Baddaginnie, but if the dog trainer was not already home when the detectives arrived, Bowker was willing to wait. With the temperature the way it was, and with his greyhounds enclosed in a metal dog trailer, it was unlikely Marshall would detour to a favourite watering hole for any length of time.

A few kilometres out the old highway, Bowker turned right and followed a series of signs to the local cemetery. 'Just a quick detour to say g'day to mum and dad,' he told Holmes. 'Planned to do it on the way back, but by the look of the sky it'll be pissing down by then.'

Bowker parked the car clear of the line of European shade trees that bordered the cemetery and the two men made their way through the red brick gateway to the accompanying sound of rolling thunder and the smell of ozone. To their left was the lawn cemetery where the Bowkers were interred. To the right was the older graveyard with granite monoliths of varying sizes standing within areas divided according to religious denomination.

Holmes patted Bowker lightly on the back. 'I'll leave you to it mate. I'll check some of these older graves and see if I can spot someone famous.'

Bowker nodded and made his way down an avenue of brass plates. Eventually he found the final resting place of his parents and dropped to his haunches. Amongst the sadness, came a flood of happy memories from days of yore. After a few minutes of silent contemplation, a bright flash and a clap of thunder snapped him back to the present. Out to the west rain was on its way and already a smattering of large raindrops had darkened the concrete plinth holding the brass testament to his parents' earthly existence. The detective stood and looked above. The anvil shaped and gun metal hued clouds had arrived more quickly than anticipated and now eclipsed the sun. Bowker estimated he had thirty seconds to reach the car before the deluge came. Holmes was already there.

As luck would have it, Marshall was just pulling up beside his dog yards when the detectives arrived at his rundown property. Bowker pulled in behind as the trainer removed a single greyhound from its mini-caravan and placed it in its enclosure. The brindle bitch in the pen next door stood on her hind legs against the dividing fence and the two canines sniffed their reacquaintance. Bowker flashed his identification and introduced his colleague. Marshall was quite a few years younger than Wilma Rice, short in stature and dressed in faded jeans with a tight white tee shirt pulled over a muscly torso. A cigarette packet was tucked up the outside of his tee shirt sleeve. He had a narrow, pinched face, his eyes seemed too close together, and a beer tan coloured his nose and cheeks. An earring in his left ear seemed out of place on a man trying desperately to appear tough, and the tattoos from his younger days were beginning to fade and lose their shape. What

Wilma Rice saw in this man perplexed both policemen. As the rain fell heavier, Marshall pointed to a small outbuilding and the three men quickly retreated to the shelter of its ramshackle verandah.

Marshall was the first to speak, practically yelling to compete with the drum of the rain on the corrugated iron above. 'If you're here about Gary Rice's murder, you'll find Wilma in the house somewhere.'

Bowker looked at Holmes then at Marshall. 'She's not here anymore, and she's not coming back, Mr Marshall. She's gone to live with her daughter. Permanently.'

Marshall exploded. 'I'll put an end to that fuckin' bullshit quick smart. So if you'll excuse me.' He tried to push past Bowker, but the detective stepped into his path.

'Not so fast, Tony. Firstly, you're not going anywhere near Wilma. The local police are aware of your violent treatment of her and she's willing to press charges if you come near her again. And secondly, within the next couple of days the courts will place an intervention order on your movements that will make it an offence to go anywhere near her.'

'This is all bullshit,' Marshall replied, kicking a large stone out into the rain.

'Ron Cloverdale doesn't think so,' Holmes added. 'He said he'd knock your block off if you come anywhere near Tatong or try to contact his mother-in-law in any way. He's a big bastard, and I don't think he'd have much trouble handling a little cock sparrow like you.'

Marshall threw back his shoulders and puffed out his chest. 'I'd like to see him try.'

'So would I mate,' Holmes replied aggressively. 'One of my pet hates is violence against women. My experience in the force tells me that men who bash women are as weak as piss. Must have a complex about the size of their dick or something. Right now, every bone in my body would like to give you a bit of your own medicine. But that would be a touch hypocritical don't you think? Me lecturing you about belting someone too weak to defend themselves and then me laying into a snivelling little runt like you.' Holmes put his hands on his hips and towered over Marshall. 'But that attitude could change pretty quickly if you stuff us around, mate. So don't push me.'

The menace in Holmes's reply surprised Bowker. Maybe it was the volume of his voice, abnormally loud to compete with the drumming of the rain and the constant rolling of thunder. But it had an effect on the normally cocky Marshall who stared at the ground and didn't reply.

'It's *you* we'd like to talk to about the murder of Gary Rice,' Bowker explained, folding his arms across his chest.

'What's it got to do with me?' Marshall replied quickly. 'I hardly knew the fucker.'

Bowker stared straight at him. 'Our information is that Wilma contacted Mr Rice as a last resort, short of contacting police which she knew would make you even more abusive. She hoped that her ex-husband might have a quiet word with you. Just man to man. She thought Rice might convince you to lay off her a bit.'

'Man to man? That's a joke,' Marshall retorted quickly. 'He was a bloody school teacher, for fuck's sake. Hadn't done a proper day's work in his life.'

'He was man enough not to bash women,' Holmes said.

Marshall didn't reply.

'What was your reaction when he requested you lay off Wilma?' Bowker asked.

Marshall feigned a chuckle. 'What do you think was my reaction? I told him to mind his own fuckin' business if he didn't want his head punched in.'

'So you threatened violence against him?' Bowker asked. 'You threatened to punch his head in, and then he's found in the lake with a fractured skull. Got your wish, eh Mr Marshall?'

Marshall put his hands on his hips defiantly. 'I didn't kill the old bastard, so don't try and pin that on me. I told him to mind his own bloody business, but that's where it ended.'

Holmes took a step closer to Marshall. 'Did it, Tony? Rice was whacked in the head from behind. That's the work of a coward. And we already know you're one of them, so the MO fits perfectly.'

'Where were you last Saturday night?' Bowker asked.

'Drinking at the Farmer's Arms in Benalla. There'd be half a dozen blokes who can back me up on that. The barman certainly will.'

'What time did you leave?' Bowker asked.

Marshall shrugged. 'Around midnight. Probably home by twelve fifteen. Wilma would know.'

'We've already asked. She doesn't know,' Bowker replied. 'She remembers you coming in, but has no idea what time it was. Which way did you drive home?'

'The way I always do. Over the stock bridge, past the tech school and onto the old highway at the roundabout.'

'Sounds like you were dodging the coppers,' Holmes said.

'I wasn't over the limit, but I wasn't taking any chances,' Marshall replied. 'If I lose my licence I can't get to the dog races. That's my living.'

Bowker unfolded his arms and put his hands in his pockets. 'We might leave it at that, for now Mr Marshall. But we'll probably be in touch, especially if you're seen anywhere near Wilma Rice.'

The two officers jogged quickly back to their vehicle and climbed in out of the rain. 'What do you reckon?' Holmes asked.

'He's a shit of a bloke, but I've got my doubts about him killing Rice. If his story checks out at the pub, I can't see how he and

Rice would cross paths on the boardwalk beside the lake. How would he even know Rice was there?' Bowker shifted in his seat so as to look directly at his colleague. 'You came on pretty strong mate. I thought you were about to dong the bastard. Not your usual easy-going self.'

'The little prick just rubbed me the wrong way, that's all. Got me in a bad mood, I s'pose.' Holmes replied.

'Something playing on your mind?'

Holmes shook his head. 'Nothing, I can think of,' he replied as he stared straight ahead. Through the rain spattered windscreen, he saw Marshall sprint to his car, then drive the vehicle and dog trailer into the lean-to car port beside the house. He thought for a moment. 'Wilma said he took two dogs to Albury. He's only unloaded one.'

Bowker nodded. 'She definitely mentioned two dogs.'

Holmes took his mobile phone from his shirt pocket and googled the results for the meeting at Albury. 'In the first race, he ran last with a dog called "Bad Agony".'

Bowker laughed. 'That's pretty clever for a bloke like him. Bad Agony, Baddaginnie. Did he have another runner?'

Holmes scrolled through the fields. 'Ran fourth in the last with "Possum Magic". Two-year-old bitch. Backed in at long odds.'

'The dog he unloaded was a male. Bad Agony, I'd presume. I wonder what happened to the bitch.'

'You sure it was a male? They all look the same to me?'

'Yep.' Bowker chuckled and was about to continue when Holmes beat him to the punch.

'Yeah, I know what you're gonna say. Stands out like dog's balls.'

Bowker smiled then thought for a minute. 'It's probably not relevant to Rice's murder, but I'm intrigued to know where that other dog finished up.' He started the car and drove up beside where Marshall was unloading his own vehicle. Bowker wound down the window and was hit by ricocheting raindrops. 'Where's Possum Magic, mate?'

Marshall was taken aback. 'Dunno what you're talking about.'

'Your dog that ran fourth at Albury. The dog backed for big money but didn't run a drum.'

Marshall thought for a little too long. 'Left her at my sister's place in Wodonga. Decided to retire her. Sister's kids seemed to love her, so I gave her to them. In the morning I'll contact Greyhound Racing Victoria and let them know she's retired and no longer in my ownership.'

'You own a gun, Tony?' Bowker asked.

'Yeah. A 22. Registered and everything. Keep it in a safe inside,' Marshall replied. 'I'm a primary producer.'

'Primary Producer, are you?' Bowker pointed to the forlorn looking wether standing in the paddock with his back to the incoming rain. 'That lousy merino count as your stock?'

'Yeah. So what's it to you?'

'Might check your gun safe while we're out here. Just to make sure it's compliant.' Bowker was bluffing, but Marshall didn't know that.

'The trainer inhaled deeply. 'Actually, the rifle might still be in the car from when I helped a mate shoot a few rabbits on his place at Warrenbayne.'

'Bet you were pretty pissed when your dog didn't run a place. Especially after you'd driven all that way and obviously had a few bob on her.' Bowker paused for effect. 'Still, I'm surprised you'd just give her away after you had such an elaborate plan to make money. She'd be handy to breed from too, I suspect.'

Holmes looked at Bowker. 'Maybe we should contact the sister and see if she's willing to sell, Greg. We could get a few blokes together at Homicide and form a greyhound syndicate. Maybe you could train for us Tony. That's unless you treat your animals like you treat women.'

Bowker laughed. 'That's not a bad idea, Sherlock. See if we can buy Possum Magic as our first runner. We'll contact your sister and be in touch,' he replied, continuing the charade.

Bowker put the car in gear and drove off, watching the stationary Marshall in his rear vision mirror through the rain dotted back window.

'He shot the dog, didn't he?' Holmes suggested.

'Yep. Did his dough and cracked it. Possum Magic will be decomposing somewhere in the bush between here and Albury.'

The rain had eased a little by the time they were approaching Benalla, but the sky was still dark and ribbons of lightning were a constant on all sides of the car. 'Tomorrow morning's interview with Dennis Lowther is a pain in the arse,' Bowker said as they passed the turnoff to the cemetery. 'We could piss off back to Melbourne this afternoon, otherwise. There's bugger-all else we can do here until the forensics arrive on Monday.' He smiled. 'One has to do one's duty, I guess. What's that song from *The Pirates of Penzance*? A policeman's lot is not a happy one. On the bright side, the christening's not till Sunday so if we get away tomorrow arvo, everything should work in fine.'

'Just drop me off in Benalla, and you head home,' Holmes suggested. 'I can handle Lowther tomorrow morning. I'll take Aaron Fleming with me. I don't think Lowther is a big player in this anyway.'

'That will leave you to drive back on your own tomorrow afternoon,' Bowker responded. 'That'd be pretty selfish on my behalf.'

'I'll stay up here for the weekend. I've got no commitments in Melbourne and Cassie won't miss me. I'll talk to Lowther in the morning, then veg out for the weekend. Maybe put together a summary of the case so far.'

'Are you sure about this mate?' Bowker asked, becoming increasingly worried his close friend had personal issues that he wasn't willing to discuss.

'Couldn't be surer, Greg. You head off and enjoy the time with your family. I'll be as right as rain up here.' He chuckled. 'It's God's country, you said.'

'Then I owe you one, OK?'

'No problem.'

Bowker left for Melbourne after collecting a few items from the motel room. Holmes sprinted across a flooding Bridge Street to the police station where he hoped to find Fleming and seek his assistance in the Lowther interview next morning. He found the detective sergeant at his desk in the CIB section in deep conversation on his mobile phone. Kirsten Larsen stood at a bank of filing cabinets against the back wall, her blond hair pulled up into a topknot and wearing a pale-blue silk blouse, a short navy-blue pencil skirt and high heels. She retrieved a file from an open cabinet drawer, closed it, turned and saw Holmes open-mouthed in the doorway. 'Back from Baddaginnie already, Darren? Cracked the case open, did you?'

Holmes shook his head, trying desperately to steady his heart rate. 'Nah. Just crossed swords with a little wife-basher,' he said casually, 'but no real progress on the Rice case as far as we can tell.' Holmes knew that it was fraught with danger nowadays to comment on a workmate's appearance, but felt he had to say something. 'You're all dressed up today,' he commented, picking his words carefully so as not to sound sleazy.

Larsen smiled and took the comment as a compliment. 'In court most of the morning.' She paused for a moment. 'Where's Greg?'

'One of his grandkid's is being christened on Sunday, so he's headed back to Melbourne.'

'Bugger of a day for driving,' Larsen replied.

'Yeah. But he's pretty careful on the roads.'

'When do you head back?'

'I've got an interview with Dennis Lowther tomorrow morning so it's not much use driving back to the city when I need to be here on Monday morning to follow up the forensic reports after they arrive.'

Fleming completed his phone call and wandered across to where the pair were speaking. Holmes went through what he'd already discussed with Larsen then added: 'Can you spare an hour or so in the morning, Aaron? I'm interviewing Councillor Lowther out at Goorambat and I'd appreciate a second pair of ears.'

Fleming screwed up his face. 'Sorry, mate. No can do. Rostered for junior cricket umpiring in the morning. That's harder to get out of than Barwon Prison. You might have to wait till Monday if you need company.'

'I can go with you,' Larsen said. 'Good experience to see how the big dogs operate.'

Holmes shook his head. 'Nah. Don't want to bugger your family weekend as well. I can do it on my own.'

Larsen chuckled. 'No family with me, Darren. The interview will give me something to do.'

Fleming appeared aggrieved. 'Surely it can wait till Monday. Bloody weekend's a bloody weekend as far as I'm concerned.'

Larsen was having none of it. 'Darren has given up his weekend at home to keep this investigation rolling, so it won't hurt me to give up a couple of hours.'

Holmes smiled. 'OK. Meet you here around nine thirty.' He was unsure whether he felt trepidation or exhilaration. Or perhaps a combination of both.

CHAPTER 11

Holmes awoke early on Friday morning and struggled to get back to sleep after a restless night. The storms of the day before had not cooled the weather and the high humidity made sleeping difficult even with the air conditioner running flat out. At 6am, Holmes surrendered to his insomnia, opting for a swim in the motel's swimming pool. Outside the day was dawning hot and windy with the sky laced with feathery high cloud. Inside the pool pavilion, the air was warm and thick with the heavy smell of chlorine. The water was cool and refreshing however, and Holmes could feel the heat leaching from his core. The pool was no more than fifteen metres in length, but long enough for him to comfortably swim up and back with some rhythm. After ten minutes and feeling refreshed, he lifted himself backwards to sit on the edge of the pool allowing his legs to dangle into the cool water. There he sat, absorbed in his own thoughts, until he was jolted from his introspection by a female voice at the door behind him.

'What's it like in?' the woman asked.

'Beautiful,' Holmes replied without looking back.

Within a few seconds, the woman stood beside him on the pool's edge. The first thing he caught in the corner of his eye were the long, tanned legs. As he followed them up searching for

116

a face to address, he had to force himself not to be side-tracked by the shiny, snakeskin-patterned swimsuit tight around her shapely body. When he finally focused on her face, he saw the smiling Constable Larsen, her long blond hair falling across her shoulders. Holmes's heart was thumping. He felt less confused by her presence than by his reaction to her. He was nearly twenty years her senior, and in all his years of marriage had taken little notice of any woman other than his wife. What had changed? he asked himself. Was he becoming one of those dirty old men he dealt with so often as part of his job. Larsen walked to the deep end, gracefully dived in and swam the length of the pool under water. When she exploded to the surface, she wiped the wet hair from her face and Holmes could not avert his gaze from the wet snakeskin that now clung to Larsen's skin. She breast-stroked over to Holmes and dragged him off the ledge by his legs. Once he was in the water, she threw her arms around his neck and pushed herself against him. He instinctively wrapped his arms around her waist feeling the slinky fabric stuck to her body.

Holmes woke to the sound of his alarm in a lather of sweat, his heart beating at a rate he'd not felt for decades. He fumbled for the buzzing phone among his sheets, craving desperately to re-enter the pool. Within a minute he was wide awake, confused at what his subconscious had conjured in his sleep. He'd had that dream before, but it was always Cassie in the pool. He had to remind himself that the woman he would meet at the police station in a little over an hour was not privy to his recent fantasy. He had to disconnect the detective constable from the milieu his mind had constructed in the wee hours of the morning.

'Still hot and muggy,' Larsen said as Holmes entered the foyer of the police station. To his great relief, and disappointment, she was wearing a less striking outfit than the day before, although she still looked attractive in tight blue jeans, a billowy navy-blue blouse with a stand-up collar, and medium heeled leather boots.

'Yeah. Not a good sleeping night, that's for sure,' Holmes replied.

She nodded. 'More swimming weather than sleeping.'

Holmes reminded himself that coincidences occur all the time and simply nodded his agreement.

By ten o'clock they were parked in front of the Nooramunga homestead. The car had barely come to a standstill before Dennis Lowther came through the front door of the house and strode purposefully towards his visitors. He was a tall thin man, slightly hunched over as he walked. He displayed the farmers' stereotypical weather-beaten skin and sported the pastoralist uniform of moleskin trousers, long sleeved button up shirt, and R M Williams elastic sided riding boots. An Akubra hat sat atop a mop of silver-white hair. His craggy face was long and horse-shaped and his eyes a misty grey. His cheeks and nose bore a network of thin spidery veins, usually characteristic of those who enjoyed a whisky or five after a hard day's work. Holmes met him with an outstretched hand. 'Detective Sergeant Holmes. I presume you're Dennis Lowther.'

Lowther ignored the officer's attempted handshake. 'I resent your presence here, Detective. And I resent the accusations you made to my wife while I was in New South Wales.'

'We made no accusations, Mr Lowther. We merely asked about your relationship with Gary Rice.' Holmes indicated his fellow officer. 'This is Detective Constable Larsen of CID in Benalla.'

Lowther stared at Larsen. 'First they lowered the physical requirements to become a policeman and now we've got women detectives.' He looked her up and down. 'And women who dress as if they're on their way to a music festival. No wonder there's a law and order problem in this country.'

Larsen smiled. 'Top of the morning to you too, Councillor.'

'Can we talk inside, Mr Lowther?' Holmes suggested. 'Too hot to be standing around out here.'

Lowther sniffed loudly, then turned and led the officers into the house. The room closest to the front door was a study-cum-office. A stack of official-looking papers and a cherrywood pipe in an ash tray sat on a large mahogany desk under the window. A silver tray with a decanter of whisky and six glasses sat on a sideboard. The walls were covered with photos and framed documents. Just above head height, a timber shelf ran around three sides of the room. Sporting trophies of various sizes were arranged along its length. On the wall opposite the desk hung a large photo featuring a younger Lowther in mayoral robes. Obviously at some stage, he'd held the top job on council. Lowther sat behind the desk and invited the officers to take chairs opposite.

Holmes pointed to the mayoral photo. 'I hear you're the present deputy mayor. Obviously from the photo, you've had the head job at some stage.' Larsen bit her lip and tried desperately not to smile. The two men missed Holmes's unintentional double entendre.

'I was Shire President before the amalgamation of the two local councils,' Lowther replied. 'Just working my way back to the top again.'

Holmes nodded. 'Looks like you're a man devoted to helping his community. There's not a lot of that these days. CFA struggling to get members, volunteer organisations running entirely on the goodwill of pensioners. Hell, I've heard of at least one footy club that has folded because they couldn't form a committee. Plenty of players, but no one wanted to take responsibility for organizing things. So my hat's off to people like you, Mr Lowther.' Holmes felt sickened hearing the words leave his mouth, but they had the desired effect.

Lowther visibly relaxed and pushed out his chest. 'Thank you, Detective. It's not often people see the little things people do these days. How about I get a jug of cold water and three glasses?' He stood up and left the room.

'Suck-hole,' Larsen said quietly after Lowther had left.

'Catch more flies with honey,' Holmes whispered as he stood and took in the memorabilia in the room. Expecting to see evidence of a lifetime of major awards, he was surprised by the certificates that had been framed and was torn between laughter and sadness. A first aid completion certificate, certificates for participation in farm chemical safety courses, a local council induction certificate and on it went. There were photos of the farmer shaking hands with people Holmes didn't recognise, certainly no one in the public spotlight. The trophies on the shelf were just as underwhelming: Runners Up C Grade Squash, Encouragement Award Benalla Junior Tennis 1963, Most improved handicap C Grade Benalla Golf Club, Most Reliable Junior Rowing Reserves Geelong College. As Holmes followed the long line of uninspiring silverware, he came to a more impressive trophy tucked in the corner and obscured by a green and yellow pennant for a D grade basketball premiership in the late sixties. Holmes moved away the pennant and rotated the bigger trophy to read the inscription that had faced the wall. Benalla Lawn Tennis Association, A Grade Champion, Women, Dorothy Sinclair. Holmes heard Dennis Lowther's footsteps in the passage so he returned the basketball pennant to its place just as Lowther entered the room.

'Ah, I see you've discovered my premiership pennant. One of my proudest days that. Nearly shot the winning basket but it lipped out and one of my mates took all the glory by dropping it in.' He placed a tray on the desk and filled three large tumblers with ice water. He sat down in his chair as Holmes resumed his seat. 'Now what can I help you with, officers?'

Holmes took a sip of his water. 'How well did you know Gary Rice, Mr Lowther?'

Lowther leant back in his chair, now confident he had the officers in the palm of his hand. 'Not very well. The first time I met him was after he was elected to Council. My secondary education was down at Geelong College, so obviously I didn't know him as a teacher.'

Holmes nodded. 'According to his wife, you and Rice didn't get on terribly well.'

'I wouldn't exactly say we didn't get on,' Lowther replied. 'It was more that we had disagreements over council policy.'

'Rates,' Holmes suggested.

'Exactly,' Lowther replied. 'He couldn't appreciate the contribution farmers make to our country, and wouldn't accept that we deserved to be rated at a lower percentage of property value. It would be accurate to describe our discussions as robust.'

Holmes raised his eyebrows. 'Mrs Rice said you threatened her husband with violence over the phone. You said you'd knock his head off, if I remember her words correctly.'

Lowther shook his head and sighed loudly. 'Total exaggeration. We had a disagreement that night, I'll admit. But I'd never threaten violence.' He paused for a second or two. 'You can see by my surrounds, I'm a man of culture,' he added with a sweep of his arm.

'Mrs Rice said you grabbed her husband by the throat in the carpark after a council meeting,' Holmes said.

'Total rubbish,' Lowther growled aggressively, leaning forward and placing his palms on his desk. 'I'm sixty-nine years old, Detective. Rice was in his seventies. Do you really believe that sort of physical altercation would have occurred?'

Larsen took a sip from her glass and placed it back on the table. 'Just for the record, Mr Lowther. Can you tell us your whereabouts on the night Mr Rice was killed?'

Lowther leant back in his chair, a self-satisfied smirk swamping his weather-beaten face. 'I attended a reception for a business delegation from China. I'm the chairman of a council subcommittee which aims to develop greater ties between the Benalla district and Chinese industry. Particularly those involving fine wool. There were fifty witnesses there who can attest to my attendance.' His smirk transformed to a wide smile. 'Sixty, if you speak mandarin,' he added with an air of self-satisfaction.

'What time did it finish?' Larsen asked.

'Well after midnight. Got a lift in and out with George Elston who owns Redwood Park, a property a couple of miles up the road just this side of Devenish. Big wool grower. He can vouch for my movements, if you don't take my word.'

Rather than returning to Benalla, Holmes and Larsen made the short trip north to Redwood Park, where they confirmed Lowther's attendance at the Chinese reception and his transport arrangements to and from the function. Passing through Goorambat on their way back, Holmes pulled over under one of the shadier gums to procure a closer look at the massive art works featured on the silos beside the railway line. It wasn't until the officers were out of their vehicle that they fully appreciated the enormous scale of the scenes above them. On one of the metal silos were painted three baldy-faced draught horses dragging an early twentieth century stripper through the dust. On the other, an old homestead sat in the distance behind paddocks of golden wheat. But perhaps the most impressive of all was a massive barking owl taking flight on one of the original concrete silos. Larsen leant backwards against the front of the car, the heel of one boot on the bumper. Holmes stood beside her, arms folded. 'Pretty amazing, eh?' he said looking up and taking in the details of the artwork.

'There's some talented people in the world, that's for sure,' Larsen replied. She shook her head. 'How they can paint little patches of colour up there and still know what it'll look like from down here's the thing that's got me beat.'

'Guess that's why they're artists and we're coppers,' Holmes said. He pointed at the draft horses on the silo above. 'Look at those Clydesdales dragging that wooden stripper. As an old bushy, I find the farming technology of the time fascinating. From that point in the harvest, everything would have been done by hand. Threshed, bagged up, the lot.' He chuckled. 'Now the modern combines do everything. With GPS systems, they don't even need a driver.'

'A lot of things change over the years though, don't they?' Larsen said, still looking up at the artwork.

Holmes's eyes dropped to the ground. 'Yeah. They do,' he said quietly. He pondered his options for a moment then looked at Larsen. 'Is there anything you need to rush back for?'

Larsen shrugged. 'Nope,' she replied airily.

'I could go a cool drink at the pub across the road, if you're not in any hurry.'

'Sounds like a plan,' Larsen replied as she stood up straight and stretched her arms towards the sky.

The Goorambat Railway Hotel was an old-style country pub and was one of the very few to survive in small settlements where farms had become bigger and the workforce smaller. Add in the ease with which local residents could travel to bigger centres meant a publican had to run an outstanding establishment to remain viable. Goorambat still having a football team made the battle a lot easier, and obvious improvements had been made to the original pub grounds to make the venue more inviting. The area out front was green and well-watered with a number of heavy wooden tables under umbrellas giving the space the look of a cool beer garden. More tables and chairs sat in the shelter of the building's verandah and several trees shaded large parts of the lawn.

There were more patrons in the lounge than Holmes had expected, and after surveying the options, he led Larsen to a table under a window facing to the east. He offered to buy the first round and returned after five minutes with a light beer and a glass of white wine. Larsen held up her drink. 'Here's to the hunt for Gary Rice's killer,' she said, quietly enough not to be overheard. The detectives discussed the investigation for the next twenty minutes, with Larsen assuring her senior colleague that Noel Sanderson was the culprit, probably with the help of Glen Brown. Holmes confessed that if forced to choose a suspect at this stage of their inquiries, Sanderson would also be top of his list. But he was not as sure as Larsen that the case was open and shut.

'What made you become a copper?' Holmes asked when they had exhausted the details of the murder case.

'Finally decided it was my life I had to live, not some dream of my parents.' She smiled widely. 'Would you believe I was six months away from qualifying as a medical doctor when I realised I didn't want to do that for the rest of my life. Meant I'd wasted six years, but in hindsight it was the right decision.'

Brains as well as beauty, Holmes thought but didn't say. 'What did your folks think about that?'

'They went ape shit, as you can imagine. Said I'd pissed two hundred thousand of their hard-earned dollars up against a wall.' She chuckled. 'They should have been used to it. My older sister did three years of law before she decided to try her hand at pottery. My brother is a dentist but chucked that in to become a musician on the pub circuit.' She looked across the table at Holmes and smiled. 'What about you, Darren? Are you a slightly underqualified doctor, too?'

Holmes laughed out loud. 'Underqualified farmer more like it. Born in the Mallee. One of three brothers. Not enough land to support Dad and Mum, let alone three grown up sons and their future families. I needed to pick something else. Only other jobs I'd seen in Murrayville were schoolteachers and the local policeman. Couldn't see myself teaching.....' He leant back in his chair and extended his arms out wide. 'So here I am.'

It was silent for a moment before Larsen spoke. 'What does your wife do?' She saw the look on Holmes's face and pointed to his hand. 'You're wearing a wedding ring,' she added a little awkwardly.

Holmes looked at his hand as if noticing the ring for the first time, then back at his colleague. 'She was a legal secretary before we had the two kids. By the time she returned to the workforce, that avenue of work had dried up with the development of computers and all. Now she's assistant office manager at a financial advice company, so it's worked out okay for her.'

'How old are your kids?'

'Our son is twenty and our daughter eighteen. Both at uni.'

'You look too young to have kids that old,' Larsen replied, maintaining eye contact.

Holmes felt his chest swell but remained matter-of-fact. 'We had them very early in our marriage. Made life hectic then, but it's freed us up now.' He drained the last of his beer.

'Where'd the two of you meet?'

Holmes laughed. 'Preschool at Murrayville. Not too romantic.' He paused for a moment. 'Sad probably, when you think about it,' he added as he stared out the window.

'Not if you still get on,' Larsen replied.

Holmes wasn't sure whether it was a question or a comment, so he said nothing. After a few moments he turned the conversation. 'What about you? Yesterday, you said you had no family commitments over this weekend. Is that the normal state of affairs or just for these couple of days?'

Larsen swirled the remains of her wine in her glass. 'Normal state of affairs. Never been married or had kids. Lived with a bloke for a few years, but that went belly up. Haven't met anyone since who's piqued my interest.' She looked up and smiled at Holmes. 'So right now, it's just me.' She looked out the window. 'Pretty depressing when you think about it, eh?' she added quietly, before draining her drink and standing up. 'My shout,' she said as she collected Holmes's empty glass and strolled confidently towards the bar, her colleague's eyes following her all the way.

CHAPTER 12

The much-awaited forensic reports arrived simultaneously at the police station and on Bowker's email as the detective inspector drove into Benalla on Monday morning. He found the rest of his team chatting in their makeshift operation centre on the second floor of the station and immediately felt underdressed in the jeans and polo shirt he had worn for the return trip. Fleming was in his usual white shirt and dark tie while Larsen wore a classy charcoal grey skirt and jacket. Under his suit coat, Holmes sported a trendy pale-blue and white shirt Bowker hadn't seen on him before. After delivering a brief summary of the previous day's family christening, he was keen to see what the forensic teams had found. Fleming handed a hard copy to the senior officer.

Bowker scanned the transcript, making comments as he went. 'Victim confirmed via DNA analysis as Gary Edward Rice. Body showed minimal signs of decomposition or prolonged exposure to the sun. Precise time of death was difficult to establish due to the body's immersion in water, but death was estimated to have occurred in the thirty-six hours prior to the body being discovered. Cause of death was a severe blow to the back of the skull causing a fracture and severe intercranial bleeding. The blow almost certainly involved the use of a blunt instrument since the severity of the wound would preclude a simple punch or kick. Given the minimal volume of water in the lungs, it can be concluded that the victim was already deceased when falling or being placed in the water. There were no other abrasions or contusions found on the body, giving weight to the strong possibility that the victim was assailed from behind and was unaware he was to be struck. Two strands of dog hair with the roots still attached were recovered from the wound, the most probable source being contamination on the murder weapon.' Bowker flipped to the next page. 'Soil granules found in clothing all consistent with samples taken at the scene. Grass fragments were also identical to specimens taken at the scene. Grass smudges on the back of the victim's shirt indicate the body had been dragged or rolled into the water.' He turned another page. 'Alcohol was found in the blood but no evidence of other drugs or toxins. Smears were taken for blood analysis. Blood group is O positive.' Bowker lowered the report and looked at his fellow detectives. 'OK, before we get into the small print, what does the summary tell us?'

'It's not so much what it tells us, it's more what it confirms,' Larsen replied. 'Rice was approached from behind on the Saturday night and belted over the back of the head with a blunt instrument. He was dead when he hit the water.'

'The presence of dog hair is interesting,' Holmes added.

Fleming smiled. 'Sanderson has a dog. A big, scary Doberman cross.'

'Unfortunately, Ron Cloverdale and Dennis Lowther and Tony Marshall all have dogs too,' Bowker reminded him. 'And the victim himself had two long haired Pomeranians.' The detective inspector raised the forensic report, read for a quick moment then smiled. 'Well done, lab techs!' he said enthusiastically before looking up at the others. 'They DNA tested the dog hair and guess what they found?'

Fleming nodded his head assuming he knew the answer. 'The hair belongs to a Doberman cross.'

Bowker shook his head. 'Nope. That would be convenient though, wouldn't it? Unfortunately, the hair belongs to a kelpie.'

'Lowther, Marshall and Cloverdale all have kelpies,' Holmes said.

'And probably so does every farmer in the district,' Larsen added.

Fleming was a little annoyed at where the inquiry seemed headed. 'Surely a couple of strands of dog hair isn't going to let Sanderson off the hook. That hair could have got there independent of Rice being sconed. Or even picked up in the grass when he fell. There are people walking their dogs beside the lake all the time.'

Bowker raised a palm. 'No one is suggesting we drop Sanderson from our inquiries, Aaron. But I've got a feeling those dog hairs might be significant somewhere down the track.' He moved to the next page on the lab report. 'Let's see what Forensics can tell us about the actual murder scene.' He read down the page quickly then looked at his team. 'DNA analysis of the blood found on the boardwalk and the grass shows a match to Gary Rice. Soil and vegetable samples taken from this site are identical to those found on his clothes.' Bowker grinned as he read a little more of the report to himself. 'You've got to hand it to them,' he said as he looked up. 'They're one step ahead. No dog hair was found in the area where the body had fallen.'

Fleming shook his head and stared at the tabletop as Bowker turned to the last page of the report. 'OK, this is the analysis of the items found in the esky that Sanderson took fishing on the day of the murder. Blood on the tyre lever is not of human origin, but rather from two varieties of fish, European carp and redfin.' Bowker read a little further then stopped, a puzzled look pervading his features. He looked at the others. 'They found traces of blood on one of the empty beer cans in the esky. The blood belongs to

Gary Rice. The prints on the can were run through the national database and they got a match.'

Fleming leant back in his chair with a self-satisfied look, arms folded across his chest. 'Noel fucking Sanderson.'

Bowker shook his head. 'Nope. His little mate, Glen Brown.'

Within thirty minutes, two uniformed officers had dragged Brown from his bed and had him seated in an interview room ready for interrogation. Bowker and Holmes entered and sat at the table opposite. Bowker activated the recording technology and identified himself, his colleague and the man they were about to interview. He then looked at Brown. 'I must inform you that you do not have to say or do anything, but anything you say or do may be given in <u>evidence</u>. Do you understand this?'

Brown folded his arms across his chest and spoke defiantly. 'Yeah. Done this plenty of times before, haven't I?'

Bowker nodded. 'I must also inform you of the following rights. You may communicate with or attempt to communicate with a friend or a relative to inform that person of your whereabouts. You may communicate with or attempt to communicate with a legal practitioner. Do you understand this?'

'What do you think I am? Some sort of dumb arse? I've got nothing to hide, so I don't need to call nobody.'

Holmes referred to his notes. 'OK, Mr Brown. Last Monday I spoke with you at your home concerning your movements the Saturday before. You remember that conversation?'

'Yeah,' Brown replied. 'But you didn't tell me that old Rice had been killed. You just raved on about springers.'

'How'd you find out about Mr Rice's murder?' Bowker asked.

'Sando told me some arsehole from homicide was at his place accusing him of knocking over the old prick. Sando sent him packin' but.'

Bowker smiled but didn't comment.

'When I spoke to you on Monday you said you hadn't seen Mr Rice on Saturday except for the dust-up in the car park,' Holmes reminded him.

'Yeah, that's right,' Brown replied.

'Are you happy to stick to that story, Mr Brown,' Bowker asked.

'Yeah. Why wouldn't I? It's the fuckin' truth.'

Bowker leant forward and folded his hands on the table in front of him. 'No, it's not, Glen. Forensics found a beer can in Noel Sanderson's esky with your fingerprints on it.'

'Big deal!' Brown replied confidently. 'That's where I threw some of my empties. There'll be others in there the same, and some with Sando's prints.'

Bowker held his gaze on Brown's eyes. 'But only one with traces of Gary Rice's blood on it.'

Brown struggled to conceal being caught out and saw attack as his only defence. 'Bullshit! You're not going to fit me up on this!'

Holmes removed a sheet of paper from a folder he had in front of him. 'It's there in black and white mate.' He tapped a paragraph halfway down the page. Bowker snuck a quick glance at where his colleague was pointing.

Brown looked at the roof, then at the tabletop, searching for a way out. He couldn't find one. 'I didn't kill him alright. I rolled him into the water, but he was already dead. I wouldn't lie to you.'

'You've been lying to us for a week, mate,' Holmes said in exasperation.

'Right now, you're looking down the barrel of a murder charge,' Bowker said quietly, 'so I suggest you tell us what actually happened.'

Brown exhaled heavily. 'I thought it was near pack up time, so I went looking for Sando. I knew he was up near the bridge somewhere, so I followed the lake along until I tripped over old Rice's body on the wooden walkway. I nearly shit myself. I thought Sando must have run into him and cracked a mental and killed the silly old prick. I just rolled the body into the water so it wouldn't be found where we were fishing.'

'Where was Sanderson when this happened?' Bowker asked.

'I eventually found him up near the footy clubrooms packing up his fishin' gear. I was all panicky and asked him why he killed Rice and he said he didn't know what I was talking about.'

Holmes shook his head. 'Why didn't you tell us this last week?'

Brown threw his arms out wide. 'Because I knew we'd get blamed for it. We always do. Sando said to shut up about the body and everything would be sweet. I didn't know I got blood on the fuckin' can, did I?'

Bowker drummed his fingers on the desk. 'Do you honestly expect us to believe this cock and bull story, Glen? Seems to me that one of three things happened.' He counted on his fingers. 'One. You found Gary Rice after Sanderson had killed him. Or two. The pair of you killed him and rolled him into the lake. Or three. You killed him yourself and you're trying to put in your mate.'

Brown shook his head vehemently. 'I had nothing to do with killing him. And Sando says he didn't kill him either. You're looking at the wrong blokes here, honest.'

After a further thirty minutes of questioning, Brown's story hadn't changed so Bowker had the suspect removed and sent to the cells. At the same time two uniformed officers were sent to collect an unsuspecting Noel Sanderson.

'Obviously, the poor bastard can't read,' Bowker said, tapping the duty roster sitting on the table in front of Holmes. 'I took a quick glance and couldn't see where it mentioned his fingerprints.'

Holmes shook his head sadly. 'The poor bastard's been behind the eight ball from the time he was born.'

The full team reconvened in their operations room where Bowker brought his local colleagues up to speed on the interview with Glen Brown. While they waited for the arrival of Sanderson, Holmes and Larsen summarised their conversation with Dennis Lowther the Saturday before.

Twenty-five minutes later, a young constable informed the detectives that Sanderson wasn't home and in a quick drive around town they hadn't been able to locate his vehicle. 'I bet Sanderson's at the saleyards shovelling shit,' the detective inspector said. 'Sherlock and I might drive over and see if he's there.'

The four officers stood and left the room as a group. Out of the corner of his eye Bowker saw Holmes and Larsen brush hands. Fleming noticed it too. Once in the car and away from the others, Bowker was keen to hear Holmes's gut feeling about Dennis Lowther's involvement. 'What do your instincts tell you about Lowther?' he asked as he started the car. 'Any chance he knocked over Rice?'

Holmes didn't mix words. 'He's a conceited, up himself bastard with an over-inflated opinion of his contribution to the world. I mentioned his trophies and certificates inside. I wouldn't be surprised if he's had his turds bronzed for posterity.' Bowker laughed out loud as Holmes continued. 'There's no doubt he hated Rice with a passion and was capable of violence to express his contempt, but I can't see where he had the opportunity to kill him. He was in a function with numerous other people and was transported home by one of the participants. Besides, the council's conference centre is over the other side of town near the airport so how would he even know Rice was walking by the lake?'

'I tend to agree. I think we can put a line through his name.'

'Probably all academic now anyway. It's looking pretty obvious that Sanderson and Brown are up to their balls in this.'

'Yep,' Bowker replied as the vehicle exited the carpark. 'How'd Kirsten perform?'

Holmes looked straight ahead. 'What do you mean?'

'In the interview with Lowther. She let you do all the talking or fire in the odd question of her own?'

'I took the lead, but she quizzed him on his whereabouts on the night in question,' Holmes replied. 'She did a good job,' he added as an afterthought.

Bowker nodded as they turned into Arundel Street and headed north. 'Got potential?'

'I think so. Has to learn not to jump to conclusions.' Holmes looked at Bowker. 'But we can all be guilty of that sometimes, can't we?'

'Yeah mate, we can,' Bowker replied.

Nothing more was said until they crossed the main Sydney to Melbourne railway line. 'How'd you fill in your weekend?' Bowker asked.

'Went through the case notes a couple of times, but nothing new caught my eye. Kirsten felt a bit sorry for me here on my own, so she invited me around for dinner on Saturday night. Yesterday I walked down to the gardens and watched the local cricket for a while. Vegged out mainly. Took the opportunity to spend a bit more time in bed.'

Bowker nodded as they crossed the stock bridge in Ackerly Avenue and passed the lawn tennis courts on their left. 'Spent many hours in there mate,' Bowker said. 'Brother and I won the open men's doubles when we were just kids. Played intertown on a Sunday against other places in the district as well. Played against a Davis Cup player one time at Whorouly.'

'Did you win?'

Bowker shook his head and smiled. 'Nuh. But only losing 8-6 was a pretty fair effort for a couple of kids, I reckon.'

They crossed the Shepparton road near the railway gates and drove slowly past the Farmer's Arms Hotel, Tony Marshall's preferred watering hole. The saleyards were around a sweeping bend and on the other side of the Yarrawonga railway line. The stock selling complex was divided between yards for cattle on the southern side and sheep to the north. The officers found Sanderson in one of the high-fenced cattle pens ladling fresh cattle manure into a wheelbarrow with a square-mouthed shovel. 'Pleasure to see a man at work, Noel,' Bowker said.

'Only reason I'm fuckin' here is that fuckin' Centrelink said they'd cut off my pay if I didn't take this job.'

'Your pay?' Holmes asked with a smirk.

'Yeah. My fuckin' benefits,' Sanderson replied as if Holmes was slow on the uptake. 'And I can thank fuckin' Rice for all this. If it hadn't been for him, I'd be running my own business. Right now, I'd be in my office doling out jobs for my workers. Waiting for my sexy little secretary to bring in my morning tea.'

'Yeah, we need to talk to you a little more about Mr Rice,' Bowker said. 'Lock up your gear and we'll go back to the station.'

'Can't we just talk here? It'll take me half an hour to set up again,' Sanderson replied.

'You may not be back today mate. Maybe not for a fair while,' Holmes said.

'What are you bastards on about? Is this about old Rice being found dead?'

'We'll talk about that at the station,' Bowker replied.

Sanderson threw the shovel against the steel gate and poured the sloppy contents of the barrow onto the ground, the spatter barely missing Bowker's shoes. He then threw the shovel back in the barrow, stowed the equipment in a tin shed and snapped closed a padlock on a sliding bolt. Within five minutes they were back in the interview room at the police station.

After similar preliminaries to the Brown interview, Bowker got straight to the point. 'You were lying through your teeth when

I spoke to you last Tuesday, Noel. We've got your mate Brown in the lockup and he said you killed Rice and he helped you roll the body into the lake.'

Sanderson jumped to his feet. 'That's bullshit and you know it. You can't find the real killer, so you're trying to hang it on me and Brown Eye.'

'Sit down Noel,' Holmes ordered. 'You're going nowhere until we've finished with you.'

Sanderson sat down slowly. 'That's it! I'm not saying nothin' from now on. It's my fuckin' right.'

Bowker nodded. 'That's correct, Noel. It is your right. But while you're sitting there exercising that right, Detective Holmes and I will lay a few facts in front of you.' He removed the forensic reports from a folder and flipped through it until he found the section he was after. 'This is the forensic report on the contents of your esky.' Bowker held up the sheet so that Sanderson could confirm the bold header at the top of the page. 'The laboratory found traces of Gary Rice's blood in your ice box.....'

Before Bowker could finish, Sanderson broke his vow of silence. 'That was fuckin' fish blood. I told you that I smashed a carp.'

'Most of it *was* fish blood, Noel. But there were traces of Rice's blood in there too.'

Again, Sanderson was on his feet. 'This is a set up. There is no way his blood could get anywhere near my esky.'

'It was on a beer can, Noel,' Bowker said quietly. 'Along with a set of fingerprints that have been identified from the police database,' he added being deliberately vague.

Sanderson shook his head, was about to speak then sat down. 'They were Brown Eye's prints, weren't they?'

Holmes shrugged. 'You tell us, mate.'

Sanderson stared into space assessing his options. 'OK. If I tell you what really happened will you believe me or just use it to put me away?'

'We're only after the truth mate,' Bowker replied. 'We don't railroad people.'

Again, Sanderson thought for a moment before locking his eyes on Bowker. 'I never saw Rice that night except earlier in the carpark. When I was packing up my gear around midnight, Brown Eye found me and was absolutely shitting himself. He said he'd seen old Rice dead beside the lake. He thought I'd killed him, so he rolled the body into the water to get rid of it. He was scollin' beer out of a can, real panicky like, then he threw it in the esky.'

Bowker looked at Holmes acknowledging with a nod that Sanderson's story matched that of Brown. And the two hadn't communicated since the forensic report came back detailing the prints on the can.

'I didn't kill the old bastard. Honest,' Sanderson said standing up again and running both hands through his hair. After a moment he bent over, his palms planted on the table. 'I didn't kill the old bastard. You believe me this time, don't you?' he said, his gaze flashing between the two detectives.

After another fifteen minutes of intense questioning, Bowker had Sanderson taken to a cell, to be held overnight with Brown on suspicion of murder. With the suspect gone, Bowker invited his local colleagues back to summarise the interview. He sat on the edge of the table rubbing his chin. 'My gut feel is that he didn't kill Rice. His story mirrors Brown's and the two haven't seen each other since Brown told us about finding the body.'

'Maybe they cooked it up earlier as a fall back if things went belly up,' Holmes suggested.

'If they did fabricate something, surely it wouldn't include Brown finding the body. That implicates them in the whole shebang. They'd have kept denying everything like they did when we first spoke to them.'

'Maybe they remembered Rice's blood was on something.'

Bowker shook his head. 'Nah. Forensics said it was just a smear and the night was pitch-black. They wouldn't have seen it. And if they did, why not just fill the can with water and chuck it into the guts of the lake?'

Fleming was harder to convince. 'If Sanderson didn't kill Rice, then it was Brown and he's cooked up this story about finding the body to deflect blame,' he said, now certain the homicide detectives were incapable of seeing the forest for the trees.

'We're not saying either is definitely in the clear, Aaron,' Holmes replied. 'Especially Glen Brown who's admitted to handling the body and whose prints were found on the bloodied can. But if he's trying to save his own arse, why does he tell us he initially believed Sanderson had rolled Rice. Surely a better story for him was to leave Sanderson out of it and say he hadn't reported what he'd found because he thought he'd be blamed.'

Bowker nodded his agreement. 'And why admit to shoving the body into the water if he didn't believe he was cleaning up Sanderson's mess?'

Larsen exhaled loudly. 'So, we're left with a third person killing Rice, and Brown merely finding the body. Sanderson is guilty of nothing more than hindering police in their inquiries.'

Bowker nodded. 'Yeah. That's my feeling at the moment. But nothing's set in stone by any means.'

Fleming frowned and shook his head. 'After all their lies, you suddenly put your faith in an account that helps neutralise the forensic evidence.'

'Individually, I'm reluctant to believe anything either of them says,' Bowker replied. 'But when they tell you the exact same story when they haven't had an opportunity to confer, I think for once they've had no option but to tell the truth.'

Fleming was annoyed. 'So we cut them loose?'

Bowker shook his head. 'We hold them on suspicion for a few days and see what else we can dig up. If we don't find anything, we'll need to release them. There isn't a magistrate in Victoria who'd commit either of them for trial on what we've got at the moment.'

Fleming looked at Larsen and rolled his eyes.

CHAPTER 13

Later in the afternoon, Bowker rang the Police Forensic Services Centre in McLeod, a northern suburb of Melbourne. His direct contact there was Erin O'Meara, a skeletal woman in her late fifties or early sixties. It was difficult to tell which. With her pinched face and pallid skin, to Bowker she was a walking corpse, a woman already dead but refusing to lie down. When the phone rang on her desk, she reached across a stack of documents and picked up the receiver in her nicotine-stained fingers.

'O'Meara,' she said in a gravelly smoker's voice as she balanced her rimless glasses on the tip of her nose and picked up a biro in readiness to take notes.

'Greg Bowker, Erin.'

'Gregory my love. Haven't heard from you since I solved that last case of yours.' She laughed then coughed and spat in a tissue. 'I could do with a fresh bottle of Johnny Walker, so what favour are you after this time?'

'I'm working the Gary Rice murder up here at Benalla. I'm just after a bit of technical information.'

'Hold on, I'll get that case up on my screen.' With a few clicks of her mouse, she had what she wanted. 'OK. Victim bashed on the head and dumped in the lake up there. What can I do for you?'

'The report mentioned strands of dog hair found in the head wound.'

'Yeah. By the location of the stands deep in the wound, it looks like the hair was probably on the murder weapon prior to the attack.'

'That's what the report suggested,' Bowker replied.

'But given the time of night the attack took place there could be another explanation for the dog hair,' O'Meara suggested.

Bowker sounded interested. 'Yeah? You've got my attention,' he replied.

'The victim may have been shapeshifting into a werewolf,' O'Meara replied laughing. 'In medieval times that could get you killed' she added before being punished with a long bout of coughing.

'Fuck me, Erin. I thought you were going to tell me something useful,' Bowker replied after he heard the coughing stop and O'Meara spit out the product.

'So what's your bloody question, then? O'Meara asked. 'Haven't got all day.'

'The dog hair. Can DNA match that to an individual dog?'

'What do you think, Greg?' O'Meara replied. 'We can do it with humans, so of course we can do it with other types of animals. You supply us with samples for comparison and we'll tell you if you've found the right dog. Just make sure the roots are attached to the strands.'

Armed with a score of plastic evidence bags, first stop on Tuesday morning was Redwood Park at Devenish. Rather than taking the shortest route via the Tocumwal road, Bowker decided to see a bit more of the countryside and use the Yarrawonga road before following back roads west to Devenish. As they turned off the highway and onto the Yarrawonga road, Bowker burst into song.

I'm going back again to Yarrawonga
In Yarrawonga I'll linger longer
I'm goin' back again to Yarrawonga
Where the skies are always blue
And when I'm back again in Yarrawonga
I'll soon be stronger, then over hunger
You can have all your Tennessee and Caroline
I'm gonna get some lovin' from that mammy of mine
I'm goin' back again to Yarrawonga
To the land of the kangaroo.

Holmes looked at his colleague open-mouthed. 'Where the hell did that come from?'

Bowker shrugged. 'Somewhere deep in the past. Mum and me and my brother used to sing it on the way to Yarrawonga when we played intertown tennis.'

'Your Dad play?'

'He was a gun apparently,' Bowker replied, 'but by the time I was playing juniors he'd moved on to golf. He played off a handicap of 2, so he was pretty handy at that as well.'

'All round sportsman by the sounds of it.'

'Yeah. Played footy for Benalla in the Ovens and Murray. Got invitations to train with Geelong and Footscray in the big league in Melbourne, but he was milking cows at the time so that was out of the question. There was no money in the game like there is now. Players left VFL clubs in their prime because they were paid more to coach in the bush.'

Holmes put his fingers through the safety handle above his side window. 'You ever see him play?'

Bowker again shook his head. 'Nah. Too young for that too.' He was quiet for a few seconds. 'Probably his biggest claim to fame was winning the Victorian clay bird championship at Ringwood in Melbourne. Shot 123 straight. The sash he won hung in our room for years.'

'Must have thought he was a chance. Long way to travel. Especially in those days.'

Bowker smiled, then chuckled. 'There's a bit of a story to it. He went to the city to buy a new shotgun. Bought a Browning five shot automatic. He asked the salesman in the gun shop if there were any shoots on in the city because he was keen to give his new purchase a try. The bloke mentioned Ringwood and one of the events was the state championship. Dad went out there and won the bloody thing, much to the disgust of the other shooters who treated him like Li'l Abner from the back blocks.'

'Holmes grinned widely. 'But he had the last laugh.'

Bowker looked across at his mate. His smile had disappeared. 'Unfortunately, not. The official prize was a canteen of cutlery and the sash. But each of the shooters put ten quid into a winner-take-all sweep. When the old man got home and opened the envelope it only had ten pounds in it. He rang up about it, but no joy.'

'Fuckin' arseholes,' Holmes replied sadly.

'Yeah. About sums it up. Boy from the bush was a bit too trusting.'

Both men were quiet as they crossed the Sydney to Melbourne railway line, Bowker slowing to a near standstill and looking both ways several times. 'A car load of people was wiped out here when I was a kid,' Bowker said. 'It was night time and the car ploughed straight into the side of a goods train.'

'Shit! The driver go to sleep or something?'

Bowker shook his head. 'Nope. There was a car coming in the opposite direction and the investigation showed its lights would have been visible under the train. The driver of the doomed car must have assumed the crossing was clear. Bang!' Bowker took a deep breath. 'Mum would always stop here when she drove up to Yarra.'

'Your parents get on alright?' Holmes asked when they'd cleared the crossing.'

Bowker frowned, puzzled by the question. 'Yeah. Why?'

'Just wondering. Sounds like your old man had his head to do what he wanted, and your mum was in charge of running the kids around. She didn't resent that?'

Bowker was intrigued where this was heading. 'Mum was an A grade tennis player herself and was normally playing in the same place. It was logical that she'd take us there. You've got to remember that things were different then. Mum didn't have a paid job like most women do now.'

Holmes looked out his side window. 'Similar situation with my folks. Dad looked after the farm and mum did everything else. But most times things were sweet. Can't complain about my upbringing.'

Bowker nodded, but said nothing.

'You and Rachael ever have rough patches?' Holmes asked, still staring into the paddocks outside his window.

I know where this is heading, Bowker thought shaking his head but not taking his eyes off the road. 'Nuh. If we have disagreements, we just talk them out.'

'So you still talk after all these years? Haven't run out of things to say?'

'Nah. Plenty of things to talk about, mate.' This wasn't the first time Holmes had hinted at problems at home. The two families didn't socialize often, but when they did, Holmes and his wife seemed perfectly content in their domestic situation. Their two kids had left the nest, their son was studying teaching and their daughter was about to graduate as a pharmacist from La Trobe in Bendigo. 'Everything OK with you and Cassie?'

Holmes turned and looked at his friend. 'Not really sure, to tell you the truth, mate. Things have changed a fair bit since the kids left home. Just me and Cass, now. Our relationship seems as flat as a pancake. Once it was all wine and song, but somehow the zing has disappeared. Once we'd be trying to sneak in a bit of nooky while the kids weren't around, now we've got all the time in the world and there's no interest.'

Bowker wasn't sure how far he should delve into Holmes's private life, but given his friend's initiation of the conversation, he felt he was on safe ground. 'You don't believe Cassie is seeing someone on the side though, surely?'

Holmes shrugged. 'I doubt it, but who knows. I'm away half the time ...'

Bowker cut him off with an apology. 'Sorry mate. If you'd yelled out, I could have brought Peter Sanders.'

Holmes lifted a palm. 'Don't apologise Greg. To tell you the truth, I'm happy to be up here.' He smiled weakly. 'I don't want you to take this the wrong way, but at the moment I enjoy your company a lot better than hers.'

And Kirsten Larsen's too, Bowker thought but didn't say.

'And let's face it,' Holmes continued, 'if she's keen on somebody else, me staying in Melbourne to keep an eye on her won't change that.'

'I think it might be time for you and Cassie to sit down for a heart-to-heart. Or get in a professional to sort things out if you reckon you can't solve it yourselves.'

'Perhaps. Something to think about I s'pose,' Holmes replied before changing the subject. 'This trip will be a waste of time if Elston didn't take his ute to the council reception.'

Bowker slowed down as he turned left onto East Road towards Devenish. 'Probably, but we need to check. Even if he took another vehicle, it's still possible it may have had one of his kelpies inside it at some stage.'

Holmes laughed. 'Not if he's anything like the cockies I know. They wouldn't let a working dog anywhere near a normal passenger vehicle. Besides, presumably Elston locked his vehicle during the reception, so how would Lowther have access to a murder weapon with dog hair on it? That's not to mention how the fuck he would get across town to belt Rice by the lake.'

'If the hair from one of the Elston dogs matches the sample found on the victim, then there'll be a lot of riddles that need solving, including whether Mr Elston himself shared Lowther's animosity towards Gary Rice.'

The driveway into Redwood Park was a grand one with white railed fences down each side of the quarter-mile strip of sealed road. The paddocks on either side were stocked with fine merinos, their heads down in the thick green irrigated lucerne. The farmhouse was far more impressive than Lowther's both in its authenticity and the way it complimented the landscape. It was much older than the house at Nooramunga, but was in first class condition, its sweeping verandas newly painted and its intricate fretwork a reminder of the skills from times gone by. Bowker drove past the house and towards a cluster of farm vehicles parked beside a large woolshed. Several hundred sheep in full wool crammed the yards adjoining. When the policemen alighted from the car, they were met by the familiar buzz of shearing machines and the bleating of sheep. Three black and tan kelpies rushed across to welcome their visitors with enthusiastic high-pitched yelps that prompted an elderly man to appear in the glass window of the shed. He surveyed the detectives, acknowledged their presence with a wave of his hand and disappeared from view.

'That was George Elston at the window,' Holmes replied. 'He's a jovial bastard and gives the impression he hasn't got two shillings to rub together. In reality, he'd probably buy Lowther three times over.'

After a few moments, Elston slowly made his way down the steps from the landing adjoining the wide doorway to the shed. He was of wiry build and dressed in torn khaki work trousers, a blue shearer's singlet and elastic sided boots. His skinny, sun scarred face matched his bony frame. By contrast to the rest of his body his eyes sparkled with life. He removed his battered felt hat to reveal large scabby lesions on his predominately bald head. He held out his bony hand towards Holmes and the two shook firmly. 'Can't stay away from the place, Detective Holmes,' he said with a wide grin.

Holmes introduced Bowker, and Elston shook the detective inspector's hand vigorously. 'Nothing against you detective inspector, but I'm disappointed the sergeant didn't bring that sexy young constable he had with him on Saturday morning. If I was twenty years younger ....' He burst out laughing. 'Actually, I'd need to be seventy years younger.' Normally, Bowker would have challenged the sexist description of a fellow officer, but he'd discovered over the years that this was counterproductive with elderly people who were a product of their time and whose comments usually carried no venom or disrespect. 'So what can I do for you, detective inspector? I've already told the sergeant here that I transported Dennis in and out for the meeting with our oriental friends. Long night it was. Ended far too late for a man of my advanced years.'

'We are just wondering what vehicle you used that night.' Bowker replied.

Elston smiled. 'Originally it was to be the Jag, but the bloody thing wouldn't start. Once you flood it, you're buggered for an hour or so. Normally I would have reverted to the Statesman but my wife had already taken it to the bridge game she plays with three friends from properties over near St James. She had an invitation to go with me to the reception in Benalla, but she said that was for wankers and she'd prefer her game of cards.' He chuckled. 'Gossip fest if you ask me. Somehow, Clara seems to know everything that happens in the district.' He looked at Holmes. 'Enjoy your afternoon in the Goorambat hotel with that scrumptious little constable?' He waved a finger in Holmes's face. 'I don't know about the city, but you don't get away with much here in the bush.'

Holmes found himself strangely defensive. 'Wasn't trying to get away with anything, Mr Elston. We were both technically on our day off, so we stopped in town to admire the silo paintings then decided to support a small country pub by grabbing lunch rather than spending our money back in Benalla.'

Bowker bailed him out of an unwanted discussion. 'So no Jag and no Statesman. What vehicle did you finish up taking to Benalla?'

'The bloody farm ute.' He pointed towards the police car. 'The one you're parked next to. Left in a hurry, so no time to clean the cab, no time to organise things on the back. Should have been bloody embarrassed.' He laughed. 'But at eighty-nine years of age, I couldn't give two hoots what people think.'

'Do you carry the dogs around in the ute?' Bowker asked.

'What do you think?' the farmer replied. 'They spend half their time up there on the tray. They think they're dropping me a hint that I should be going around the sheep.'

'How many kelpie's have you got?' Holmes asked.

Elston held up three fingers. 'Three. The three that probably greeted you when you drove in.'

Bowker explained the reason for their visit and their intention to take hair samples from the three dogs for comparison with hair found on the victim. 'This has nothing to do with you, Mr

Elston. We're just checking that nobody took something from the tray of your ute and used it as a murder weapon.'

'Somebody like Dennis Lowther, you mean.' Elston shot back.

Bowker put his hands in his pockets. 'Why would you mention Dennis Lowther?' he asked.

'Because the detective sergeant and the 2012 Miss Police Force were here on Saturday confirming that he travelled with me to the reception. And everyone knows he hated Gary Rice's guts. Even had a physical encounter with him, if the rumours are correct.'

Holmes scratched his ear. 'What did you think of Gary Rice?'

'To be honest, I quite liked the bloke. Didn't know him that well, mind you. He was writing a family history and he asked me questions about my family and the story of Redwood Park,' Elston replied. 'Look, just like the next bloke, I don't want to pay more in rates. But Dennis's carry-on was way over the top. It became a bloody obsession. A change was never going to get through council anyway, so why make such a big deal about it.' He shook his head. 'The whole thing's got me beat, to be honest.'

Bowker nodded. 'Thanks, Mr Elston. We'll pull a few hairs off each of your dogs and let you get back to your shearing.'

'Just crutching at the moment, so there's not a lot of pressure,' Elson replied.

Bowker thought for a moment. 'You wouldn't be a relation to the Elston who played fullback for South in the fifties?'

Elston smiled. 'One and the same George Elston mate. Over a hundred games for the Bloods. Footy in the winter and cricket in the summer. You could do both in those days. Played district cricket for South Melbourne as well. Even cracked it for the odd game for Victoria when one of their regular fast bowlers went down.'

Holmes was amazed that this withered up old man was once

a league footballer and a Sheffield Shield cricketer. 'Love to see your trophy cabinet, mate.'

'Haven't got one,' Elston said. 'My experience is that people who show off their trophies haven't done much worth skiting about.'

Holmes smiled, knowing Elston was referring to Lowther. 'Dennis Lowther's wife must have been a handy tennis player.'

'More than handy mate,' Elston replied. 'She could have been anything. Played Margaret Smith from Albury a couple of times when they were both teenagers and there was bugger all between them. She won the A Grade singles in Benalla at seventeen, married Dennis at eighteen and hasn't been on a tennis court since. Never see her out and about anywhere much, except when she goes into Benalla to get groceries and the like. Before the Goorambat general store closed, I don't reckon she ever left the district.' He rubbed the side of his grey stubbled face. 'In her quieter moments, I wonder if she ever thinks about what could have been.' He raised his eyebrows. 'But I suppose that can be said about a lot of people.'

The farmer called his dogs and the detectives systematically took a small sample of hair from each and dropped them in individual plastic evidence bags. The names Sophie, Dan and Mongie were written on the labels of each satchel.

Elston followed the detectives to their car. Holmes checked the tray of the ute and took note of the many items that could have been used as a weapon. His quick survey returned no obvious sign of blood. As he was about to climb in the passenger seat, he asked Elston one last question. 'Did you notice if Dennis Lowther left the reception at any stage?'

'He told me he was going outside for a smoke towards the end of the night,' Elston replied. 'He's pretty addicted to that cherrywood pipe of his.'

'Where abouts did you park the vehicle?'

Elston thought for a moment. 'In the public parking area. Not far along from the main bridge.'

Holmes was confused. 'Wasn't the function in the Convention Centre in Samaria Road. On the other side of town?'

Elston shook his head. 'No. It was at the art gallery.'

Elston shook his head. 'No. It was at the art gallery.'

CHAPTER 14

A flock of pink galahs lifted from a patch of spilt grain on the road as the detectives drove back towards Goorambat and their next stop at Dennis Lowther's property. The Rice case was becoming more complex by the hour with the guilt of prime suspects not established and the innocence of peripheral players unconfirmed. At this time last week, the investigation found five persons with motive to kill Rice. Sanderson and Brown were top of the list, but Lowther, Marshall and Cloverdale were also of interest. At this point, Cloverdale and Marshall had a line through their names, albeit one drawn with pencil. Lowther would have been crossed off that list as well, if not for the revelation that he was at the art gallery on the night of Rice's death, a venue that stood less than fifty metres from the scene of the murder.

'Bloody great detectives we are, Sherlock,' Bowker said. 'Just assuming the reception would be at their arts and convention centre.' He shook his head. 'What's a major rule in our job?'

'Assume nothing,' Holmes replied. 'But if you're a local mob trying to impress overseas visitors, surely your modern whiz-bang radical architecturally-designed community centre is the place.'

'Unless you have a fancy gallery containing works from some of the biggest names in Australian art history. One that overlooks a beautiful lake on one side and award-winning botanical gardens on the other.'

Holmes raised his eyebrows. 'Touché,' he replied.

'Touché for us both mate.'

The pair were quiet for a few moments as they passed a farm truck travelling in the opposite direction and demanding both vehicles retreat to the road's gravel verges.

'So if Lowther is our man, what's the chain of events?' Holmes asked. 'He leaves the reception for a smoke, sees Rice making his way home beside the lake, grabs something from the back of Elston's ute, or from somewhere else, then follows Rice and belts him.'

'If he did do it, then logically that's the way it would unfold. But how would Lowther have known that Rice would pass by, or at what time?'

Holmes screwed up his face. 'Not very likely, is it?' he suggested.

'No, but we've seen less likely things happen,' Bowker replied.

Holmes wound down his window a few centimetres as they slowed down to enter the Goorambat township.

'Serve a decent meal?' Bowker asked, nodding towards the pub on their right.

'My steak sandwich was nice,' Holmes replied without looking at his partner. He wound the window down completely and let the breeze flow through.

'What'd Kirsten have?'

'Salt and pepper squid.'

Bowker nodded. 'Good company?'

Holmes stared out his open window. 'Yeah. Good company.' He pointed at the painted silos. 'You'd wonder how they do those pictures, wouldn't you?'

Bowker took the hint and let the topic of Kirsten Larsen drop. 'Yeah, mate. Dunno how they get them so realistic.'

Dennis Lowther was sitting with his wife on the verandah when the detectives pulled up in front of the house. Pop-up sprinklers were spraying a fine mist over the lawn area creating rainbows in the bright sun. A pair of magpies jumped in and out of the spray, fluffing their feathers after each expedition. Two kelpie dogs barked from kennels under nearby melaleucas. The policemen walked along the verandah to the elderly couple, neither of whom rose from the steel lace table to meet them halfway. Holmes introduced Bowker to Lowther and the two men shook hands.

'At least you've brought a real policeman with you this time,' Lowther snarled to Holmes. 'Not some little flibbertigibbet. Anyway, what are you out here for? I've told you everything I know about Rice's death.'

Bowker leant a shoulder against the verandah post and folded his arms. 'We've just come from George Elston's place at Devenish.'

Lowther picked up an iced drink from the table then put it down again. 'And I presume he told you he'd driven me to and from the council reception two Saturdays ago.' He nodded towards Holmes. 'Just like I told the detective sergeant here.'

'He also told us you went outside for a smoke very late in the evening?' Bowker replied.

Lowther picked up his pipe from the table and waved it at the detective inspector. 'That's right. Bloody boring the whole show was. Had to get out for some fresh air and light my pipe. What's that got to do with anything?'

'So where did you go for your fresh air?' Holmes asked. 'Out on the lawns? In the carpark, perhaps?'

Lowther replaced his pipe on the table. 'I went out on the balcony deck and sat at one of the café tables there. Overlooks the lake. Bloody beautiful at night with all the town lights reflecting in the water.'

154

Bowker stood up straight and put his hands in his pockets. 'You didn't go down the external stairs for a closer look?'

'There are no external stairs,' Lowther snarled. 'So get your bloody facts straight before you come here casting aspersions.'

'We're not casting aspersions, Mr Lowther,' Holmes replied. 'Just trying to establish where people were on the night in question.'

'So you were on the balcony?' Bowker reiterated.

'How many times do I need to repeat it, detective. I sat at one of the café tables, lit my pipe and took in the views of the town.'

'While you were sitting up there, did you see any people out and about,' Holmes asked.

'Saw three young blokes chiacking as they crossed the bridge from the main street. Probably intoxicated, going by what you hear about young people these days. I also heard a few cars leaving the football club on the other side of Bridge Street.'

'See anybody on the boardwalk beside the lake?' Bowker asked. 'It would have been visible from where you were sitting?'

'No,' Lowther snapped back. 'The night was as black as pitch and the lighting is terrible down there. I'll have to bring it up at council.'

Lowther's wife squirmed in her seat but said nothing.

'You didn't see Gary Rice on the boardwalk, did you Mr Lowther?' Bowker asked, staring into the old man's eyes. 'He had a limp and used a walking stick. Even in bad light you'd notice if it was him.'

'I told you I saw nobody on that path.'

Mrs Lowther stood up suddenly. 'I've got things in the oven. You'll have to excuse me.' She left without looking at her husband.

Bowker and Holmes exchanged glances.

'Always on the go, that woman,' Lowther said. 'Thought she'd be bored stupid once the kids left home, but she manages to fill in her time pottering around the kitchen and helping me with stock occasionally.'

'George Elston mentioned she was a brilliant tennis player in her youth,' Holmes said.

'Yes, but she needed to give that away when we married.' Lowther sniffed loudly. 'You know, setting up a home and all that. Then the children came along and that made playing tennis impossible. I played golf of a weekend, so someone needed to be home with the kids.' He began loading his pipe with tobacco from a leather pouch. 'One can't expect to have everything they want in life, can they? She came from a humble working-class family in Benalla and married into one of the more prominent pastoral dynasties in the district.' He snapped open a cigarette lighter, sucked in the flame and leant back contentedly in his chair, blowing smoke towards the eaves above.

Bowker fought the urge to relocate Lowther's pipe to somewhere south of his tonsils. 'We'll leave you to it, Mr Lowther. If you think of anything else you might have seen that night, give us a call.' He removed a business card from his wallet and placed it on the table in front of the farmer. 'I'll just pop inside to say goodbye to your wife and we'll be on our way. Probably won't need to talk to you again.'

Lowther nodded and took a long drag on his cherrywood.

Bowker looked at Holmes and winked. 'Won't be a minute mate. How about you wander over and have a yarn to those two kelpies under the tree.' He walked in the front door as Holmes made his way back to the car to collect a pair of rubber gloves and two evidence bags.

It took Bowker a few tries to locate the kitchen in the labyrinth of passageways inside the house. The room was empty and the stove cold when he put his hand against the oven door. Through the window onto the rear verandah, he could see the back of Mrs Lowther's head. He opened the flywire door and found the farmer's wife sitting in a cane chair staring into the gum trees bordering the nearby Broken Creek.

'Just come to say we'll be on our way, Mrs Lowther.' The detective took another business card from his wallet and handed it to the woman. 'Thought you looked a bit uneasy with your husband's account of the night in question. And I notice the oven is stone cold.' Mrs Lowther's eyes remained on the creek in front of her. 'If you've got anything that might be useful to our inquiry, you can call me on that number.' Again, the woman's eyes didn't move. Bowker started to walk away, then turned. 'George Elston said you were an extremely talented tennis player. Do you ever regret giving it away?'

The woman's head turned slowly, and she stared directly at the policeman. 'Me giving it away is not an accurate description of what happened, detective. And do I have regrets about what happened. Oh, Yes. Especially each time I saw pictures of Margaret holding up a trophy in Paris, or New York or London or even Melbourne.' Tears welled in her eyes. 'At the same time, a big trip for me was in to Goorambat to buy bread and milk.'

'I'm sorry, Mrs Lowther,' was all Bowker could find to say.

'I may not have made it all the way to those giddy heights detective, but I was on a par with those top girls. I would have just loved the chance, that's all.' She looked away as Bowker nodded, turned and left.

Holmes was already in the passenger seat when Bowker returned to the car and slid in behind the wheel. 'Lowther is a piece of shit,' the senior officer said as he pulled on his seatbelt. 'Ripped the dreams away from that poor woman and believes he's done her a favour by allowing her to be part of his family. It was all I could do not to grab the leg of his chair and upend the prick.'

'Yeah, I saw the look on your face,' Holmes replied with a smile, then changed the subject. 'We're just going through the motions with his kelpies, aren't we? He travelled in Elston's vehicle, not his own.'

'We're just covering all bases. I don't think we'll get a match, but you never know. There might be some cross contamination. Dog hairs on his shoes or clothes that have somehow transferred onto a weapon. While we were out this way, I thought grabbing a quick sample wouldn't hurt.'

They were just short of the turn onto the Tocumwal-Benalla Road when Bowker's phone rang. He tapped the green phone icon on the vehicle's video display to switch to hands-free mode. He didn't recognise the number, but knew it was local. 'Detective Inspector Bowker.'

A woman's feeble voice replied. 'It's Dorothy Lowther, Detective Bowker. I need to speak quickly. My husband is loading bales of hay onto the ute. He won't be more than a few minutes, I dare say.'

Bowker looked at Holmes before speaking. 'OK Mrs Lowther. What's on your mind?'

'My husband was lying when he said that he didn't see Gary Rice when he was sitting on the deck at the art gallery. A few nights ago, he told me that he saw him on the path and saw a couple of other figures in the gloom as well.' She hesitated for a moment. 'Don't get me wrong detective, I'm sure my husband didn't kill anyone, but the sooner this thing is cleared up the better.'

'Why do you think he lied to us?' Bowker asked.

'He believes he's one of the big wigs in this district and he doesn't want to become tangled up in this. He said it would hurt his prospects of getting re-elected and becoming the next mayor. Plus deep down, I think he's worried you'll charge him if he admits to seeing Mr Rice near where the killing took place.'

'I'm sorry Mrs Lowther, but we're going to have to front him with this.'

'I realise that, detective. I should have had enough courage to mention it when you were here. I'm being secretive with this call because he'd stop me from using the phone if he heard me talking to you.'

Bowker performed a U turn and was back at the Lowther's property within ten minutes. The farmer was at his hay-laden ute gesticulating with his wife when they arrived.

'Looks like she's given him the good news,' Holmes said as Bowker pulled the police vehicle in beside Lowther's Toyota one-tonner.

Bowker nodded as he turned off the engine and unbuckled his belt. 'If any physical ramifications flow from this I'll charge the old bastard with assault. See how that goes down when the council elections come around. Both men alighted from the vehicle slamming their doors in unison behind them. Before they could say anything, Lowther approached them quickly, eager to get onto the front foot.

He held up both palms in concession. 'I apologise for not acknowledging that I'd seen Gary Rice by the lake on the Saturday night, but I was keen to keep my name out of the whole nasty business. I again assure you that I had nothing to do with his death, and I felt my admitting that I'd seen him on that path would add nothing to your investigation. You knew he'd met his fate down there already.'

Bowker was having none of that. 'Whether it was important to our investigation or not was our decision to make, not yours Mr Lowther. Right now, I'm tempted to charge you with obstructing the investigation. I can imagine how that would play with your precious electorate. Whether I go ahead with that charge will depend on how honest you are in the next few minutes.' Lowther looked at the ground and quietly kicked a few stones away with the toe of his boot. 'So, tell me about your sighting of Gary Rice.'

Lowther looked up. 'Like I said before, I was on the balcony looking across the lake. I noticed Rice walking the path from under the bridge. I couldn't see him properly in the half-dark, but as you suggested, he was easy to identify by his limp and the fact that he used a walking stick.'

Holmes leant back against the Toyota, his arms folded. 'Did you witness an attack?' he asked.

Lowther shook his head vigorously. 'Absolutely not. He walked further along the path, out of my field of vision I suppose you'd call it. You've got to remember that I didn't hear he'd been killed until the next day, so at the time it was no big deal that I'd seen him walking home. I remember hoping he'd fall in the lake and drown, but of course the prospect of him being killed in the next little while never entered my head.'

Bowker leant backwards against the tray of the ute. 'Your wife said you saw other people on the path that night.'

Lowther looked at his wife then at Bowker. 'Yeah. Two people. The first one was about twenty metres behind Rice and walking quickly. He went out of my view not long after Rice.'

'Any guesses on who it was?' Bowker asked.

Lowther shook his head. 'No. It was too dark. Besides, Benalla's got a population of over nine thousand and I probably know less than a hundred. All I can tell you is that I'm pretty sure it was a male by the way the person walked. Not an overly tall person, but I'd estimate probably taller than most women.' He thought for a moment. 'Yes, I'd be ninety-nine percent sure it was a man.'

'So in your estimation, this person would have caught up with Gary Rice not long after he went out of your view?'

Lowther nodded. 'Within a second or two, I'd imagine.'

'Did you hear any noises from down there?' Holmes asked.

'There were cars leaving the school reunion and going over the bridge, so it wasn't all that quiet,' Lowther replied.

'The second person,' Bowker asked, unfolding his arms and putting his hands on the tray of the ute, 'what can you tell us there?'

'Small in stature, carrying a fishing rod. At first, I thought it was a kid, or maybe a woman. When he yelled out something, I realised it was a man.'

Bowker smiled, immediately thinking of Glen Brown, the failed jockey.

'Do you remember what he yelled out?' Holmes asked.

'I thought he might have been drunk,' Lowther replied. 'He was calling out "where are you, Santa" or something like that. I thought it was a bit early for Christmas.'

Holmes looked at Bowker then back at Lowther. 'It wasn't "where are you, *Sando*"?'

Lowther thought for a moment then nodded. 'Yeah, it could have been that I guess. Words drift a bit in the night air. Anyway, the little bloke went out of my vision and next thing I hear him swearing. Maybe fifteen seconds later I see him high-tail it back along the path under the bridge.'

'How long after Rice and the first bloke went past did the small man appear?' Holmes asked.

Lowther shrugged. 'Three or four minutes probably. Maybe five.'

Bowker thought for a moment. 'Did you describe what you'd seen to anybody else? To George Elston on the way home, perhaps?'

'Why would I?' Lowther said with a puzzled look. 'Nobody at that stage knew that Rice had been killed. All I'd seen while I was smoking my pipe were a few people walking across the bridge, and three people on the boardwalk. To tell you the truth,

I never gave any of them a second thought until I heard about Rice's murder. There were a lot of things from the reception that were more worthy of discussion on the way home than three men walking beside the lake.'

'Once you heard about Rice, you didn't think it a good idea to tell us what you'd seen?' Bowker asked with a tone of annoyance. 'Would have saved us a lot of legwork and a few others a fair bit of grief.'

'I heard his body had been found beside the dam wall up near the stock bridge. It seemed irrelevant what I'd seen up near the gallery.'

Bowker was becoming increasingly annoyed and pointed a finger at Lowther's chest. 'You were worried about becoming involved, especially given your history with Rice. And most importantly, you didn't want your precious reputation to come into question. What a pity you don't have the same community awareness and courage as your wife.'

Lowther quietly kicked away another stone but didn't reply. Bowker turned and addressed the farmer's wife. 'Thanks for your help Mrs Lowther. You've saved us hours of work and helped clear several suspects we've been pursuing.' He looked again at Lowther. 'I still haven't decided whether to lay a charge of lying to police and obstructing justice. I guess it will depend on what your reaction is after we leave. I don't think you recognise what your wife has given up to make your life the breeze it's been. Not the least of which was forfeiting a potential professional tennis career so you could improve your golf handicap and climb out of D Grade.' Bowker nodded at Dorothy Lowther who, for the first time, allowed the faintest of smiles.

Holmes stood to his full height and hitched his trousers up by the belt. 'We'd like you to attend the Benalla police station in the next two days and provide a sworn written statement. If we're not there, Detective Fleming or Detective Larsen will do the honours.'

Bowker and Holmes walked around the rear of the one tonner to their police vehicle leaving Lowther staring into space and his wife trudging back towards the house.

CHAPTER 15

On the way back to the station, Bowker and Holmes visited the art gallery and were shown to the balcony deck by a volunteer worker. Several tables were occupied by patrons consuming coffee and cake while taking in the vista across Lake Benalla. The detectives' observations from numerous positions on the deck supported Lowther's assertion that the murder scene was just out of sight from these vantage points.

Following a quick sit-down lunch at Hides Bakery in Bridge Street, it took less than fifteen minutes for the homicide detectives to update their local colleagues on their discussions with Elston and Lowther. 'So the upshot is we turn Sanderson and Brown loose,' Bowker said in summary.

Fleming was annoyed. 'Why? Lowther confirms Brown was on the boardwalk at the same time as Rice. What more do we need?'

'Yeah, he was there, but three or four minutes later, maybe five,' Bowker replied. 'And he said that he heard the little bloke, let's assume it's Brown, swear out loud immediately after he went out of view. He then said the same bloke reappeared running in the other direction fifteen seconds later. Let's do the maths. In the four or five minutes before Brown appears, if Rice was still alive he would have been at least another hundred metres further down the path. Even if Brown was another Usain Bolt, there is no way he could catch Rice, kill him, and be back in Lowther's view fifteen seconds later.'

'And remember,' Holmes added, 'Forensics have established where the murder took place. That point is just out of the vision of where Lowther was sitting that night, not a hundred yards down the path.'

'Maybe Rice stopped at that point to admire the view. Maybe he was tired and wanted to rest and Brown killed him there,' Fleming replied.

Holmes shook his head vehemently. 'I'm sorry Aaron, but that doesn't make any sense. Rice departed from a venue no more than a hundred and fifty metres from the murder site. If Brown saw Rice leaving, or already on the path and wanted to follow, why was he three or four or five minutes behind. He would have caught him in thirty seconds if he'd seen him walking along there. Plus, if Brown was four or five minutes behind Rice, then Rice was way gone in the dark before Brown could have spotted him.'

'And if Rice did need a breather, there's a bench seat ten metres further along from the murder site,' Bowker added.

Larsen spoke for the first time. 'And if Brown was to follow Rice with evil intent, he'd hardly take his fishing rod and a can of beer. Or yell out "where are you Sando?".'

Fleming looked down at the tabletop, searching for an explanation that would make Lowther's observations consistent with Brown's and Sanderson's guilt, but was struggling to come up with a believable scenario. If Lowther was telling the truth, then Fleming's prize suspects were in the clear, particularly Glen Brown. If Lowther was lying, then this threw more suspicion on the farmer and logically lessened that on Sanderson and Brown. Either way, the foundations of Fleming's certainty on the pair's guilt were being washed away. But at this stage he was reluctant to acknowledge that.

'Let's summarise this,' Bowker said putting both palms on the table. 'If what Lowther tells us is true, and I tend to think it is, then I think we can rule out Lowther himself, Glen Brown, plus Ron Cloverdale who is a man-mountain and doesn't fit the stature of the male Lowther saw walking immediately behind Rice. There's no doubt in my mind that this mystery male is the one who committed the murder. Going on Lowther's explanation, he would have caught up with the victim at the exact spot where the killing occurred and no one else was seen on the boardwalk until Brown arrives several minutes later and flies into a panic.'

'Somebody could have come from the other direction, passed Rice, turned around and hit him from behind,' Fleming suggested as an alternative.

Holmes started to say something, but Larsen beat him to the punch. 'But then our mystery man would have been a witness. I don't think it happened that way, Aaron.' Larsen flashed a glance at Holmes who winked back.

'I'm sorry if it doesn't fit your assumptions, Aaron, but I think we have to assume the bloke following Rice was the one who killed him,' Bowker said. 'So our task now is to identify said mystery man. Was it Sanderson, who may I say at the outset, I believe it was not because everything about his and Brown's story continue to check out? Could it be Tony Marshall? I have my doubts because of his flimsy motive and his inability to know Rice was on that path that night. Or was it somebody new? That's where my money sits at present.'

'Fuck,' Fleming said quickly. 'The last thing I want to do is start all over again.'

'What's the alternative, Aaron?' Bowker asked brusquely, arms spread wide. 'Just charge Sanderson and move on?'

Fleming wasn't intimidated. 'I'm not as convinced of his innocence as you are. Just because his story matches with Brown's doesn't mean it wasn't concocted to cover his arse.'

'It not only matches with Brown's story,' Bowker replied, 'but it matches what Lowther saw. Brown goes looking for Sanderson, finds Rice's body and bolts back to Sanderson assuming his mate has earlier committed the murder.'

Fleming held his ground. 'What if your unidentified man was Sanderson and he kills Rice. Brown finds the body and sprints back to where he thinks his mate will be.'

'Lowther didn't see anyone heading back to the bridge before Brown arrived on the scene,' Holmes said.

'What if Sanderson didn't go back to the bridge after he killed Rice, but just continued following the path?' Fleming asked.

Bowker looked puzzled. 'Why would Sanderson continue up the path when his fishing gear is back on the other side of the bridge and so is his mate? Besides, we now believe Brown sprinted back to where he says he found Sanderson packing up his stuff near the footy club.'

Fleming slammed his palms on the table. 'So we just turn him loose? We swallow his story and let him go?' he asked defiantly.

Bowker sat up straight in his chair. 'We don't hold people without cause, Aaron. We'll charge Brown by summons for stuffing around with the body.'

Fleming stood up and left the room in a huff.

Larsen raised her eyebrows then looked at Bowker. 'So where to now?'

'We'll need to tidy up any loose ends around what we've done so far,' the detective inspector replied. 'We'll get samples of hair from the dog at the Cloverdales and the old kelpie at Tony Marshall's place in Baddaginnie. I don't think either of these will prove a match but we'll make it official. Then we'll go through everything again and see if anything points to someone we've missed.'

'What did you make of Fleming's reaction when you told him to release Sanderson and Brown?' Holmes asked as they headed out the Samaria Road towards Tatong.

'His reluctance to see beyond Sanderson didn't surprise me, but him spitting the dummy and walking out of our meeting I thought was a bit childish,' Bowker replied. 'But to his credit, he caught up with me in the dunny a few minutes ago and apologised, so I'll cut him a bit of slack. Sounds like there are few problems at home. Apparently, his teenage daughter is giving him and his wife buggery. She resents the fact that her father's a cop. She says it stops her being included in all the good stuff because the other kids are worried she'll dob to her father. Sounds like bullshit to me, but then again, when I was a country cop, my kids were still in primary school.'

'Sounds like the girl may be playing the mind games with her parents, and at this stage she's winning.'

'Yeah.'

Bowker flicked on his blinker and overtook two professionally kitted-out cyclists making every effort to look like they were part of the Tour de France and had just broken away from the peloton.

'This case is not going to be solved any time soon, is it? Not if we're looking for new suspects,' Holmes said, staring out his window at a group of Hereford cattle standing in a circle and tearing tufts of hay from a circular steel feeder.

'We've obviously missed something, Sherlock. If there's no match for any of these dog hairs, I reckon we go back to Rice's wife and go over his life with a fine-tooth comb. There has to be someone else who gains from the old bloke's death.'

'There's always the possibility of a random act of violence.

How many cases have we investigated where death has come from a king hit?'

Bowker nodded. 'But ninety-nine times out of a hundred it involves some weak prick showing off to his mates. Who follows an old bloke with a walking stick for a hundred yards and king hits him for no reason. Rice's wallet was still in his jacket, so the motive wasn't robbery.'

It was quiet in the car for a mile or two before Holmes spoke. 'If something doesn't break quickly, looks like we're up here for another weekend. You heading back to Melbourne if we haven't wrapped it up by Friday?'

Bowker thought for a moment. 'Depends if we've got any new leads to follow up.' He looked across at his partner. 'What about you, mate?'

Holmes shrugged. 'Same as you. If nothing's on the go here, then I guess I better put in an appearance for a couple of days.' He chuckled, half to himself. 'See if Cassie has noticed I've been away.'

Bowker wasn't sure how to respond, so he said nothing.

Holland Flat looked its normal picturesque self as the detectives pulled up beside the historic homestead. Alison Cloverdale and her mother were in the front garden dead-heading the roses when they arrived and strolled across to meet the detectives as they made their way across the lawn. Wilma Rice looked like a different woman from the one the officers had rescued less than a week ago. Her face appeared ten years younger, and she carried a smile that was absent when she lived in Baddaginnie.

'Have my knights in shining armour come out to check on me,' she said, her face beaming.

'Actually, we came to take a hair sample from one of your dogs,' Bowker replied with a chuckle, 'but you're looking a million dollars. The change of address must be good for you.'

'It's done wonders for us all,' Alison Cloverdale replied with a puzzled look. 'Why the hair samples?'

'Your father had a few strands of kelpie hair embedded in the wound on his head. Forensics believe they probably came from the murder weapon. They're keen to DNA test the hair from kelpies owned by anyone connected with this case, whether suspects or not.'

Alison Cloverdale looked horrified.

Holmes held up a palm. 'I know police often say that certain inquiries are just routine, Mrs Cloverdale, but in this case that assurance is accurate,' he explained.

Mrs Cloverdale relaxed a little and shrugged. 'OK. If you say so,' she said hesitantly.

'Tony has an old kelpie, Bessie's her name' Mrs Rice said, her forehead wrinkling. 'Not that I'm saying he had anything to do with Gary's death,' she added.

'That's our next port of call, Mrs Rice,' Holmes replied. 'Does he ever carry Bessie in the car with him?'

The older woman nodded. 'She goes with him most times unless he's off to a greyhound track. She sits on the back seat.' She seemed to hesitate before continuing. 'He keeps a baseball bat behind the front seat for self defence reasons. Or that's his story anyway.'

Bowker looked at Holmes, then back at Mrs Rice. 'We'll check that out when we take a sample from the dog.' He thought for a moment. 'I assume there's been no contact since you've been out here?'

Wilma Rice shook her head. 'Nothing, thank God.'

'Wise move on his part,' Bowker said looking towards the yard at the rear of the house. 'Now, where would we find Ron? Down the back paddock with the dog we want, I bet.'

Mrs Cloverdale shook her head. 'Ron's not home. He's

shot through to Albury to see a little bitch he's become besotted with.'

Bowker was about to admit he knew of her husband's dalliance with the Sydney real estate agent who had used the Albury airport less than a fortnight earlier, when Alison finished her explanation. 'Old Bluey, our cattle dog, is near the end of his tether I'm afraid. Ron saw this ad for a well-bred female blue heeler in *The Stock and Land*. So off he's trotted to check her out.'

Bowker still believed his suspicions about Cloverdale's trip had merit, but kept his counsel. The detectives left the women to their roses and within ten minutes had taken hair samples from a jumping, attention-seeking kelpie.

'Nearly put my foot in it,' Bowker said as they headed to Baddaginnie via backroads through the district of Warrenbayne. 'Not that I feel any obligation to protect the adulterous bastard.' Out of the corner of his eye he saw Holmes's face flinch and immediately wished he hadn't used that term.

Holmes turned his head and stared out the window. 'I didn't sleep with Kirsten Larsen, if that's what you're thinking. I spent Saturday with her and had dinner at her place, but I didn't stay there.'

Bowker kept his eyes on the road. 'OK,' he said, unemotionally.

'Not that I didn't want to,' Holmes continued. 'She invited me to stay.'

'So why didn't you?' Bowker asked.

Holmes looked across at his colleague. 'Old fashioned stuff, I suppose. I'm a married man and I've never cheated on Cassie.' He chuckled. 'I've never had sex with anyone else, would you believe?'

'Nothing old fashioned about being faithful, mate,' Bowker replied.

'Plus, I'm forty-eight and Kirsten's thirty-one.' Holmes looked out his window. 'The term silly old fool comes to mind. Or dirty old man.'

'It's only seventeen years and she's a big girl, so don't be too hard on yourself.'

'If anything came of it, when I turn seventy, she'll be fifty-three. Still in the prime of her life and I'd be about fucked.' Holmes paused for a few seconds. 'Shit, mate. Let's put it into perspective. When I started Year 12 at Murrayville, she wasn't even born.'

'For what it's worth, I think you did the right thing,' Bowker replied. 'Before you cross any bridges, get things sorted out with Cassie. If you both agree it's time to pull up stumps, that's the time to consider a new relationship. If that's with Kirsten Larsen, I don't think age has much to do with it.'

Holmes nodded and stared back out his window at a kookaburra sitting on a fence post. He felt sure the bird was laughing at him.

The first thing the detectives noticed when they arrived at Marshall's ramshackle hobby farm was the baby stroller under the carport. Three greyhounds barked from their enclosures and the old kelpie bitch struggled her way out from under the house to greet them. Her tail wagged more slowly than it would have done in years gone by, but she was doing her best to welcome the visitors. This was more than could be said for Marshall who came storming from the house towards the police car as it came to a halt.

'You bastards come out to take away another woman,' he yelled from a distance.

'Shit, Sherlock. How do these useless bastards attract females,' Bowker muttered to Holmes as they climbed from their vehicle. 'Come to have a look at your old kelpie actually, Mr Marshall,' he said loudly.

'What the fuck's she got to do with anything?' Marshall shot back angrily.

'There was kelpie hair on the murder weapon used to kill Gary Rice,' Holmes replied. 'You've got a kelpie and you had it in for Rice, so if you put two and two together,' he added to see Marshall's reaction.

That reaction came quickly. 'Don't try and put that murder on me,' Marshall roared. 'I never saw Rice on that weekend, let alone kill him.' He shook his head theatrically, put his hands on his hips and stared up into the sky. 'That's typical of you bastards. You can't find the fuckin' killer so you start looking for someone to pin it on.'

Bowker removed an evidence bag and a pair of rubber gloves from the back seat of his vehicle. He looked down at the old dog who was watching him expectantly. He patted her on the head then pulled a sample of hair from the back of her neck and placed it in the plastic zip lock bag. 'There you go old girl. Didn't hurt a bit.' He patted her again and the old dog tried to jump up, but her paws barely left the ground.

'We'd like to have a look in your car, Mr Marshall. Have a look for stray dog hairs just to confirm that the dog's been in there,' Holmes lied.

Marshall threw back his head and exhaled loudly. 'Of course there'll be fuckin' dog hairs in there. Bessie comes with me most of the time,' he said angrily.

Holmes opened a rear door of the old Commodore, rifled through the junk on the back seat and quickly located the baseball bat that Wilma Rice had mentioned. He walked back to the police vehicle and retrieved a rubber glove which he used to take the bat from the car.

'You play baseball, Mr Marshall?' Bowker asked sarcastically.

'I keep it in the car for self-defence,' Marshall responded angrily.

'I'm on the road a lot with the dogs. You never know who you might run into.'

Holmes indicated a brown stain near the end of the bat. 'Where'd the blood come from? Ran into someone on the road, did you?'

Marshall put his hands in his jeans pocket and shrugged. 'No fuckin' idea where it came from, mate. Old Bessie cut her foot when we were out and about one day and she bled a bit on the back seat. I killed a king brown that was hanging around the dog pens a month or so ago. Bailed him up in the corner and belted him with that bat. Angry bastard he was too.'

Bowker smiled and leant against the car. 'Gutsy effort taking on a snake with a baseball bat. Especially when you carry a gun in your car.'

'The gun was locked in a safe inside,' Marshall replied. 'It's against the law not to have it locked away,' he added mockingly.

'It's also against the law to kill snakes,' Holmes replied.

Marshall took his hands from his pockets and held his wrists together in front of his waist. 'Arrest me then, smart-arse.'

Holmes slid the baseball bat into a large plastic bag and placed it on the backseat of the police vehicle. 'Let's see if the lab confirms it's snake's blood before we go down that track.'

A grossly overweight and barefooted woman in her late teens or early twenties exited the front door and wandered across with a crying baby swaddled in her arms. Her greasy hair was coloured green and she wore a badly stained tee-shirt teamed with torn baggy shorts. On her arms and legs she sported tattoos of flowers and mythical animals. Metal rings pierced her nose and eyebrows. Her face was round and podgy, her eyes sunken and a trio of cold sores lined her bottom lip.

'Who's this? Your granddaughter?' Bowker asked, already knowing the answer.

Marshall put his arm around the woman's shoulders when she reached the group. 'This is Imagen. She's moved in with me after her nutcase boyfriend round in Palmerston Street kicked her out. Just trying to do the neighbourly thing.'

Bowker looked at the woman. 'Got your own room, have you Imagen? Just for you and the bub.'

'No need to. Plenty of room for us in Tony's room,' the young woman replied. She looked at Marshall. 'What time are we headin' to Benalla for Maccas? Jayden will need a sleep before we go.'

Bowker looked at Holmes with an overwhelming feeling of despair, not just for the young woman, but for her son whose papers had already been stamped. Knowing there was little more to be gained from their visit, they drove back to Benalla with no more than a few words passing between them.

'Got a bit of good news for you,' Fleming said as they found him in the CID section of the station and about to knock off for the day.

'Could use some,' Bowker replied. 'Just come from Baddaginnie. Wilma Rice has been gone less than a week and Tony Marshall has already replaced her with a new female. She can't be older than twenty. Already got a baby of her own.' He shook his head sadly. 'Bloody depressing, Aaron.'

Fleming frowned. 'Twenty? He's got to be in his sixties. What would a girl that age possibly see in him?'

'Booted out by the boyfriend,' Holmes replied. 'Nowhere else to go. You know the story. Any port in a storm.'

Kirsten Larsen entered the room. 'Whose port, whose storm?' she asked.

'Apparently Tony Marshall has already hooked up with another woman,' Fleming replied. 'Someone a hell of a lot younger.'

Larsen shot a glance at Holmes. 'Age is no big deal if they're compatible.'

'She'd be lucky to be twenty and has a babe in arms,' Bowker replied.

Larsen closed her eyes and shook her head. 'Shit. Nothing good can come out of that.'

Bowker clapped his hands together once and looked at Fleming. 'OK. Let's hear the good news, Aaron.'.

Fleming scratched his cheek. 'Perhaps good news is a bit optimistic, but at least it's something. An elderly couple were walking by the lake and spotted Rice's walking stick in amongst the reeds. Read about us looking for it in the *Ensign* and gave us a call. Had enough brains not to handle it and a couple of our uniforms fished it out and bagged it. We've checked it with Rice's wife, and she confirmed it belonged to her husband. Not sure it'll be much help, though. It's been in the water for over a week now.'

'You might be surprised,' Bowker replied. 'Especially in a lake like that. Fresh water, basically no currents, very few pollutants. Best conditions for a submerged print to survive.'

'What's the plan going forward?' Larsen asked.

'I think we've gone about as far as we can with our original list of suspects,' Bowker replied. 'In the morning, I'd like a longer chat with Rice's wife and see if there's an angle we've missed.' He shrugged. 'Other than that, our best prospect of a breakthrough probably lies with the forensic samples we need tested. I think the quickest way to get those results is to head back to Melbourne and drop them off at the lab in McLeod. There are a couple of other cases we're working on that I'd like to catch up on, anyway.'

'Will you be heading back or staying up here again, Darren?' Larsen said taking a seat on her desktop and putting her feet on her chair.'

Out of the corner of his eye, Holmes saw Larsen's short skirt ride up on her long legs as she sat up on the desk. His brain screamed that he wanted to stay, but his words said otherwise. 'I'd better go back and say hello to the family.'

Larsen nodded and then stared at the floor. Fleming smiled and looked away.

CHAPTER 16

The Rice residence resembled a giant garage sale. A large rubbish skip rested on the nature strip and a removalist's truck was backed up the drive. Various pieces of furniture littered the lawn awaiting loading and a wall of cardboard storage boxes were stacked under the verandah. Two muscly men in branded singlets, shorts and steel capped boots went in and out of the house like worker ants carrying items back to their nest in the truck. The oldest of the two men intercepted the detectives as they walked up the front path. His powerful bare arms carried tattooed scenes of the South Pacific complete with palm trees and hula girls. The two Pomeranians ran excitedly around the lawn, barking at anything and everything.

'The old girl's inside if that's who you're looking for,' the man said. 'Snapping out orders like she's an officer in the fuckin' Gestapo.' He grabbed the six-wheeled hand trolley from the other side of the path. He nodded towards the dogs. 'And it's only a matter of time before I give one of those little shits a good kick in the guts.' He pulled the trolley up the steps and into the house.

'Nice tats on his guns,' Holmes said. He pulled up his sleeve and flexed his bicep. 'Might have to consider getting some.'

'They'd look alright at the moment, mate,' Bowker replied, 'but

178

when you're in your seventies they'll look like a condom full of vomit.'

Holmes laughed out loud as he followed his colleague through the front door and up the passage towards the kitchen. There they found Arabella Rice sitting on a lone kitchen chair barking orders to the movers as they manoeuvred an upright freezer onto the trolley.

'Found my husband's killer yet?' she said, bypassing any form of pleasantry.

'Good morning to you too, Mrs Rice' Bowker replied. 'Unfortunately progress has been slow, but we have made some headway by eliminating a number of people we thought may have had a reason to murder Gary.'

The woman watched the freezer disappear up the passage before responding. 'So what you're telling me is that you know who *didn't* kill my husband, but can't tell me who did. I'd hardly call that progress. I could have given you a hundred names of people who didn't kill him.'

Holmes closed his eyes composing himself before seeking to explain to the woman. 'We know when and where he was killed, Mrs Rice. We have a witness who saw the killer just ten seconds before he hit your husband over the head.'

Mrs Rice turned and stared at Holmes. 'Well why isn't he arrested? I don't understand.'

'The sighting was in poor light,' Bowker responded. 'We know it was a man, but we're still searching to identify him.'

'So you're no closer than you were a week ago really, are you?' She rolled her eyes and exhaled tiresomely. 'So what do you want of me? I've told you everything I know. That truck will be gone by this afternoon and I will be in my car behind it. The sooner I get back to civilisation the better, and then I can put this house on the market and be done with this town for good.'

'Other than the council and the Rotary Club, what else was your husband involved in?' Bowker asked. 'Any little connection may be a big help.'

'He filled in at bowls every now and then, but I've never heard him speak of any conflict at the club. He was forever on about me joining because everybody was so friendly, so I doubt there was any issues there.'

'But you didn't join?' Holmes asked, already knowing the answer.

'Don't be ridiculous. Silly white dresses and unbecoming hats.'

'So not the sporting type, I take it?' Bowker said, inviting more invective.

'I played a little social tennis on our neighbour's court in South Yarra, and I often accompanied my first husband when he played polo at the equestrian centre at Werribee. But playing sport up here? Really? Come on.'

'Did your husband own a computer, Mrs Rice?' Bowker asked.

'Only a cheap laptop he used for council business and writing his silly family history.'

'We'd like to take that with us, if you don't mind, Mrs Rice,' Bowker said. 'It might give us a clue as to who else may have wished your husband harm. It will be returned when we've finished with it.'

'It's on the backseat of the car with other fragile items.' She looked around to see that the coast was clear. 'I wouldn't trust these baboons not to break something or take things for their own benefit.'

'Did your husband make notes or keep hard copies of his research into his family?'

Mrs Rice rolled her eyes and threw her head back melodramatically. 'There are two cardboard boxes full of the stuff. Photocopies, handwritten notes of interviews, photos of old gravestones in the cemetery, you name it. There's one box for each branch of the Rice family.'

Bowker frowned in confusion. 'How do you mean, two branches of the family?'

Mrs Rice looked at the detectives and sighed heavily, making it obvious she thought they were wasting her time. 'It goes back to the squatting days of the 1860's. Two Rice brothers, Albert and James journeyed from England to Australia and took up land in the Benalla district. James settled in the Tatong area and Albert took up land near Greta.'

Bowker nodded. 'OK. Are these boxes on the front verandah or already loaded into the truck?'

The woman scoffed. 'Why would I keep that rubbish. If you want it, you're welcome to it. But I'll leave it to you to fish it out of the skip.' She thought for a moment then added, 'the less reminders I have of that man, the better. Right now he'll be laying in his coffin laughing at my expense.'

Bowker glanced at Holmes then looked back at the woman. 'Not sure what you mean, Mrs Rice,' he said, knowing exactly what was coming.

'His will,' she said angrily. 'For over a year I pressed him to make changes. Finally he said he'd been to the solicitor and fixed it up.' She chortled sarcastically. 'Fixed it up, alright. Not only do I not inherit the farm, but now the proceeds from the sale of this house need to be shared with his first wife. A gold-digging hussy living in sin somewhere in the backwoods, I've heard.' She paused, then stared out over the lake. 'I've already engaged a solicitor in Melbourne, so this is not over yet. Not by a long shot.'

Bowker collected the laptop from Mrs Rice's car and nominated Holmes to climb into the skip and search for the discarded boxes of Rice's research material. All the victim's clothes had been jettisoned by his wife, wardrobe items still on their hangers. Holmes heaved the stack of clothes aside and located two cartons partially squashed underneath. He pulled aside the cardboard flaps on the first and confirmed it contained documents relating to the Rice history. He passed it out to Bowker who placed it in the rear of the police vehicle. The other box contained kitchen requisites including unopened packets of flour and sugar as well as a large assortment of herbs. It took Holmes several minutes of sifting through the junk before he located the second box sitting snugly in the corner of the skip, obviously having been one of the first items deposited. The carton was covered in spilt yogurt or stale cream so he passed it carefully to Bowker before climbing out and brushing himself down. The Pomeranians abandoned their aggressive posture and descended on the second box, licking it clean before Bowker placed it with its mate in the rear of the vehicle.

The sky filled with heavy cloud as the detectives approached Melbourne, the first spits of rain hitting the windscreen as they passed through Kalkallo on the outskirts of the city. It was raining steadily by the time they turned left at the end of the Hume Freeway to follow the Ring Road around to the Plenty Road exit. In spite of the threatening weather, they were through security and parked in the Victorian Police Forensic Centre compound within two and a half hours of leaving Benalla. Erin O'Meara was in her office when Bowker and Holmes entered, her nose up close to her computer monitor.

'You need new glasses,' Bowker said as he knocked and came through the open door.

O'Meara leaned back in her chair and smiled. 'I need a lot of new things, Gregory. Glasses are the least of them, let me tell you.' She looked at Holmes. 'Ah, Detective Sergeant Holmes. Long time, no see.' She gestured for the officers to pull up the two chairs sitting against a side wall.'

'G'day Erin,' Holmes replied as he placed a cardboard box on the edge of her desk before grabbing a chair and sitting down. 'Haven't been out here for a couple of years, but spoken to you a few times over the phone.'

O'Meara wasted no time in getting down to business. She patted the box. 'All the way from Benalla, I assume. What have you got for us, gentlemen?'

'Four separate samples of kelpie hair, a baseball bat with blood on it and the victim's walking stick that was found after a week in the lake,' Bowker summarised.

O'Meara nodded. 'OK. Six items in all.'

Bowker lifted both palms. 'You don't have to tell us, Erin. You're flat chat here and we'll have to wait our turn?'

O'Meara raised her eyebrows. 'You've never waited your turn yet, Gregory. Usually a bottle of scotch gets your jobs knocked up the list.' She smiled. 'However, on this occasion you won't need the bribes. It's as quiet here as I can remember, so we should be able to knock over your stuff in no time.'

Bowker winked at Holmes.

'So tell me what we're looking for?' O'Meara asked, removing her glasses and massaging the bridge of her nose.

Bowker nodded to Holmes to answer. 'We're looking for a match between the dog hair we've sampled and the hair found in the victim's head wound, and whether the blood on the baseball bat has come from the victim. We're also hoping you can lift fingerprints off the walking stick.'

'Easy-peasy,' Bowker added as he stood up.

O'Meara donned her glasses. 'Before you go. Have you run into a detective in Benalla named Kirsten Larsen?'

'Yeah,' Bowker replied. 'Part of our team on the Rice case. What's the go?'

'She just impresses me as very sharp in the dealings she's had with us,' O'Meara replied. 'Some of her hunches have turned out to be spot on when we've done the forensics. I think she's got too much talent to be up in the bush chasing stolen bikes and two-bob assaults. Should get her down to Homicide.' She smiled. 'You've got too many swinging dicks in there. Need a few more women to lift the standard.'

'We'll keep a close eye on her, eh Sherlock,' Bowker said to Holmes, then wished he hadn't phrased it that way.

Bowker sprinted through the rain from the garage to the back door of his North Caulfield home. As he shook the raindrops from his jacket, Rachael entered the kitchen arms outstretched and sporting a wide smile. The two embraced for an extended moment before catching up with family matters while Rachael boiled the kettle and made coffee. She retrieved a tin of homemade biscuits from an overhead cupboard, removed the lid, and placed it on the kitchen table in front of where Bowker was seated. When the drinks had been made, she transported the mugs of instant coffee to the table and sat down opposite her husband.

'I didn't expect you home until the weekend,' she said.

Bowker picked up his coffee and blew across the top of the mug. 'We've run out of leads up there unfortunately. There were a few items we needed tested in the lab, so we thought we may as well kill two birds with the one stone and drive back to the city.'

'You had half a dozen suspects. No joy with any of them in the end, I take it?' Rachael asked picking up her coffee in two hands.

Bowker brought his wife up to date with their investigations, particularly the progress generated by Lowther's account of events on the boardwalk. At the end of his discourse, he smiled. 'It's not very often a big breakthrough like that can set you back to square one.'

'So you're pretty sure you're chasing someone new?' his wife replied.

Bowker nodded. 'Yeah. And we haven't got a clue who that might be.' He took a sip of his coffee and took a biscuit from the tin. 'I've brought home the victim's laptop and the notes he was using to write a family history. The laptop might give us a clue. There may be something in the council correspondence he stored on there, but I doubt there'll be much of value in the family material.' He smiled. 'Still, being an old Benalla boy, it'll make interesting reading, I suppose.'

Rachael stood up from her chair and walked around behind her husband. She leant down and rested her head on his shoulder and wrapped her arms around him. 'It's good to have you back anyway, Big Boy. I bet Darren is pleased to be home. He didn't get back last weekend, did he?'

Bowker clasped his wife's forearms. 'I think Sherlock's preference would have been to stay in Benalla.'

Rachael disengaged her arms and returned to her seat with a concerned look on her face. 'Do you think there are problems between him and Cassie?'

'Sherlock reckons they've grown apart since the kids moved out. It was his decision not to come home last weekend.' Bowker took another sip of his coffee. 'Plus, between you and me and the gatepost, there's a complicating factor.'

Rachael stared into Bowker's eyes. 'What sort of complicating factor?' she said with trepidation.

Bowker breathed in deeply, assessing the most politic way to explain the situation. 'There's a female detective in the Benalla CID who we're working with.' He watched his wife roll her eyes, obviously aware of what was coming. 'She's a fair bit younger than Sherlock, but they get on like a house on fire.'

'How much younger?' Rachael asked quickly.

'Seventeen years. She's thirty-one.'

'Is she married?'

'Nope.'

Rachael leant back in her chair and looked up at the ceiling. 'Has anything happened?'

'Sherlock says no. They conducted an interview with a suspect last Saturday morning, then spent the rest of the day together, including dinner at her place that night.'

'Did they sleep together?'

Bowker shook his head. 'Not according to Sherlock. But apparently she asked him to spend the night there. He passed up the offer because he's married, but he told me his preference was to stay.'

'Isn't this workplace stuff banned?' Rachael asked. 'Power differentials and all that?'

'It's hardly a power differential when she's the one suggesting they have sex.' Bowker took another biscuit and dunked it in his coffee.

Rachael thought for a moment. 'So what's Darren going to do? Presumably you'll both be in Benalla again in a few days.'

Bowker shrugged. 'Talk to Cassie, I think. Not about the woman in Benalla, but about their situation in general. See if there's any future in their relationship.'

Rachael slid her hands across the table and gently clasped her husband's fingers. She smiled. 'I hope you don't get these temptations when you're off doing these far-flung investigations.'

Bowker laughed. 'Shit, I've got more than I can handle here.'

Rachael grinned flirtatiously. 'We'll see about that after dinner, shall we?'

CHAPTER 17

With Rachael having departed early the next morning for her kindergarten and with the weather cool and showery, Bowker made the decision to work from home and away from the distractions of the Spencer Street centre. His first obstacle after setting up base on the kitchen table was the password protection on Rice's laptop. He expected he'd ultimately need IT specialist assistance to gain entry, but before heading down that track, he assessed there was little to lose by throwing the computer a few educated guesses. Bowker knew Rice was elderly and not computer savvy so was unlikely to have had password security continually drummed into him. He also knew that most casual users chose passwords that were easy to remember and could often be guessed within a few attempts. Bowker tried the letters in the names of Rice and his wife in various combinations, but with no success. He suspected the names of the Pomeranians were also a possibility, but since he was ignorant of what they were called that thought got him nowhere. On a worldwide basis, the most commonly used password was the word "password". He tried that, but again the laptop refused to open. He tried the same word with a capital P, then used all capital letters. Once again, no joy. As a last resort he typed in "pa$$word" and, as if by magic, Rice's digital world opened before his eyes.

There were only a few applications on the machine, with the Microsoft Office suite the most prominent. After a cursory inspection of the various directories, it appeared to Bowker that most of Rice's work was stored on the desktop. Three folders sat in a cluster in the centre of the screen with the titles "History", "Council" and "Personal". Bowker opened the Personal file first. Inside there were only four documents. He read each in turn. Two were letters of complaint to the state ombudsmen concerning an overcharge on his power bill, the other two were invitations for former colleagues to attend the school reunion. Bowker recorded the names and addresses of the invitees with a view to cross referencing them with those on the attendees list. He doubted much would result, but for the moment the investigation had stalled and anything was worth a look.

The council folder held substantially more documents. Most were routine articles of correspondence between the city and its councillors, but a subfolder contained material specific to Rice's campaign to equalize rates. Bowker spent the next sixty minutes reading through every document and was satisfied there was nothing new to see, except for the depth of dislike that had evolved between Rice and Dennis Lowther. He stood up, stretched and walked to the bench to make himself a cup of coffee. His mobile rang and Holmes's name was on the screen when he checked. He tapped the accept button.

'Sherlock.'

'Yeah, mate. You not coming in today by the look of it?'

'I'm working my way through the stuff on Rice's laptop. Thought I could do that at home just as easily as lugging everything into Spencer Street.'

'Find anything so far?'

'Nothing we didn't know already. Correspondence between Rice and Lowther became pretty heated towards the end. The rest of the stuff is just normal council business. Haven't looked at his emails yet, or the material he's assembled for his family history.'

'Maybe something will turn up where you least expect it.'

Bowker flicked on the electric kettle. 'It's starting to feel like one of those cases that hang on for years without a breakthrough.'

'That's what we felt about the Cocamba investigation last year. Then out of the blue, bingo. Something drops out of the sky.'

'Hope that happens this time. But you know as well as I do mate, that the more days that pass, the less chance there is of finding something.' Bowker paused, contemplating a move from the professional to the personal. 'How's Cassie? Happy to see you?'

Holmes sniffed. 'She was civil. Hardly exuberant at my appearance.'

'Not a big, passionate reunion?' Bowker replied, comparing Holmes's description with the reception he'd received from Rachael.

Holmes laughed sarcastically. 'Passion? What's that mate?'

'You have a yarn about how things are travelling with the two of you?'

'Didn't have to really. As soon as she got home from work, she drops it on me that the company where she works is opening a branch across the ditch. They're sending her boss over to run the show. He's asked Cassie to go with him to New Zealand and be his PA. She's already accepted the offer. There's an old battle axe in the same office who's more senior, so why not take her? How many guesses do you need?'

'You might be reading too much into this, mate,' Bowker replied as he shovelled a spoonful of instant coffee into a mug. 'Is Cassie's boss married?'

'Divorced. Much the same age as me and Cass.'

'Did she say why she's taking up the offer.'

'Great opportunity, she tells me. Once in a lifetime chance to climb the ladder.' There was quiet on the line for just long enough. 'Nothing to keep her here now the kids have moved out, she said.'

'Do you think maybe it's her way of finding out one way or another if you see any future in the marriage. To see whether you're willing to fight tooth and nail to hold things together.'

It was a moment or two before Holmes answered. 'Maybe. But it didn't come across that way. The whole thing has the smell of a *fait accompli.*'

'So how'd you respond when she told you about the kiwi job?'

'Just flew a kite to see where I stood. Said that I could get a job with the homicide squad over there.'

'How'd she react to that?'

'Didn't take me seriously. She said I love my job here too much to pull up stakes and move over there.' There was a pause. 'I didn't tell her this, but she's spot on with that one.'

'And she's officially accepted the offer?'

'Yesterday, apparently. No discussion with me. Just bang, I'm off, thank your mother for the rabbits.'

Rice's family history directory contained a series of subfolders. The largest in volume housed the draft of his narrative. Bowker decided to read this first as an overview of Rice's research and the individuals who had contributed information. The prologue detailed what the detective had been told by Arabella Rice the day before, that two brothers, James and Albert Rice had journeyed from England in the 1860's to take up land around a settlement that later became known as Benalla. The brothers' family owned a thriving foundry works on the outskirts of Sheffield in South Yorkshire. Neither James nor Albert saw their future in the grimy coal and steel industries and departed the foundry to follow their dream of becoming land owners on the other side of the world. Gary Rice's narrative detailed information concerning the family background in England and the brothers' voyage to Australia, but despite the fascination he felt with the brothers' intrepid journey, Bowker chose to skip the minutia knowing it had little relevance to his inquiries.

Chapter 1 described the area into which the brothers decided to settle and its history prior to their arrival. Unlike many chronicles of the past, Rice allocated space to the indigenous peoples who were the region's inhabitants for thousands of years. He then described Hume and Hovell's 1824 expedition and Major Mitchell's exploration ten years later that effectively opened the area for European settlement. He detailed the first pastoral runs and the establishment of the Broken River settlement, the precursor to the township of Benalla. Bowker was entranced by the history of his old town, but fearing being side-tracked by information irrelevant to his investigation, he flipped to the end of the chapter.

There, the Rice family tree was laid out over a double page in spreadsheet form. On the left-hand side were the descendants of James Rice in a lineage that stretched all the way down to Gary and his daughter, Alison. Sub-branches shot off in all directions in an exponential pattern as the tree grew further from its immigrant roots. Certain cells in the spreadsheet were shaded pink to denote the history of ownership of the Tatong property as it passed from generation to generation. Seeing nothing of value to his investigation he turned his attention to the right-hand side of the layout.

Unlike his brother James, where the Rice family name had survived through an unbroken series of sons all the way down as far as Alison in the present day, the Rice name had disappeared from Albert's lineage only two generations after he arrived from England when his grandson produced three daughters. The eldest of these married Joseph Faraday and ultimately the couple inherited the Greta pastoral run. Bowker tracked the blue shaded rectangles that indicated ownership of the property down the page until three generations later a family with an only child, a daughter, appeared. This daughter, Irene Faraday, married an Edward Oosterman and they inherited the Greta farm on her father's death. This marriage produced a son and a daughter but generated no new blue-shaded cells on the spreadsheet, perhaps indicating that the property had been sold. A bell was ringing somewhere in Bowker's subconscious, and he stared up at the ceiling willing his mind to reveal what it was. After unsuccessfully searching his memory for a minute or two, he returned his attention to the document. The Oosterman daughter married a Matthew White, and a boy and a girl, now teenagers, were born of that union. Her brother Paul's branch however was a dead end. There was apparently a partner, Denise, but no descendants. In superscript beside Paul's name was a tiny 4, denoting the existence of a footnote. The list of notes was on the next page, but a sudden flash of memory told Bowker what 4 would explain. Paul Oosterman committed suicide on the slopes of The Granite in Lurg. What set the detective's heart aflutter was not his own teenage involvement in finding Oosterman's body all those years ago, but what Gary Rice had typed in red print at the end of the footnote. A long series of question marks.

'So you found the body? When you were a kid?' Holmes asked when Bowker rang him to suggest he may have found something to chase up, even when tenuous seemed too strong a description.

'Yeah. My brother and I often rode our horses up around that area when we were teenagers. Shootin' rabbits and basically piss-fartin' around. You would have been the same up at Murrayville. Shoot through after breakfast and arrive home just in time for tea.'

'So what are you saying here?' Holmes asked. 'Gary Rice is writing a family history, finds something suss about a distant cousin's suicide, then gets knocked on the head for asking too many questions?'

'It's a long shot, but what else have we got at present? We're talkin' about forty years ago mate. The local police probably followed the tried-and-true method we still use most of the time today. If it walks like a duck and quacks like a duck, then you can be pretty sure it's a fuckin' duck. But they didn't have the tools we've got today. If we suspect the duck might be a swan, we can do a DNA test to make sure. Maybe Rice found something the coppers back then missed. Or maybe he's spoken to someone the police didn't know about.'

'It's a possibility I s'pose. And if the bloke was murdered rather than simply topping himself, then the killer wouldn't want somebody sniffing around asking questions after all these years. Especially if they feared Rice might point the finger at them.'

'I'm gonna keep digging,' Bowker said. 'I'll let you know if I find anything new. You got anything to keep you busy in there?'

'Yeah. The bloody O'Brien case. What sort of a bastard kills the poor old prick and leaves him to be eaten by his own dogs? From all accounts, he was a grumpy old shit, but nobody deserves to go out like that.' He paused for a moment. 'Yell out if you need a hand or another set of eyes.'

Bowker scrolled through a number of chapters, pausing occasionally to read something that caught his eye. For example, Rice detailed that in 1890 on a farm adjoining Albert Rice's pastoral run, a twenty-five-year-old farm worker from England used a razor to cut the throat of his boss's eleven-year-old daughter and then proceeded to kill himself in identical fashion. It was totally premeditated. The worker left a note confessing his love for the young girl and that God wanted them to be together in Heaven. Bowker looked up from the laptop and stared out the kitchen window for a few seconds. He shook his head before scrolling through multiple pages until he found the first relating to Paul Oosterman's family. Rice's flowery narrative put meat onto the bones Bowker had gleaned from the spreadsheet. Irene Faraday, a direct descendant of Albert Rice had married Graham Oosterman and they set up house on the Oosterman's family farm, *Melaleuca Springs*, no more than ten miles distant from Irene's father's Greta property. The couple produced a son, Paul, and a daughter Margaret. After some twenty-five years, the Greta property passed to Irene on the death of her father, and she and her husband moved into the homestead there, leaving their son Paul to manage *Melaleuca Springs* at Upper Lurg. By this time, their daughter Margaret had married and moved into Wangaratta. A year later, Paul married Denise Macklin, the Commonwealth Bank manager's daughter from Benalla, and the couple moved from running sheep to Black Angus cattle. The chapter came to an abrupt end with a series of notes in italics.

Trouble Brewing
Denise leaves Paul???
Paul Suicides ????
Oostermans sell up both properties

Bowker scrolled to the end of the document, but the remaining page was empty. Something about Paul Oosterman's suicide had side tracked Gary Rice and Bowker felt certain it was an avenue worth following. But he needed more background before he began digging through Rice's mountain of notes. With the number of decades that had passed since Paul Oosterman's demise, he knew that any record of the police investigation was unlikely to have been retained at the Benalla station. The next best thing was a chat with someone who was around at the time and might still have memories of the incident. The only person he could think of was Sid Wilson, the stock and station agent who once lived on a small farm in the lane opposite the Bowker family property and who Ron Cloverdale said was still plying his trade in the town.

Bowker lifted his phone from the table and quickly found Wilson's number via yellow pages. The call was picked up on the second ring.

'Sid Wilson,' came the answer in an elderly gravelly voice.

'G'day Sid. Greg Bowker here. You probably don't remember me, but forty years ago I used to live opposite you on Kilfeera Road.'

'One of Malcolm Bowker's boys,' Wilson replied quickly. 'Used to ride your horses down the lane past my place when I lived out there. You the older one, or the younger one?'

'The older one.'

'Rode a dappled grey mare,' Wilson said. 'Bit flighty.'

Bowker was amazed at his recall. 'That's right, Sid. You've got a hell of a memory.'

Wilson laughed. 'For some things, yeah. My wife reckons I only remember what I feel like remembering.' He was quiet for a quick moment. 'You and your brother were the kids who found Paul Oosterman's body on The Granite after he topped himself, weren't you?'

'Yeah, that's what I want to pick your brain about,' Bowker replied.

Wilson was confused. 'Are you trying to relive your childhood or something? I thought findin' Paul Oosterman would be an occasion you'd want to forget.'

'I'm a homicide detective these days Sid. I'm ringing you from Melbourne in connection with a case I'm working on.'

'Shit you've done well for yourself, young fella,' Wilson replied. 'I'm not sure I can help you with much, but I'll do my best to see what I can remember.'

'I'd appreciate whatever you can tell me.'

'Paul Oosterman was married for a while before he and his wife split up. Denise was her name. When I was with Goldsboroughs, Denise worked in the office. Nice lady. Then one day she up and left. Didn't even take her car. No one has heard from her since, I don't think. The general feeling was that's the reason why Paul shot himself. He was pretty devoted to her.' He paused for a moment. 'Well, more jealous than devoted, to be quite honest. He'd even blow his top if another bloke asked her for a dance at one of the district balls we all went to in those days.'

'You do their stock work?' Bowker asked.

'I was Paul's grandfather's agent for the place out at Greta. But when the old bloke died, the place was left to Irene. Her and Graham then used Dalgetys for both properties. I was really pissed off to lose that account. They were one of my biggest clients.'

'What happened to the two properties?' Bowker asked.

'Sold. Both of them. On the market not long after Paul died. They had a massive clearing sale. Everything was sold. I bought Denise's lime-green Toyota Celica. Cheap as chips. Drove it until it died with over four hundred Ks on the clock. Great little car.'

'I remember you driving it,' Bowker replied with a chuckle. 'Put me and the horse into the scrub a couple of times you came so close to me up the lane.'

'That nutcase mare of yours would have done the same thing if a mozzie had flown past.' Wilson laughed at his own joke. 'I bought a top of the range chain saw at that sale too. There were no reserves on anything. Some blokes bought virtually brand-new farming machinery for half price.'

Bowker nodded to himself. 'Yeah. My old man bought a slasher from that sale.'

'Losing their only son broke the Oostermans' heart, I reckon,' Wilson continued. 'Especially occurring up there on The Granite.

The bloody thing's visible from both properties. Would have been a constant reminder of what happened.'

'And nothing has been heard of Denise in all the years since she disappeared?'

'Not to my knowledge,' Wilson replied. 'Of course, there were rumours that Paul may have done her in because he was such a jealous bastard, but the police couldn't find any evidence to support that theory. They were even planning to excavate dirt from the sheep dip, thinking Denise may have been buried in the bottom of that. But the dip had been filled in a month before Denise shot through after two kids had drowned in a plunge dip over in the Wimmera. In the end, the police concluded that she'd just left the district looking for a better life.'

'Thanks mate,' Bowker replied, 'what you've told me helps fill in a few gaps.'

'This to do with the Gary Rice murder?' Wilson asked. 'Gary was a distant cousin of Paul Oosterman. But I s'pose you know that. Be a big coincidence if Paul Oosterman's name comes up for another unnatural death somewhere.'

'You're on the ball Sid,' Bowker replied with a grin. 'We're running into dead ends everywhere, so I'm just flying kites at the moment. Plus, when I heard Rice was related to Paul Oosterman, the old memories of finding his body came flooding back. To tell you the truth, the questions you've just answered are more mine in the personal sense, than anything relating to the Rice murder. But you never know.'

CHAPTER 18

Bowker closed the file and moved to Rice's email application. Most of his incoming and outgoing emails related to council business, although a folder name pointed to correspondence relating to the family history. Several emails were exchanged with the State Library in Melbourne and a number of local historical societies. Bowker read each and found they mainly contained requests for copies of documents or photos, or answers to sets of questions he had posed. An email to Paul Oosterman's sister Margaret requested access to any historical material that had been passed down through the family. Margaret's reply expressed excitement at Rice's plan to write the history and her delight in making available the material he had requested. She also flagged her intention to include the documentation her father had accrued around the death of her brother, much of it from the police and of a nature that would be unavailable to the public under today's laws. She expressed the whole family's unwillingness to accept the coroner's finding that Paul had suicided. They believed Paul would never have contemplated taking his own life and that they found numerous anomalies in the evidence. Bowker scanned the remaining emails and found nothing that immediately activated his radar.

Bowker hurried to his vehicle in the carport, retrieving the carton containing the information concerning the Albert Rice side of the family. As he unpacked the box on the kitchen table, it became obvious that many of the bundles of documents and photos, particularly the older ones, still had Margaret's original binding, suggesting Rice had not perused them. On the other hand, the information pertaining to Paul Oosterman's death was untidily thrown into a manilla folder. Many pages had red biro notations in the margin that Bowker presumed were Gary Rice's thoughts as he perused the individual pages. Bowker carefully removed each document and laid it on the table in front of him. At the back of the folder was a report on the disappearance of Oosterman's wife Denise, which he placed on the floor beside his chair.

Bowker first read the incident scene report and smiled when he saw his name, and that of his brother, recorded for posterity as the finders of Oosterman's body on the slopes of The Granite. The report confirmed Bowker's vague memory that they found Oosterman about half-way up to the summit and that a rifle was in his hands with the barrel close to his face. The early estimate was that the body had lain there on the hillside for at least a couple of days, maybe three. Photos were taken of the scene and the weapon bagged for fingerprinting and ballistic examination. The term "suicide" was used repeatedly throughout the report and Bowker sensed the officers had made up their minds quite quickly that Oosterman had taken his own life. Rice's red biro notations indicated he had not missed this point either. The area was searched for anything that could aid with the investigation, but nothing of value was found. No footprints were discovered, which Bowker thought was unsurprising due to the flint-hard, gravelly nature of the soil on the hill. It wasn't called The Granite for nothing, he thought to himself. One spent shell was found in the breach of the rifle with a second live round in the five-shot magazine. Bowker leaned back in his chair in thought. Why have a second bullet, if you planned to shoot yourself in the head? he asked himself before surmising that if Oosterman did in fact suicide, his only thought would have been to ensure that the gun was loaded. If there were more bullets in the magazine, so what? There was nothing in the report to suggest that the attending officers looked for drag marks on the ground or on the clothes of the deceased. No mention was made of soil or vegetation samples being taken either, so Bowker made the assumption the officers were certain the body's location was where the fatal shot had been fired. He placed the report to the side, a little disappointed in its brevity and the superficial treatment of the incident scene. It was like so many crime-scene reports he's read in the past, where conclusions had been drawn before the evidence was collected when it should have been the other way around. He wondered if the officers on The Granite that day had specifically looked for any evidence that would support a finding other than suicide, or were they just dotting the i's and crossing the t's in what looked like and open and shut inquiry?

There weren't a lot of photos of the scene, certainly not the hundreds that were taken as part of modern-day investigations. The first few images were of The Granite and the track leading up to where the body was found. Over the years, Bowker had seen literally thousands of photos of dead bodies in various states of mutilation or decomposition, but the sight of Paul Oosterman lying in his own dried blood made his stomach churn. It is amazing what the mind hides in the deep dark recesses of the brain and this photo dragged a traumatising childhood image back to the front of the detective's consciousness. He stared at the lifeless Paul Oosterman, the clothes he was wearing and the location of the rifle. The clothes were totally at odds with the bush around him. A light pair of tracksuit pants, a navy-blue shearer's singlet and a pair of sheepskin moccasins looked out of place, but who thinks about what they are wearing when they are about to extinguish their own existence? But it was Oosterman's disfigured head that drew Bowker's closest attention. He lifted his mobile phone from beside the photo and opened the camera app. He trained the lens on Oosterman's mouth and used two fingers to enlarge the image on the screen. He stared at the phone. Oosterman's front teeth were broken away along with parts of his gums. This couldn't have happened when he hit the ground, since his head was half turned upwards. There was no doubt in the detective's mind that the teeth had been blown away in the rifle blast. He took a sip from his coffee which was now too cold to drink. He walked to the sink, poured the remaining liquid down the plughole and flicked on the kettle. While the water boiled, he scooped two teaspoons of instant coffee into his mug and leant on the sink, staring out into the back garden. Suicides carried out with firearms always entailed two methods. If a handgun was used, a shot through the temple was the most popular, where the muzzle of the gun was placed against the skull. In cases involving a rifle or a shotgun, the barrel was invariably inserted into the mouth and the shot directed up through the back of the skull. Bowker had never seen or heard of a case where the shot was fired from outside the mouth, through the teeth. Never.

When his coffee was made, Bowker raided the biscuit tin and retrieved three of his favourite homemade ANZAC's. He resumed his seat, placed his morning tea to the side and moved on to the forensic findings. The report was much shorter than those of today, but he expected that, given that this document was written half a lifetime ago before the advent of modern laboratory processes in areas such as DNA, insect evaluation and advanced fingerprint analysis. The time of death was estimated at seventy-two hours before the body was examined, the cause of death being a bullet fired through the roof of the mouth from very close range. Powder burns were found on the face, but no residue on the hands. This did not surprise Bowker, since a rifle trigger is a reasonable distance from the muzzle of the gun. The report commented on the shot-away teeth and concluded, like Bowker, that the rifle barrel had been outside Oosterman's mouth when it was fired. The forensic experts believed the likely cause was the deceased inadvertently pulling the trigger before he had the gun in the right position. This conclusion was supported by ballistics experts who reported that the rifle had a "hair trigger". The gun was dusted for fingerprints, with only the deceased prints being lifted from the stock, fore-end and trigger assembly of the weapon. There were no prints on the barrel. This last finding bothered the detective inspector. Most times, rifles are picked up by the barrel and its metal composition gives the optimal surface to retain prints. Could the gun have been wiped clean before it was placed in the dead man's hands if foul play was involved? he wondered. He read the next page but found nothing that piqued his interest until the report moved to the examination of the Oosterman house at the bottom of the hill. Before reading on, Bowker searched through the various documents until he found the write-up of the police visit to *Melaleuca Springs*.

The document reported little in Oosterman's house to contradict an assumption of suicide. A short, handwritten note was found on the kitchen table, scribbled on the back of a SEC power bill. A low quality photocopy of the note was attached to the report.

SORRY, MUM AND DAD
WITH DENISE GONE AND NO KIDS
THERE IS NO POINT TO MY LIFE.
YOU WILL FIND ME ON THE GRANITE
WHERE I CAN LOOK OUT OVER WHAT IS NOW MEANINGLESS
WHAT I AM ABOUT TO DO

I CAN DO IN GOOD CONSCIENCE.
I ASK ONLY THAT THIS WEDDING PHOTO BE HUNG IN THE
FAMILY HOME
AS A MOMENTUM OF OUR SHORT LIFE TOGETHER
LOVE TO EVERYONE. PAUL

Bowker read the note twice and wondered how a life could be summed up in such a few lines. The misspelt word jumped out at him, but he quickly conceded that if a bloke is really about to top himself, he probably deserves a bit of slack on his English expression. Bowker took a sip of his coffee then demolished one of his biscuits in two bites. He brushed the crumbs from the table in front of him and went back to reading the report on Oosterman's home. It noted that a page of *The Sun* daily newspaper sat on the table beside the note and a framed wedding photo. It was folded in half with the crossword puzzle completed in the same ink and capital letters as the note. A copy of the puzzle page was attached. Bowker looked at the date on the top of the page and saw it matched the date of Oosterman's demise, the paper no doubt being delivered with the mail earlier in the morning. Bowker leant back in his chair, closed his eyes and folded his hands behind his head. Who completes a crossword before going outside and killing himself? he thought. The line of question marks scribbled in red biro in the margin indicated that Gary Rice had agreed with him. There were a lot of things associated with Oosterman's death that didn't make sense. Police found nothing outside the house they felt was of interest except that the dogs were in dire need of water, giving further weight to their theory that Oosterman had died a couple of days before. But in Bowker's experience, no farmer would leave his dogs to die of thirst even if he was about to punch his own ticket.

Bowker drained his coffee as he perused the photos taken inside

Oosterman's kitchen. Nothing appeared out of place, although dirty dishes were stacked up on the sink. A picture taken from above the kitchen table showed the relative positions of the wedding photo, the newspaper and the suicide note, each with a red biro circle drawn around them. One of the chairs was slightly pulled out and on the seat he could see a red biro circled plastic tag that had come adrift from its key. Once again, Bowker used his phone's camera to magnify the handwritten symbols on the slip of paper inside the plastic case. Once fully enlarged, Bowker could make out the capital letters MS which he assumed stood for the property's name *Melaleuca Springs*. The labelling would allow the farm's keys to be distinguished from those used at the Greta property. Whether the tag was once attached to a key for the house, or one of the sheds or even the tractor was impossible to determine, especially with the passing of decades and at least one change in the farm's ownership.

Returning to the forensic report, Bowker read that the kitchen was dusted for fingerprints along with the photo, newspaper and SEC bill on which the note was written. Of the prints that were usable, most belonged to Paul Oosterman himself, a few were matched to those found on cosmetic products in the bathroom which the police assumed belonged to his wife Denise. A small number of fingerprints were ultimately found to belong to the deceased man's parents. The owner of one set lifted from the back door could not be identified and given that the case was already assumed a suicide, little was done to trace the owner. A photocopy of the mystery prints accompanied the transcript.

The Coroner's Report summarized the findings of the forensic analysis and the police records, and officially concluded that Paul Oosterman had taken his own life in the wake of his wife's disappearance. Bowker placed the document on top of the others and removed a stack of sympathy cards from the box. As expected, most came from relatives and friends, but a few were sent by local businesses who'd dealt closely with the Oostermans. These included cards from the local branches of the State bank, Dalgety stock and station agency and their competitors Goldsborough Mort. Attached to the latter by paperclip was a small black and white photo taken at the Benalla Agricultural Show. "Better Times" was written underneath. Pictured was Paul Oosterman proudly standing beside a Black Angus cow and being presented with a Goldsborough Mort-sponsored winner's sash by a young Sid Wilson. Bowker read all the cards carefully and, satisfied they added nothing to his inquiry, dropped them back in the box. He stood up and walked to his office. He returned with a pen and a notepad. He scribbled down a list of things that had worried him about the assumption of suicide.

Crossword prior to taking own life???
Muzzle of gun outside mouth???
No prints on Barrel?
No prior signs of Oosterman's depressive state of mind
The suicide note written in capitals? Copied from puzzle?
No farmer leaves animals without water

He dropped the pen on the pad and stared into space. If Oosterman didn't suicide, then obviously someone else shot him. But why? Who had a motive? Did his estranged wife come back when everyone thought she was out of the picture? Bowker's head was spinning with ifs and buts. But one thing he did know. If Oosterman *was* murdered, and if Rice had unearthed the truth in the course of his research, then someone had a very strong motive to silence Rice before the truth came out. The detective returned to the laptop and found a phone contact in an email from Paul Oosterman's sister. He tapped the number into his mobile and was pleasantly surprised when the call was answered.

'Good morning, Mrs White. This is Detective Inspector Greg

Bowker of the homicide squad. I'm investigating the death of Gary Rice in Benalla a fortnight or so ago.'

'Oh yes,' the woman answered timidly, but with a puzzled tone.

'We're looking into every aspect of Mr Rice's life in search of a motive for the murder. As you know, he was writing a family history and at the moment I have his notes in front of me. His research seems to have stalled around the time of your brother's death. It appears he was troubled by the assumption that Paul committed suicide.'

'The whole family was troubled by that finding, detective,' the woman replied. 'Paul wasn't suffering from depression or any other mental condition. He just wasn't that type of person. He was loud and self-opinionated. Arrogant at times, I guess you'd describe him. Never willing to admit when he'd made a mistake. He'd have felt himself too important to deprive the world of his presence, so the idea that he would commit suicide is just preposterous. That may sound harsh coming from his sister, detective, but that's the way he was.'

'How did he react to his wife up and leaving?'

'Angry. Certainly not depressed. It was a rocky relationship at the best of times.'

'And they had no kids?'

'No. But it wasn't through design. They tried pretty hard in the early years. Paul was frustrated that Denise couldn't get pregnant and sent her to Melbourne for tests.' She chuckled. 'Turned out the problem wasn't with her, it was Paul. He'd had a serious case of mumps when he was a teenager, but normally that will have minimal impact on the chances of becoming a parent. But Paul was one of those rare cases where he was rendered totally infertile.'

Bowker scratched out notes on his lined pad. 'Do you think that might have been why Denise left? Perhaps feeling the need to be a mother?'

'Who knows,' the woman replied.

'Was there any domestic violence?'

The woman didn't respond for a moment, perhaps answering Bowker's question before she spoke. 'To be honest, I'd be surprised if there wasn't. As I've already mentioned detective, my brother could be an angry bugger. And a controlling prick too, at times. Denise was quite an equestrian in her youth, but Paul wouldn't let her keep a horse on their property. Unproductive animals have no place on a working farm, he said. Occasionally she climbed The Granite to destress.'

'Apparently her leaving all happened pretty suddenly.'

'Yes. She left for work in Benalla, parked her car under a shady tree near the railway station and she's never been seen or heard of since. I suspect she's up in Queensland. That's where her family originally came from. Up there on the coast somewhere. She was always on about us all going up to see the reef.'

Bowker nodded to himself. 'Besides his personality, were there other things that made your family doubt that Paul took his own life?'

'Lots of things,' the woman answered quickly. 'The suicide note for a start. I'd never seen Paul use capital letters to write anything, and neither had dad or mum. And if my brother was to leave a note it would be filled with recriminations against everyone and anyone. It certainly wouldn't be an ode to lost love.' She laughed. 'And the bit about the wedding photo is not him either. I think Paul saw Denise as a chattel more than a soulmate. If you want my opinion, someone trumped up all that sentimental stuff to provide a reason for why my brother would kill himself.'

'OK,' Bowker replied as he scribbled more notes.

'And really, detective. Who does a crossword prior to killing themselves? Plus, there's no way Paul would have left the dogs chained up and likely to run out of water before anybody came to the farm looking for him. I could believe he'd leave Denise without water, but not the dogs.'

'So why do you think the police failed to dig a bit deeper?' Bowker asked.

'Because on the surface it looked like suicide and it was easier to leave it at that then spend time trying to find another answer.'

'Your parents were obviously distraught?'

'Yes. The apple of their eye had been taken from them,' the woman answered with the hint of bitterness. 'They sold *Melaleuca Springs*, as well as *Sheffield Park* over at Greta and left the district.' She hesitated for a moment or two before continuing. 'It worked out alright for me in a selfish sort of way. I inherited everything so I'm now a wealthy woman, but I would have loved dad to ask me if I'd be interested in taking over the farm and maintaining the family connection.' She sighed. 'But I'm a female, so that would have never crossed his mind.' She chuckled quietly. 'At least I wasn't rejected on competency grounds.'

'Well Mrs White, if you disagree with the finding of suicide then you must think your brother was murdered. I mean it's hardly conceivable that he accidentally shot himself in the face at that angle.'

'Totally agree, detective,' the woman replied. 'But if you're going to ask me who actually shot my brother, I can't help you much. He had a few run-ins with people over the years, but I wouldn't think any were serious enough to warrant murder.'

'You'd be surprised sometimes, Mrs White. I've seen people murdered over a throw-away line, or over a dog that barks in a neighbour's yard. Can you give me any names of people Paul may have clashed with?' Bowker had his pen poised.

'He had a big run-in with Jack Templeton over an Angus bull Paul bought off him. Ironically Paul reckoned the bull had a low sperm count when a few of his heifers failed to get in calf. Old Jack died about twenty-five years ago so you won't get much sense out of him.'

'Any others?' He asked.

'He hated this bloke called Brian Gottfried. He worked in the Lands Department in the Benalla Shire. He attended all the dances around the district and always asked Denise for a dance when they played the modern waltz. Denise was quite a dancer and the floor used to clear when Brian and Denise did their thing. Stirred Paul up something shocking. Led to a punch-up outside the Molyullah hall one night. Gottfried then started serving notices on Paul about scotch thistles in his back paddock and blackberries in the creek that ran through his place.'

'Is Gottfried still alive?' Bowker asked.

'Wouldn't know. Those Lands Department blokes were moved around a lot in those days. It's not called that anymore either. Name's been changed heaps of times. Was Conservation Forests and Land at one stage but couldn't tell you what it goes by now.'

'OK,' Bowker replied as he continued to scribble.

'The only other person I can remember that Paul hated with a passion was Dennis Lowther.'

Bowker sat up in his chair, his interest piqued. 'The farmer out at Goorambat? Deputy Mayor?'

'That's him. Was Shire President before the amalgamation of the councils,' the woman replied. 'My brother was a hopeless footballer, but he really enjoyed the social side of it. He played in the reserves for Thoona and every time they came up against the Goorambat seconds there's be a blue with Lowther. Not sure what it was, neither of them was any good but they seemed to rub each other the wrong way and you'd be certain they'd start a brawl whenever those teams played one another. Both would invariably get suspended for a couple of games and threats would fly. But a motive for murder would be stretching it a tad.'

Bowker's initial reaction was that maybe Lowther had a second motive to kill Rice. Maybe it had nothing to do with rates, but rather preventing the exposé of a crime from decades prior. But as his thoughts settled, he remembered he had already cleared Lowther and was now using the old man's observations from the art gallery deck as the basis for further inquiries. He thanked Margaret White for her assistance and left his number in case she had further thoughts. He jotted a few notes in summary of the conversation then retrieved the Denise Oosterman file from the floor beside him.

CHAPTER 19

The Denise Oosterman file documented what Bowker judged a cursory investigation at best. She was reported missing by her husband when she failed to return from work on a Tuesday following a long weekend. Prior to contacting police, Oosterman had rung Bill Crouch, the manager of Goldsborough Mort, only to be told she hadn't reported to the office that morning. Crouch also informed Oosterman that he had attempted to ring *Melaleuca Springs* several times during the day to check on Denise's whereabouts as it was so out of character for her not to contact the office if she was ill or indisposed. Oosterman explained to police that he had been drenching cattle for much of the day and thus must have been out of the house when the calls came in. A search of the town found Denise's lime-green Toyota Celica parked under an elm tree in the street opposite the railway station. Police could find no one who'd seen the Celica arrive or had noticed Denise Oosterman in the street. A railway employee believed he'd seen the Celica parked under the tree at 7am but couldn't be sure. Oosterman deemed that impossible since Denise did not leave for work until 7.45am. Police dusted the car inside and out for fingerprints but found only those belonging to the Oosterman couple. There was no sign of blood or anything out of place in the Celica, with the car clean and tidy except for a little dried mud in the back and a rubber smudge mark on the wall of the rear deck. Oosterman explained a flat tyre had been thrown in after the spare was removed from its well and fitted to the rear. Bowker instinctively went searching through the report for evidence of the tyre being repaired and a forensic report on the composition of the rubber smudge and analysis of the mud. He quickly reminded himself that at this point, the investigation had related to a woman who had been missing for less than a day and that the forensics of forty years prior were nothing like they were now.

Bowker refreshed his coffee and again raided the biscuit tin before he returned to his reading. The officers at the time believed the most likely scenario was that Denise had driven into town, deposited her car near the railway station and then caught a train to Sydney or Melbourne before disappearing into thin air. A photo of Denise was shown to railway station staff, with a young ticket clerk believing he had sold a Sydney ticket to a lady resembling the pretty woman in the picture. Logic told the police that if she was heading to Queensland by train, Sydney would be her next connecting stop. Although the report showed no evidence that the police suspected Paul Oosterman of foul play, when Denise Oosterman hadn't reappeared or made contact with the family after three days, they did the professional thing by searching his Upper Lurg house and property for any clues to his wife's disappearance. The search revealed a missing suitcase and what Paul Oosterman thought was a small quantity of her clothing. As Sid Wilson had earlier mentioned to Bowker in their chat, the police contemplated excavating the sheep dip before Oosterman assured them it had been filled with dirt for weeks. On close inspection, officers were satisfied there was no disturbance of the surface in the days prior. With no evidence of foul play, the investigation ground to a halt and Denise's disappearance was filed under missing persons, although the accompanying report suggested that she was most probably in northern Queensland. In the margin of the report, Rice had scribbled the word "Cairns" with a question mark.

Bowker poured the dregs of his coffee into the sink and grabbed a can of Diet Coke from the fridge. He went up the passage to his office and turned on his desktop computer. He snapped open the can as he waited for the iMac to load. He knew what he was about to do was a Hail-Mary, but that was about all he had left. And occasionally a Hail-Mary worked. Very, very occasionally he had to remind himself. He opened the White Pages website and typed in the surname Oosterman for the city of Cairns in far north Queensland. As expected, no names came up, except for a David with that surname who lived in New South Wales. But with the trend towards unlisted mobile phone numbers and with many fixed line subscribers opting for silent numbers anyway, Bowker was not surprised. Finding her with a simple phone call was an extreme longshot, especially when he added in the possibility that the woman who disappeared so effectively forty years ago may still not wish to be tracked down. She had probably dropped the Oosterman name anyway. Still, the detective thought, it was worth a try. Deep down however, he knew he was probably chasing a ghost, but not the spectre of a person who died after leaving Benalla, but one of a woman whose remains still lay in that district.

After making himself a tomato and cheese sandwich for lunch, he rang Holmes in Spencer Street. It took him a good ten minutes to explain what he had discovered among Rice's papers.

'So you're convinced Oosterman was murdered and the scene set up to look like he'd walked through the self-checkout?' Holmes asked after he'd heard the full explanation.

'That's my gut feeling, Sherlock.'

'Who does your gut say did it?'

'It has no bloody idea, to tell you the truth, mate.'

'The wife, perhaps?' Holmes surmised. 'Treated like shit, staged her own disappearance then came back and popped him?'

'Or the other way around. Oosterman kills her then pretends she's done a runner.'

'So who punched his ticket?'

'Dunno, mate. Somebody who knows Oosterman killed his wife and murders him in revenge. Or alternatively it may be totally independent of the wife's disappearance.'

'The wife's the obvious candidate mate,' Holmes replied. 'Battered wife syndrome and all that.'

'Maybe. But if the family history is the key to all this, that would imply she also killed Gary Rice to shut him up. But nobody has seen her for nearly forty years so how the hell would she know about Rice's research. And why would she worry anyway, she's been untraceable since she disappeared from Benalla.'

Holmes exhaled loudly enough for Bowker to hear him over the phone. 'When you put it like that, it probably does count her out.' He paused for a moment. 'Wasn't her old man a bank Manager in town? Maybe he knew Oosterman killed his daughter and squared things up.'

'If one of her parents did it, neither would be a threat to Gary Rice. The old man has been dead for years and the mother's in God's waiting room out at the hospital.'

'Rice was the least of their problems, eh?' Holmes replied with a chuckle.

'If Rice's research did lead to his murder, then we need to work out what he stumbled on that triggered the chain of events that followed. It couldn't have been simply a theory that Oosterman's death wasn't suicide, it must have pointed a finger at an individual.'

The two detectives chatted for a few minutes, before resolving to discuss the case further at Spencer Street in the morning.

Bowker was already at his desk when Holmes arrived at headquarters. With two McDonalds coffees in hand, Holmes wandered across and handed a cup to his senior colleague. He put the other on Bowker's desk and pulled up a chair. He patted the two boxes stacked one on top of the other. 'Get through all that yesterday, did you? Big bloody effort.'

'Spent the afternoon going through the paperwork I'd bypassed in the morning. It's all memorabilia from generations past. I don't think any of it is relevant to Rice's murder. But the stuff relating to Paul Oosterman's death and his wife's disappearance might hold the key to this whole bloody mystery.' He raised his coffee. 'Thanks mate, just what I need.'

'This investigation is becoming bigger than Ben Hur, Greg,' Holmes said. 'One murder investigation has suddenly morphed into three.' Holmes sipped his coffee. 'You reckon we could be chasing two killers?'

Bowker shook his head as he placed his coffee on the desk. 'Just one killer, mate. The other one is dead. I reckon Oosterman killed his missus and was subsequently murdered as a result. That same person then knocked Rice on the head to cover that up. So our task hasn't changed really, except now we've got more to go on in terms of a motive.' Bowker leant back in his chair and folded his hands behind his head. 'If I'm wrong about a link to these earlier events then we're no worse off than we are now, because at the moment we've got zilch-else to go on.'

'You realise the whole house of cards is built on two big pieces of speculation, both of which are contrary to the original police conclusions?'

Bowker nodded. 'Yeah, but you tell me where you see a

weakness in my reasoning. Let's start with Denise Oosterman being murdered by her husband rather than just disappearing into the ether.'

'The Celica,' Holmes replied immediately. 'It's sitting in town at 7am on the day of her disappearance. How does Oosterman dump the car in Benalla without a way of getting home? That's assuming he's had no help, which I think is a safe assumption at this stage.'

'I reckon he put a farm bike in the back of the car. The police report mentions dried mud and a rubber smudge on the rear deck.'

Holmes wasn't convinced. 'A Celica is a bloody sports car Greg. You wouldn't fit a motor bike in the back.'

'On most models, you're right. But Denise's had a big hatchback. With the backseats down you could manoeuvre one of those lightweight farm bikes in there. You could even put the front passenger seat forward if you needed. It'd be tight, but we're not talking about a road bike.'

Holmes was a little dubious but happy to move on. 'OK what about the missing suitcase and clothes?'

'Oosterman was the one who claimed they were missing,' Bowker replied. 'That was likely just bullshit to reinforce the idea that she's shot through.'

Holmes nodded. 'What about the ticket clerk at the railway station? Didn't he ID her?'

'He said there was a lady who looked like the woman in the photo,' Bowker replied. 'Hardly a positive identification.'

'Well if Oosterman did kill her, her body has never been found.'

'The coppers barely looked, except for a walk around the house and sheds. The farm was over a thousand acres. That's a lot of area to bury a body. And there's bush over the road from the house. He could have disposed of her anywhere.' Bowker thought for a moment. 'She was reported missing on the Tuesday after a long weekend. Nobody except Oosterman had seen her since the Friday afternoon. Shit, he could have topped her any time over that weekend with plenty of time to dispose of her body and work out a scheme to cover his tracks.'

Holmes took a long draw on his coffee. 'OK, you've convinced me. Now tell me again why you don't buy Oosterman giving himself a Remington mouthwash.'

Bowker went through what caused his doubts around suicide; the absence of a depressive state of mind, the crossword puzzle, the suicide note, the lack of water for the dogs, the physical anomalies around the fatal wound itself.

'So, what's our next move?' Holmes asked after five minutes of discussion.

Bowker closed his eyes and thought for a moment. 'Back to Benalla, I think. We won't solve this thing sitting here. First off, we'll have another look at the register of attendees at the school reunion. I'm ninety-nine percent sure the person who killed Rice was at that function and followed him when he left to walk home. And logic tells me that Rice must have alerted the killer of his suspicions on that same night.'

Holmes frowned. 'We've looked at that list a dozen times.'

'Yeah,' Bowker replied with a grin, 'but now we know what age group we are looking for. I was sixteen or seventeen when Alex and I found Oosterman's body. It makes sense that whoever shot him was at least a few years older than me. That eliminates three quarters of the people who were at that function.'

'So that gets us down to forty people,' Holmes replied with a half grin.

'Some of them will be spouses that aren't from the district.' Bowker smiled. 'And I could live to regret saying this, but I reckon we can put a line through the women. Blasting a bloke's face away halfway up a scrubby hill is more a bloke's thing, I reckon. And so is smashing in someone's head.'

Holmes downed the last of his coffee. 'When do you want to head back to the North East?'

'What's today?' He looked at his watch. 'Friday. How about Monday morning? We'll have the weekend off.'

'Sounds like a plan,' Holmes replied.

'I can take somebody else if it suits you better to hang around the city. You know, for personal reasons.'

'May as well go to Benalla,' Holmes replied looking at the floor. 'Cass and I had a long talk last night.' He shrugged. 'She's keen to have a trial separation. Her New Zealand gig is a twelve-month contract with the option to extend. At the end of that she reckons we'll both have a better idea if there's anything left of our relationship worth coming back to.'

Bowker wasn't sure whether to respond with optimism or with a tone of solace, so he chose a more neutral path. 'What are the terms of the separation?'

Holmes shrugged again. 'Play it by ear, I guess.'

'So when we go back to Benalla and you run into Kirsten Larsen and she's all legs and smiles, what's your plan?' Bowker asked. 'And don't say you'll play it by ear. There's a lot of truth in the old saying that God gave men a big head and a little head but not enough blood to run both at the same time.'

Holmes burst out laughing, but didn't respond.

Bowker was about to continue when his phone rang. The call was from Erin O'Meara in McLeod. 'I've got those forensic results you were after,' she said following the usual banter.

'Beautiful,' Bowker replied. 'I've got Sherlock Holmes here with me so I'll put you on speaker.'

'You've always been a thinker, Gregory. How are you Darren? Still making Bowker look good?'

'Doing my best. But it's a massive job,' Holmes replied winking at Bowker.

O'Meara chuckled then fell into a spasm of smoker's cough. After she regained her breath, the detectives heard her blow her nose and then she was straight down to business. 'OK. First up, the dog hair. Doesn't match the hair found on the victim.' She laughed. 'How many kelpies are left up there to sample? Surely you'll run out soon!'

'We'll get the other five thousand samples down to you by the end of next week,' Bowker replied with a grin. 'What about the baseball bat? It relates to the same suspect as the dog hair.'

'The blood on the bat is not human. Combination of greyhound and possum, would you believe? There were also fragments of greyhound and possum hair embedded in the bat's wood grain, meaning that these animals were probably bashed with it. The techs also found a few kelpie hairs on the surface of the handle that matched the sample you sent. They were most likely left there by incidental contact rather than the dog being mistreated.'

'The bastard trains greyhounds and he's already been in trouble with the authorities for cruelty and live baiting,' Bowker replied. 'We'll pass on your report to the powers-that-be.'

'Did you have any luck with the walking stick?' Holmes asked.

'Just getting to that,' O'Meara replied. 'Being in the water for a few days made the process a bit difficult, but we managed to lift three sets of prints. One lot we can't match to anyone on the National Database. They were of a left hand and overlapped the prints belonging to the other two. This person was almost certainly the last one to handle the stick. Find who owns those prints and I reckon you're well on your way to nailing your killer.'

'I assume one of the other sets belonged to the victim,' Bowker asked.

'Correctamundo, Gregory,' O'Meara replied.

'And the third?' Bowker asked, anticipating a breakthrough.

'They were very faint, but they belong to the victim's wife. Arabella Jean Rice.'

Holmes frowned at Bowker with a puzzled look. 'We haven't fingerprinted that stuck-up bitch.'

'Her prints were on file,' O'Meara replied. 'We traced her name changes through Birth Deaths and Marriages. She had a series of historical convictions in the sixties for soliciting for the purposes of prostitution.'

CHAPTER 20

Monday dawned wet and windy. A strong northerly brought low dark cloud in from the north west and whipped heavy rain sideways across the freeway in front of the detectives. In spite of the enhanced safety provided by a divided road, the conditions were still treacherous. The massive tyres of semitrailers and B Double's generated clouds of swirling mist, and overtaking these mechanical monsters meant taking a leap into the unknown. Windscreen wipers struggled to move the massive quantities of water thrown up from the trucks and any obstacle on the road ahead, an animal, a shredded truck tyre, a stalled car, would be impossible to see, much less avoid. But at least Bowker drew some comfort from knowing that there was no oncoming traffic. This hadn't been the case a few years earlier when he'd travelled with a young constable on a narrow country road in similar conditions. The pair had followed a cattle truck for miles, when inexplicably the young officer had lost patience on a steep rise and pulled out to overtake across double lines. By the time Bowker could react, the car had passed the point of no return and he watched helplessly as they speared headlong into the swirling white maelstrom on the wrong side of the road. If death was to come, it would come without warning, the detective thought. An oncoming Land Cruiser materialised from the haze just as the police car cleared the front of the truck and swerved back into the left lane. The constable said nothing, putting on his left-hand indicator and pulling over into a farm gateway allowing the truck to roar past him. His hands shook as he looked at Bowker, his face ashen and his eyes damp. 'You'll have to drive sir,' he mouthed several times.

There was no sign of a break in the weather when they reached the Benalla police station, forcing the detectives to scurry quickly from the car park to the shelter of the building. They found Fleming and Larsen in the CID squad room on the second floor in discussion with uniformed colleagues about the robbery of a tobacco store that had occurred over the weekend. Larsen was wearing tight shiny black leggings, a white lacy top and high heels. Her face lit up when the homicide officers entered the room, but Bowker noticed her eyes never left Holmes.

'Some action in the town over the weekend, by the sounds of it,' Bowker said.

'Break-in at a tobacco and gift shop in the main street,' Fleming replied. 'A few cartons of smokes stolen, along with a big figurine of some bloody mythical dragon.' He shook his head. 'Who buys that shit anyway?'

'Any suspects?' Holmes asked, looking at Larsen.

'They've already been charged and in the lock up,' Larsen replied proudly. 'Your mates, Noel Sanderson and Glen Brown.'

Bowker was amazed. 'That was quick. Did they just walk in and confess?'

'May as well have,' Larsen replied. 'Brown posted a selfie of himself on Facebook holding up the dragon inside the darkened tobacco shop. We picked him up and went around to Sanderson's dive and found the cigarettes stacked in his passage.' She chuckled. 'And people accuse coppers of being dumb.'

Bowker laughed then invited the local members of their team to the makeshift operations room along the corridor. Larsen entered the room first and Holmes quickly sat beside her when she took a seat on the far side of the table. Bowker spent the next fifteen minutes bringing the locals up to speed on the new avenue of investigation.

At the end of Bowker's spiel, Fleming leaned back in his chair and exhaled loudly. 'So the long and the short of it, is that you left here last Wednesday with one unsolved murder and now you arrive back with three.' He shook his head. 'If the coppers back then couldn't see a murder, what makes you think we can do anything about it forty years later?'

Holmes folded his hands on the table and Bowker noticed that he'd dispensed with the wedding ring he was wearing when he was picked up earlier that morning. 'Rather than complicating things,' Holmes said, 'I reckon these other deaths might be our key to solving the Rice case.'

Fleming was far from convinced. 'So where to from here? Send a forensic team up to The Granite,' he asked sarcastically.

Bowker ignored the comment. 'After lunch, Sherlock and I will go through the list of those attending the school reunion. We'll narrow down the names to those who would have been around Benalla as adults when the Oosterman saga occurred.'

Fleming seemed relieved. 'If you don't need us for the moment, that'll work out well. The ceramic mural by the lake has been vandalized, again.' He paused for a moment and looked at Bowker. 'It may not be a big murder case, but at least it's solvable,' he added as an afterthought.

Larsen stood up from the table, ostensibly steadying herself with a hand on Holmes's shoulder. 'If there's anything you need, just yell out.' She collected the notepad she had in front of her and left the room.

Fleming watched her leave then raised his eyebrows and said quietly. 'If I was twenty years younger and not married with kids…..' Holmes looked away then stared down at the tabletop, as Fleming continued. 'She's a good detective with a keen mind. Has a real knack in getting confessions out of even the toughest of blokes. Somehow, she gets them to think with their dick rather than their brain, and next thing you know they're signing away their freedom with a big smile on their face.' He chuckled as he stood and exited the room.

Luckily the record of attendees at the reunion contained one column that provided all the information the detectives were seeking. Its header requested the years the participant studied or taught at Benalla High School. Many of those at the function had left that blank, suggesting they were a guest of someone associated with the school. The names of any persons who were enrolled at the time or after the death of Paul Oosterman were discarded by the detectives as being too young to have been involved in any foul play, leaving only those who had left school prior to the apparent suicide on the slopes of The Granite. Bowker took a ruler and drew a pencil line through the attendees who they determined fell outside their parameters. But one name he was about to delete stopped him in his tracks and exposed a flaw in their logic.

'Fuck, fuck, fuck,' Bowker exclaimed as he threw his pencil down and leant back in his chair. 'I was about to put a line through Brian Gottfried.' He looked at Holmes. 'Remember, he was the Lands Department officer here at the time of Paul Oosterman's death and according to Oosterman's sister the two hated each other. Oosterman reckoned Gottfried had the hots for his wife and apparently the two had clashed physically at one of the district dances. Gottfried served a number of notices on him for noxious weeds, so there was no love lost there.' Bowker leant forward and tapped the entry on the list. 'He didn't go to school in Benalla, but his wife did. She left three years after the Oosterman death so I was about to cross them both off. Gottfried was in his early thirties when he was here. Fuck, he must have been a cradle snatcher.'

'Yeah, probably thirteen or fourteen years difference,' Holmes shot back. 'Could have been worse, I suppose. Could have been seventeen or eighteen.'

Bowker winced internally, but then pointed at the sheet in front of him. 'They're obviously still together and probably as happy as pigs in mud,' he said, trying to make the best of his faux pas. 'Let's extend that period of schooling for the women to five years past the time of Oosterman's death so we pick up those sorts of relationships, but it's unlikely there'll be too many others like Gottfried.'

At the end of the exercise, the detectives had pruned the list to thirty-two. 'I think we can scratch the women,' Holmes suggested. 'Dennis Lowther is adamant the person he saw following Rice by the lake that night was a male. Plus, if Rice's murder is tied to the Oosterman business, I can't see a woman shooting our mate halfway up a rocky hill.'

Bowker nodded in agreement. 'Yeah. I reckon you're right.' He drew a line through the women's names. He counted those left. 'That leaves us with ten blokes if you don't count Gary Rice.'

'Shit, that was a savage cull. So twenty-three of the thirty-two were women?'

'Yep. A lot of them came on their own, either by choice or because their husbands didn't make it for one reason or another.' He didn't think it politic to add that most men marry women who are younger than them, and die at an earlier age. By the look on his partner's face, Bowker knew Holmes was probably thinking that himself.

'So who have we got left?' Holmes asked.

'Mick Sargood, Dan Wetherall, Sid Wilson, Graham Tucker, Brian Gottfried, Selby Allen, Gerry Brady, Ian Carthew, William Downie and Charlie Benbow.'

'Other than Gottfried, do we know anything about the rest of them?'

Bowker took a notebook from his coat pocket. 'Ron Cloverdale mentioned a few of those blokes being at the reunion.' Bowker flipped through the pages until he found the notes he was looking for. 'Sargood is apparently an old cocky from out near Lurg where the Oostermans once lived. Carthew is a former wool classer and Wetherall is an ex-butcher.' He looked from his notes to Holmes. 'And I've known Sid Wilson since I was a kid. He lived on a farm in the lane opposite our place. He's a stock agent, so he was one of dad's mates. Used to be with Goldsboroughs before they merged with Elders. Now he's out on his own. He'd have to be one of the oldest agents in the state I reckon.'

Holmes consulted their list. 'So we know nothing about Tucker, Allen, Benbow or Brady?'

Bowker shook his head. 'Not yet. But we'll need to talk to them all unless something breaks first.' He thought for a moment. 'I think I'll give Sid another ring. If anyone knows who these blokes are, it will be him.' The detective took out his mobile, consulted the list of recent calls and punched the call button. He looked at Holmes while the phone dialled. 'If he's out looking at stock we'll be lucky to get hold of him.'

Wilson answered. 'Sid, here.'

'G'day Sid. Greg Bowker. I need to pick your brains again.'

'What can I do for you this time, young fella,' Wilson replied cheerily.

'We're still investigating Gary Rice's death, but we're not getting very far,' Bowker replied. 'I've got the names of four blokes around your vintage who were at the school reunion a couple of Saturdays ago. I've got one of my colleagues here beside me, so I'll put you on speaker so I don't have to repeat everything.'

'Fine with me, mate. I can probably name most of the blokes you'd be asking about. There were about ten or twelve, but tell us who you need the good oil on.'

'Let's start with Graham Tucker,' Bowker replied.

Wilson chuckled. 'Ah, Friar Tucker, as we used to call him. Left school at the end of fourth form and got an apprenticeship in the air force working with aeroplane engines. Nobody from around here had seen him since school until he turned up at the big shebang. His mum was a widow and when Friar left to start his course at the Williamson base in New South, she moved to Melbourne. To be near her sister, from memory. Her husband was a livestock carrier and most of the agents around here used his trucks to transport animals. Sheep mainly, but occasionally cattle. After he was killed in a big smash up near Wang, she only hung around Benalla until her son finished school.'

Bowker shook his head at Holmes who scrawled a line through Tucker's name. He hadn't been in the district when Oosterman died. 'What about Selby Allen?'

'Got a job on the railways when he left school. According to what he said at the dinner, he quit that when he got married and moved onto his in-law's grape block up around Mildura somewhere. Trains the odd trotter, his missus said. Got four kids apparently.' He chortled. 'Just between you and me, I reckon Selby must have knocked her up with the first one. He was pretty good-lookin' in his day, but his wife has a face that would send a steam train up a dirt track.'

Holmes had to bite his knuckle not to laugh as he put a line through Selby's name. 'Charlie Benbow?' he asked.

'Charlie's still around. Fourth or fifth generation farmer at

Boho South, up towards Strathbogie. Left school as soon as he could. Good bloke. See him at the sheep markets occasionally.'

Bowker made a face to Holmes indicating an interest in speaking to Mr Benbow. He could stay on the list for now. 'What about Gerry Brady?'

'He still lives in the district too. Sour old bastard with a chip on his shoulder.'

Bowker looked at Holmes and raised his eyebrows.

Wilson continued. 'Can't blame the poor bugger though. Got polio as a kid. Been on crutches or in a wheelchair ever since. Had a job at the post office for a while sorting mail.'

Bowker shook his head sadly as his colleague deleted Brady's name. There was no way he could have killed Oosterman halfway up the steep slope of The Granite and his disability would have been obvious to Lowther if he'd followed Rice by the lake. 'The last one we know nothing about is William Downie?'

'Never heard of him,' Wilson replied quickly.

'He didn't go to school here, but his wife did.' Bowker read from the original attendee list. 'A Glenda Downie, nee Wilkinson.'

'Oh, Glenda Wilkinson. She was a sexy little piece, three or four years behind me at school. She was the town bike before she married a visiting Presbyterian minister from Melbourne. Fair bit older than she was, if my memory serves me correctly. Surprised he's still alive, to tell you the truth. I thought Glenda would have killed the old bastard by now. Not a bad way to go, though.' He laughed.

Holmes deleted Downie from their list. 'There were three other blokes there that Ron Cloverdale said he saw talking to Gary Rice,' Bowker said.

'Rotten Ronny?' Wilson replied with a chortle. 'Good bloke. One of my best clients. If he ever put on a kilt, you'd reckon he was Braveheart or some mad Scotsman. Especially if he came out of the mist up there in Tatong on a winters morning.' He chuckled again at his own words. 'Who'd he spot at the do? They'd have to be locals. He wouldn't have a clue about the blokes we've just spoken about. Except for old Gerry perhaps. Or maybe Charlie Benbow. We all went through school well before Ronny's time.'

Bowker reeled off the three names left on his list. Wilson's pen picture of town residents Dan Wetherall the ex-butcher, and Ian Carthew the former wool classer, raised no flags but they'd need to be interviewed just to make sure. Mick Sargood, the farmer from Lurg was a different story.

'Mick is an old bachelor from out at Upper Lurg,' Wilson said. 'His property adjoins *Melaleuca Springs* where the Cashmans live now. They bought it from the Oostermans after Paul topped himself and the family left the district. Mick reckons the Cashmans are the ants' pants compared with Paul Oosterman.'

'They didn't get on, I take it?' Bowker replied.

'They had a few blues about boundary fences and stray stock over the years. What riled Mick was Oosterman calling him a poofter because he wasn't married and lived on his own. Nobody could give a dead rat's clacker nowadays, but back then that was a malicious thing to call a bloke. Especially out here in the bush.'

'Is he gay?' Holmes asked.

'There's always been rumours. As a young bloke he was a good lookin' rooster and the eligible ladies of the district threw everything at him bar their garters. Probably them as well, but all to no avail. Nobody has ever seen him with a woman, but that doesn't prove anything. He used to go to Melbourne pretty often which created its share of gossip, but I know a few other blokes who went to Melbourne a lot too and they were visiting ladies of the night. So who knows? Who cares really?'

'Did you notice Gary Rice speaking to any of the men we've mentioned?' Bowker asked.

'I reckon he spoke to just about everyone who was there. Those he knew from school anyway.'

'Did he mention the family history he was writing?'

'Yeah. He was carrying on about how he'd turned up new information about Paul Oosterman's suicide, but most of the blokes were half-pissed and couldn't give a rat's arse about his family.' Wilson was quiet for a moment with the sound of sheep bleating and dogs barking in the background. 'Got to go mate. I've got a lamb buyer with me and the sheep are just coming into the yards.'

Bowker thanked the agent and hit the red disconnect icon. 'What do you reckon Sherlock?'

Holmes pushed the list of names towards Bowker who looked down noticing that his colleague had circled the initials of one particular individual. Mick Sargood. Bowker raised his eyebrows. 'MS. The letters on the key tag in Oosterman's kitchen. Perhaps I went a bit early assuming it related to *Melaleuca Springs*.'

'Most likely a coincidence, but it's food for thought.'

'If there was no love lost between Sargood and Oosterman,' Bowker replied, 'then it's definitely worth a trip out to Lurg in the morning to see what he's got to say.' He looked at his watch. 'In what's left of the afternoon we may as well pay Wetherall and Carthew a visit.'

The detectives found both men to be amiable chaps, but of little value in their investigation. Both recalled Rice speaking about his family history but had little interest in hearing the details of his research. Carthew had never classed wool at either of the Oosterman properties, and only knew of the family by reputation. Wetherall remembered Rice addressing Oosterman's death, but the conversation had been side tracked by news that Benalla was about to appoint a recently retired Collingwood player as the team's next coach. A nauseous wife had caused Wetherall to leave the reunion earlier than his old mates. He put his wife's condition down to the wine that had flowed freely during the evening, particularly down her throat.

'We can put a line through him as well as Carthew unless something else comes up,' Bowker said as they walked to the car.

Holmes's mobile phone rang. He removed it from his breast pocket, glanced at the screen and smiled. He leant on the roof of the car as Bowker climbed into the vehicle on the other side. After a minute or so, Holmes opened the passenger door and clambered into his seat. 'That was Kirsten. She's suggested a counter-tea at The Royal. I told her we had nothing planned and we'd meet her in the bistro at six-thirty. That alright with you?'

'Sounds like a plan. I've heard they put on a good spread,' Bowker replied cheerily, knowing his partner would be more than happy to meet the detective constable on his own.

CHAPTER 21

arsen was sitting on a stool at the bar when the casually dressed homicide pair arrived at The Royal. She had exchanged her shiny leggings and lacy top for a black mini dress, the hem of which was riding up her long legs as she sat with her high heels resting on the foot rail of the stool. After a round of drinks, the trio adjourned to a table in the bistro and ordered their meals with a teenage waitress. While waiting for their food, they discussed the Rice case and the possible connection to Denise Oosterman's disappearance and her husband's apparent suicide. Bowker's mail about the quality of the hotel's food had been spot on and following the clearing of plates, he made his way to the bar to buy the next round. On his return, he found Holmes and Larsen on their feet. 'We're off to the gaming room to take on the pokies,' Holmes said. 'Never know, could be our lucky night. You interested in risking a few dollars, mate?'

Bowker handed a drink to each colleague. 'Nah, you guys go for your life. I'll sit here and finish my drink then wander back to the motel and ring Rachael.'

'I'll catch you in an hour or so mate,' Holmes replied.

'See you at work, Greg,' Larsen added.

Bowker raised his hand in acknowledgement and sipped his

Diet Coke. Holmes and Larsen wandered off into the pokies room with Bowker suspecting that wasn't be only game being played that night.

Bowker had the perception he'd been asleep for less than an hour when he was woken by Holmes opening the door. 'Hit the Jackpot did you mate?' he said, rubbing his eyes in the darkened room. Holmes didn't reply. 'To tell you the truth, I didn't think I'd see you until the morning the way you and Kirsten had cozied up.'

Holmes dragged open the curtains and bright sunlight flooded the room. Bowker threw a hand over his eyes. 'Fuck mate! What time is it?'

'Bit after seven,' Holmes replied as he unbuttoned his shirt.

Bowker lifted his phone from the bedside table and double checked. 'Shit. I thought it was about midnight.' He rubbed his eyes again. 'So obviously you did hit the jackpot.'

Holmes smiled. 'Not on the pokies, if that's what you're referring to.'

'How long did you stay at the pub after I left?'

'About ten minutes. Fifteen p'haps.'

'Not feeling lucky?' Bowker replied as he lifted off the doona and sat on the side of his bed in his boxer shorts.

Holmes slipped off his shirt and exchanged it for a clean business shirt from a hanger. 'Not a big fan of gambling. Neither is Kirsten, as it turns out.'

Bowker just nodded as he stood up. 'Mind if I pinch the shower?'

'Go for it. I had one before I came back.'

I bet it was a good one too, Bowker thought but didn't say. If Holmes wanted to elaborate on his night's adventure, then that was up to him to bring it up.

'What's on the agenda today?' Holmes asked. 'Out to Lurg to talk to the 1981 Bachelor of the Year?'

'Michael Sargood. Yeah. We'll go out via Kilfeera Road and I'll show you the farm where I was brought up.'

Holmes nodded, then spoke hesitantly. 'You know Rice's family history stuff that's in the back of the car? Do you mind if Kirsten takes a look at it? You know, another set of eyes.'

Bowker shrugged, wondering where this had come from. 'Sounds like a good idea. Can't do any harm that's for sure.' He walked towards the bathroom.

'It's just that she doesn't really feel part of the investigation. Except for the original Lowther interview with me, she and Fleming have only been involved in the updates.'

Bowker turned to face his colleague. 'Does Fleming feel the same way?'

'Not according to Kirsten. She says he's happy to sail along and leave the legwork to us.'

'I suspected that. We'll drop the boxes into the station before we leave for Lurg. Kirsten can review the stuff to her heart's content. There's so much of it, there's bound to be something I've missed.' He turned back towards the bathroom.

'Thanks mate. Appreciate it.'

Bowker wasn't sure why Holmes should be thanking him, but suspected pleasing Detective Constable Larsen was a higher priority than double checking the information.

The handover of the two boxes was completed with exaggerated professionalism between Holmes and Larsen, with just a surreptitious tap on the young detective's backside the only overt sign of affection Bowker was able to detect between the two. The journey out of Benalla took them past the aerodrome to the east. When they reached the gateway to his old farm, Bowker pulled off the side of the road. He pointed to the left. 'That's the house I was brought up in, mate. The new owners took me through it after Dad had sold the home paddock to fund the new build in town. It was hard to recognise, it had so many walls taken out and features added.'

'Lost its rural charm?'

Bowker laughed. 'Wasn't much rural charm left when we last had it. Old lath and plaster walls where the render would fall away if it was damaged, which happened pretty regularly with two boys in the house. I remember a bat used to live in our bedroom wall and it would occasionally come out at night and flit around the room. You could feel the breeze being fanned by his wings.' Bowker laughed. 'Sounds like Dad and Dave when you think about it now. But gee we had some fun as kids. Besides all the stuff on horses, we made tree houses, made rafts for the dam out of forty-four gallon drums, climbed up the top of the windmill, trapped rabbits.' He looked at Holmes. 'Never once missed having an iPad or a mobile phone.'

'It's a wonder you two survived,' Holmes replied.

Bowker nodded. 'I wonder too, sometimes, when I think about what we got up to.' He pointed out his driver's side window to a track opposite that headed to the south. 'That's Standish's Lane. It runs all the way down to Hollands Creek. That house you can see used to belong to Sid Wilson, the stock agent we were talking to yesterday. He had a couple of hundred acres where he used to punt cattle. You know, buy a pen-full when he thought they were going cheap then sell them when prices rose. That was the plan, anyway.' He swept his arm to the south. 'Standish's owned the property on the other side of the lane all the way down to the river. Alex and I used to ride our horses down to the creek and go fishing. Or shoot a few rabbits or ducks or bronzewing pigeons.'

'Boys' own adventure stuff, by the sounds of it,' Holmes replied. 'It was similar up at Murrayville, except there weren't too many creeks up there.'

'I can remember one year there'd been a shitload of rain and rivers were in flood right across the north east. Both the Broken and the Hollands had broken their banks and half the paddocks were underwater. My brother and I decided it would be a fun idea to see how far we could get down the lane before the water got too deep for our horses.' He laughed. 'Bad move.'

Leaden clouds hung low overhead with more rain imminent. Either side of the lane, stock stood in raised islands above the sheets of water covering most of the paddock surrounding them. The track down the lane was gravelled and raised above the waterline as far as the gateway into Sid Wilson's property. Judging by the cars behind his house, Sid was home, his Ford ute and lime green Celica parked side-by-side in the large lake that was the back yard and as close as possible to the backstep of the house. There were cattle and a chestnut thoroughbred gelding in the house paddock, so the front gate was closed. The first obstacle the young Bowker brothers encountered was one they had negotiated many times before. A massive red gum had fallen several years prior, cutting off the lane beyond Wilson's entrance. The giant tree had not died and had sprouted a wall of small vertical branches from its horizontal trunk. The tree had once stood close to Wilson's fence and while some of its roots remained in the earth, its massive base was now perpendicular to the ground with a tangle of broken roots protruding towards the fence. A horse and rider had room to squeeze between the roots and the barbed wire topped fence only if the rider lifted both feet atop the horse's wither.

With the fallen tree successfully negotiated, the pair splashed through fetlock-deep water, the older brother's grey mare becoming flightier with each step. After half a mile with spits of rain blowing in on the stiffening northerly, they cantered the mares sending spray in all directions. By this point, the fence bordering the Standish property was on its side and the lane was effectively subsumed into the paddocks adjoining. Ahead was a green knoll above the water level where hay had been fed to cattle and the remnants formed golden discs on the sodden grass. Greg's grey mare's ears twitched back and forwards, her eyes widened and she snorted loudly, sending strings of saliva into the air. Her rider recognised the signs immediately. The horse's disposition had changed, and he knew her actions were now unpredictable. While the younger brother walked his toffee-coloured mare past the hay, the grey mare would have none of it. Head down and walking backwards against her rider's furious urgings, somewhere in her mind she made the decision that home was the safest place to be. She spun in a half circle, reared up then bolted back down the lane.

For Greg, the first half mile was fun. His steed was in a full stretch gallop, water was being thrown up in all direction and both horse and rider quickly became saturated. He saw himself in the Marlboro cigarette ad on television, where the Marlboro Man galloped his horse in slow motion through the shallows on a beach, sending spray up over himself and the palomino he was riding. This wasn't the first time Connie had bolted and the scenario was always the same. She was spooked by something entirely of her own imagination and had taken off, her hard mouth making her difficult for any rider to manage. The fact that she was an uncontrollable bolter probably explained why the boys' father had bought such a beautiful looking horse so cheap. Usually with these episodes, once she was in the home paddock she would gradually slow down and come to a full stop at the rear of the house where she had been saddled. No doubt the same thing would transpire today, Greg thought. But suddenly the reality of the situation struck the teenager. Getting home wasn't a simple gallop across a few paddocks. Three major problems needed to be solved within the next minute or so. The furthest obstacle was the closed gate into the farm. Just prior to that, the Kilfeera Road needed to be safely crossed, a task filled with danger at any time, let alone at a full gallop with possible road traffic intersecting at speeds of sixty miles an hour. But the problem at the forefront of the boy's mind was the fallen red gum. If the tree hadn't sprouted branches it would have still been a hell of a jump for his mare to negotiate, but the thicket of regrowth created a wall of timber ten or twelve feet tall. For the horse to retrace her steps around the end of the fallen tree was equally impossible at a full gallop, certainly with him still aboard on the other side.

In the few hundred metres of thinking time he had left, he resolved to steer the mare straight at the middle of the fallen tree. His hope was that common sense would prevail, at the same time accepting he was pinning his hopes on a quality his horse was normally short on. The mare pricked her ears when she saw the obstacle looming closer but there was no slowing down. Greg felt her change legs as she approached the fallen tree and the boy sensed her readying herself to jump. She'll hit the wall of branches halfway up, he thought as they approached the point of no return. Then to his amazement, the mare applied the brakes, skidding the last ten metres on the slippery ground to stand quivering with her head in the foliage of the gum. The lad climbed slowly from his trembling mount and took a short grip on the reins under her jaw. He patted her on the neck to assure her all was well and resolved to lead her home. Ten seconds later his younger brother arrived at a flat gallop but totally in control. 'Geez, that was fun,' he said with a wide smile.

The detectives were on Brocks Road and on a beeline to The Granite by the time Bowker had finished the narrative of his mad ride through the floodwaters.

'We didn't have horses on our place in the Mallee,' Holmes said. 'We had farm bikes. A lot bloody safer than something with a mind of its own.'

'Sometimes that mind comes in handy, mate. Never heard of a horse galloping head-first into the trunk of a tree.'

Holmes nodded. 'I s'pose there's good and bad with both.' He looked out his side window. 'What'd you say is the name of Sargood's place?'

'*Granite View*, according to the senior sergeant on the front desk. He said it's to the Glenrowan side of *Melaleuca Springs*.'

As they followed a sweeping bend to their right, Holmes hunched his neck and pointed through the windscreen towards a stony hill rising up ahead of them. 'I presume that's The Granite.'

'That's it Sherlock. Hasn't moved for billions of years.'

'I'm underwhelmed,' Holmes replied. 'I expected something more like Hanging Rock with massive stone monoliths.'

'Sorry mate. It's just a big rocky hill covered in scrub. We'll have a closer look on the way back. I'll take you up to where Alex and I found Oosterman, if I can remember the way.'

Holmes upturned his palms. 'Shit mate. We're not really dressed for mountain climbing.'

Bowker laughed. 'It's not exactly Everest. Just a nice walk in the bush.'

Holmes took another look at the sharply rising slope. 'Yeah, I believe you,' he said sarcastically. 'Thousands wouldn't, but I do.' There was a pause. 'It looks pretty steep. Don't forget we're not teenage kids anymore.'

'We're both still pretty fit,' Bowker replied. 'Unless you're totally shagged out.'

Holmes didn't answer.

Granite View was set among rolling hills that were a light brown at this time of year but in autumn would remind an English visitor of the old country. The homestead sat at the end of a long elm-lined driveway. The residence was an old, but well-maintained weatherboard with a verandah on all sides. It stood in extensive gardens and spacious lawns with The Granite rising up behind to provide a dramatic backdrop. Several sheds were a few hundred metres away. With the car windows down, the detectives could hear dogs barking and the occasional deep bellow of cattle. Beyond the sheds at the end of a dirt track, they found an elderly man drenching cattle in a small complex of steel yards set under a line of shady oaks. The man released an angus steer from the crush, placed his drenching gear atop a fence post and wandered over to where the officers had parked their vehicle.

'Can I do something for you fellas?' the old man said, removing a battered straw hat with the crown missing. He smiled. 'By the way you're dressed, I assume you're lost.' He was short in stature, no more than five-foot-eight or nine. He was almost entirely bald, with just a small arc of hair around the back of his head. He wore a goatee beard that was in need of a trim, and black horn-rimmed glasses tied on with elastic behind his head. His attire was a typical farmer's outfit of jeans, a worn-out long-sleeved shirt and elastic sided boots that had seen more than their day. Like his boots, the legs of his pants were caked in cow manure and provided a congregation point for a thousand flies. Two blue heelers yapped at his side.

Bowker proffered his right hand. 'I'm Detective Inspector Greg Bowker of the homicide squad and this is Detective Sergeant Holmes. I presume you are Michael Sargood.'

The old man was puzzled as he shook the officers' hands. 'That's right. My friends call me Mick. What brings homicide detectives out this way? I can only presume it has to do with Gary Rice.'

Bowker nodded and put his hands in his pockets. 'You guessed it in one. We're just having a chat with anyone who was at the school reunion the night he died.'

Sargood slapped away the flies with his hat. 'Not sure I can help you much, but I'm happy to try.'

'You speak to Rice that night?' Holmes asked.

'Yes. A lot of us did. He taught most of us many years ago,' Sargood replied. 'I think he was in his first year of teaching when I finished school at the end of Form 5.' He thought for a moment. 'I also knew him when we were kids, but he was a half a dozen years older than me of course. His father had a property over at Tatong and dad knew him through Apex. Even if they didn't go to school together, back then a lot of the country kids got to know each other through the annual Molyullah sports.'

'What was the topic of conversation at the reunion?' Bowker asked.

Sargood brushed away more flies. 'Old times mainly. As you'd imagine at a do like that.'

'Did he mention he was writing a family history?' Bowker then asked.

The farmer nodded. 'Yes. He said he'd been through some old papers and come up with the theory that my former neighbour Paul Oosterman had been murdered. But I don't think anybody took much notice of him. The police had investigated it and there'd been a coroner's inquest.'

Bowker took his hands from his pockets and folded his arms across his chest. A pair of white cockatoos screeched loudly as they dipped down overhead. 'How'd you get on with Mr Oosterman?'

Sargood chuckled. 'I can see where you're going with this. You reckon I might have killed Oosterman and then murdered Gary Rice forty years later to shut him up.'

'I'm not accusing you of anything Mr Sargood,' Bowker

replied seriously. 'I'm just interested in how you got on with Paul Oosterman.'

Sargood used a palm to wipe the top of his head. 'Everybody in the district knew we didn't get on. He was a prick of a bloke and not much of a farmer either. His stock were always getting onto the road or into my property. He refused to share the cost of replacing boundary fences and wouldn't do anything to stop the spread of noxious weeds into my place. Not even when the Lands Department served notices on him.'

'And I hear he abused and insulted you personally as well?' Holmes asked.

Sargood laughed under his breath. 'That was his style. Get angry and abuse people.' He looked directly into Bowker's eyes. 'I'll tell you something else too, detective. His wife Denise never ran away.' He pointed towards *Melaleuca Springs*. 'She'll be buried somewhere on that farm next door.'

Holmes leant against the car. 'What makes you so sure?' he asked.

'Just a feeling in the gut,' Sargood replied. 'The way he treated her, the way she disappeared without a trace, the way she's never been heard of again.'

Bowker leant against the car beside Holmes. 'You say you agree with the police that Oosterman committed suicide. But why would he do that if he was such a self-centred bastard? Surely not over the disappearance of his wife, especially if he had killed her himself as you suspect.'

Sargood shrugged. 'Dunno. I've never thought too much about it. As I said, the police concluded it was suicide, so did the coroner, so I just assume they got it right. Denise's disappearance on the other hand was pretty open-ended. People just assumed she'd run away with no evidence to back it up.'

'Were you worried when Gary Rice suggested that Oosterman had been murdered?' Holmes asked.

'I thought it was an interesting theory. But worried? No. Why would I be?'

'There are police photos of Oosterman's kitchen. They were taken after his body was found,' Bowker said. 'In one of them there's a key tag with MS written on it. We thought maybe that stood for Michael Sargood. Or Mick Sargood to his friends.'

Sargood shook his head. 'Wouldn't have been mine. Never used tags on my keys. I've only ever had four. One for the car, one for the ute, one for the tractor and one for the house. They're all different shapes so why put tags on them? If you lose one, it only tells the finder where to go to pinch stuff. Besides, I wasn't in the district the weekend Paul Oosterman died.'

Holmes and Bowker exchanged looks. 'OK,' Bowker said slowly. 'Where were you?'

Sargood exhaled heavily. 'I was at a thirtieth birthday celebration over that long weekend. At a holiday house in Lorne.'

'Family, friends, someone we can check with just so we can exclude you from our enquiries?' Bowker asked.

'Let's not play games with this, detective. If you've interviewed a series of people around my age, you will have heard rumours concerning my lifestyle. Well they're true. I am a gay man. For most of my life I have had to hide my sexuality to survive in a rural area like this. I've done better than many others in my situation. I haven't taken my own life, although I'd hate to think how many times I've contemplated it.' He sighed loudly. 'At least in the twenty first century we can talk about these things in an honest and open way.' He chuckled to himself. 'A religious man I know in Melbourne says he has more difficulty telling his friends he's a Christian than he does telling them he's gay. How things have changed, eh?'

'Thank goodness most of that crap is behind us,' Bowker said. 'But unfortunately, we've still got a way to go with a lot of people.'

'I can give you the names of men I remember were in Lorne that weekend. Being a birthday party, and at that particular location, will no doubt jog a few memories.' Sargood again exhaled loudly. 'Unfortunately, at least two have passed away since that time.' A blue heeler bitch jumped up and put her front paws on the old farmer's hip, licking the back of his hand and looking for attention. Sargood patted her on the head. 'You're a good girl, aren't you Lucy?'

Holmes pointed to the other heeler, now laying on the ground behind his master. 'What's the other bloke's name?'

'Bluey,' Sargood replied with a chuckle. 'Pretty imaginative, eh?'

'Got any other dogs?' Bowker asked.

'Na. Just these two,' the farmer replied.

'No kelpies?' Bowker asked.

Sargood shook his head. 'Nuh. Only run cattle. No need for kelpies.'

Sargood led them back to the house and furnished them with the names and contact details of five men who he remembered were with him in Lorne the weekend of Oosterman's death. Bowker folded the written details and placed the sheet in his trouser pocket, doubting there was any value in making contact. He was already convinced that Sargood wasn't their man.

CHAPTER 22

The Granite towered above as the detectives clambered through the wire fence and surveyed the climb confronting them. Clouds drifted across the blue sky overhead creating the illusion that the hill itself was moving. A murder of crows squawked appropriately in a tree nearby and two hawks circled high above. It didn't take long for Bowker to locate the semblance of an animal track he hoped would lead up the slope. Within fifty metres it had disappeared, leaving the policemen to bush bash their way through the scrub. Bowker was surprised by how much he remembered from his last climb off the hill on that fateful day four decades prior. He eventually led Holmes to the sheer rock wall that had punctuated the boys' descent and it was just a matter of following it laterally until he located the site where Paul Oosterman had died. Although it was more overgrown than he remembered, the rocky overhang made the spot unmistakable.

'This is where Alex and I found him.' Bowker dropped to his haunches and motioned with his hands. 'He was laying crossways with his head down here. The rifle was in his right hand with the butt near that rock. You couldn't see the poor bastard for flies. And the stench. You have no idea mate.' He chuckled. 'Although after your years in Homicide you probably do.'

Holmes scratched his cheek as he assessed the bush around him. 'If it was murder, how the fuck did the killer get him up here without him bolting into all this scrub?'

'Maybe Oosterman climbed up here on his own and the killer followed after. Or maybe Oosterman knew his killer and assumed they were just chasing rabbits and foxes.' Bowker stood up and pointed to a spot. 'I'm sure there was a more defined track back then. Alex followed it down looking for help, and we both used it when we took off home to tell our folks.' Bowker placed his hands on his hips and surveyed the slope above him. 'Oosterman's sister said that Denise occasionally climbed to the top when things were getting her down at home. So there'd have to have been a better track back then. I can't see her picking her way through the scrub each time.'

Holmes nodded and stretched his back.

'How are you feeling?' Bowker asked. 'Fancy a climb to the top? Magnificent view from up there.'

Holmes shrugged. 'We've come this far so we may as well keep going.' He smiled. 'I'm sure you'll entertain me on the way up with more stories of your teenage escapades.'

Bowker chuckled as he pushed his way around the base of the rock wall. 'As a matter of fact, we did whistle up a fox the same day we found Oosterman.'

After twenty-five minutes of scratches and grazes they were standing on a flat rock at the summit, transfixed by the 360-degree Panorama. Passing clouds cast moving shadows over the patchwork landscape that stretched to infinity. The two men said nothing for several minutes, happy to just take in the vista.

'Worth the climb, eh?' Bowker finally said.

'Bloody specky alright,' Holmes replied without looking at his partner. 'Don't get views like this in the Mallee, that's for sure.'

Bowker sat down on the ground and stared out towards the Australian Alps. 'You can't blame Denise Oosterman if she came up here to get away from it all.'

Holmes sat down beside him and nothing was said for a minute or two. 'We haven't got a lot of irons left in the fire with this case, have we?'

'Can't disagree there, mate,' Bowker replied. 'But we still haven't spoken to Mr Gottfried, our Lands Department mate. He was likely present when Gary Rice was spouting forth about Oosterman's suicide being a possible case of murder.'

'Well if he comes up clean, we're basically rooted,' Holmes said.

'Yeah. The term "square one" comes to mind.'

Holmes sighed loudly. 'Maybe we're just chasing shadows trying to connect the Oostermans to the Rice killing. It's highly probable Rice's murder has nothing to do with the events of forty years ago. Maybe Oosterman did top himself. Maybe his wife is in Cairns like Rice suggested in his notes.'

Bowker continued to stare at the horizon. All of a sudden, his brow wrinkled and his face contorted.

Holmes saw the look on his face. 'What?'

Bowker climbed to his feet, walked over and put his hand on one of the two neat stone pyramids. 'Maybe the cairns Rice referred to wasn't the city in Queensland, but one of these?'

Holmes burst out laughing. 'You're yanking my chain, right?'

Bowker was deadly serious. 'Think about it for a moment, Sherlock. We're told Denise came up here after she'd been abused by her husband, or just needed to clear her head. What if he followed her up here and lost it completely? He kills her, then faces the problem of what to do with her body. He can't risk dragging her back down the hill in case a car comes past when he gets to the road at the bottom. He can hardly bury her. The topsoil here is about two inches thick with solid granite below that. Covering her with rocks would be his only alternative, particularly if he planned to stage her disappearance.'

'I know we're grasping at straws Greg, but you're not suggesting we demolish these bloody things on the basis of what they're called?'

'It's more than that. Returning up here today has taken me back to when Alex and I were here as kids. Something really stunk that day, but we put it down to a dead roo or fox until we found Oosterman's decomposing body on the way down. But maybe, just maybe, what we smelt up here came from under one of these cairns.'

Holmes saw that Bowker was serious. 'So we dismantle the bloody things and then rebuild them again when it turns out we're wrong?'

'You got anything better to do at the moment?'

'I can think of a hundred things,' Holmes replied with a sigh of resignation, knowing Bowker's will would prevail.

Bowker focussed on the smaller of the two structures that sat atop the second highest point of The Granite about twenty metres away. 'We'll tackle that one first. Its half collapsed, which could be the result of a body gradually decaying underneath and compromising its structural integrity.'

Holmes stood and reluctantly agreed to dismantle the cairn. The majority the stones were easily thrown aside by men of the detectives' stature, and the exercise was relatively hassle free. Bowker believed if the cairn did contain Denise Oosterman's remains, the absence of large heavy rocks, similar to those in the other pyramid, could be explained by Paul Oosterman working on his own.

The detectives received their first surprise three layers of stones from the bottom with the sudden exposure of a fired-up red-bellied black snake. Once the hissing reptile had been convinced to relocate, it took less than ten minutes for the base layer of rocks to be revealed. A rectangle of large stones created the border of the pyramid's base. Inside this perimeter were smaller stones some of which were a good six-inches lower than those around the edges.

A sweat-beaded Bowker looked at Holmes. 'I bet when this cairn was built, or rebuilt probably, the height of these smaller stones was level with the perimeter. They've since gradually sunken down.'

'Sunken down into what? We're on a granite base,' an anxious Holmes replied.

Bowker placed his knees on the stone border, leant down and lifted a stone from the centre of the base. He looked up at Holmes, the blood drained from his face. 'Fuck, mate.'

It was late afternoon by the time the forensic team had exhumed and bagged the human remains. Since the crime scene was forty years old, other forensic sweeps of the surrounds were of limited value. After four decades of decomposition, the body would require sophisticated analysis before any identification was possible either by DNA or dental records. At this stage, all that the detectives could be safely told was that the remains belonged to a female. Severe trauma to the skull suggested she had been bludgeoned to death, but further testing would be required to confirm the cranial damage had occurred at the time of death rather than at some time post mortem in the construction of the cairn.

Back at the police station the team assembled to discuss the ramifications of the find.

'So reading the word "cairns" with a question mark in Rice's notes was enough to make you pull down a stone pyramid?' Larsen said. 'That's what I call inspired detective work.'

'It's what I'd call arse,' Fleming added.

Bowker ignored Fleming's snipe. 'It wasn't just the word, Kirsten, but the word in combination with a location Denise was known to frequent. My memory of the smell was the additional factor that convinced me we should have a look.'

'So now it's official. We've got two murders to solve, rather than one,' Fleming replied without the hint of a smile. 'You blokes stay here much longer and we'll be the murder capital of the state.' He leant back in his chair and rubbed his face. 'Of course there's no guarantee the remains belong to Denise Oosterman. It may be an old cold case we'll never solve.'

'The remains would have to belong her, you'd think,' Larsen said. 'Went missing without a trace. Known to visit the top of that hill.'

'It's her,' Bowker replied adamantly. 'But we'll have to wait for a positive ID before it's official. Forensics are visiting the geriatric wing at the hospital. They'll ask the medical staff to fabricate some reason to swab the mother for a sample. No point upsetting the old girl until it's confirmed the remains belong to her daughter.'

'Even if it is Denise Oosterman, it doesn't help solve the Rice case though, does it?' Fleming said. 'Finding her body might validate your theory that Oosterman killed his wife, but it gets us no closer to finding Rice's killer.'

'Revenge is a strong motive for someone to cap Oosterman though,' Holmes replied. 'Once we find that someone, I'm willing to bet we'll have found the bastard who belted Rice over the head.'

'You've interviewed half the residents of Victoria and learnt fuck-all,' an irritated Fleming replied.

Bowker straightened but remained matter-of-fact. 'We've still got a few possibilities left on our list, including Brian Gottfried.'

'And if you draw a blank there, what then?' Fleming asked, lifting upturned palms.

'We go through it all again,' Bowker replied civilly. Fleming threw up his hands in response. Bowker leaned forward, placing his elbows on the desk, hands folded tightly, knuckles blanching. 'Then what would you do, Detective Fleming?'

'Not keep flogging a dead horse anyway,' Fleming replied.

Bowker smiled insincerely. 'Well, Aaron. As far as I'm concerned, there's still plenty of life left in this particular nag.' He paused for a moment assessing whether to push back. 'Seems like you're keen to see the end of us, mate?'

This took Fleming by surprise and he shook his head. 'Not at all. I just get frustrated when we have meeting after meeting and really nothing has changed.'

Bowker nodded an acknowledgement towards Fleming, then moved his gaze to Larsen. 'Anything grab your attention in the Rice documents?'

'Just started, Greg. Gone right back to the beginning. One thing I have found out is that life in the nineteen-century was bloody hard, even for the people with money.'

Bowker was impressed that she was starting with the documentation he'd only glossed over. He thought it likely a futile exercise, but there was always a chance something from those early days might be relevant. After several minutes of further discussion, Bowker informally adjourned the meeting, but asked Fleming to stay behind for a quick chat. He waited for Holmes and Larsen to clear the room.

'Why the haste to wind up this investigation, Aaron?'

'No haste, just looking at the reality of the situation, that's all,' Fleming replied tentatively. 'We're no closer to solving Rice's murder than when we started.'

'We just found a dead body that has ties to this case,' Bowker said, folding his arms.

'Tenuous link at best, I would say,' Fleming replied, without looking at Bowker. 'It's a forty-year-old cold case with no prospect of solution.'

Bowker rubbed the back of his neck. 'Can't just let it go through to the keeper though, can we?'

'Kirsten and I can ask a few questions and keep our ears to the ground. Can do the same with the Rice case. Free up you blokes for more pressing matters in Melbourne. I heard on the news there was another murder down there overnight.'

Bowker thought carefully before he continued. 'Is it me or Holmes who is giving you the shits?' he asked out of the blue.

Fleming stared at Bowker with a confected look of bewilderment. 'Not sure what you're talking about.'

'I think your negativity has nothing to do with this case. It's something more personal, and you'd like to see Holmes and I pack up and piss off back to Melbourne.'

Fleming didn't respond for a long moment, then looked directly into his senior colleague's eyes. 'I've got nothing against you, Greg. But the sooner I see the back of Holmes the better. I'm very close to filing a workplace sexual misconduct complaint.'

Bowker suspected this was coming. 'In relation to Kirstin Larsen, I presume.'

Fleming put the palms of his hands on the table and nodded. 'Yeah. The two of them are acting like teenagers around each other. Shit, Holmes is old enough to be her father.'

'And why do you see this as a problem?' Bowker asked. 'It doesn't seem to be affecting their work.'

'Kirsten is just a kid and I don't want to see her taken advantage of by someone with, what do they call it,' he twirled his fingers looking for the right term, 'a positive power differential.'

'She's thirty-one. That's hardly a kid,' Bowker replied. 'And you said yesterday that if you were unmarried and a few years younger you'd be interested yourself.'

'That's the point,' Fleming said irately, clenching his fists on the table. 'I *am* married and I'm *not* a few years younger, so Kirsten is out of bounds as far as I'm concerned. And even if I wasn't married, my senior position would prohibit me from pursuing a romantic relationship anyway.'

'If there is something developing between Sherlock and Kirsten, I think you'll find Kirsten is the one who initiated it.'

'Only because she's hell bent on joining the homicide squad and thinks Holmes might give her a leg up. I don't want Holmes taking advantage of that just to get his *leg over*.'

'Holmes has no influence in who gets assigned to homicide,' Bowker replied.

'I'm not sure she knows that?' Fleming mumbled.

Bowker assessed his options before deciding to dig a bit deeper. 'Are you sure you're not a tad jealous about the attention Holmes is receiving from Larsen. I'm not suggesting anything inappropriate on your behalf, but the detective constable is pretty easy on the eye and I imagine you enjoy the close working relationship you have with her.'

'She's a good friend and I don't want to see her get hurt, that's all,' Fleming said. 'If that means I have to file a complaint against Holmes then I'm willing to do it.'

'From my observations, that would impact Larsen as much as Holmes. And to be honest, I don't see any abuse of power here.'

Fleming walked towards the door. 'It would be better for everyone if you sent Holmes back to Melbourne and brought in another detective. If that's a female, all the better.'

'That's not going to happen Aaron, so I advise you to think

carefully before you do anything drastic. Have a chat to Kirsten and see where she sits before you drag her into an enquiry.'

Fleming didn't reply, just turning and leaving the room. Bowker knew he was in a tricky situation. The new protocols were introduced to protect vulnerable employees from workplace predators, particularly females who were vulnerable in a male dominated service. Bowker had seen some of these malignant situations himself, but he had also witnessed countless successful and lifelong relationships develop between work colleagues. He was wary of Holmes and Larsen being thrown out with the bathwater of an official enquiry.'

Bowker found Holmes downstairs chatting with the duty officer at the front desk.

'I've retrieved Brian Gottfried's address from the list of reunion attendees,' Holmes said. 'We could pay him a visit while we wait for The Granite forensics to come back.'

'You've read my thoughts, mate. Where's he live these days? Hopefully not interstate.'

'Within driving distance. Over in Bendigo.' Holmes opened the folder he was carrying. 'Burn Street in Golden Square, to be more precise.'

'I'll ring the Bendigo CID and ask them to whip around and make sure Gottfried will be home tomorrow. It's a couple of hours from here, so I'd hate to drive all that way and he's away somewhere. If they give us the all-clear, we'll head off first thing in the morning.' Bowker looked at his watch and saw that it was later than he thought. 'Any preferences for tea tonight?'

Holmes blushed like a caught-out schoolboy. 'I mentioned to Kirsten that I'm a sucker for lamb shanks. She's had some in the slow cooker all day and she's asked me around to pass verdict on her recipe.'

Bowker nodded, assessing whether to relate the discussion he'd just finished with Fleming. Given the awkwardness of the hour, he resolved to postpone the conversation until the morning when there'd be plenty of time to talk during the journey to Bendigo. 'You take the car mate.' He pointed across the road. 'I'll grab something to eat in the restaurant at the motel.' He patted Holmes on the shoulder. 'Good luck with the shanks.'

'You calling it quits for the day?' Holmes asked with a tinge of guilt.

'As soon as I ring Bendigo,' Bowker replied.

Once inside his motel room, Bowker threw off his dirty shoes, took out his mobile phone, then crashed onto his bed. After a few rings, Rachael answered and the couple exchanged chit-chat before Bowker asked about his wife's day at the kindergarten. She related the usual stories about toileting accidents, sick kids and the occasional light bulb moment from one of her infants. Bowker wished the last twenty-four hours for him were as straightforward and manageable. Before he could outline the new developments in the case, Rachael was keen to get one thing cleared up.

'Did Darren come back to the motel after we spoke last night?' she asked.

'Yeah. About seven o'clock this morning,' Bowker replied.

'Oh,' Rachael said after a slight hesitation. 'So obviously he's not with you at the moment?'

'Nope. Kirsten has cooked him up a special tea.'

'And you weren't invited?'

Bowker laughed. 'Come on Rach. Use your imagination. This has nothing to do with the meal. I doubt they'll even get to that, unless it's a half-time snack.'

Rachael was quiet for a moment. 'They're not crossing any lines though, are they? She's single and he's now officially separated.'

'Aaron Fleming reckons they are. He's Kirsten's detective partner up here and he reckons Sherlock is using his senior position to elicit her affections.'

'Is he?'

'She's the one doing the chasing.' Bowker laughed. 'Not that Holmes isn't happy to be caught, mind you. Fleming is older than Kirsten and married with kids. I don't think he'd ever try it on with her, but I suspect he resents Holmes getting her attention.'

'Will you broach the subject with Darren?'

'We're interviewing a suspect in Bendigo tomorrow, so I'll have a yarn with him on the way. Personally, I don't think he's crossed any lines, but if things go belly-up, who knows how people will view it. Especially in this day and age where people are finally calling out older blokes using their position to harass women or cultivate their affections. I think a few up the top of the force would be happy to kill one to educate a thousand, as the old Chinese proverb goes.'

Bowker finished the call with a detailed explanation of finding the woman's body at the summit of The Granite and their dependence on the forensic analysis for a breakthrough in what was developing into a complicated and possibly unsolvable set of killings.

CHAPTER 23

Bowker woke before seven o'clock, smiling to himself when he focussed on Holmes's undisturbed bed. His partner arrived twenty minutes later as Bowker dressed after showering.

'Lamb shanks must have been good,' Bowker said with a wry grin.

'Yeah. Excellent,' Holmes replied, rejecting the opportunity to address the subliminal gist of Bowker's question.

Kirsten Larsen's name wasn't mentioned until the detectives had cleared Benalla and were heading west towards Bendigo. 'Aaron Fleming was in my ear yesterday about you and the detective constable.'

Holmes was driving and stared straight ahead. 'Yeah? What's his beef?'

'Reckons you might be taking advantage of your position to take Kirsten to places she doesn't want to go.'

Holmes chuckled sarcastically and looked across at Bowker. 'That's bullshit and you know it, Greg. She was the one who made the first move.'

Bowker raised both palms. 'I know. I know. I'm just telling you what Fleming said. But I should warn you, he's making noises about lodging a report alleging sexual harassment in the workplace.'

Holmes exhaled audibly. 'Against who? We're both consenting adults.'

'You both are *now*. But what if things go pear-shaped? Is Kirsten the type to change the narrative if things don't end well?'

Holmes shrugged. 'I wouldn't think so.' He thought for a moment. 'What's his motive in threatening this bullshit?'

Bowker cocked his head to the side. 'He says he's protecting Kirsten from getting hurt. You know the story. A big homicide dick comes to town, has his way with an innocent young thing and leaves a wreck behind when he moves on to a new case.'

'Do *you* believe that?' Holmes asked.

'What he says, or the reason why he says it?'

'Both.'

'Well, I certainly don't believe you'd ever behave in the way he described. You're one of the most honourable men I've ever met. In terms of his motive, I think he has a bee in his bonnet about missing the undivided attention of an attractive woman.'

'OK,' Holmes replied.

There was silence as Holmes pulled out and overtook a struggling motorhome blowing blue diesel smoke out its exhaust.

'What plans do you and Kirsten have after we finish up in Benalla?' Bowker asked.

'Keep seeing each other as much as we can until Kirsten gets the transfer to Melbourne that's she's after. Then who knows. Maybe we'll set up house together.'

Bowker chose not to mention Fleming's theory about Larsen and the Homicide Squad, so he let the discussion peter out and they moved on to other topics.

The door to the modest Golden Square residence was opened by a woman of middle age, vivacious and attractive. She was dressed fashionably in a style more often seen on younger women but carried the look with an understated panache. Her hair was short but well styled, her face unwrinkled and her wide smile revealing perfect teeth. She proffered her hand. 'I'm Petrice Gottfried. I assume you are the officers wishing to speak to my husband.'

Following introductions, the woman looked quizzically into the senior officer's face. 'There was a Greg Bowker who attended Benalla High School many years ago.'

Bowker grinned. 'That was me. I think I would have been three or four years ahead of you.'

The woman smiled and nodded. 'The longer you live, the more you realise what a small world we live in. Follow me gentlemen, and I'll take you through to my husband.'

A shrunken and withered elderly man sat in an old-fashioned armchair in the lounge room. He climbed unsteadily to his feet as his wife introduced the detectives. As Bowker shook his hand and felt his bony and arthritic fingers, he immediately doubted Gottfried's capacity to follow and kill Gary Rice just weeks before. The officers were invited to sit on the couch opposite, while Gottfried's wife placed a coffee table between them and adjourned to the kitchen to make hot drinks for the visitors.

'I presume you are here about Gary Rice's murder. Petrice and I attended her school reunion in Benalla that evening.' the old man mumbled in a trembling voice.

'That's right, Mr Gottfried,' Bowker replied, sitting forward on the couch. 'We're interviewing anyone who was talking to Mr Rice that night.'

'I spoke to him only briefly,' Gottfried said. 'Being of similar age, obviously I wasn't one of his students, nor was I a fellow teacher either. I've worked for the Lands Department or its various incarnations all my life. But I knew him from sport when I lived in Benalla. We crossed paths playing tennis on the odd occasion.'

'Can I ask what you chatted about?' Holmes asked.

The old man shrugged. 'Nothing earth-shattering that I can recall. We had a laugh about our sporting highlights, or rather the lack of them, and how decrepit we'd become since the golden days of our youth.'

'Did he mention he was writing a family history?' Bowker asked.

Gottfried shook his head. 'Not that I recall. As I said, our conversation was quite brief. Except for the odd chat with a couple of farmers I had dealt with in my time in Benalla, I spent most of the night listening to Petrice relive old times with her schoolmates.'

'Which farmers were they?' Holmes asked, removing a notebook from his jacket.

The old man thought deeply for a moment, rubbing the rough stubble on his chin. 'Mick Sargood and Charlie Benbow were the main ones.'

'Mick had problems with Paul Oosterman, we're told,' Bowker suggested.

Gottfried's face darkened. 'Everyone had problems with Paul Oosterman. I'd describe him as a pig of a man except that would be doing the pig a major injustice. I had a series of altercations with him over the noxious weeds on his property. He was an angry bastard. Kicked me off his place a couple of times when I was just trying to do my job.' Gottfried gave Bowker a puzzled look. 'What's Paul Oosterman got to do with Gary Rice's murder? The bastard cashed his own chips forty years ago.'

Bowker wasn't keen to give too much away so early in the interview. 'When we spoke to Mick Sargood, he mentioned

Oosterman in passing, that's all. And that a lot of people celebrated when he took his own life.'

'We're told you had a blue with him at a dance one night,' Holmes said. 'Things got pretty physical apparently.'

'He became upset because I'd always ask his wife for a dance when the band played the modern waltz. Except for a couple down Longwood way, Denise and I were the only ones who could do it properly, so we'd put on a bit of a show for the crowd. Paul couldn't handle that.' He coughed heavily into his fist.

'Then one day his wife just disappeared,' Bowker said.

'Don't blame her really,' Gottfried replied. 'If he treated her the same way he treated everyone else then her marriage wouldn't have been much chop.'

'Any idea where she ended up,' Holmes asked, crossing his legs and resting the notepad on his thigh. 'She didn't contact you after she disappeared?'

'Why would she?' Gottfried shot back. 'I had the occasional dance with her, that's all.'

Bowker leant back on the couch and folded his arms. 'There was no other relationship between the two of you?'

Gottfried scoffed. 'Of course not. She was a married woman.' He was still bewildered by this line of questioning. 'I don't understand why you're interested in my dealings with the Oostermans.'

Bowker looked at Holmes then back at Gottfried before explaining the possible link between the forty-year-old death and Gary Rice's murder. He decided against revealing that a body had been found atop The Granite that they suspected belonged to Denise Oosterman.

Gottfried was pensive for a moment as he digested Bowker's explanation. 'As I mentioned earlier, I hadn't heard Rice was writing a family history.'

'Do you own a dog, Mr Gottfried?' Holmes asked.

Gottfried shook his head. 'Haven't had a dog since I stopped working. We've got two cats though. I'm surprised they're not in here now climbing all over you.'

Bowker was winding up the interview when Gottfried's wife appeared with a silver tray supporting four coffee mugs and a plate of hedgehog slices. Gottfried took a coffee with two unsteady hands before his wife handed each officer a cup and placed the tray on a coffee table. She perched on the arm of her husband's chair and Holmes immediately absorbed the physical disparity between them. The age gap, that would have been hardly perceptible thirty-five years before, was now a yawning chasm. Gottfried was knocking at death's door while his wife was ready to take on whatever life offered.

'Were you at the school reunion too, Greg,' Mrs Gottfried asked.

Bowker took a sip of his coffee before answering. 'Yes, I was there. But I don't think too many people remembered me. I was a pretty quiet kid at school.'

'I loved catching up with old friends. Luckily Brian was well enough to come.' She glanced down at her husband before continuing. 'I'm not sure whether he mentioned it, but he's being treated for cancer. A lot of the time he's too weak to travel anywhere.'

After cheerful discussion about the old days in Benalla while finishing their coffee, the detectives bade their farewells with wishes of good luck for the old man in his health battles.

Fifteen minutes later they were seated in the lounge of the historic Shamrock Hotel on Pall Mall in the heart of Bendigo.

'There is no way Gottfried killed Gary Rice,' Bowker proclaimed as he perused the lunch menu. 'He's so bloody weak he could hardly support his coffee cup.'

Holmes looked up from his own copy of the menu. 'Forty years ago he would have been fit enough to shoot Oosterman.'

'Yeah, but if that happened, there goes our motive for someone to top Rice.'

Holmes thought for a moment. 'If the deaths are connected, I agree we can scratch Gottfried off our list. But there's still a real possibility there's no link between the cases and we're really chasing two killers. Can't afford to have tunnel vision. That's what you always say, isn't it mate?'

Bowker smiled. His partner was right.

The detectives ordered their meals at the bar and returned to their table, each carrying a pot of ice-cold diet Coke. Holmes played with his glass before speaking. 'I should have taken a photo of Gottfried sitting in that lounge chair with his wife daintily balanced on its armrest. Could have shown Kirsten what's in store for us if our relationship does go anywhere. Half dead old bastard sitting there like a millstone around the neck of a younger woman with plenty of life still to live.' He took a long swig of his soft drink, put the glass down and stared at the table.

'I bet there were a lot of good years in between,' Bowker replied.

'My case is more selfish. Had the good years with Cassie, then I hook up with someone younger for *her* good years with the expectation that she'll blow a chunk of her life looking after me in my dotage.'

Bowker took a sip of his drink before answering. 'I reckon you're over-thinking this a bit at the moment, mate. You've spent two nights in the cot with Kirsten and you're already visualising what things might be like in thirty years. Just sort out how you feel about each other and whether there's more to it than an enjoyable roll in the hay. If it's meant to be then the future will take care of itself.'

Holmes nodded and took another sip of his drink.

'How about we go back to Melbourne from here?' Bowker suggested. 'There's nothing much more we can do in Benalla until the forensics come through. We'll see what's on the agenda at Spencer Street. There was a double murder in Glen Waverly on Monday night and I'd like to see how far the team have progressed on that. And the O'Brien case is still open.' He looked at Holmes. 'Hope this doesn't interfere with your social life.'

'Give me some thinking time,' Homes replied. He then chortled and held up his glass. 'Plus a good chance to build up my strength again.'

Rachael was thrilled by the unexpected arrival of her husband and threw her arms around him as he came through the back door. 'This is a surprise,' she said as she kissed him gently on the lips.

Bowker dropped his briefcase on the floor and placed both hands on his wife's backside. 'Yeah, we went to Bendigo for an interview which came up blank, so we decided to come home until the science on the woman's remains comes through.'

'Well I'm glad you did,' Rachael said. 'Gets lonely here when you're away.' She kissed him again, then released her arms. 'I'll make us a coffee and you can give me an update on the investigation.'

Bowker pulled out a kitchen chair and sat down at the table. 'That won't take long. In a nutshell, we're getting nowhere. This morning, we interviewed a former Lands Department officer who was friendly with the woman whose remains we believe were hidden on The Granite in the eighties. Even if he was involved in the death of her husband, there's no way he killed Rice a few weeks ago. He's now a withered, cancer-riddled old man who not only would have been incapable of killing Rice, but given his medical prognosis would have little to gain by silencing him.'

Rachael retrieved two mugs from an overhead cupboard as the kettle began to boil. 'Any other leads to chase up?'

'Nothing concrete,' Bowker replied. 'There's an old farmer from the opposite side of Benalla who spoke to Rice at the reunion we haven't talked to yet. And we haven't checked the Alibi of a man who claims he was away on the weekend Oosterman died. My gut tells me neither of these will lead anywhere.'

Rachael poured the hot water onto the instant coffee in the mugs and carried them over to the table. 'This is becoming like the silo murders at Cocamba,' she said. 'You had plenty of leads, but they all turned out to be dead ends.'

'Thanks Love,' Bowker said as he took the steaming beverage from his wife. 'What's been the go while I've been away?'

Rachael smiled as she sat down. 'After you rang last night, I had a phone call from Cassie Holmes.'

Bowker was intrigued. 'Yeah?'

'Yeah. She told me that she and Darren had separated, which of course I knew, but didn't let on. She's a bit worried about how Darren will react to it all.' Rachael giggled. 'She was hoping you might be able to keep his spirits up until things settle down and he gets his head around the new reality.'

Bowker burst out laughing. 'I think his spirits are pretty high already! While Cassie was making that call, Sherlock was rooting himself silly in Benalla.'

'Well speaking of such matters, I'm glad you're home.' She raised her mug and clinked it against Bowker's.

CHAPTER 24

I t wasn't until Friday that the post mortem results for the remains found atop The Granite came through. Erin O'Meara phoned and delivered a summary to Bowker as he sat at his desk in Spencer Street.

'Female, in her mid-twenties when she died,' O'Meara reported. 'DNA matches that taken from a Sheila Macklin, a resident in the geriatric wing of the Benalla Hospital. Birth records confirm the remains belong to a Denise Elizabeth Oosterman. But I bet you suspected that anyway.'

Bowker nodded to himself. 'Yeah. But it's still sad to hear it confirmed.'

'If the body hadn't been hers, it would have belonged to some other unfortunate woman, so don't spend too much time mourning the individual.'

'It hits a bit harder when you know their history, that's all. You see them as a person rather than just a set of bones.'

'You're turning soft in your old age, Gregory,' O'Meara replied. 'Anyway, she's estimated to have died around forty years ago, going by the level of decomposition and the environmental factors pertinent to the body's location.'

266

Bowker scribbled furiously on a pad in front of him. 'Any conclusions on cause of death?'

'Crushed skull. Hit with something blunt and heavy on the back of the head,' O'Meara replied. 'But she also had a broken jaw that most likely occurred independent of the blow that killed her.'

'Like maybe she was punched before the fatal blow was delivered?' Bowker suggested.

'Or when she hit the ground,' O'Meara replied. 'But the position of the fracture would indicate a punch is the most likely scenario.'

'There were strong rumours that her husband was physically abusive.'

'That would explain a couple of other things that were found. Two historical rib fractures were identified, along with a healed crack in her cheekbone.'

'Poor woman,' Bowker replied sadly.

'One last thing,' O'Meara said. 'She was pregnant. About four and a half months, by the bone development of the foetus.'

'Fuck!' Bowker blurted out.

'I think we can assume that,' O'Meara replied in bad taste.

Bowker frowned. 'Her husband was supposedly infertile. The result of mumps as a kid. A really serious case, apparently.'

'Then the plot thickens,' O'Meara replied. 'We'll need to sample his DNA.'

'He's been dead forty years himself.'

'Is there any family still alive?' O'Meara asked. 'Easier than digging up the bastard.'

'I spoke to his sister a week or so ago. I've got her mobile number on my phone.'

'That'll do. You forward that to us and we'll arrange to get a sample from her.'

Bowker thought for a moment. 'Did the techs find anything of use at the scene?'

'Nothing really. Forty years on the top of a windswept hill wouldn't leave much of value. They did note that the rocks used in the cairn hiding the body were of a smaller size than the other one.'

'Yeah, we noticed that too,' Bowker replied. 'Easier for a man on his own to handle.'

'So if he dismantled the old cairn, how did he manage the larger rocks on his own. And where are they now? Our team found no evidence of them discarded close by, so they reckon either the cairn has always comprised smaller rocks or that there was originally only one cairn until a second was constructed to hide the body.'

Bowker laughed to himself. 'Never gave any thought to how the killer might have got rid of the original stones. But it did surprise me that there were two cairns up there. Only ever seen one on other hills.'

Bowker thanked O'Meara, disconnected the call and wandered over to where Holmes had his head down over a stack of papers. He pulled up a chair. 'Just got off the phone to O'Meara. The results of the post mortem and DNA tests have come through.'

Holmes pushed aside the papers and turned to face his partner. 'Was it Denise Oosterman?'

Bowker nodded. 'Yeah, mate. Died of head wounds as we suspected, but had other older injuries as well that suggest she was physically abused.'

'Confirms Paul Oosterman was a piece of shit,' Holmes replied.

'She was also four and a half months pregnant. About the time she'd be starting to show,' Bowker added.

Holmes momentarily closed his eyes before exhaling loudly. 'Wasn't Oosterman supposed to be sterile?'

'That's what his sister told me,' Bowker replied. 'But apparently mumps can cause different degrees of infertility. Maybe in amongst the blanks, he produced the odd live bullet.'

'It'd be a strong motive for a self-centred bastard to attack his wife if he knew she was pregnant and assumed some other bloke had cut his lunch. Achieved what he was incapable of doing himself.'

Bowker nodded his agreement. 'And if some other bloke is the father, then it provides an enhanced motive for that person to seek revenge.'

'Assuming he knew of the pregnancy,' Holmes replied.

Bowker scratched his neck and thought for a moment. 'We'll know more in the next couple of days. Forensics will contact Oosterman's sister and obtain a DNA swab. If they can't tie the family DNA to the foetal remains, then we're looking for a male who does match.'

Holmes scoffed. 'Good luck with that. We can't even identify a suspect we're half confident about, let alone one that a court would allow us to DNA test.'

Bowker drummed his fingers on Holmes's desk as he thought for a long moment. 'Maybe you're right, Sherlock. Maybe I am becoming a bit too tunnel visioned and getting too hung up on a link between Oosterman and Rice? Perhaps Brian Gottfried did kill Oosterman when he was young and fit and liked to squire Denise around the dance floor. Maybe they added the horizontal tango to their dance card? Maybe the family history is a wild goose chase and it's merely a coincidence that Rice gets topped at a time he's rabbiting on about Oosterman being murdered?'

Holmes shrugged. 'It's all possible. But you do realise that takes us back to where we were a fortnight ago? So do we reinterview Sanderson and Brown? Dennis Lowther? Tony Marshall? Ron Cloverdale? Keep in mind Greg, we've already put a line through all of these blokes.'

'Maybe we missed something,' Bowker said. 'On Monday, I think we'll head back to the North East and work through our notes again with Fleming and Larsen. I'd also like a yarn with Charlie Benbow, the cocky from Boho South who was chatting to Rice at the reunion. And we need to confirm Mick Sargood's alibi at the gay thirtieth birthday party.' He looked at Holmes. 'You happy to go back to Benalla? I can take someone else if you're tied up here.'

Holmes tried to suppress a smile. 'No, Benalla sounds good.'

Bowker and Holmes were in Benalla by eleven o'clock on the Monday. Their meeting with Fleming and Larsen brought the local detectives up to speed with Denise Oosterman's post mortem and their interview with Brian Gottfried. Holmes and Larsen sat on the same side of the table. Fleming and Bowker both noticed the subtle touching of shoulders.

'So at least the remains now have a name,' Larsen said after Bowker had finished his summary.

'Solves the mystery of her disappearance, so I suppose that's one step in the right direction,' the detective inspector replied.

Fleming sniggered. 'No closer to finding Rice's killer though, are we?'

Bowker was nearing the end of his tether but managed to ignore Fleming's sustained negative campaign and outlined his plan to talk to Charlie Benbow and to verify Sargood's alibi. He then turned to Larsen. 'How far into Rice's documentation have you got?'

'A fair way,' Larsen replied. 'I've read all the early historical material on both branches of the family tree, but so far nothing has jumped out at me. I'm about to attack the information Rice assembled on Paul Oosterman's suicide.'

Holmes moved his shoulder an inch to make contact with Larsen. Fleming's face reddened. 'You won't have much time for that now that he's back, will you?' he blurted out, pointing at Holmes.

Larsen was stunned. 'What the hell's going on, Aaron?'

Fleming moved his finger to point straight at her across the table. 'I can't believe you're taken in by this bastard. He's twice your age and you're carrying on like a lovesick schoolgirl.'

Holmes stood up and leant forward with palms on the table. 'Just watch what you say, mate. Our private lives are none of your fuckin' business, so butt out!'

Larsen remained perplexed. 'What's come over you, Aaron? Who I choose to socialise with is none of your business.'

Fleming climbed to his feet. 'It is when I see you being taken advantage of by a senior officer,' he said heatedly.

'I'm a big girl, Aaron,' Larsen said irately. 'I'm not a young cadet and I don't appreciate being told what I can do in my own time.'

Fleming wasn't backing down. 'Seems to me, Holmes is telling you what he'd like you to do. A whistle blower report for workplace exploitation will be emailed to Personnel in Melbourne before I leave the station tonight.'

'Jealousy's a curse, mate,' Holmes shot back.

The palm of Bowker's hand hit the table with a loud bang. 'Alright! Everybody sit down and listen to me. This is the way it is going to be from here on in. Detective Holmes and I will work the day to day aspects of this case from here on in.' He looked at Larsen. 'Kirsten, I'd appreciate you continuing with your analysis of the Rice documents.' His gaze switched to Fleming. 'Aaron, once the easy suspects were eliminated, your heart's never been in doing the hard slog to get this case solved. So I'm going to do you a favour. I'm cutting you loose from this investigation.'

Fleming stood up and looked at Bowker. 'Thank God. It's a fuckin' waste of time anyway.' He turned to leave.

'It's your prerogative if you want to pursue a complaint against colleagues,' Bowker said as Fleming walked to the door, 'but I'd think carefully about what your motives are before you do.' When

Fleming had slammed the door behind him, Bowker looked at the officers across the table and spoke in a softer tone. 'I can't instruct you on how you spend your private time, but while you're at work I need the height of professionalism. I don't want the slightest display of affection at work, or anything that can be construed as compromising the professional conduct of your duties.'

Holmes and Larsen nodded but said nothing.

Bowker and Holmes split Sargood's list of party-goers between them. Of the five witnesses Sargood had nominated, only three could be traced but each vouched for the farmer's presence at the Lorne event. While the birthday party had occurred some forty years prior, each could remember Sargood's shirt catching alight as he carried in a giant cake topped with thirty oversized candles. In terms of Paul Oosterman's death, Mick Sargood was in the clear.

Before making the trip southeast to interview Charlie Benbow, Bowker tracked down Fleming in the CID area and invited him into an interview room for a quiet chat, hopeful that the local detective had settled down after his earlier outburst.

'Let me say from the outset, Aaron, that speaking to a senior officer in the way I was addressed this morning is totally unacceptable.'

It was obvious Fleming had reassessed his behaviour. 'I apologise unreservedly. The way I reacted was totally inappropriate and unprofessional.' He took a deep breath. 'Having said that, I won't retreat from my complaint about Detective Sergeant Holmes. It is still my belief that he is manipulative and exploitative in his relationship with Detective Larsen, and it is still my intention to submit an official report to this effect.'

Bowker nodded. 'That is certainly your right and your duty if you are convinced that lines have been crossed. I am not sitting here to convince you otherwise since that would be unprofessional in the extreme. More especially in this instance which involves a colleague and personal friend. To intercede on his behalf would be to pervert the course of your complaint and only serve to reinforce a community perception of male officers protecting predators within their ranks.'

Fleming thought for a moment then spoke in a surprised tone. 'So you're not instructing me to drop the whole thing?'

Bowker shook his head and folded his hands on the table. 'I have no authority to do that, even if I wanted to. The only advice I have is to consider the same questions that the arbiters of the complaint will ask. Has Kirsten gone into the relationship with her eyes open and of her own free will? At this point in time, she will no doubt attest that she is a mature woman exercising her right to spend her own time with a person whose company she enjoys. It will be very difficult to convince a tribunal that exploitation has occurred when the supposed victim rejects any suggestion she has been manipulated. Without the support of the alleged victim, I am worried that the person who may suffer most in all this is the officer who filed the complaint. The last thing you want is all this backfiring on you, Aaron.'

Fleming looked puzzled. 'Backfire? What do mean?'

'If Larsen officially denies your assertions then you run the risk of your complaint being labelled as the revenge of a middle-aged officer spurned by an attractive younger colleague.' Bowker watched Fleming drop his head. 'It's your decision where to go from here, but think everything through carefully before you put any wheels in motion.' Bowker stood up and patted Fleming on the shoulder as he walked towards the door leaving his colleague staring into space behind him.

The trip to Boho South took less than thirty minutes. They found

Charlie Benbow on a tractor slashing dry grass around ramshackle sheds behind a dilapidated house. He was a knock-about sort, straight out of the pages of a Steele Rudd tale. Dressed in khaki bib-and-brace overalls over a grey-haired bare chest, he was unshaven and his hair protruded like grey straw from a filthy blue towelling hat. His toes were visible out the front of worn-out football socks and elastic-sided work boots. In a slow drawl, he informed the detectives he had only known Paul Oosterman by sight and had no social or commercial dealings with him. Yes, he had attended the school reunion and had spoken briefly to Gary Rice who had taught him in Form 2, the year he had finished school. There had been no discussion of a family history, with Rice interested in what the farmer had been up to since he went shearing all those years ago. Benbow had departed the function around 10.30pm with his wife Thelma and their next-door neighbour Maggie Price whom they'd given a ride to and from the reunion. The only dogs the farmer owned were two purebred border collies who jumped all over the detectives as they stood chatting to their master.

The excursion convinced Bowker that Benbow was irrelevant to their inquiries, but in order to draw a permanent line through his name, they dropped in on his next-door neighbour to confirm she had travelled with him to and from the school reunion. In contrast to Benbow's decrepit farm, Maggie Price, a widow, lived in a well-kept home amidst a small but manicured garden with the blue haze of the Strathbogie ranges as a backdrop. Since her husband's death, she had leased out her property on a share-farming basis. A large, jovial woman, Mrs Price affirmed she had travelled with the Benbows to the reunion and that she was home by eleven. This confirming that they had left the function well before the time Rice was killed. The detectives were again back to square one.

On the way back to Benalla, Holmes raised his altercation with Fleming for the first time. 'What did you think of this morning's shit show?' he asked without looking at Bowker.

'Unseemly, unnecessary, unprofessional,' Bowker replied. He looked across at Holmes. 'You shouldn't have let yourself be sucked in. You should've let what he had to say go through to the keeper, or at least played a straight bat. Getting involved in a slanging match doesn't help anybody.'

Holmes was annoyed. 'He was treating Kirsten like she was a little kid and accusing me of predatory behaviour. I wasn't going to sit there and take that shit.'

Bowker held up a hand. 'I know how you felt mate, but there are times when it's better to bite your lip and let a person get a few things off their chest. Often, that's all they want. Have their say and feel they've been listened to.'

Holmes was silent for a few moments. 'I saw you take him to the interview room. Did you rip him, or what?'

'I reprimanded him about the way he spoke to fellow officers, particularly the way he addressed me.'

Holmes turned sideways in his seat so he could address his partner more directly. 'Did you tell him to forget submitting that bullshit report he's on about?'

Bowker shook his head vigorously. 'Nope. You know as well as I do, I can't do that. Regardless of a complaint's accuracy, the shit would really hit the fan if a senior officer kyboshes a report to protect his mate.'

Holmes frowned. 'So, what? You gave him the green light to go ahead with this bullshit?'

'I told him it was his right to submit a complaint,' Holmes tried to protest but Bowker quickly stopped him with a raised left hand, 'but I warned him that if Larsen rejects its substance, then he risks sullying his reputation when questions are asked about his motive in exposing his partner's private life.'

Holmes's face relaxed a little. 'What do you think he'll do?'

Bowker shrugged and returned his left hand to the steering wheel. 'Hopefully, whatever he decides will follow some self-reflection on his part.'

'Should Kirsten and I dial it down a touch,' Holmes asked.

'Far be it for me to tell two mature adults how they should spend their spare time. What do you think?'

'May as well be hanged for a sheep as a lamb,' Holmes replied with a grin.

CHAPTER 25

The results surrounding the paternity of Denise Oosterman's unborn child came early the next morning with Erin O'Meara's phone call from the police forensic centre.

'Gregory, my good man. We acquired a cheek swab from Paul Oosterman's sister on Friday and run the relevant tests over the weekend. I don't know whether the results will help or hinder your investigation, but there is no DNA connection between the remains of that foetus and the Oosterman bloodline.'

'So Paul Oosterman wasn't the father,' Bowker replied.

'I can see why they made you a detective,' O'Meara said in a sarcastic voice before laughing at her own joke which in turn triggered a fit of coughing.

'OK, OK. It's still early up here in the bush, alright,' Bowker said with a smile, holding up a palm that O'Meara obviously couldn't see. 'And it doesn't match other DNA you have on file either, otherwise you'd be crowing about how you've solved another one of my cases.'

'Shit, Bowker. What percentage of the population do you think we've got DNA for?' She sighed heavily. 'But if it helps, I can tell you the father wasn't Gary Rice. He's the only one associated with your inquiry whose genetic data we've sampled. And before you ask, yes, we've run the foetus DNA against our database hoping to fluke a match with something we've collected in relation to other matters.'

'No joy?'

'It was a longshot, but occasionally longshots pay off.' O'Meara laughed and immediately started coughing again. 'The doctors told me I'd be dead with lung cancer by now, and here I am still fit as a fiddle.' She broke into another bout of coughing. 'Listen, I might have a way to break this case wide open.'

Bowker was suddenly energised. 'Tell me. I can do with some help right now.'

'If you can get me a cheek swab of every male who was in the Benalla district forty years ago, I'll guarantee I'll identify the father of that unborn baby.' She laughed out loud again. 'See ya,' she added cheekily. All Bowker could hear as he disconnected the call was O'Meara coughing and spitting.

'So now we've got Denise Oosterman getting a bit on the side,' Holmes replied when told of O'Meara's call. 'We're slowly establishing a chain between her disappearance and the murder of Gary Rice.' He held up one hand, making a small gap between his thumb and index finger. 'Just missing one teeny-weeny link. The fucker that the whole chain is wrapped around!'

'We'll get him eventually, Sherlock,' Bowker replied before grinning. 'Hopefully the bastard won't die on us first.'

'A national register of DNA would make our job a lot easier.'

'Well, that ain't going to happen, is it? And it probably shouldn't, if we value our privacy.'

'What a pity we're not investigating a confined geographic region. Remember that murder on Norfolk Island a few years ago? All the residents volunteered their DNA to help nail the killer.'

Bowker nodded. 'Yeah, but there's a big ethical difference

between that and keeping a permanent database. We'll just have to continue narrowing down our suspects. If we find sufficient grounds, we can apply to have them DNA tested. The father of that unborn baby may not be our killer, but if we knew his identity it would give us something new to work with.' Bowker rubbed his chin. 'I'll take anything at this stage.'

Bowker knew they were clutching at straws when he and Holmes were ushered into the archives room of the *Benalla Ensign* the next morning. Holmes had the easier task, scanning digital records of recent newspaper stories that referenced Gary Rice. The digital archive's search function made the exercise straight forward. Bowker's undertaking promised to be much more laborious, a manual inspection of fading newspapers from around the time of the Oosterman deaths. His mission hoped to unearth any relevant material that had been missed by Rice in his research. Both officers accepted they were searching for needles in haystacks without any confidence that a needle even existed. But at this stage of their investigation there was little better to occupy their time and if nothing broke soon, Fleming would get his wish to see Bowker and Holmes put the case on indefinite hold and return to Melbourne.

Within five minutes, Bowker recognised the temptation of becoming side-tracked by stories from the times of his youth. He quickly found himself gravitating to the sports pages and he knew he'd gone back too far when he read multiple articles celebrating the Benalla Demons' 1973 premiership in the Ovens and Murray League. He flipped through editions to the early eighties and found his name mentioned in the A grade tennis results even though he was just a kid at the time. Finally, he found references to the Oosterman family. The first appeared in the police column, where the local officers were seeking the whereabouts of a Denise Oosterman who had disappeared a few days earlier. A small photo showed the face of a smiling young woman. Coverage of Paul Oosterman's death came two weeks later. A lengthy article Bowker had read while perusing Gary Rice's material was accompanied by a photo that Bowker had not seen. In fact, he couldn't even remember it being taken. It featured he and his brother on their horses at the foot of The Granite under the headline "Brothers' Grizzly Find." A week later the newspaper quoted a police source announcing there were no suspicious circumstances surrounding Oosterman's death, and the case was now closed awaiting a coronial inquest. A family death notice with funeral arrangements appeared among the classifieds. Given what he now knew about Paul Oosterman, Bowker wasn't surprised by the dearth of obituaries posted by friends or community organisations. The final mention of the family surrounded marketing of the two properties and the associated monster clearing sale.

After an hour, Bowker stood up straight and stretched his back. He wandered over to where Holmes sat at a computer terminal. 'Anything of interest?' he asked.

Holmes turned his swivel chair. 'Not really,' he replied. 'Prior to an article reporting his murder, the only reference I can find to Rice is in a series of puff-pieces the paper published leading up to the reunion. He and half a dozen ex-students and teachers were interviewed about their memories of the school and what they've done in later life. Sort of a "Where Are They Now" format.' Holmes smiled. 'Obviously, you didn't make the cut, mate. Sorry,' he said with a chuckle.

Bowker grinned. 'Did Rice mention anything in the interview that could help us?'

'Well, he announced he was writing a family history in his retirement. Part of that involved research on a branch of the family he knew little about. The reporter asked if he had found any skeletons in the closet. Rice's answer was fairly cryptic. He said he had uncovered a couple of things that were contrary to the family narrative. He laughed that off with a throw-away line about every family having their secrets. You just needed to dig deep enough.'

Bowker thought for a moment and scratched his cheek. 'So you didn't have to attend the reunion to know Rice had found something.'

'There were no names mentioned in the article. I think most people would take family secrets to mean romantic trysts, or a person's real father not being the man married to their mother.'

'Not if you've killed Oosterman, and you've been shitting yourself for forty years that someone will uncover your secret,' Bowker replied.

'Fuck, Greg. If that's the case then we could be looking beyond the reunion to anyone who read that article.' Holmes rubbed his forehead. 'This is starting to make my head hurt, mate. Where would we even start trying to narrow that one down?' He chuckled. 'I'll let you be the one to tell Fleming we now suspect anyone who reads the local paper.'

Bowker smiled. 'For the moment we'll keep flogging the horse we're riding. When its heart stops completely, we'll change course.'

'Have you found anything from the eighties?'

Bowker shrugged. 'Lot of nostalgia from my younger days, but the only article about Oosterman was the same one we found in Gary Rice's collection. There was a photo of Alex and me as the kids who found the body, a couple of death notices and a police statement confirming no suspicious circumstances. He wasn't a popular bastard, if the scarcity of obituaries is any indication.'

'Do you want me to keep looking?'

'Bowker consulted his watch. 'Let's give it another half an hour.'

He wandered back to his seat at the large wide table and resumed his search at the point he had left off. For several minutes he leafed through issue after issue without finding any reference to the Oostermans or any others who could be linked with their deaths. Dennis Lowther, whose name was associated with the Gary Rice case, appeared regularly in dispatches as a Shire Councillor and later as Shire President. Nothing in those references provided any link to the Rice murder, which didn't surprise Bowker since they'd already eliminated him from their inquiries.

The *Ensign*'s coverage of the floods Bowker had witnessed as a teenager immediately piqued his interest and challenged his memory. The map of the inundation showed an area much larger than he recollected and the photos of the flooded shops came as a shock. As a kid, he saw the wide expanses of water as an invitation to have some fun, but for those in the town the rising water levels must have been terrifying. Bowker had narrated his floodwater adventures to his wife and kids more times than they wished to remember, and their response was always the same. He was exaggerating his deeds and had read *The Man from Snowy River* a few too many times. Bowker smiled to himself as he picked up the bound issues of the newspaper. This was his chance to validate his stories and so with the assistance of the receptionist he photocopied the map and the double page of spectacular photos. Who would have the last laugh now? he thought.

As he folded the photocopies to place them in his briefcase, the date at the head of the page jumped out at him. The major Benalla flood hadn't occurred when he was still living on the farm, but rather after he had completed school and moved to Melbourne to begin his police training. It now made more sense why the map and the pictures he had photocopied looked foreign to him. But if he was remembering an earlier flood, why wasn't it headlined in the paper? Surely contemplating his premature death as his horse bolted through the floodwaters and approached the fallen gumtree wasn't a figment of his imagination. Bowker bookmarked the issue corresponding to the week he left for the city and flipped his way back through the issues. After five minutes, he found a small article he had missed when he was searching for stories about the Oostermans. A brief report was attached to a picture of cattle huddled on a grassy knoll in an inundated paddock. The flood was not a major catastrophe like those seen in 1906 or a few decades ago in 1993. There had been heavy rain in the high country and the Hollands Creek had burst its banks causing low lying farms to receive a deluge. But with only minor flooding along the Broken River, Benalla was spared a major disaster.

Bowker smiled as he tapped the article with the tips of his fingers. Faith was restored in his memory and, at least for now, there was no evidence of early onset dementia. However the more thought he gave to his watery ride the more his brow furrowed. He rechecked the date on the article in front of him. He leaned back in his chair and closed his eyes, the fingers of his right hand rubbing his forehead. Finally, he stood and dragged a chair across to Holmes.

'I just found a short article about that flood when my horse took off on me as a kid.'

Holmes turned on his chair and faced his colleague. 'Glad to see you didn't make it up,' he replied with a straight face.

'Remember I told you that Sid Wilson owned a small farm along that lane?'

Holmes nodded and smiled. 'Yeah, the stock agent. I remember. Cattle and a horse standing on rises in the front paddock. Water lapping up to the back door. The ute and the green Celica parked up close to the rear of the house so his shoes didn't get saturated before he got inside.' He laughed. 'You tell a good story mate. I'm surprised you didn't tell me the exact time you shat yourself when the horse bolted. I got every other bloody detail.' He looked at Bowker who was only half paying attention and was staring into space. 'You alright mate? That article stir up scary memories?'

Bowker didn't address his partner's question. 'I've got a problem with that green Celica being at Sid's. The date of that mini flood was a month before Paul Oosterman died. At that stage, the Celica belonged to Denise Oosterman who was still alive and kicking.'

Holmes frowned. 'So why was it parked behind Sid Wilson's place?' he asked, suspecting he might already know the answer. 'That's what we need to find out,' Bowker replied.

CHAPTER 26

Stock agents are normally out and about visiting clients or at livestock sales, but by a stroke of good fortune Sid Wilson was in his Carrier Street office when the detectives dropped in for their chat. Wilson's ute was parked out the front, a chained kelpie sheepdog on the tray licking Bowker's hand enthusiastically as he patted its head as he walked past. The business had no receptionist, and agricultural merchandise was spread higgledy piggledy around the filthy showroom floor. An old-fashioned bell above the door rang as the officers entered. An elderly weathered-beaten man came from an office at the back. He was stopped in his tracks by the sight of the two large men dressed in suits. Bowker had twice spoken to Wilson on the phone in the last fortnight but had not laid eyes on the man for over four decades. Time had taken its toll. The individual who now stood before Bowker was a frail shadow of the man mountain he knew as a teenager. That same former man mountain had played in the ruck for Benalla and put the fear of God into opposing players. Wilson was now hunched over, his arms covered in skin lesions of various types and his hair thin and grey. His deep blue eyes were still sharp but set back behind protruding cheekbones. His lips were cracked by sunburn and his ears flaking with sun damage. When Bowker introduced himself, the old man's face lit up and he shook the detective's hand furiously. As he was introduced to Holmes, his eyes remained on Bowker. 'Malcolm's eldest boy, eh? Done a lot better for yourself than staying on the bloody farm.' He shook his head. 'Some of the things you and your brother did on those horses would make the hair stand up on the back of your head.' He looked at Holmes. 'Has he ever told you what they got up to?'

'Many times,' Holmes replied with a grin.

'It's one of those times I'd like to talk to you about,' Bowker said.

'Back when you were a kid?' Wilson asked. 'Shit, you'll be testing the memory mate, but I'll do my best. Fire away.'

'When I was sixteen years old, the Hollands burst its banks and the paddocks at your place in Standish's Lane were mostly underwater,' Bowker said.

Wilson scratched the side of his head and frowned as he thought back. 'Was that the big flood that nearly washed the town away, or the smaller one a few years earlier?'

'The smaller one,' Bowker replied. 'My brother and I rode our horses through the water down past your place. We never quite made it to the creek.'

Wilson smiled and looked at Holmes. 'I told you they did some dickhead things.' He looked back at Bowker. 'I remember the water lapping up on my backdoor step. What do you want to know?'

'When we rode past that day, I remember Denise Oosterman's lime green Celica parked in the water behind the house.'

'I'm not surprised, I bought it from the clearing sale when the Oostermans left the district,' Wilson replied.

Bowker shook his head. 'No, this flood occurred before Oosterman's death. At that stage, the car would have still belonged to Denise.'

'Then she would have been at my place feeding her horse,'

Wilson replied. 'She was a keen equestrian, but her prick of a husband wouldn't let her keep a horse. I mentioned over the phone that she worked in the office at Goldsboroughs when I was there. I felt a bit sorry for her and offered agistment for her big chestnut showjumper out at my place. She'd come out every now and then to ride him, or bring out some chaff. With most of the paddocks underwater, I suspect that's probably why she was there that day. Make sure he had enough tucker.'

This all made sense to Bowker. Margaret White had mentioned her brother not allowing Denise to keep a horse, and Bowker remembered the big chestnut in Wilson's paddock. 'You've probably heard on the grapevine that a body was found up on The Granite last week.'

Wilson looked surprised. 'I've been up in New South buying ewes. Got in late last night. I bet it was some city bastard shootin' rabbits. I wager the gun went off as he got through a wire fence.'

'We found the forty-year-old remains of Denise Oosterman,' Bowker said watching for Wilson's reaction.

Wilson looked shocked. He shook his head. 'It couldn't have been Denise. She pissed off around the time Oosterman topped himself. Moved up to Queensland somewhere.' He looked at Bowker. 'You're sure it's her?'

'Absolutely,' Holmes replied. 'Her DNA was matched to her elderly mother in the geriatric wing at the hospital.'

A pained look came over his face. 'Fuck. She was such a nice lady.' He was speechless for a moment. 'Helps explain why she never contacted me about what to do with her horse.'

'So, the horse was the only reason she went to your place?' Bowker said, choosing his words carefully.

'What other reason would there be?' Wilson replied. The look on his face changed as he realised what Bowker was asking. 'Surely you don't think I was on with her?'

'Somebody was,' Bowker said. 'She was pregnant when she died.'

'She was a married woman,' Wilson replied staring into Bowker's eyes. 'Unless you've missed something in your education, married women have a habit of getting pregnant.'

'DNA shows it wasn't Oosterman's child,' Holmes said.

'Whose was it, then?' Wilson asked.

Bowker shrugged. 'Dunno at this stage. Would you be willing to provide a DNA sample sometime down the track if we think it would help with our inquiry?'

Wilson was taken aback. 'If I need to, I would, yeah. But I didn't realise it was now a crime to knock up a married woman.'

Holmes folded his arms across his chest. 'It's theoretically possible the father of the unborn child may have been involved in the deaths of one or other or both of the Oostermans and was worried Gary Rice's family history research might expose his actions after all this time.'

Wilson shrugged. 'Well do whatever you need to do testing wise, but I can assure you that other than working at Goldsboroughs, Denise and I did nothing together except keeping an eye on her horse.'

'Did you ever see Denise with particular men when she was in town?' Bowker asked. 'Were there any blokes who came into the Goldsborough office on a regular basis but spent more time chatting her up than actually doing business?'

Wilson thought hard for a few moments. 'Shit, it's a long time ago Greg. But I do remember she was pretty popular with the younger cockies. They'd all be old bastards now, of course.'

'Any one bloke in particular, you can think of?' Bowker asked.

Wilson shook his head. 'Not really. Although the Lands Department bloke used to drop in fairly often.'

'Brian Gottfried?' Holmes asked.

'Yeah, that's him,' Wilson replied. 'Always a social visit and he spent most of his time yakking to Denise. Bought nothing from us. All his chemicals were supplied by the government. I know it used to upset the boss that Gottfried was wasting Denise's time when he didn't spend a penny in the shop. He was willing to put up with the cockies flirting at the front desk because most of them were our clients or were at least in to buy merchandise.'

After another five minutes of chat, the detectives had exhausted their questions. Wilson's reactions and responses to the matters they had raised were all reasonable. Tending to her horse as an explanation for Mrs Oosterman's visits to Wilson's farm was in keeping with the known facts, and the stock agent's readiness to consent to a DNA swab suggested he had nothing to hide. In summary, the Wilson connection had all the hallmarks of another dead end. After exchanging farewells, and with the detectives halfway out the door, Wilson had a question of his own.

'You said Denise's remains were found on The granite. Just out of interest, whereabouts on The Granite?'

To Bowker, this seemed like an odd question and he hesitated before answering. 'Up the top. On the summit, if you could call it that.'

'What? Buried in solid rock?' Wilson asked with a puzzled look.

'No. The body was under a pyramid of stones,' Bowker replied.

'Who found her,' Wilson asked.

Holmes pointed a finger back and forth between himself and Bowker. 'We did. But it was Greg who had the idea of looking there, so he deserves most of the credit.'

'That's why you blokes are detectives, eh?' Wilson said. 'Look at all the possibilities. Your average bloke wouldn't think of checking under one of those cairns.'

Bowker tapped his temple with an index finger. 'Yep. We've got it all up here.' He shook hands with Wilson a second time and the detectives returned to their car. As they passed Sid's ute, Bowker again patted the dog, this time ruffling its neck and making sure he had a few kelpie hairs in his hand before he walked to their vehicle.

'He knows a lot more than he's letting on,' Holmes said as he snapped on his seatbelt.

'Yeah, I'd written him off as a suspect until he asked about where we found the body,' Bowker said as he placed the dog hairs inside a plastic evidence bag he'd retrieved from the glovebox. 'It struck me as strange that he was so interested in where the remains were located, but I was happy to put that down to natural curiosity. But when he mentioned the hard rock surface and the cairns, it gave me the distinct impression that he'd been to the top of The Granite at some stage and had paid a lot of attention to what he saw up there.'

Holmes was nodding his agreement. 'And mentioning us checking under *one* of the cairns tells us he knew there were more than one up there, even though major hills normally only have the one cairn or trig point at the summit. That's if they have any.'

'Precisely. It was the novelty of the two cairns that led to us finding the remains.' Bowker connected his own seatbelt and started the car. 'So why has Sid been up there?'

'His curiosity around the location of the remains seem to rule out him killing her and hiding her body up there.' Holmes smiled. 'Of course, he could have just been on The Granite chasing rabbits.' His smile widened to a broad grin. 'I heard a couple of kids were silly enough to climb up there doing that very same thing.'

Bowker chuckled. 'For someone with a vehicle there are a million better places to shoot rabbits.' The smile disappeared. 'My guess is that sometime after Denise disappeared, he was up there searching for some trace of her. If they were close, she might have told him what a prick Paul Oosterman was and that The Granite was her sanctuary when things erupted.'

'Do you want to print him and see if we can link him to Rice's walking stick? Maybe apply to take a DNA sample to see if Denise was carrying his child.'

Bowker slipped the car into gear. 'He's not going anywhere. Let's just think this through before we do anything.' The detective backed out of the angle park and headed back towards Bridge Street and the Benalla Bakery.

CHAPTER 27

The tabletop in the investigation room was entirely covered in neat stacks of documents, photos and handwritten notes. When the homicide detectives entered, Larsen was bending across the table arranging items on the opposite side. She wore calf-length navy-blue wet-look leggings matched with a lacy cream-coloured top and black stilettos. Holmes instinctively moved to tap her buttock, but luckily remembered Bowker was beside him and was able to clumsily disguise his movement as picking up a photograph from the table. Larsen stood up straight and smiled when she heard her colleagues behind her.

'I think I might have found the breakthrough we've been chasing,' she said as she turned and leant her backside on the edge of the table.

'We might have made some progress too,' Bowker said. 'But you go first, Kirsten. Ours is more speculation that a breakthrough.'

The two men pulled up chairs either side of Larsen so that they could both see what she had in front of her. 'OK, this is all to do with what I found in Rice's research around Oosterman's supposed suicide.'

'So obviously I missed something.' Bowker speculated.

'I missed them the first time through too. I read everything in the box from start to finish, but uncovered nothing to add to what you'd already found. So I put all the historical family stuff away and concentrated solely on what looked to have become Rice's obsession with Paul Oosterman's death. On the second time through I found two things that I think might finally lever this case open.'

'You've certainly got our attention,' Bowker said hoping a conclusion to this saga was imminent.

Larsen retrieved a copy of the suicide note from a manilla folder. 'We've all seen and read this. I refer you to the last two lines.' She read them out. '"I ask only that this wedding photo be hung in the family home as a *momentum* of our short life together." The word "momentum" jumps out at us, right? As we know, the correct word to use in this context is "memento"'

Bowker nodded. 'Yeah, I think I wrote something to that effect in my notes. That it was strange for a person with Paul Oosterman's expensive education to have made such an elementary error, even if he *was* contemplating suicide at the time.'

Larsen pulled a sympathy card from her folder. It was the one sent by the staff of Goldsborough Mort with the small black and white photo taken at the Benalla Agricultural Show attached with a paperclip. The picture depicted a proud Paul Oosterman standing beside a Black Angus cow whilst being presented with a Goldsborough Mort-sponsored winner's sash by a young Sid Wilson. Underneath was written "Better Times". Larsen slid the card across to Bowker.

'Yeah, I've seen this card too,' the Homicide detective said. 'Nice touch coming from an agency who didn't handle the Oosterman family business.' He looked at Larsen mystified. 'What's our interest here?'

Larsen pulled the photo from the paperclip, turned it over, and placed it back in front of her senior colleague. Bowker's eyes widened as he read what was written in blue biro on the back. "A momentum of Paul winning our prize at the Benalla show." It was signed by Sid Wilson. Bowker closed his eyes and threw his head back. He exhaled loudly. "'A momentum of Paul winning our prize'" he repeated. 'How the hell did I miss that? How many hours did that oversight cost us?' he asked himself out loud. He opened his eyes and turned to Larsen. 'Bloody magnificent, Kirsten.'

Holmes put his hand on Larsen's shoulder, more a congratulatory gesture than one of romantic affection. 'Well done, detective,' he said warmly.

'I know I'm stating the bleeding obvious, but there's only one reason why Sid Wilson would write that suicide note,' Bowker said. 'To cover up killing Paul Oosterman.'

'There's something else I found,' Larsen said as she took one of the original crime scene photos from her folder. The picture showed Oosterman's kitchen table with the various items sitting atop it. Bowker had perused the same photo many times on his own journey through Rice's research. Circles in red pen had been scribbled around the image of the suicide note, the crossword and the key tag with the initials "MS".

Larsen tapped the circle around the suicide note. 'See how Rice has made this circle?' she said. 'He's put the pen above the image he wants to highlight, then draws a quick circle around the object in an anticlockwise direction before roughly connecting with the point where he started.' She then pointed to the crossword. 'He's done the same thing here.' She moved her finger to the key tag. 'But look at this circle.'

'He's started his circle from below the key tag,' Holmes presumed.

'That's what I assumed until I did this.' Larsen turned the photograph through 180 degrees. 'The circle now could be drawn the same as the other ones. But look what else has changed when we rotate the picture.'

Bowker looked at the key tag inside Rice's circle. With the photo's new orientation, the key tags lettering was transformed. It now no longer read "MS" but rather "SW".

'SW,' Holmes blurted out. 'Sid Wilson!'

Fleming intercepted his fellow detectives on their way downstairs. 'Can I have a word in private, Greg?'

'Sherlock, can you send a couple of uniforms out to pick up Sid Wilson,' Bowker asked. 'Hopefully he'll still be in his office, otherwise he could be anywhere. When he gets here print him and take a DNA swab.'

Holmes nodded and accompanied Larsen to the ground floor. Bowker retraced his steps with Fleming, trailing him into their small investigation room.

Bowker pulled out a chair and indicated that Fleming sit opposite. 'What's on your mind, mate?' he asked.

'Kirsten said she'd found a couple of things among Rice's stuff that points towards Sid Wilson having a role in Paul Oosterman's death.'

'That's right,' Bowker replied.

'And that would give him a motive for killing Rice to shut him up?'

'That's the way I see it.

'So you're close to winding up the investigation?' Fleming asked tentatively.

Bowker folded his arms across his chest. 'Where are you heading with this, Aaron?'

Fleming took a deep breath. 'I've decided if you're close to finishing here, then I won't pursue the complaint against Holmes.'

Bowker frowned. 'There's either substance to your accusations or there's not, Aaron. It has nothing to do with timelines.'

Fleming sniffed and rubbed his nose with the back of his

hand. 'The way I figure it, if Holmes is gone, then any danger of Kirsten being hurt goes with him. The longer the relationship continues, the more involved she'll become.'

'She doesn't seem too damaged at the moment,' Bowker replied.

'My wife is a schoolteacher, Greg. She was friendly with a young female graduate. It's a few years ago now. Natalie McArdle was her name. Same thing happened. An older married bloke decides he'd like something with a younger taste, they have a romp in the hay, things go belly up and now she's lost to teaching and spends half her time in psychiatric care. I don't want something like that happening to Kirsten.'

'Are you sure you're not using our Wilson breakthrough as an excuse to shelve your complaint? That way you won't look to have backed down.' Bowker rubbed his chin. 'What was Kirsten's reaction to your outburst yesterday?'

'What do you think,' Fleming replied. 'Told me to mind my own business.'

Bowker thought for a second. 'To be honest, Aaron. I think you might be the only one in danger of being hurt at the moment.'

'I'm not worried about me. Kirsten's welfare is my main priority in all this.'

Wilson was still at his office when two uniformed constables picked him up and brought him back to the police station. After having his fingerprints scanned and his DNA samples collected, he was placed in an interview room. Running the risk of overkill, Bowker asked Larsen to join he and Holmes in the questioning of the stock agent, judging her efforts in progressing the case too important to see her sidelined at this point. When the trio entered the room and sat down, Wilson's face tightened knowing something serious was afoot.

'What's all this about, Greg?' Wilson asked. 'I told you everything I know about Denise Oosterman's car.'

'This isn't about the car, Sid,' Bowker replied. 'We can now place you in Paul Oosterman's kitchen on the day he supposedly took his own life.'

'He *did* take his own life,' Wilson blurted out. 'The police said he did, and so did the coroner.'

'Can you explain why you were in his kitchen that day?' Bowker asked.

'I was nowhere near Lurg when he killed himself. We didn't have clients out that way.'

'We've got two prints that put you in the room. One was on a photo that had been placed on the table that day,' Bowker said, willing to take the punt that the unknown prints belonged to the stock agent. It would take only a short while to have that confirmed after the photocopied print was compared to those lifted from Wilson a few minutes earlier. The images had already been emailed to McLeod with a priority label.

Wilson shook his head vigorously. 'I honestly don't know what you're talking about. I've never been inside that house. Ever. So it's impossible that I could have left fingerprints on the wedding photo so...' He stopped mid-sentence realising his *faux par*.

'I didn't mention it was a wedding photo, did I Sid?' Bowker replied. 'I think we better start at the beginning. The constables have just taken a cheek swab to sample your DNA. Is there any chance that this will confirm you as the father of the unborn child found with the remains of Denise Oosterman?'

Wilson picked at the rough skin on his fingers. 'The baby was mine.' He replied, half under his breath. 'Denise told me a few weeks before she disappeared.'

'Were you having an ongoing affair with Mrs Oosterman, or did the pregnancy result from a one-off sexual encounter?' Holmes asked.

'It had been going on for eighteen months,' Wilson replied without looking up. 'It started out as her keeping her horse at my place, but over time it developed into something more.'

'How were you going to keep it secret when the pregnancy started to show?' Larsen asked. 'Her husband would have known the child wasn't his.'

'We planned to leave the district together. The idea was to return to her home state of Queensland. I had already sussed out possible transfers to Goldsborough branches up there.'

'When did you first suspect that things were not going as planned?' Bowker asked.

Wilson looked up at the detective. 'It should have been when Denise didn't show up for work one morning. But when the boss couldn't contact her and her car was found abandoned, that's when I really got worried.'

Holmes leant back in his chair and folded his arms. 'Were you worried she might have done a runner without you?'

Wilson shook his head. 'No. I knew something terrible had happened. I waited another day to see if Denise made contact. When she didn't, I just assumed that Oosterman had found out about the pregnancy or our affair and had done something terrible to her.' He looked at Holmes. 'There were a few times in the past when I'd been on my way to confront him after he'd smashed her around. Each time, Denise stopped me.' His gaze dropped to the table. 'Pity she had, as it's turned out.'

'So you went up to Lurg looking for her? You say two days after she didn't show for work?' Bowker asked.

'Probably the morning of the third day,' Wilson replied.

Holmes looked at his notes. 'That would match the date on the crossword,' he said.

'So tell us what happened,' Bowker said, folding his hands together on the table in front of him.

Wilson leaned back and stared at the ceiling. 'I drove out to *Melaleuca Springs* and parked on the track between the house and the sheds. The dogs were barking like crazy and I heard Oosterman yell to them to shut up, so I suspected he didn't realise he had a visitor. His ute was parked beside the back door and I noticed his rifle on the front seat with a box of bullets. I could see him through the kitchen window with his back to me writing on something at the table. I knocked on the back door and walked in. He turned around in surprise and asked what I was doing out there. I told him my boss had sent me out to check if there was any sign of Denise.'

'How did he react to that?' Larsen asked.

'He told me to give my boss a message. To tell him to mind his own fuckin' business. Tell him to find another whore to work on his front desk.'

Bowker looked him in the eye. 'How'd you take that?'

Wilson thought for a moment. 'Did the block. Went out the back door and collected the rifle from his ute, made sure it was loaded and went back inside and bailed him up.'

'OK,' Bowker replied. 'Then what? You obviously didn't shoot him and then drag him halfway up The Granite.'

'I told him I wanted to know what had happened to Denise. He went as white as a sheet then started screaming at me.'

Larsen leant forward. 'About what?'

Wilson exhaled loudly. 'About how he now realised who the motherfucker was who'd been rooting his wife. About how I must be the one who got her up the duff. And how she'd got what she'd deserved.' Wilson swallowed deeply. 'I think at that point it suddenly struck him that I might actually pull the trigger. So he asked me what I wanted.'

299

'What did you say?' Bowker replied.

'I told him that I reckoned he'd killed Denise and that I wanted to see where he had left her. He said he hadn't killed her and she'd just run away to Queensland.'

'OK,' Bowker said. 'Then what?'

'I said that I didn't believe him, and that I wanted to see where he'd left Denise. I said unless he showed me, I'd shoot him then and there.' He took a deep breath. 'I think he saw the look in my eyes and believed I'd do it. And I would have too if he hadn't led me up the side of The Granite. I knew that's where she'd be. When she needed to get away from him, that's where she'd go. She'd told me that a dozen times.'

'So what made you shoot him, half way up?' Holmes asked.

'I didn't plan to. He spun around and tried to grab the gun. It's got a hair trigger and it went off in his face.' Wilson shrugged. 'No one would have believed it was an accident, so I set it up to look like he'd shot himself. Then I walked to the top of The Granite and searched for any sign of Denise. If I'd found her body, I may have come clean about killing Oosterman. But I didn't find a thing up there.'

'So you went back to the house and wrote a suicide note in capitals to match the letters in the crossword,' Larsen said.

Wilson bowed his head. 'Yeah. And I put the wedding photo beside it to make it look like he was heartbroken after being abandoned by his wife.'

Bowker took out his notebook and wrote the word "Momentum" in large letters. He slid it across to Wilson. 'What does that word mean, Sid?' he asked.

Wilson frowned not knowing where this was going. 'It's got two meanings. One is like the force of something. You know, when a car starts rolling it has some momentum. The other meaning is like a souvenir.'

'A *memento* is like a souvenir, Syd. Not a momentum,' Bowker explained. 'That's where you made your mistake. Plus, you left a key tag with your initials on it in his kitchen.'

Wilson dropped his head.

Bowker looked at his fellow detectives, then took a deep breath. 'Sidney Wilson, it is my intention to charge you with the murder of Paul Oosterman. You have the right to remain silent. If you do say anything, what you say can be used against you in a court of law. You have the right to consult with a lawyer and have that lawyer present during any questioning. If you cannot afford a lawyer, one will be appointed for you if you so desire. Do you understand?'

Wilson thought for a few moments as he absorbed the seriousness of the situation. He suddenly sprung to his feet and shouted. 'I told you! It was a bloody accident!'

'You can argue that in court, Sid. Do you wish to call a lawyer?' Bowker asked.

Wilson stood stunned for a moment or two before falling back into his chair and dropping his face into his hands. 'Not at this stage, no,' he mumbled.

Bowker rubbed his chin. 'Then we'll move along to the murder of Gary Rice.'

CHAPTER 28

The moment Bowker mentioned Gary Rice's murder, Wilson's demeaner changed. He held up both palms. 'Whoa, whoa, whoa. I had nothing to do with that.'

'Come on Sid,' Holmes said. 'At the school reunion Rice was telling anyone who would listen, that his family history research pointed to Paul Oosterman being murdered.'

'And we've got several witnesses who have confirmed that you and Rice had a long conversation during that evening,' Bowker added.

Wilson shook his head slowly and deliberately. 'He never mentioned Oosterman to me personally. He asked me about how Ron Cloverdale was managing *Holland Flats*. Rice owns that property, you know.' He looked down at the tabletop. 'Or he did.'

Larsen opened her manilla folder on the desktop and tapped it with her fingertips. 'We discovered everything that implicated you among Rice's research documents, Mr Wilson. He found those same things. He wrote notes to that effect among the documents and he circled items in photos that pointed straight to you. He not only knew that Oosterman was murdered, but he knew you killed him.'

Bowker shrugged. 'Pretty strong motive for another murder, eh

Sid'. He looked at Holmes. 'What's that saying of yours, Detective Holmes. 'May as well hang for a sheep as a lamb?'

Wilson slammed his fist down on the table in his first real sign of emotion. 'I didn't kill Gary Rice!'

'I think the risk-rewards were all in your favour Sid,' Bowker said, raising his eyebrows. 'You're nearing seventy years old. If Rice gets to tell his story, you go to jail for the rest of your life. If you shut him up, things go on as normal. And you risk nothing by killing him. If you get caught and your killing of Oosterman comes out, sure you'll get done for two murders, but in terms of jail time what's the difference between twenty and forty years when you're already seventy?'

'So I guess you've got nothing to lose by telling us the truth here, Sid,' Holmes added. 'Might even go in your favour with the courts.'

'I didn't kill Rice,' Wilson shouted. 'And Paul Oosterman was an accident.' He dropped the volume of his voice. 'Look, don't get me wrong. I wasn't unhappy that Oosterman was dead. And if we'd made it to the top of The Granite and I'd found Denise's remains, then there's a fair chance I would have pulled the trigger on purpose.' He looked at Bowker. 'I think I'd like to call a solicitor before I say anything further.'

'It's probably a good time to have a break, anyway. There're some forensic results I'd like to see before we resume.' Bowker looked at Wilson. 'You'll be held in custody on a charge of murdering Paul Oosterman and on suspicion of killing Gary Rice. A uniformed officer will be here shortly to arrange calls to a solicitor and your family before you're taken to the cells.'

Wilson dropped his head onto his arms on the tabletop as the three detectives left the room.

Aaron Fleming was at the sink in the empty staffroom when

Bowker wandered across to make himself a coffee. 'Did you charge Sid Wilson?' he asked casually as he washed his cup.

'With killing Paul Oosterman, yeah. Need to see the forensics before we take the Rice case any further.' Bowker shovelled instant coffee into a mug.

Fleming sighed heavily. 'If he killed Oosterman then he killed Rice to prevent being found out. That's been your theory all along. Why change now? How much more do you need?'

Bowker filled his mug with hot water from the urn and began stirring the contents with a teaspoon. He looked at his fellow detective. 'What more do I need, Aaron? Well for a start, I'd like to have something a little more substantive than just a motive to link him to Rice.'

'Wilson was at the reunion less than a hundred metres from where Rice got whacked,' Fleming replied.

'So were a couple of other suspects,' Bowker shot back.

'But you've eliminated them,' Fleming replied.

'And I'm going through the same processes to see if I can eliminate Wilson,' Bowker said, his voice starting to betray his annoyance. 'If I can't eliminate him, then I'll look for things to prove he committed the crime. Investigation 101, Aaron.'

'You may never find those things,' Fleming retorted quickly.

'Well then he won't be charged. That's how the law works. Innocent until proven guilty.' Bowker looked straight into Fleming's eyes. 'First you had Noel Sanderson in the gun, now it's Sid Wilson. I know you want Holmes and I out of your hair, but I won't compromise the investigations just so you get Kirsten Larsen all to yourself again.'

Fleming was incensed. 'I resent that comment.'

Bowker was in no mood for conciliation. 'Well if she's not the reason, then why else do you want someone fitted up for this murder?'

Fleming put his hands on his hips and stood up straight invading Bowker's personal space, which only served to exaggerate his nine-inch deficit in relative heights. 'I'm not wanting anyone fitted up for the murder of that sanctimonious prick. I've a good mind to ...'

Bowker cut him off mid-sentence. 'Sanctimonious prick, was he? I heard you attended Benalla High as a kid. Did Gary Rice give you a hard time at some stage? Make you feel inferior?'

Fleming took a step backwards away from Bowker, a scowl pervading his reddened face. 'Are you suggesting I might have topped Rice?' he snarled angrily.

Bowker shrugged and cocked his head. 'Sounds like you harboured a fair amount of resentment towards the man. And you've been working pretty hard to put somebody, or should I say *anybody*, in the frame for his murder.'

Fleming's anger boiled over. 'You're another sanctimonious prick!' He turned and walked halfway to the door. 'You and Holmes can both fuck off as far as I'm concerned.' When he reached the door, he turned for a final word. 'Report me if you want. I couldn't give a shit if I lose my job if I have to put up with self-righteous big city know-alls like you.' He slammed the door and was gone.

Bowker sat at his motel table the next morning checking his emails when Holmes arrived after spending the night with Kirsten Larsen. 'Another romp in paradise mate?' he asked with a big smile as his partner sat down opposite. 'When we get back to Melbourne, we'll need to spell you in a paddock of lucerne.'

Holmes chuckled under his breath. 'Sorry about leaving you on your own again mate. I should have called you over to Kirsten's after dinner. We had a few drinks to celebrate her breakthrough in the Oosterman case. You should have been there for that,' Holmes replied.

Bowker shook his head. 'Nah. Don't want to be the third wheel. But it was great work her finding those anomalies among Rice's stuff. She cracked the case. Privately, she'd be pretty chuffed with what she did, I'd imagine.'

Holmes screwed up his face a little. 'Yeah. But she sees everything in the context of joining the homicide squad.'

'She's a good detective. If she applies, she'll certainly be in the mix.'

'I told her that. She applied for a vacancy a month or so ago but hasn't heard back as yet. She's got this idea that appointments to Homicide are based around jobs for the boys.'

Bowker smiled. 'Then how did our female colleagues get there?'

Holmes held up both palms. 'I know. I know. But she reckons she's got a better chance if I put in a good word for her. Or I ask one of the big boys to push her case. One of the big boys like you.'

'That's what referees are for,' Bowker replied.

'I told her that too.'

Bowker's phone beeped. He looked at the screen. 'Email from forensics. This will be the report on Sid Wilson's fingerprints.' He opened the document and silently read its contents before reporting to Holmes. 'One of Wilson's prints is a match for the one they lifted from Oosterman's wedding photo forty years ago.'

'No surprise. He's already admitted he was there,' Holmes replied. 'But it doesn't hurt to have physical evidence in case he changes his story.'

'Now for the bad news. Or good news if you're Sid Wilson. His prints don't match any of those found on Rice's walking stick. Doesn't mean he didn't kill him, of course.' Bowker read the last part of the email before closing down his phone. 'Forensics are fast-tracking the DNA from both Wilson and his kelpie.'

'Where's your money on Wilson killing Rice?' Holmes asked.

'That he didn't do it.'

'That's where mine is too. Once he'd made the slip up about the wedding photo, he was happy to tell us the whole Oosterman story. Given his age, it makes no practical difference really whether he gets sentenced for one or two murders. And yet he denied killing Rice so vehemently.'

Bowker upturned his palms. 'Or you can look at it the other way. If he hopes a court will see Oosterman's death as an accident, then admitting he followed Rice and killed him in cold blood sort of makes that Oosterman verdict irrelevant.'

Holmes nodded. 'Yeah, there's definitely two ways to come at it, that's for sure.'

'When we get back to the station, I'd like another squiz at the attendees list for the reunion,' Bowker said. 'If Wilson didn't kill Rice, then we're back to where we started.'

The attendees list was now so familiar to Bowker that he felt he knew it off by heart.

Holmes was intrigued. 'Looking for anyone in particular mate, or just waiting for a bolt of inspiration?'

'Aaron Fleming. But I know I would have noticed his name if it was on the list, but I'm just checking whether his wife was at the show. If she was, then maybe Aaron came to pick her up at the end of the night.'

Holmes's brow creased and his eyes narrowed in bewilderment. 'Fleming? Why would you be interested in the movements of that turd?'

'He's been pushing me to close the Rice case even if that means charging the wrong bloke or pulling up stumps and leaving it unsolved altogether.'

'That's because he's pissed off about me and Kirsten,' Holmes replied.

'That's probably true, Sherlock. But yesterday he let it slip that Gary Rice had taught him at school and apparently treated him like shit. A sanctimonious prick was how Fleming described him. I thought maybe if the two crossed paths at the reunion, something nasty might have transpired.'

Holmes scratched the side of his head. 'You were there. You would have seen him.'

'There were hundreds packed in the room. I met Fleming the same time as you. Here, on the Tuesday after Rice was killed.' Bowker resumed his perusal of the list until he stopped on a name. He closed his eyes, deep in thought.

'You find him?' Holmes asked.

Bowker shook his head slowly. 'No. But there's a name on here that I've heard just recently.' He drummed his fingers on the table. 'Bruce McArdle. I'm trying to place where I've heard it before.'

'Can't help you mate. Never heard of the bloke.'

Bowker stared up at the ceiling, desperate for a memory to materialise. After a few moments, he slapped the desk with his right hand. 'Fleming mentioned a McArdle, but it wasn't Bruce. McArdle was the surname of a graduate teacher who had an affair with an older colleague at the high school. It finished up mentally destroying her.'

'Why'd Fleming bring that up?'

Bowker laughed. 'You're not going to like this mate. But he said he was worried Kirsten would end up the same way when you dump her and leave town.'

Holmes threw himself back in his chair and folded his arms across his chest. 'Pity he didn't spend a bit more time doing his fuckin' job than stickin' his nose into other people's personal business.'

'Apparently the McArdle girl went downhill after the affair,' Bowker reported. 'She quit teaching and has spent time in psychiatric institutions.' The detective flipped to the last page of the list to where the reunion organiser's contact details were listed. He took out his mobile and dialled the daytime phone number for Emily Gladsen. 'I've got a gut feeling about something,' he said to Holmes as the phone rang.

The call was answered quickly. 'Benalla College. This is Emily.'

'Emily Gladsen?' Bowker asked.

Yes,' the woman answered hesitantly.

'Good morning, Emily. This is Detective Inspector Greg Bowker. I'm hoping you can be of assistance in a couple of things that are relevant to an investigation I am conducting at present. You were one of the organisers of the reunion a few weeks ago?'

'That's right,' Gladsen replied. 'One of those many unexpected tasks a receptionist is allocated under the heading of duties as assigned by the principal. And if my memory serves me correctly detective, you were one of the ex-students who attended that function.'

'Your memory is accurate, Emily. I need to pick that memory in relation to a name I've come across on your list of attendees.'

'And that name would be?'

'Bruce McArdle.'

'An ex-student of around thirty years ago,' Gladsen replied quickly. 'Runs a farm out Dookie way. Nice fellow. Tragically lost his wife to cancer last year. He still holds a few sprinting records here at the school, as I'm reminded each year when I type up the program for the house athletic sports.'

Bowker was careful how to phrase his next question. 'There was a young graduate teacher with the same surname who taught at your school.'

The detective could hear the hesitation in the receptionist's voice as she answered. 'That's right. It was quite a few years ago now. Natalie McArdle. From memory, she taught history and legal studies. Was only here for a year.' She hesitated again. 'I probably shouldn't make comment, but since you're a police officer I guess it's alright to give you all I know.'

'That would be appreciated,' Bowker replied.

'Well Natalie had a terrible time here. The kids ran all over her. It was just dreadful some of the things they did. One class jammed a rubbish bin on her head when they were studying Ned Kelly. Often when she wrote on the board the kids would sneak out of the room one by one. It was just terrible. I can't tell you the number of times I saw her curled up in the staffroom in tears. She was a timid little thing who should never have become a teacher.'

'And she was in a relationship with one of the married men on staff?'

It was a moment before Gladsen replied. 'Yes. It apparently began a few months after she started here. It was common knowledge around the school and the kids gave her hell because of it.'

'And the married teacher was Gary Rice?' Bowker asked.

'Yes. And he took advantage of her, if you ask me.'

'Is Natalie McArdle any relation to Bruce McArdle?' Bowker asked.

'Daughter.'

Bowker nodded to Holmes who was following the gist of the conversation. 'Was Natalie an ex-student of the school as well?'

'No. The way the buses run out their way, it was easier for her to go to Shepparton, I think.'

'Bruce McArdle's email address is on my sheet here. You wouldn't have a postal address?'

'I might have something. I'll need to pull up the reunion details on my computer.' After half a minute when Bowker could hear the clacking of keys, the receptionist was able to provide an RMB address.

'Thanks for your time, Emily,' Bowker said as he wrote down McArdle's home address. 'Listen, before I go, one of my colleague's wife works at your school, is that right? Aaron Fleming.'

'Yes. Sally. Teaches maths.'

'Sally Fleming?'

'No. Sally Wright. She's stayed with her maiden name when she teaches.'

Bowker looked down at his reunion list and circled that name.

CHAPTER 29

No sooner had Bowker disconnected than the phone rang. He looked at the screen. 'Erin O'Meara,' he said to Holmes as he put the phone on speaker mode and pushed the receive button. 'Erin. Got some news for us?'

'You said you wanted it pronto, so you can put me down for a bottle of Johnnie Walker,' O'Meara replied before laughing and then rasping as she coughed.'

'How'd we go with Wilson's DNA?' Bowker asked.

'He's confirmed as the father of that forty-year-old foetus, if that's what you're asking. But he doesn't match anything on the national database.'

'Since we did the swab he's admitted to an affair with the mother,' Bowker replied. 'Your tests now confirm paternity. There was always the chance the husband had fired a live bullet or she was playing around with more than just Wilson. What you've found fits with the story we've put together.'

'Glad we can justify ourselves some of the time.' O'Meara coughed loudly. 'Now, the strands of dog hair you sent down.'

'They came from Wilson's kelpie,' Holmes said.

'Is that you Darren? Bloody hell. Are you and Bowker joined at the hip?'

'Something like that,' Holmes replied with a chuckle.

'The dog hair doesn't match that found on Mr Rice's head wound,' O'Meara reported. 'So you're still looking for the mystery hound.' She laughed. 'Would have been a shit load easier if the perp had owned a rarer dog. A wolfhound-chihuahua cross might have made your job easier.' Another bout of coughing ensued before Bowker passed on his appreciation for the swift processing of the tests and ended the call.

Holmes leant back and folded his hands behind his head revealing patches of sweat under his arms. 'She has to be on borrowed time by the sound of that cough.'

'She's been like that for twenty years, mate,' Bowker replied, tossing his pen on the sheets of paper in front of him. 'When she does fall off the perch, it'll be a hell of a loss. She's as rough as guts and not very well liked by some in the force, but she'd done me some big favours over the years. I can remember half a dozen cases that wouldn't have been solved without her personal involvement.'

Holmes massaged the back of his neck as he stared up at the ceiling. 'The prints on Rice's walking stick didn't tie Sid Wilson to the crime scene and now the dog hair doesn't either. I think he's telling the truth about not topping Rice. Either that, or he's been super lucky with the forensics?'

'I agree that the science is in his favour, but there's nothing to say the print on the walking stick wasn't left there by someone innocently touching it at the festivities. And there's always the chance that Sid grabbed the murder weapon from someone else's vehicle.' Bowker rested his forehead on the fingers of his left hand with his elbow on the tabletop. He picked up the pen in his right hand and tapped the list in front of him. 'Fleming's wife was at the reunion, but not him. I wonder if he picked her up from the function? That would place him close to the venue at the right time to see Gary Rice head off home.'

'Do we ask him or his wife?'

'Either way will be tricky and cause Fleming to go ape shit,' Bowker suggested. 'But it's probably only fair to give him first chance to detail his movements that night.'

'Do we do it together, or does one of us have a chat with him just one on one?'

Bowker chuckled. 'I've already had a big run-in with him and you're public enemy number one as far as he's concerned. Either way will cause angst.' He thought for a long moment. 'I'll do it. I'll tell him forensics can't tie Wilson to Rice and then ask him if he picked up his missus and whether he'd seen Wilson poking around.'

'Good luck with that' Holmes replied. 'He'll ask how you knew his wife was at the reunion when she doesn't carry his surname.'

'If push comes to shove, I'll tell him he's under suspicion.' Bowker laughed. 'I've practically told him that already, so it shouldn't come as any surprise that I'm checking his movements.'

Bowker found Fleming at his desk, writing furiously. 'Drafting up an apology, Aaron?'

Fleming looked up, and his face tightened. 'You're the one who should apologise, Bowker. You all but accused me of murder yesterday. I'm a good cop. I don't go around topping people.'

Bowker remained standing to maintain his towering position over his colleague. 'Good cops don't lose their tempers like you did yesterday. And if you can lose it over that sort of discussion, then you can lose it with a former teacher who you feel treated you like shit.'

'And when would such a conversation have taken place, detective inspector?' Fleming growled. 'If you're as good an investigator as you think you are, then you'll have checked the list of guests at the reunion and confirmed I didn't go.'

Bowker decided a statement, rather than a question was the best approach. 'But you *were* at the football club to pick up your wife at the end of the night.'

Fleming answered the question with another question. 'You saw a Mrs Fleming on the list, did you?' He shook his head and chuckled. 'I don't think so.'

'I saw a Sally Wright's name,' Bowker replied smugly. 'That's your better half, isn't it?'

Fleming stared down at his desk. 'OK, I picked her up after the show. She planned to have a few shandies and didn't want to risk driving home.'

Bowker put his hands on his hips. 'So why are you trying to bullshit me around? Tell me about picking her up and maybe we can all move on. Did you sight Rice at all that night?'

Fleming exhaled loudly. 'I waited on the steps for Sally and he came out for a smoke. He complimented me on becoming a police officer. Then kindly added that he thought I'd spend most of my life in jail, given the family I'd come from.'

Bowker frowned. 'Nice. How'd you react to that?'

'Told him to go fuck himself and to be careful with his driving because it's amazing how often a police officer is watching when you do something wrong.' He looked at Bowker. 'Pretty childish, I know.' He shrugged. 'I couldn't stand being near the prick, so I decided to wait for Sally by my car. And that was the last I saw of the arrogant bastard.'

'So why haven't you told me this before? Surely you know it's relevant to our investigation.'

'Because I didn't want to be dragged into the bloody enquiry on the basis of my hatred for the victim. It was better to shut up about seeing Rice, keep my name right out of it and not run the risk of being fitted up for his murder in the event the real killer couldn't be found.'

Bowker was visibly annoyed. 'That doesn't happen, Aaron. Not on my watch anyway. You're the one who's been playing fast and loose with the facts, suggesting we charge people when the evidence hasn't been there. You shouldn't judge other people's standards by your own, mate. There's no excuse for not telling us you'd spoken to Rice on that night.'

Fleming took a deep breath through clenched teeth. 'Me telling you that I'd briefly spoken to him would have added nothing to what you already had. You knew that he'd attended the reunion, and you knew that at some stage he'd left to walk home. And you knew that he was killed soon after. What relevance was knowing he had a smoke on the steps?'

Bowker rolled his eyes in frustration that his lecture on ethics was getting nowhere. 'And Sally will confirm Rice was still there having a smoke when you left?'

'Of course, she will,' Fleming replied angrily.

'Because she's your wife?'

'Because it's the fucking truth!' Fleming snarled back.

It was lunchtime at school when the detectives parked at the Barkly Street campus of Benalla's P12 college. The physical landscape had changed dramatically since Bowker had attended the then High School. In his day, students were forced to cross a busy street for classes in the technical studies wing. A building now sat where the crossing had been, and the old thoroughfare was now part of the school grounds and home for tall trees and mature shrubbery. The policemen followed a series of signs to the general office where two middle-aged women were seated behind a polished timber counter. Bowker surveyed their name tags and introduced himself to Emily Gladsen, the woman he had spoken to over the phone. He explained they were seeking a quick chat with Sally Wright, who they hoped was on her lunch break. Emily called the staffroom and after a moment a short plumpish woman with tightly curled hair and bright red lipstick arrived and invited the detectives to a nearby interview room. She wore oversized tracksuit pants, a faded Year 12 branded windcheater from several years prior, and worn-out sandals. After pleasantries were exchanged and the purpose of the officers' visit revealed, Wright's podgy face darkened.

'So you're double checking my husband's account of picking me up that night?' she said irately. 'You're not willing to accept the word of a fellow officer?'

'We're just wondering if you might have seen something that could help us in our enquiries,' Bowker replied.

The woman sighed loudly as if her time was too precious to waste on such trivialities. 'When I came out, Aaron was standing with his elbows on the roof of a car about twenty metres from the bottom of the steps. He was looking back across the oval watching some of my Year 12 kids fart-arsing around on the cricket pitch area when they should have been home in bed. Or even better, doing their bloody homework.' She pursed her lips before continuing. 'If you want all the intimate details, I snuck up on Aaron and put my hands around his waist and suggested we pop off home quick smart, if you get my drift? I'd had a few to drink so I was in the mood for a bit of fun.'

Fleming would need a few drinks too, Holmes thought but didn't say. 'Where was Gary Rice at that stage?' he asked instead.

Wright closed her eyes in thought. 'Halfway down the steps smoking and looking out over the lake. As I passed him, he butted his cigarette on the steps and headed down towards the bridge.'

'Was anybody else outside at this point?' Bowker asked.

'Only Bruce McArdle. He came through the door at the same time as me.'

CHAPTER 30

The day was hot and steamy with no relief forecast for the next two days. The trip out to Dookie took forty minutes by the time the detectives found the right RMB address on the Nalinga-Dookie Road. Sheep roamed the paddocks either side of the potholed drive, many of them with peeling layers of dirty wool dragging on the ground. Traces of wool snagged on fence wires and tree guards further evidenced a severe lice problem on the property. The McArdle farmhouse was a white weatherboard building set in an expansive garden that had been allowed to overgrow with grass reaching a metre high in areas that looked to have once been lawn. Looming as a backdrop was the treeless Mount Major with its communication towers overlooking the plains than extended for many miles around it. A line of sheds stood behind the house with a set of sheep yards further along and partly shaded by a large gum. A cacophony of birdsong tried desperately to lift the spirits of a property that appeared trapped in a death spiral.

A woman of indeterminate age sat on the front verandah of the house, staring towards the horizon. As the detectives approached, her faraway gaze never wavered. She was skeletal to the point of being anorexic, oversized clothes hanging loosely from her bony frame. Her hair was greasy and unbrushed, her hands unwashed and her bare feet filthy. Finally she looked up at the visitors, but said nothing, her sunken eyes bereft of life.

'Natalie McArdle?' Bowker asked, struggling to come to grips with the sight of this broken woman.

There was the slightest movement of her head in acknowledgement before she resumed her thousand-yard stare.

'We're looking for your father,' Holmes said.

The woman moved a finger slightly. 'Shed,' she muttered almost inaudibly.

Bowker nodded his thanks, and the officers made their way to the rear of the house. 'Fuck, how can someone be that dead and still be alive,' Holmes said quietly as they approached the sheds. A Falcon ute was parked in a bay beside a dust-covered later model Holden Statesman. Two tan kelpies were tied up in the bay next door that housed a John Deere tractor, it also covered in layers of dust. The clinking of glass brought the detectives to the last bay of the long shed where an unshaven, ill-kempt man in torn overalls sat on an oil drum drinking from a long neck beer bottle. An opened carton of bottles sat one side of him, a forty-four-gallon drum three quarters filled with empties sat on the other.

'Bruce McArdle?' Bowker asked as he led Holmes into the shed.

'That's me,' McArdle said wearily before taking a long draw from his bottle.

Bowker made the introductions and explained they wanted a quick chat about Gary Rice.

'A ten-seconds look at my daughter will tell you everything you need to know about that bastard,' McArdle said, eyes focussed on the label of his beer bottle. 'Thanks to him, she's totally fucked. Won't eat. Won't talk. If she makes it to Christmas, it'll be a miracle.' He took another swig. 'Probably better for her if she doesn't.'

'Had troubles at work, I've been told,' Bowker said. 'Then the affair with Rice tipped her over the edge.'

'All that, plus the miscarriage, if that's the way it really happened. She won't talk about it,' McArdle replied, staring at the ground.

Holmes put his hands in his pockets and exchanged glances with Bowker before speaking sympathetically to the broken farmer. 'And you're struggling to cope as well, by the looks of it,' Holmes said pointing to the top of the empties drum.

'Living from day to day since my wife died of cancer eighteen months ago. Done nothing on the farm or around the house.' He looked up at the detectives. 'What's the point? Natalie's on borrowed time, my wife's been taken from me by that fuckin' disease and I've got nobody to leave the place to.'

'But you went to the school reunion I heard,' Bowker said.

'Yeah. But shouldn't have. I thought I'd catch up with a few old school mates who might raise my spirits, but none of them were there. Everybody was so happy-go-lucky which made me feel more out of it.' He looked up. 'Don't get me wrong, most people were sympathetic about me losing Carol and what has happened to Nat, but you know .....' His voice tailed off.

'Where'd you park?' Holmes asked.

'Why do you want to know that?' the farmer replied without looking up.

'Just interested,' Holmes said.

McArdle shrugged. 'Not far from the clubrooms,' he replied before taking another gulp of his beer. 'I had to squeeze in between two trees on the riverbank. The main carpark was overflowing.'

'Did you speak with Gary Rice?' Bowker asked.

McArdle shook his head. 'I didn't go near him, and he had enough brains to stay well clear of me. I'd have killed him if he had come over and tried to smooth it over about Natalie.'

'*Did* you kill him, Mr McArdle?' Bowker asked. 'We have

320

a witness who says that you were coming out the door of the function room as Rice left the reunion. You didn't follow him along the lake and whack him over the head?'

'Of course I bloody didn't,' McArdle said quietly. 'I go to jail and who looks after Nat? She's struggling to get through the day even with me here. How would she cope on her own?' He took a deep breath. 'I saw Rice leave and head down towards the bridge, but I went straight to my ute and drove back here.'

Bowker pointed towards the bay with the cars. 'You took the ute and not the Statesman?'

Tears welled in McArdle's eyes as he looked up at the detective. 'I haven't driven that car since I took Carol to the hospital and didn't bring her home.'

Bowker noticed that McArdle was holding the beer bottle in his left hand as he made to deposit the long neck in the empties drum. 'I wonder if you'd mind placing that bottle on the ground in front of you Mr McArdle. We found unidentified left-hand fingerprints on Gary Rice's walking stick. We've fingerprinted quite a few people in relation to this, and one way or another, we'll need to take your prints. If you'll allow us to take this bottle it will save you a round trip to Benalla to be scanned.'

McArdle shrugged. 'Be my guest.' He placed the bottle on the ground in front of the detectives, then pulled another empty from the drum. He wiped it on his flannelette shirt then clasped it in his right hand. 'You may as well do my right hand as well,' he said as he placed the second bottle on the ground beside the first.

'And we'll need samples of hair from your two sheepdogs,' Bowker added.

McArdle looked at the detective with eyes devoid of amusement. 'Do you suspect one of my dogs might have killed him?'

'There was dog hair embedded in the fracture that killed Mr

Rice,' Holmes replied. 'Our forensic people suspect it originated from the murder weapon.'

'I'm sure the dogs will appreciate the attention,' McArdle said. 'They haven't had a lot from me lately.'

Holmes returned to the police vehicle and collected evidence bags. Within a few minutes the bottles and dog hair were bagged and tagged. As the detectives drove away, McArdle flicked the top off another long neck and drank half the bottle in one hit.

'Depression plus, that place,' Holmes said as he steered the car out of McArdle's drive and back onto the road past Dookie Agricultural College. 'I don't think he's trying to hide anything, do you?'

Bowker shook his head. 'Nuh. Happy enough to give us the forensic stuff we wanted. Poor bastard. How do you face that every day?'

'Where to from here?' Holmes asked as he slowed down to pass a stray ewe hunting the green pick on the side of the bitumen.

'Wait for these forensics to come back. Dig around and see if Fleming's story holds up.'

As luck would have it, a local sergeant was travelling to Melbourne for detective training early the next morning. While the McLeod forensic centre was a fair distance from the Police Academy in Glen Waverley, he was nevertheless happy to drop off the McArdle samples with a written plea to Erin O'Meara for a rapid turnaround. In what was left of the afternoon, the homicide detectives spent their time writing up the interviews for what had been a busy, but most likely unproductive day. After an hour of documentation, Holmes stood and stretched his back. 'If you're alright with finishing the McArdle stuff, I might slip out and see what Kirsten's got planned for the evening.'

Bowker smiled. 'I can tell you exactly what she'll have planned.'

Holmes grinned as he left. 'I hope so, mate,' he called over his shoulder.

Bowker had just signed the McArdle summary when Holmes returned smiling broadly.

'If you zipped off for a quickie, I don't want to hear about it,' Bowker said raising a palm.

Holmes sat down and folded his hands on the table. 'Kirsten just received notification that she's been accepted into the homicide squad. She's on an absolute high. I've just booked a table for three at that swanky restaurant in the main street to celebrate.'

Bowker leant back in his chair and knitted his fingers behind his head. 'Well good on her. She's a good detective. And it'll make things a bit easier for the two of you if you're both in the same city.' He thought for a moment. 'Look, count me out for dinner mate. Third wheel again and all that. I'll grab a takeaway and have a chat with Rachael'. He smiled. 'You could always ask Fleming to join you if you don't want to cancel the third seat.'

Holmes chortled. 'As if,' he said as he sorted through the papers on the table. 'Are we just about finished here?'

'Just a few bits and pieces to tidy up. You go mate. I won't be long.'

'Are you sure?'

Bowker waved his hand. 'Yeah. You go and get yourself dolled up.'

Holmes nodded in appreciation. 'Thanks, Greg. Probably see you in the morning.'

It wasn't the morning, but just after eight that evening when Holmes arrived at the motel and threw his bag on the vacant bed. 'What's the go, mate?' Bowker said, as he lay on his bed reading the local rag. 'I thought with Kirsten's promotion you'd be in for a long night.'

Holmes gave a fake chuckle. 'Me too. But I think reality might have hit. I'm an old bastard, and now Kirsten's got what she wanted, I'm expendable by the look of it.'

Bowker sat on the side of his bed and placed the newspaper on the bedside table. 'What happened?' he asked sympathetically.

'Had a nice meal, a few celebratory drinks and everything seemed honky-dory.' Holmes sat down onto his own bed, hands folded between his knees. 'When it was time to leave, Kirsten kissed me on the cheek like some elderly uncle and said we shouldn't continue the relationship now that we'd be working together at Homicide. It would just complicate things, she said.'

'It didn't seem to worry her that you're working together here.' Bowker retorted quickly.

Holmes shrugged. 'I mentioned that, but she said this was only a short-term investigation and we should regard it as a bit of fun while it lasted.' He scratched his cheek. 'Funny, because we'd had a few conversations about how we could make things work in the long term.'

'So you feel you may have been used? That she thought you could help her get into homicide?'

Holmes thought deeply before answering. 'Yeah. Even though I was very upfront and said we had zero input into those decisions.' He chuckled to himself. 'No fool like an old fool, eh? Fancy thinking a stunner like her would be interested in a bloke as old as me.'

'Don't beat yourself up, mate. Perhaps you should look on the bright side. Kirsten turned a potentially boring few weeks up here in the country into something worth remembering. I'm not sure whether it helps, but they say it is better to have loved and lost than never to have loved at all.'

'Maybe. But one thing she's wrong about though. Calling it quits is not going to make things easier for us down at homicide. Every time I see those legs, my concentration will turn to shit.'

Bowker's phone rang and he saw Rachael's name light up the screen. He looked at Holmes. 'Rachael.'

'Take the call mate. I'm fine. A cold shower and I'll be a hundred percent.'

Bowker pressed the green receive icon and wandered outside to speak with his wife. For him, life was suddenly so simple.

The Thursday morning detectives' meeting was a subdued affair. Larsen set the tone with her conservative attire, a grey pants suit with flat shoes and her hair rolled up in a bun. The dialogue between her and Holmes was civil and professional, but any spark had gone. Bowker congratulated Larsen on her appointment and acknowledged that they'd probably be working more cases together in the future. He outlined the previous day's visit to the McArdle property and that they were just waiting on forensic results to officially put a line through that avenue of inquiry. He didn't feel the need to mention his scrutiny of Fleming's movements on the night of Rice's murder, not wishing Larsen to doubt her colleague when there was no evidence to support any of his suspicions.

With little to occupy their time until the forensic report arrived, Bowker decided on another trip to the school to finally kill off any lingering doubts he had concerning Fleming's movements after the reunion. Again, he asked to speak to Sally Wright. Again, he was lucky. She had a spare period before launching into Maths for the rest of the day. She was indignant when she arrived at the office to find Bowker and Holmes waiting. Bowker explained they wanted to speak to the Year 12 boys Wright had seen on the oval on the night in question. Wright closed her eyes in frustration. 'I'll go and get them, if you like. They're in the chem room.'

Bowker requested their names and then walked to the receptionist's counter and asked Emily if she would fetch the boys from their class. He explained that the boys were not in trouble and there was no need for parent involvement. He had one simple question to ask. Emily rose from her chair and headed out and across the verandah-enclosed quadrangle.

'What's with sending Emily,' Wright said irately. 'Were you worried I'd word the boys up or something?' She looked at Holmes. 'And you're the one who Aaron's complained about taking young Kirsten for a ride. A man of your age should be ashamed. And now you're covering your own bum by putting my husband in the gun.'

Before Holmes could reply, Bowker suggested Wright return to her tasks as her presence was no longer required. The stocky woman waddled off, mumbling to herself. After a few moments, Emily returned with three tall boys. Bowker questioned two of them about the night of the reunion while Holmes took the third lad outside for a word on his own. All three boys freely admitted they were on the oval late that night after attending the movies earlier in the evening and wandering around town for a couple of hours. They said the area near the clubrooms was well lit and they saw Sergeant Fleming and Miss Wright after the former yelled that they should be home studying their maths. They all attested to seeing the couple climb in the car and exit the showgrounds into Arundel Street. Bowker thanked the boys and sent them back to class knowing he could finally drop Fleming from his list of suspects.

As the boys walked away, they stopped and came back. If it was any help, one of them said, they'd noticed a man coming through the pedestrian gate from Bridge Street before he circumnavigated the oval and disappeared into the car park near the football clubrooms. They were too far away, and it was too dark for them to describe the person they'd seen in any detail. Bridge Street was very quiet, the boys said, and they didn't remember any cars stopping to drop off the mystery person. Again, Bowker thanked the boys and they disappeared across the quadrangle chatting intensely.

'Could have been our killer,' Bowker said. 'Whacked Rice, disappeared up through the gardens behind the art gallery, crossed Bridge Street and returned to his vehicle via the pedestrian gate.'

'Well, at least we know it wasn't Fleming,' Holmes replied.

CHAPTER 31

The call from Erin O'Meara came mid Friday morning as Bowker and Holmes were making arrangements to return to Melbourne for the weekend and possibly much longer if the stalemate continued.

'Solved another one for you, Gregory.' O'Meara said before a short cough.

Bowker had the call on speaker and he and his partner exchanged bewildered looks. If the McArdle samples were positive, why did he hand them over without the slightest protest? 'You're talking about the samples a Benalla officer dropped off yesterday?' Bowker asked to ensure there was no confusion.

'Yeah, the stuff labelled Bruce McArdle of Dookie, wherever the hell that is. Two beer bottles and two lots of dog hair,' O'Meara replied. 'A print on the beer bottle matches the one on the victim's walking stick. DNA sequencing matches the hair from one of the dogs to the strands we found embedded in the fatal wound of the victim. You can inform the other dog he's in the clear.' Her laugh deteriorated into a rasping cough.

Within ten minutes Bowker and Holmes were in a car and on their way to Dookie to arrest Bruce McArdle. His daughter Natalie would be brought back to Benalla as well, hopefully to be housed in a shelter or at worst admitted to the local hospital as a temporary measure. Under no circumstances could she be left on the farm to cope on her own. As a cool change arrived, light rain was falling and beginning to pool in the potholes as they drove up McArdle's drive towards the house. The two kelpies were off their chain and sprinted towards the police vehicle as it entered the gravelled turnaround area beside the house. Much to Bowker's relief, Natalie was not sitting on the front verandah exposed to the cold wind that was now gusting in from the west. McArdle's ute hadn't moved since their visit and except for the rain on the shed roof the place seemed eerily quiet. The lousy sheep in the front paddocks had made their way under the shelter of trees along the dividing fences and the birds were noticeably silent. Distant thunder rolled in the west, and the heavy smell of ozone was carried in on the breeze. Holmes checked the sheds, while Bowker walked through the garden gate he had forced open only days before and made his way to the front door. He knocked loudly before shouting for someone to open up. With no response after three or four tries, he circled the house to the back door. Again he knocked and shouted. With no response, he turned the door handle and was relieved to find it unlocked.

After thirty-six hours of sweltering heat, the atmosphere inside the house was stifling. The kitchen was a mess with piled up dirty plates and saucepans on the sink, and food scraps on the benches. Bowker left the kitchen and checked the lounge room. It wasn't a big improvement on the kitchen. Father and daughter seemed content to live in a pigsty, but Bowker suspected they just didn't care any longer. McArdle's bedroom was down the corridor and featured a large wedding photo above the bed. A much younger, black-suited Bruce McArdle, arm in arm with a pretty young woman in a white lace bridal gown, smiled back at Bowker as he entered the unkempt room.

It was in Natalie's room that he found what he had feared since he'd seen the dogs off their chains. The buzz of flies had prepared him for the scene before he'd pushed open the door, but it still hit him hard. The farmer's daughter was tucked up in bed, her eyes closed, a bullet hole through her temple. In spite of the blood on her pillow, she somehow seemed at peace. Bruce McArdle was slumped in the cane chair beside his daughter, a rifle held across his body by a finger caught in the trigger guard. A bullet had passed through the roof of his mouth and out through the back of his head. Blood and brain matter was spattered on the wall behind him. A framed picture of him and his wife with a baby Natalie had slipped from his grasp and lay broken on the floor.

Bowker took a few moments to process the scene and his mental paralysis was broken by the sound of Holmes knocking on the front door. 'You in here mate,' Holmes yelled. 'No sign of anybody in the sheds, but I found something where the kelpies had ripped a dog food bag apart.'

Bowker opened the front door to find Holmes holding up a bloodied pipe wrench with a gloved right hand. 'Leave that on the verandah and come inside. But prepare yourself for shit.'

Holmes followed Bowker into the bedroom then stopped dead in his tracks. 'Fuck!'

'Yeah. Fuck.' Bowker thought for a moment. 'Explains why he was happy to hand over the forensic samples in spite of knowing they would incriminate him. He was playing for time.' He nodded towards the bodies. 'Time to do what he needed to do.'

Holmes took a deep breath, but his eyes were on McArdle. 'Yeah. If he'd come straight out and admitted we had him cold, we'd have arrested him then and there. He'd go to jail and Natalie would be left to face her nightmares on her own.'

'Go back to the car and call it in, mate,' Bowker said as he walked onto the verandah and sucked in the cold air.

EPILOGUE

I t was three months to the day when Bowker received the last of the coroner's reports on the five deaths they had investigated in Benalla. The coroner agreed with the homicide team that Denise Oosterman was in all likelihood murdered by her husband who in turn was killed by her lover Sid Wilson. In a series of plea bargains, Wilson had been charged with manslaughter, his explanation of accidental death muddied by his elaborate efforts to hide his involvement in Paul Oosterman's demise. The coroner deemed Bruce McArdle responsible for the murder of Gary Rice on the basis of unequivocal forensic evidence, particularly the pipe wrench which carried Rice's blood and McArdle's fingerprints. Hot off the press this morning, or the email in this case, was the coroner's official findings in relation to the deaths at the McArdle property. As expected, she found a clear case of murder-suicide. Bowker walked across to Holmes and dropped a printed copy of the report on his desk in front of him. 'Pretty much as expected,' he said.

Holmes picked up the document and flicked to the last page. He read for a few seconds then dropped it back on his desk. 'All done and dusted. Five people dead and only one person goes to jail. Pretty unusual, but given the chain reactions in all this, there was no other logical outcome.'

Bowker looked across their Spencer Street squad room to where Kirsten Larsen was sitting at her newly acquired desk. 'We better let Kirsten know,' Bowker said.

Holmes nodded, but didn't reply as Bowker called Larsen across for a quick update. Larsen said little as Bowker outlined the coroner's latest findings. 'A job well done by all of us,' he said in summary as he collected the report from Holmes's desk and wandered back to his own. Holmes waited for Larsen to depart, but she lingered until he turned around and looked her in the face.

'A celebratory drink might be in order after work, don't you reckon?' Larsen asked awkwardly.

Holmes nodded. 'Sounds good. I'll wander over and tell Greg.'

Larsen smiled. 'I'd prefer it was just you and me.'

New Found Books Australia Pty Ltd

www.newfoundbooks.au

NEW FOUND
BOOKS

Milton Keynes UK
Ingram Content Group UK Ltd.
UKHW041303270924
1887UKWH00007B/21